PRAISE FOR *THE EDGE OF WORLDS*

"The venerated pulp spirit in science fiction and fantasy has dwindled since the golden age of the 1920s to '50s. Yet an atavistic craving for adventure remains, and it is this need that Wells's books in general and the Raksura books in particular satisfy. The stories are straightforward adventure, but what makes Wells's 'new pulp' feel fresh is its refusal to take the easier storytelling routes of its forebears. Rather than thinly veil an existing human society as alien others, for example, Wells—a master world builder—creates a multicultural world of humanized monsters . . . The result is breathtakingly surprising and fun. So for readers who missed earlier entry points to this delightful series, now is the time to get on board."
—*The New York Times*

"That rarity—a completely unique and stunning fantasy world."
—Hugo Award-winning author Elizabeth Bear, author of *Karen Memory*

"A feast for the imagination . . . As a fan of the series, I really enjoyed *The Edge of Worlds*. The ending left me pumped for the next book and I can't wait to see what happens next. The Three Worlds is one of my favorite places to escape to, and this book delivers."
—*Roqoo Depot*, 5/5

"With sure-handed prose, Martha Wells provides unforgettable characters, gripping action, and fantastical vision. An addictive mix."
—Carol Berg, author of the Rai-Kirah series

"The Three Worlds is unlike any other fantasy world I've ever encountered. It's wildly imaginative and beautifully depicted."
—*The Illustrated Page*

"An irresistible tour-de-force of excellent storytelling and fine characterization . . . I consider *The Edge of Worlds* to be one of the most addictive and entertaining fantasy novels of the year."
—*Rising Shadow*

of the novel—the universal human themes of loneliness, loss, and the powerful drive to find somewhere to belong."
—Sharon Shinn, author of *Troubled Waters*

"I loved this book. This has Wells's signature worldbuilding and wholly real character development, and her wry voice shines through. I can't even explain how real the world felt, in which each race and city and culture had such well-drawn back story that they lived on even outside the main plot."
—Patrice Sarath, author of *Gordath Wood* and *Red Gold Bridge*

The Serpent Sea

"With these books Wells is writing at the top of her game, and given their breadth, originality, and complexity, this series is showing indications it could become one of the landmark series of the genre."
—*Adventures Fantastic*

"Wells remains a compelling storyteller whose clear prose, goal-driven plotting, and witty, companionable characters should win her fans among those who enjoy the works of writers such as John Scalzi and Lois McMaster Bujold."
—Matt Denault, *Strange Horizons*

"A worthy sequel to *The Cloud Roads* and it features all of the strengths (fantastic world-building, great story, awesome characters) of that first novel. It is so easy to fall in love with this series and the reasons are manifold."
—*The Book Smugglers*

The Siren Depths

"I really loved Book 3, which wound up as my favorite book of the trilogy . . . I'll be pushing it on everybody who loves great writing, ornate worlds and wonderfully-drawn nonhuman characters."
—Rachel Neumeier, author of *Lord of the Changing Winds* and *Black Dog*

"*The Siren Depths* has more of what I've come to love about the Books of the Raksura—a compelling story, great world-building in a unique setting, and lovable characters with very realistic problems. In my opinion, it's also the most satisfying installment in the series."
—*Fantasy Café*

"Truly inventive and stunningly imaginative world-building perfectly melded with vivid, engaging characters make the Books of the Raksura one of my all-time favorite science-fiction series."
—Kate Elliott, author of The Spiritwalker Trilogy

Stories of the Raksura: Volume One

"Wells is adept at suggesting a long, complex history for her world with economy . . . Longtime fans and new readers alike will enjoy Wells's deft touch with characterization and the fantastic."
—*Publishers Weekly*

"The worldbuilding and characters in these stories are as wonderful as the novels and I had no difficulty immersing myself into Wells's world and societies again."
—*SF Signal*

Stories of the Raksura: Volume Two

"Immensely pleasing . . . the shorter stories still encompass everything that makes the novels so satisfying, from the daily interactions between Raksura to the incredible creatures, mysteries and landscapes of the Three Worlds, and if Martha Wells were to never write anything other than Raksura stories from now on, as much as I love her other work, I can't say I'd complain."
—*A Dribble of Ink*

"I wonderfully enjoyed these stories . . . I urge readers with any interest in secondary world fantasy who have not done so to pick up *The Cloud Roads* and begin there and work your way to this volume. And then, like me, you can hope and wait for future volumes set in Wells's rich and endlessly entertaining world, peoples and characters."
—Paul Weimer, *Skiffy and Fanty*

The Edge of Worlds

THE EDGE OF WORLDS

MARTHA WELLS

Night Shade Books
NEW YORK

A hardcover edition of *The Edge of Worlds* was published 2016 by Night Shade Books. First trade paperback edition published 2017.

Night Shade books may be purchased in bulk at special discounts for sales promotion, corporate gifts, fund-raising, or educational purposes. Special editions can also be created to specifications. For details, contact the Special Sales Department, Night Shade Books, 307 West 36th Street, 11th Floor, New York, NY 10018 or info@skyhorsepublishing.com.

Night Shade Books™ is a trademark of Skyhorse Publishing, Inc.®, a Delaware corporation.

Visit our website at www.nightshadebooks.com.

10 9 8 7 6 5 4 3

Library of Congress Cataloging-in-Publication Data

Names: Wells, Martha, author.
Title: The edge of worlds / Martha Wells.
Description: New York : Night Shade Books, [2016]
Identifiers: LCCN 2015050039 | ISBN 9781597808439 (hardback)
Subjects: | BISAC: FICTION / Fantasy / General. | FICTION / Fantasy / Epic. | FICTION / Science Fiction / General. | FICTION / Science Fiction / Adventure. | GSAFD: Science fiction.
Classification: LCC PS3573.E4932 E34 2016 | DDC 813/.54--dc23
LC record available at http://lccn.loc.gov/2015050039

Edited by Jeremy Lassen
Cover art by Yukari Masuike
Cover design by Lesley Worrell

Hardcover ISBN: 978-1-59780-843-9
Paperback ISBN: 978-1-59780-897-2

Printed in the United States of America

To my husband Troyce, for everything

CHAPTER ONE

Moon knew he was dreaming.

In the real world, he was in Jade's bower, lying on the furs near the metal bowl of the hearth, just close enough to feel the heat of the warming stones on his skin. Chime lay nearby, breathing deeply, a book unrolled across his chest. Jade was up in the hanging bed, and he could hear the faint rasp of her scales against the cushions as she stirred in her sleep. The damp night air was laced with the familiar scents of the court, the flowers floating in Jade's bathing pool, and the ever-present musky sweetness that was the scent of the mountain-tree that housed the colony.

In the dream world, he was watching the Fell destroy the Indigo Cloud court.

He could see the central well, spiraling up through the heart of the great tree, lit by the soft glow of snail shells that were spelled for light by the mentors. Fell stench was thick in his lungs and the walls were alive with hundreds of dark shapes as dakti swarmed up the polished wood walls. Three massive major kethel climbed up from the greeting hall, their claws catching on the carved balconies, gouging through the stairs that curved up the walls, cracking the delicate pillars. They plunged their clawed hands into the bower doorways, and Arbora screamed and blood splattered against the wood and jeweled inlay.

The perspective changed and Moon watched dakti flow through the passages of the teachers' levels. He tried not to see faces and couldn't help it. There were Rill and Bark and the soldier Ginger, piled up at the mouth of a chamber they had tried to defend, their eyes blank with death but their mouths open in snarls of furious terror. And the warrior Vine, lying in a junction of bowers, caught between his scaled form and his groundling one, half soft brown groundling skin and half-scaled, one wing twisted under him, his stomach ripped open and guts spilling out. A scream of rage rang out from further up in the central well and Moon knew it was Pearl, the reigning queen.

Where's Jade? Moon thought. *Where am I? Where's Stone? Why aren't we doing anything?* That thought almost broke him out of the nightmare, and for a moment he lay on the furs again. He could see his favorite carving, the one of the Raksuran court that covered most of the bower's ceiling. In different colored woods and gemstones it depicted queens, consorts, warriors, and the wingless Arbora, all their bodies entwined or flowing apart, separate pieces making one whole.

He tried again to turn the dream into something else, tried to wake, but the rulers flowed down the stairs to the teachers' hall, past the mutilated, blood-streaked bodies of Arbora and warriors, took the passage that led toward the nurseries—

"Moon, wake up," Balm said.

He snapped out of the dream. He was on his feet, breathing hard in terror and fury. Chime yelped and shifted, sat bolt upright, dumped the book off his lap, and kicked a stray piece of pottery across the room. Jade flipped out of the hanging bed and landed on her feet, spines lifted for battle.

Balm leapt back a pace, dropped her spines and held out her hands. "Sorry! I'm sorry, I didn't mean to startle you!"

The relief was so intense, Moon's knees almost gave out. He said, "No, sorry, no, it was me." He shifted back to his groundling form, scales dissolving and reforming as soft skin, and he felt a chill cold enough to make him shiver. It was the thwarted fight-urge from the dream, still running through his blood. He had had plenty of nightmares but he rarely shifted while he was asleep. It was a long ingrained habit from all the turns of self-control while he had been living in groundling settlements, pretending to be anything but a shapeshifter. "I was having a nightmare."

Chime struggled to his knees and rescued the book and the cup. "So was I," he said, following Moon's example and shifting back to his groundling form. His hand trembled as he set the cup next to the others beside the hearth bowl. "It must be something in the air."

"I wasn't sleeping well, either." Jade settled her spines self-consciously. Queens didn't have a groundling form, shifting to a smaller Arbora-like shape with softer scales, no wings, and fewer spines. That was the form they slept in, and Jade must have shifted to her winged form at some point between leaping out of the hanging bed and landing on the floor. Moon's heart was still pounding. The relief of seeing her and Chime alive and well was almost as intense as if the dream had been real.

Balm should have been looking at them as if they had all lost their minds. Moon knew he was still twitchy from his turns of living like a feral solitary, but waking him usually didn't cause this much of an outburst. Especially considering it was Balm, Jade's warrior clutchmate and one of Moon's oldest friends in the court. But Balm looked worried, the gold scales of her brow furrowed. She said, "Were you all having nightmares? About the Fell attacking the colony?"

Startled, Moon said, "Yes."

Jade flicked her spines in an affirmative, then glanced at Moon. "What, you were too?"

Rolling the book back up into its cover, Chime looked up. "Uh, so was I."

They didn't have a moment for the strangeness of that to settle in, because Balm said, grimly, "So did almost everyone down in the teachers' bowers, and maybe everyone in the court. Some of the younger mentors woke up screaming. Heart wants to talk to you and Pearl right away."

"I know it's odd," Chime was saying as they went out into the queens' hall, "but it's theoretically possible for a mentor or a queen to share a dream with the rest of their bloodline and related bloodlines."

"Theoretically possible doesn't mean any mentors or queens know how to do it, or if they have, they never mentioned it to me." Jade's spines and expression were somewhere between appalled and angry.

As sister queen of the court, she should know. Of course, Moon was her consort, and technically he should know too, but he hadn't been raised as a Raksura, and most of the time it seemed everything he learned about his own people had to be acquired the hard way. "I think if Pearl could do it, we'd know by now," he said. It might be theoretically possible, but the idea made his skin creep.

The queens' hall, meant to impress visiting queens and consorts, was still quiet except for the water falling into a fountain pool against the far wall. The huge sculpture of a queen, her scales set with bright sunstones and her outspread wings stretched out to circle the hall and meet tip to tip, was suddenly an uncomfortable metaphor, at least for Moon. The open gallery of the consorts' quarters was above the sculpture; Moon, Stone, and Ember, the only adult consorts currently in the court, had bowers up there, but they seldom slept in them. From the well that led down through the center of the tree came the faint sounds of movement and voices. Raksura, especially Arbora, didn't always sleep through the night, but this was the noise of disturbance, uneasy voices and people calling out to each other.

Jade stepped to the edge of the well and unfurled the deep blue expanse of her wings. "Balm, you wake Pearl. Chime, find Stone." She jumped off the ledge and cupped her wings to control her fall.

Chime looked uneasy at the prospect of disturbing Stone. "If he's having the same nightmare we were . . ."

"Just make sure he's awake before you get close," Moon told him. Stone was the court's line-grandfather and could be cranky at the best of times, let alone when he was caught in a vivid dream about the Fell eating all his descendants.

Balm went toward the reigning queen's bower to wake Pearl, saying, "I think I'd better stand in the doorway and call to her."

Moon shifted to follow Jade and used his wings to drop straight down through the central well.

The dream was still too close for Moon to be able to look at the stairs curving up the spiral well and the carved balconies without wincing. He kept expecting to see dead bodies lying in the round doorways.

It wasn't as if the dream had been of some far-fetched, impossible circumstance. The Fell existed by feeding on groundling settlements and cities and had destroyed Raksuran colonies and killed entire courts. Moon was a survivor of one of those attacks; it had been the reason he had spent most of his first forty or so turns of life alone. A Fell flight had nearly destroyed Indigo Cloud's old colony to the east before the court had fled here to the Reaches.

Moon landed on the floor of the greeting hall a heartbeat after Jade. This was the first chamber visitors to the colony tree would see when they entered through the twisting passage that led in from the knothole, and it was designed to be impressive, as well as easily defended. Directly across from the entrance a pool of water was fed by a small fall from a higher channel, and the shell-lights glinted off all the warm colors of the carved wood.

Warriors and Arbora, some in their scaled forms and some in groundling, were out on the balconies that looked down on the hall, their voices rising in worry as more of them woke from the dream. Arbora soldiers were on watch in the hall all day and night, gathered around the hearth bowl near the pool. Usually they traded off turns sleeping but now they were all awake, on their feet, and watching Jade's arrival with relief. She said, "Ginger, you all had the dream too?"

Ginger flicked her spines in an affirmative. "Four of us were sleeping, and we all saw—" She stopped and her throat worked as she swallowed uneasily.

"We thought it was just us, but Balm said it's everyone," Sharp added.

Jade made her voice reassuring. "Send someone to find Knell." He was the leader of the soldiers' caste, and one of Chime's clutchmates. "Tell him to have the other soldiers check through all the bowers, make sure everyone's all right." She glanced up at the warriors gathered on one of the upper balconies. "Sand, Aura, Serene, the rest of you. Get down here and help the soldiers guard the entrance."

As the warriors dropped down to the greeting hall floor, Sharp said, uneasily, "You don't think the dream is going to become real . . ."

"No," Jade said, absently enough for it to be convincing. "But if it's a warning of some danger, we want to be prepared."

There was something Moon had to check on first, before worrying about the rest of the court. "I'm going to the nurseries."

5

Jade flicked a spine in acknowledgment and Moon dove down the stairwell into the teachers' hall. The round hall was crowded with uneasy Arbora, all talking nervously. They barely noticed as Moon flashed past and flung himself down the passage that led to the nurseries.

He slid to a stop in front of a round doorway with a lintel carved with the figures of baby Arbora and Aeriat, took a deep breath, and shifted back to his groundling form. He couldn't hear any crying or screaming inside, which was a good sign.

Moon stepped through into the first big low-ceilinged chamber and almost ran into Blossom. She lifted her hands and said, low-voiced, "It's all right. It didn't affect any of the clutches, whatever it is."

Moon let out his breath, the tension in his chest easing. He hadn't realized how afraid he was until this moment.

Everything was quiet, though some sleepy Arbora toddlers played near one of the several shallow fountain pools. Doorways led off into a maze of smaller rooms, and teachers were moving in and out of them, checking on their charges, a few being trailed by querulous Aeriat fledglings. The inhabitants of the nurseries had changed over the past two turns in the colony tree. Several Arbora had clutched, producing new Arbora babies and warrior fledglings, and the court's population balance was finally on its way to becoming more stable. Moon asked, "Did it happen to you?" From what the others had said, everyone's version of the dream was a little different. The one thing in common had been the overwhelming violence of the attack, the helplessness, the sense that the court had been caught with no warning at all.

Blossom's nod was grim. She was an older Arbora, though the only sign of age yet was the threads of gray in her dark hair. Raksura lost all their coloring as they got older, and Blossom's skin was still a warm bronze. She was the teacher Jade and Moon had chosen to be in charge of the care of their first clutch. "The Fell attacking the Reaches." She lifted her shoulders, not quite shuddering, and turned to lead the way across the room. "It was like the old colony all over again, but worse."

At the far end of the main room was another small chamber with a pile of furs and cushions. Moon and Jade's clutch was in the center of the pile, three female and two male, sleepily climbing on each other and tugging on one another's frills. It was more and more likely that they were queens and consorts. Mixed gender clutches were unlikely to produce warriors. They were with the other royal clutch, the last three survivors of the Sky Copper court. The two fledgling consorts Bitter and Thorn were half-awake, leaning on each other, and Frost, the little queen, sat in front of the babies to guard them. "What's going on?" Frost demanded. "Blossom said everyone's having the same dream."

Blossom shushed her. "Keep your voice down, some of the others are still sleeping."

In a piercing whisper, Frost repeated, "Is everyone really having the same dream?"

Moon sat down beside the nest and untangled Cloud's still soft claws from Fern's frills. At a little over a turn old, the clutch couldn't talk much and were mostly concerned with playing, along with eating and sleeping and other bodily functions. "It looks like it, but we don't know why yet. You didn't have the dream?"

Frost shrugged her spines. She was in her Arbora form, small and deceptively soft. Her scales were green, and as she had grown over the past turn, the yellow tracery was becoming more pronounced. All queens had a second contrasting web of color across their scales, and it was a sign that Frost was finally maturing. She was still a long time from officially leaving the nurseries, whatever she thought. She said, "We dream about Fell all the time." Thorn and Bitter sleepily nodded.

The Sky Copper clutch had survived the Fell attack on their colony to the east, only to be captured by a Fell flight. It would have been a horrific event for anyone to go through, let alone fledglings, and they still bore the effects of it, though it wasn't as obvious now. "But you weren't dreaming about them tonight?" Moon asked, just to make sure, as Sapphire lunged into his lap and started to chew on the cuff of his pants. Queens shared mental connections to their courts; it was how they brought the court together, how they could hold other Raksura in their groundling forms and keep them from shifting, and other abilities Moon still wasn't so certain about. But Frost wasn't in the Indigo Cloud bloodline, so even if it was possible for a queen to give a nightmare to the whole court, he didn't think it could have come from Frost.

"Blossom already asked that," Frost informed him. "We weren't dreaming."

"If any of the clutches did have the dream," Blossom said as she lifted Solace and Rain out of the nest and deposited Rain in Moon's lap, "they don't remember it. When we started to wake them, they all wanted to play or eat or go back to sleep. They weren't shifting, either."

When fledglings and baby Arbora were frightened, they shifted at random, even in their sleep. As proof he hadn't been upset, Rain curled up in Moon's lap and hissed out a contented breath as he fell asleep. Bitter crawled into the nest, pulled Cloud and Fern against his chest, and followed suit. Frost gave Thorn a push and he joined them, curling up in a ball. Moon arranged Solace, Sapphire, and Rain next to Thorn. It calmed abraded nerves just to come down here and touch their little soft-scaled bodies. He felt better able to think about this logically now. "I need to get back to Jade." She was going to want to know the nurseries weren't in chaos, for one thing. "Frost, keep an eye on everyone, all right?"

When the Sky Copper clutch had first come to the court, Frost had been, off and on, an incorrigible terror. Over the past couple of turns, Frost had gradually been getting better, either from growing more secure at Indigo Cloud or just getting a little older.

Moon had expected her, and maybe the two fledgling consorts, to be jealous of his new clutch, but it had just seemed to make all three of them happier and easier to deal with. Bitter, who had refused to speak to anyone but his clutchmates, had even started to talk to the new babies. Maybe a new royal Aeriat clutch, along with the clutches that the Arbora had produced, had been another sign of security in their new court and colony.

Frost hesitated, clearly torn between wanting to watch over the other clutches and wanting to be a part of whatever was going on. She said, grudgingly, "Someday I'll be big, and I can fight the monsters."

"It's not a monster." Moon pushed to his feet, and thought, *Probably not a monster*. In the Reaches, anything was possible.

Blossom followed him out to the doorway. Keeping his voice low, Moon said, "So whoever did it, didn't want to upset the clutches."

"Which means it was one of us. Unintentionally, I mean." Blossom eyed him a moment. "Could it be Chime?"

Moon hesitated. Before Moon had come to Indigo Cloud, Chime had been an Arbora and a mentor. The Fell influence at the old colony had caused disease and a drop in warrior births, and one day, Chime had shifted and found himself a warrior. This was apparently a natural process that happened in courts on the decline, but that hadn't made it any easier for Chime to cope with. Warriors never had mentor powers, and so Chime had also lost his ability to heal, to augur, and to manipulate rocks and flora to produce heat and light. But the change had affected him in odd ways, and he had gained the ability to hear things he shouldn't be able to, and to get odd insights about groundling magic.

Those insights had warned them of traps, but had also lured Chime into dangerous situations. It wasn't beyond the realm of possibility that something had made Chime do this. But while Chime could hear strange things, he had never shown any ability to make anyone, including other Raksura, hear him. Moon said, "Maybe, but I doubt it. I think he'd know if he did."

Blossom nodded thoughtfully. "That's true. He always does seem to know."

Another consort whipped through the passage down from the teachers' hall, not quite with the speed Moon had. Ember jolted to a halt and shifted to his groundling form. He said, "They said you were already here. Is everything all right?"

"They didn't have the dream," Moon told him. "Did you?" Ember was Pearl's consort, given to Indigo Cloud by the court of Emerald Twilight. His skin was a lighter bronze than usual for the Aeriat of Indigo Cloud or Emerald Twilight, and his hair was a light gold-brown. He was young and had been gently raised, but had a comprehensive knowledge of court politics in the Reaches, which made him nearly the opposite of Moon in every respect. Moon liked him, but Ember made him feel large, awkward, and like the feral disaster that most of Indigo Cloud had considered him when he had first arrived.

Ember nodded, stepping past Moon and Blossom to look worriedly into the nurseries. "So did Pearl. I saw Floret on the way down and she said she did too." He told Blossom, "I'll help you get the babies settled." Like a real consort, Ember was good with clutches. Pearl was probably only waiting another turn or so for him to mature a little more before she had another clutch herself.

Moon left them and went down the passage back to the teachers' hall. It was a big chamber with walls carved with a forest of spirals, plumes, fern trees, and other varieties, their branches reaching up to the domed ceiling and their roots framing the round doorways that led off to other chambers. It wasn't as large as the greeting hall, but it was less drafty and somehow more intimate, as if the tree carvings made you feel sheltered and protected. This was where both Arbora and Aeriat tended to come in the evening, to share food and conversation and stories. Now it was crowded with disturbed Arbora and warriors, gathered around Jade and Pearl.

The reigning queen, Pearl was the birthqueen of both Jade and Balm, though Moon had never been able to see the physical resemblance that was obvious to other queens. She was a head taller than Moon, and her scales were brilliant gold, overlaid with a webbed pattern of deepest indigo blue. The frilled mane behind her head was a golden sunburst, and there were more frills on the tips of her folded wings and on the triangle-shape at the end of her tail. Like all Raksuran queens, she wore only jewelry. Her relationship with Jade had become notably more tranquil since Jade had clutched, and she didn't hate Moon nearly as much as she had when Stone had first brought him to the court.

Pearl flicked her spines and several of the warriors turned to shift and leap up the stairs toward the greeting hall, probably going to join those who were guarding the entrance. Moon started through the crowd, and the Arbora made way for him until he stood beside Chime and Bell, Chime's other clutchmate, and chief of the teachers' caste. Bell leaned in to whisper to Moon, "They told you none of the clutches had the dream? It's strange."

"It's not that strange," Chime countered, and several Arbora hissed at him to be quiet.

Heart, the chief mentor, sat on the floor near the hearth bowl, staring at the warming stones. Or staring at the way the heat rising from the stones bent the air. She was a small female Arbora, in her groundling form, her brow knit in concentration. The spell-lights in the room shone on her dark amber skin and found highlights in her bronze-colored hair. She was using a quick and dirty method of scrying for danger or other momentous happenings that Moon had seen mentors use in emergencies. Jade and Pearl both watched her, their tails moving restlessly.

Keeping his voice low, Moon asked Chime, "Where's Stone?"

"He went outside to take a look around, see if there's anything out there." Chime was back in his groundling form, and lifted his shoulders uneasily, unconsciously twitching the spines of his scaled form. "You don't think the Fell are really about to attack . . ."

"No." Moon gave him a reassuring nudge to the shoulder. There hadn't been any Fell stench in the draft coming through the knothole entrance. The one thing the Fell could never disguise was their odor. He didn't think there was any reason to panic now. But what the vision might be telling them was that there was plenty of reason to panic later.

The other two young mentors, Merit and Thistle, watched Heart intently. Most of the other Arbora waiting worriedly were teachers, the soldiers and hunters having either gone up to guard the greeting hall or to search the colony on Jade's orders. Most were in their groundling forms, their skin various shades of bronze and copper, their hair dark or light or reddish brown. Arbora were shorter and often rounder and heavyset compared to the taller, thinner Aeriat. Seasons in the Reaches tended to be cool and more rainy or warm and less rainy, and this night was warm and damp, so most of the Arbora were dressed in brief kilts.

Bone, the chief of the hunters' caste, came in from one of the doorways on the far side of the room. The crowd parted to let him make his way toward Pearl and Jade. His groundling form showed the signs of age, with his hair turning white and an ashy cast to his dark bronze skin. He was stocky and heavily muscled, and he had a ring of scar tissue around his neck where something had once tried to bite his head off. He reached Pearl and said, quietly, "The doors in the lower part of the tree are still shut, and nothing's disturbed them."

He meant the doors out to the root levels, on the forest floor. Pearl flicked a spine in acknowledgment.

Then Heart looked up. "I can't see anything. If it was happening somewhere now, or about to happen here, I'd know."

Merit's shoulders slumped in relief. Thistle said, "No one could fail to see it, let alone Heart."

Pearl tilted her head and looked at Jade. Jade said, "Stone will be back soon. He can confirm it."

Pearl turned to regard Heart again. Moon would have twitched uneasily under the fixed predatory intensity of her gaze, but as an Arbora, Heart didn't have the same reflexes. Pearl said, "So what was it?"

Heart rubbed the back of her neck and glanced at Merit and Thistle. She said, "They think it was a shared dream."

Merit was close to Heart's age, but to Moon he had always seemed younger. In his groundling form, he had wide-set eyes, warm brown skin and fluffy light-colored hair. He was a little on the easily distracted side, but, like Heart, Moon had seen how powerful a mentor he was on a few memorable occasions. Thistle was young too, part of the copper-skinned and reddish-haired bloodline of Indigo Cloud, with a determined chin. Merit said, "That's a dream that comes to one of us, and is so . . . powerful, it spreads through the rest of the court, everyone who's asleep."

"That's what I said," Chime muttered under his breath.

"Everyone, but not the clutches," Moon said.

Everyone looked at him, then back to Merit.

Merit lifted his hands. "Arbora babies don't show mentor potential until they're at least ten turns old, sometimes older. Maybe fledglings and babies don't develop their connection to the rest of the court until they're older."

"It must be rare," Jade said, watching them with the scales of her brow furrowed, "considering we've never heard of it before."

"It is rare," Thistle said. "We've seen mentions of it in the mentors' histories, but that's all."

"If Flower hadn't made us read everything the court has, we wouldn't know about it," Merit added.

Not for the first time, Moon wished Flower were still here. She had been the court's oldest mentor, the one who helped guide them out of the east and to the Reaches. She had been dead for nearly two turns now.

Pearl's expression suggested shared dreams weren't rare enough. "It has never happened to this court, not in our memories. Why now?"

Merit and Thistle turned to Heart, who said, "We just don't know."

Then Jade cocked her head, and a moment later Moon heard voices from the stairwell up to the greeting hall. Jade said, "Stone's back."

Pearl turned and took the stairs in two bounds. Jade followed and Moon went after her, everyone else trailing behind him. He noticed he was getting better at this part, at realizing what his place was and taking it. Two turns ago he would have stood there a moment, waiting to go with the warriors and Arbora, while they stared at him awkwardly.

Stone was in the greeting hall with Knell and some of the other soldiers and warriors. He was in his groundling form and a little damp from the light rain outside. Raksuran queens and consorts grew larger and stronger as they grew older, and Stone was old enough to remember when the court had first left the Reaches, generations ago, so his winged form was too big to easily get through the part of the knothole entrance where it narrowed. Tip to tip his wings were more than three times Moon's twenty-pace span.

In his groundling form Stone was lean and tall, like all the groundling forms of Aeriat. One of his eyes was partially blind, with a white haze across the pupil, and his skin and hair had faded to gray with age. He wore battered gray pants and an old shirt, with absolutely no concession to the idea that consorts were supposed to dress to do credit to the court. But one of the benefits of being a line-grandfather was that you could do pretty much whatever you wanted. As Pearl came toward him, he said, "There's nothing out there."

There were murmurs of relief from the Arbora and warriors, and Jade's and Pearl's spines flicked, shedding tension. Pearl said, "You're certain?"

Stone said, "There's nothing in the air. It's not as damp as it was last night and there's a breeze. I can scent the redflower that just opened on the next mountain-tree, but no Fell."

The Fell's distinctive stench permeated their surroundings and would be carried on the wind even over long distances. It was probably one of the reasons they relied on less scent-sensitive groundling species as their main prey. If they were anywhere nearby, their odor would be hard to disguise, and Stone's senses were far more acute than an ordinary Raksura's.

"So," Pearl said. She looked around at all the anxious faces. Moon knew he didn't feel much relieved. "I'm not going to tell you to go back to sleep as if nothing happened. But there is no immediate threat, and there is no point to behaving as if there was."

For Pearl, that was an inspirational speech. All the Arbora and warriors here had grown up with her, and they knew it was an attempt to reassure them, as well as a not so subtle hint that they should shut up and stop panicking.

Pearl turned to go, collecting a few of her warriors with a dip of her spines. She exchanged an opaque look with Jade, who turned to follow. Yes, Moon figured they were probably going to talk over what had happened.

As Jade passed him, Moon caught her wrist. "I'm going to spend the rest of the night in the nurseries."

Jade didn't question it. She brushed the back of her hand against his cheek. "Just try to get some sleep."

Moon didn't make any promises, as he was pretty certain that wasn't going to happen.

Jade and Balm both leapt up the wall onto the first balcony level with Pearl to head up toward the queens' hall. Chime was climbing down the steps back to the teachers' hall with Heart and Merit and the others, still arguing about the characteristics of shared dreams. Moon found himself standing next to Stone. Keeping his voice low, he asked, "Did you have it?"

Stone eyed him. "Did you?"

"Yes." Moon didn't ask Stone exactly what he had seen. Stone was the one responsible for Moon being the first consort of Indigo Cloud rather than a feral solitary, and also the closest thing Moon had ever had to the relationship many groundlings had with their male sire. Moon didn't want to know what form Stone's vision of the destruction of the court had taken, and he didn't want to talk about his own. The images were still too vivid.

Stone jerked his head toward the stairwell down to the teachers' hall. "Do the mentors know what it was?"

"They said it was a shared dream, not a vision. And no, they don't know why it happened." Moon still felt uneasy to the core. "You've never heard of anything like that?"

"No." Stone looked away from the Arbora and the warriors who still gathered at the far end of the room, all restless and talking anxiously. "This isn't just chance. Things like this don't happen for no reason."

Moon wished he could believe Stone was wrong.

CHAPTER TWO

One Change of the Month Later

H unting was normally the Arbora's job, though in the Reaches it was necessary to have warriors present to keep watch and help transport them and their prey to and from the colony tree. Moon had wondered occasionally why they didn't just let the warriors do the hunting themselves, and attributed it to a combination of tradition and warriors being lazy. It had turned out the answer was that the warriors were terrible at hunting.

Moon crouched on the branch, his foot claws caught in the rough bark. "If you let me go down there and be the bait, we could get this over with." The warriors were only doing the stalking today because their prey was a creature who had been pursuing the Arbora on their hunts and scaring away the usual game. It was just too big and too fast for the Arbora to deal with on their own, and it had already injured too many of them. The Arbora who had been attacked hadn't been able to describe the predator well, and the hunter who had seen it best was still in a healing sleep back in the colony tree.

Chime, perched on the branch collar a little further down, said, "Uh, the hunt would be over with, all right. We'd have to spend the rest of the day recovering your body."

Annoyed, Moon settled his wings. It was raining lightly, which wasn't helping anyone's temper. The already muted light falling through the multiple layers of leaves in the mountain-tree canopies was dim and more gray than green. The court had been tense since the shared dream, with everyone braced for it to be repeated, or for the event that it foretold to occur. Neither had happened. Nothing had turned up in the mentors' augury, despite their best efforts. Jade had sent messages to their two closest allies, Sunset Water and Emerald Twilight, to see if they had had any similar experiences. The answer had been no, and the messages, delivered by warriors, had been too polite to convey what the other courts were actually thinking: that Indigo Cloud had collectively lost its mind.

Below, on a lower branch, one of the warriors startled a nest of flying lizards, sending them fleeing in a small explosion of multicolored squeaking, alerting half the Reaches to his presence. Moon hissed in frustration. He had been hunting for survival since he was a fledgling, while most of these warriors had still been playing in the nurseries. It had taken them three days to follow the signs and traces from the platform where the Arbora hunters had been attacked to here, and now they weren't even sure where the thing had gone to ground. He told Chime, "I've been bait before—"

Chime nodded. "I know, and I find that terrifying."

"—and I wasn't talking to you." He looked up at the smaller branch arching above them.

Jade perched up there, partially concealed from this angle by the drooping fronds of a fern tree that had taken root on the broad branch. She said, "Not every problem can be solved by you trying to get yourself killed."

"Not every problem," Moon agreed. He looked down toward the platforms nestled in the branches across from their vantage point. "But this one could be."

The suspended forest was made up of layers and layers of these platforms, formed when dirt built up in the entwined mountain-tree branches until it had enough depth to grow grass, form ponds and swamps, and support entire forests of smaller trees. The platform their quarry might have gone to ground in was unusual in that another mountain-tree had taken root in it. Usually when this happened, the sapling mountain-tree died off or fell when its weight grew too heavy. This one was apparently intending to survive.

It was already a few hundred paces tall, its smaller canopy mingling with that of the mountain-tree that supported the platform, and its trunk was a good hundred paces around. Its roots had grown through the dirt of the platform and twined around the branches below it, and there was plenty of room to hide in that extensive and complex structure.

Jade said, definitively, "If anyone's going to be bait, it's me."

Moon twitched his spines at her. "That is not fair."

Jade snorted. "You sound like Frost."

Moon had been teaching Frost and some of the older fledglings how to hunt, but there was no way he would have let any of them even come along to watch this. He had had to grow up the hard way, and while he was determined to teach all the fledglings how to take care of themselves in an emergency, he meant them to have a more normal Raksuran upbringing, which included comfortable nurseries guarded by determined Arbora and no fights to the death with suspended forest denizens. He pointed out, "Frost hasn't done this before. I have."

Jade's sigh was part hiss of irritation. It didn't sound like she would change her mind anytime soon.

Chime said, "This thing is too smart to be lured out by a Raksura acting as bait. If it wasn't, we would have killed it already." He added, "Maybe we need a mentor."

He had a point. Moon just wished they could get this over with. He had been restless enough lately, worrying about the dream.

Ferns fluttered on the branch above, and Jade said, "I am not dragging a mentor all the way out here to tell us this damn thing is hiding under that sapling. We already know that."

Moon had to say, "Probably hiding under the sapling."

Jade swung down onto the lower branch to stand next to him. Exasperated, she said, "If we still can't find this thing by twilight, I'll—"

Then Chime said, "Wait."

Moon turned. Chime had kept his gaze on the arched roots winding through the platform. He continued, "There was movement. Wait . . . There it is again."

Jade stepped to Chime's side and crouched to follow his sightline. She said, "At the base of the root that's almost at the edge of the platform."

"Yes." Chime's spines flicked in excitement. "I thought I saw the ground ripple. Now there's a furrow."

Moon saw it now, a too-perfect circle in the moss-covered dirt, next to one of the sapling's roots. It shaped the outline of something with a big round body. Too big. But the Arbora had all agreed that the creature had attacked from under the top dirt and moss layer of a platform. *Maybe they only saw a small part of it*, Moon thought. Maybe the rest of it had been hidden. It would explain the warriors' difficulty in following its trail.

Jade dove off the branch collar and spread her wings to drop silently. Moon jumped after her, and heard Chime's claws scrabble on the wood as he scrambled to stay with them.

Jade landed on a branch a hundred or so paces down. It was closer to eye level with the platform that had the sapling, though still far enough away to keep the predator there from sensing their presence. At least, Moon hoped so.

As Moon landed beside Jade and furled his wings, Balm climbed out of concealment behind a big knot of red tree fungus. She said, "You saw something?"

"Chime did." Jade pointed out the furrow for Balm, then glanced around at the surrounding branches. Another dozen or so warriors were hidden in various spots around them, some well-concealed, others peeking curiously out. "Now we just have to figure out how to do this."

Balm leaned back to pass the word along to Briar, who was still crouched behind the fungus. Chime said, "Can we just . . . leap on it? All that dirt on top of it should keep it from reacting too quickly."

Sometimes it was easy to tell that Chime had come late to being a warrior. His knowledge of how to attack things from the air was still sporadic. Keeping his voice low, Moon started to explain, "Digging itself just under the surface like that is probably an attack position—"

The predator burst out of the ground, spraying dirt and moss clumps, with so much force the mountain-tree sapling shook. It leapt forward off the platform, the round armored body blossoming with grasping limbs. Diagonal bands of flesh snapped out from under the upper shell. Moon snarled in astonishment. Chime said, a little unnecessarily, "Wait, it's got wings!"

Jade launched herself into the air as the predator dove toward them. Moon knew she was going for the eyes or the head, and he leapt off the branch and aimed for the chest.

Moon swept in as the limbs on this side flailed at him. He twisted under and in toward the predator's lower body, getting a brief glimpse of small mouths surrounded by tiny tentacles lining each jointed limb. It jerked at the last second and he missed, hitting its side below the first row of limbs instead of the underbelly. Then its body snapped upright as something knocked the creature backward; that had to be Jade, landing on the head. Hopefully an irritated Raksuran queen was more than this thing had counted on.

Moon held on with all his claws, trying to see a vulnerable point. He had temporarily lost his bearings and wasn't sure which way was up and which down; the sinking feeling in his stomach told him they were freefalling. The thing must be a glider and Jade had knocked it right out of the air.

A limb groped for him and he slashed it away, then managed to get a look up toward the head. Jade ripped at the predator's face but she was far too close to that wide mouth. The limbs reached up to drag at her. The armor around the cheeks moved and Moon's heart thumped in terror; the creature might be able to extend its jaw to close on her.

Before he could yell a warning, Jade planted a powerful clawed foot in the creature's jaw hinge. Moon heard a gurgling noise go through its body. That would hold it for a moment, but they were still falling and running out of time.

Moon couldn't see any vulnerable point nearby and scrambled down the armored body, headed for the back end. If there was any other opening, it might be down there.

He reached the rear section and saw a thin spot in the armor around a puckered opening. He stabbed his claws into it. The predator jerked, its body contracted, and Moon looked back in time to see Jade swing out of range of its mouth.

Then he heard Balm shouting, "Drop, drop, now!"

Moon yelled, "Jade, drop!" and let go.

The predator tumbled away, but a stray limb slapped Moon in the head. He rolled and managed to get his wings out, his eyes filling with pain-tears. He squinted to see and made out Jade, just a blurry blue shape cupping her wings to slow her fall.

The predator fell toward the mist barrier hiding the lower levels of the forest. It rolled upright and shot its wings out—and then something large, dark, and fast knocked it out of the air.

Moon let his breath out in relief, flapping to stay aloft. He had wondered where Stone was.

There was a flurry of motion, some of the predator's limbs went flying, and the two combatants fell below the mist. Moon landed on the nearest branch, a little winded.

Another warrior dove down, aiming to land beside him. Moon saw the vivid green scales with the blue undersheen, and growled.

River landed anyway. One of his virtues was that he wasn't afraid of Moon, even though every time they had fought, Moon had won. River said, in disgust, "That was typical."

Over the past couple of turns River's position had moved from insisting that Moon was embarrassing the court by existing to insisting that Moon was embarrassing the court by not behaving like a proper consort. Moon said, "You need to find another reason to hate me and we can just talk about that all the time."

"There's so many to choose from, I get confused." River flicked spines in derision.

Moon sighed. He decided to try honesty. "You thought Jade and I were going to get killed and it scared you and this is the only way you know how to say it."

That worked. River snarled and fled the branch.

Stone reappeared, flapping up through the mist, carrying the creature clutched in his front claws. Its lower body hung open, guts dripping out. Stone circled around and dropped it on the platform.

Moon jumped off the branch and banked down to land nearby. Jade beat him there. As Chime, Balm, and the other warriors swept in, Stone shook his spines out and dragged his claws through the tufts of grass to get the foul-smelling ichor off them.

Stone shifted down to groundling to say, "Were you trying to kill it or just annoy it?"

"I didn't have time to choose a better approach. I didn't want it to get away." Jade circled around toward the creature's head.

Moon told Stone, "We were slowing it down for you, because you're old."

Stone's expression was eloquent of the wish to slap Moon in the head. He said, "Slowing it down by throwing yourselves into its mouth? Did you think it was a picky eater?"

Chime said helpfully, "I think it only looked like they were doing that from a higher angle."

Jade prodded a broken gliding wing with her foot-claws. "Why didn't we know this thing could fly?"

Balm looked pointedly at Briar, whose spines drooped in dismay. Briar had been in charge of the group of warriors who had tracked the creature here. Briar said, "We thought it was climbing between platforms on branches. I guess this explains why we kept losing its trail."

It did explain that. Moon was inclined to be sympathetic, especially now that they knew the warriors hadn't actually lost their quarry and they hadn't been stalking an unoccupied platform all this time.

Jade seemed to agree. She let her breath out and looked around at the gathered warriors. There were twenty of them here, female and male, older and more experienced like Vine and Sage, and younger and possibly even more experienced like Song and Root. After three days taking turns hunting and tracking, they all looked tired and bedraggled. Jade said, "No one's dead, and we got the stupid thing. That's all that matters."

The warriors all flicked spines in relieved agreement. Stone didn't look impressed, but then he usually didn't.

Sand, who had been watching the surrounding branches, said, "Jade, Aura's coming back."

Moon turned to look. The four warriors who had been scouting the surrounding clearings were circling down toward the platform. Jade stepped forward as they landed. Their spines all twitched anxiously, but none of them seemed to be hurt. Aura said, "Jade, we found something you need to see. There's a groundling flying boat."

Everyone stared, the dead predator temporarily forgotten.

"Serene found it," Aura continued. Behind her, Serene nodded, her spines signaling excited confirmation. "She heard something and went to check it out, and there it was."

As Aura paused for breath, Moon asked, "Golden Islanders?" The Indigo Cloud court had had to borrow wind-ships from a Golden Islander family of scholars and traders for the long journey from the old colony in the east to the Reaches. Moon had friends among them that it would be good to see again. From the way Chime's spines had just lifted with excitement, he felt the same way.

"No, not them." Aura still looked worried. "It's not a wind-ship, not anything like one."

That wasn't such good news. Jade frowned. "What was it doing? Did you see what sort of groundlings were aboard?"

"It's just floating there," Serene said.

"We couldn't see anyone aboard," Aura added. "We didn't get too close. We didn't want them to see us, and we were afraid they might be looking out through the window openings."

This . . . could be a problem, Moon thought. He found himself meeting Stone's sour gaze. Yes, the Golden Islanders were the only groundlings who would be visiting the Reaches for a good reason. And if this flying boat wasn't just hopelessly lost, it might be looking specifically for the Indigo Cloud colony tree.

"It's not a leaf boat?" Chime asked. There were groundlings who lived in the lower, swampy parts of the Reaches on the forest floor, who could build some forms of flying transports. But they never came up as far as the top of the mist, let alone the suspended forest. "Does it look like it's from the swamps?"

"It could be from the swamps, but it doesn't look anything like a leaf boat." Aura's expression showed she knew that that was not a good sign. "I don't think it's from the Reaches at all."

Jade hissed through her fangs. "Balm, you and Chime, and Vine, Aura, and Serene come with me and Moon. The rest of you get back to the colony."

"You don't think—" Chime began, and then settled his spines. "No, of course not," he answered his own question.

Moon was certain he had been about to say, *You don't think this has anything to do with the Fell*. This was the first unusual thing to happen since the night of the shared dream and it was hard not to wonder. Though it was also hard to imagine what a strange groundling boat would have to do with the Fell. It couldn't be a request for help; strange groundlings usually thought Raksura were Fell.

Stone said, "I think I'll come along too."

Jade flicked her spines at him. "I was counting on you."

They flew through the green caverns of the suspended forest, following as Aura and Serene led them toward the flying boat.

A queen wouldn't have expected an ordinary consort to come with her to investigate a possible incursion by strange groundlings. But if Moon had been an ordinary consort, he would never have been out here in the first place. In the past couple of turns he hadn't really gotten the court away from the idea of "young consorts don't risk themselves, don't do anything except sit around the colony and look pretty" but had got most of them to come around to "but Moon is not a normal young consort, and never will be."

Since Pearl had taken Ember, and Moon and Jade had had their first clutch, the court's future was far more secure. There was less pressure on Moon to be well-behaved, and less on Jade to make him act the way other courts thought he ought to. Though for most of the past turn, there hadn't been much for Moon to do except take care of fledglings.

The flying boat wasn't far away; if they hadn't been so focused on the hunt, they might have sensed its presence sooner. But then that was why Jade had sent Aura and the others to scout the area, to make sure nothing else dangerous had been attracted by the presence of the warriors.

As they drew closer Moon saw the boat had stopped in a sun shaft. These were places where a mountain-tree had collapsed from old age and had left a large open spot in the canopy, where the sun had penetrated all the way to the ground, burning away the mist layers. They weren't common and could harbor unknown and therefore even more dangerous fauna than usual; they also caused a whole host of different sun-loving flora to flourish, including plants and small trees that rarely grew in the Reaches at all. Moon had never had a chance to explore one, and didn't expect to have the opportunity now. The strange flying boat was excitement enough for the moment.

They landed and took cover on an upper branch of one of the mountain-trees surrounding the sun shaft. From this vantage point they could look down on the flying boat, but were screened from view by the hanging curtains of leaves. Moon crouched between Jade and Chime, with Balm on Jade's other side. Vine, Aura, and Serene hung back a little, and Stone landed on the branch above them, settling down into a crouch. His tail hung down behind Moon and the others, moving in slow thoughtful circles.

Low-voiced, Chime said, "Aura is right, that's nothing like a Golden Islander boat."

The craft was big, and not made out of wood or plant fiber like the other groundling trading and exploring boats they had encountered. It looked like it was made of moss, or some sort of dense wiry plant material very like it. It had a pointed bow with a triangular spine sweeping up to form the main hull and the square stern. It had multiple decks on either side of the spine, balconies in the lower hull, and clear coverings for the window openings like an Aventeran flying boat, but the shapes and angles and materials were completely different. And Aventeran boats always had air bladders, and this one clearly didn't.

There was no one out on the deck, but there was no scent of death in the air, either.

Vine said, "At least it's not Fell." Aura and Serene murmured agreement.

Chime said to Jade, "It could just be lost."

"It could be, but it wouldn't have come into the Reaches accidentally." Jade twitched her spines uneasily. "If they wanted to trade with one of the amphibian races, it's in completely the wrong place."

"Maybe it's completely lost." Moon edged along the branch, trying to get a better view through the screen of leaves. It was a possibility, but he didn't think any species capable of building—or growing—and piloting a craft like this would be inept enough to lose their way this drastically. Whoever this was, they were probably looking for a Raksuran court. "We need to get a better look."

Jade hesitated, but Moon could tell how much she wanted to figure this out before they had to return to the colony. He said, "It looks
pretty stable. They wouldn't notice if we landed on the side."

Jade glanced at him, brows lifted ironically. "And you're sure of
this?"

Moon snorted. "No."

She smiled, and unfurled her wings. "It's worth a try."

Above them, Stone stirred but didn't shift to argue with their decision. There was no way he could land on the boat without the groundling crew being aware of it.

Jade said, "Moon, you take that lower set of windows and I'll take
the upper. I'll go first. The rest of you stay here," she added, as Balm,
who probably wanted to go too, drew breath to protest.

Jade crouched and leapt, and landed on the side of the flying boat.
She clung to the hull and Moon let out a hiss of relief; the boat hadn't
moved, as far as he could tell. Whatever was keeping it in the air held
it remarkably still. It might be held aloft by a tiny fragment of flying
island, like a Golden Isles wind-ship. Jade waited a few moments, her
head held to the hull to listen for anyone calling the alarm. Then she
signaled to Moon.

Chime whispered, "Careful."

Moon crouched and made his own leap. His claws caught on the
rough hull. It was like moss to the touch, but it wasn't damp and felt too
dense for vibrations to travel through.

Above him, Jade climbed toward the nearest window. The clear
crystal insets were probably another reason why the inhabitants
hadn't heard anything. Moon swung down to the one below him and
peered through.

The crystal distorted the view a little but he could see it was an
empty room. There were shelves built into the far wall with cushions
for padding and blankets, and a few odd belongings strewn around,
including a colorful wrap or shawl, and a stacked collection of crockery.
This was someone's, or multiple someone's, living quarters. He climbed
along to another set of windows and found another empty sleeping
room, and then the next few rooms stacked with bundles and casks.
But then the next held something more interesting.

Moon gripped the edge of the window with one hand and leaned back, waved until Jade glanced down and started toward him.

Moon pulled himself back to the window. Inside, a groundling sat on the floor, half turned away from the window, hunched over and writing in a book. There was something familiar about his shape. He was small, with long white hair tied back, gold skin, a beard long enough that he had flung the end back over his shoulder to get it out of his way. He turned a little so his profile was visible and Moon felt his spines twitch in startled reaction. It was Delin-Evran-lindel.

Moon leaned back from the window. Jade crouched on the hull just above him, holding on with all her claws. He whispered, "It's Delin."

She frowned. "What is he doing in this thing?" Delin was a Golden Islander, and they had never seen him use a flying boat like this.

Moon could think of at least one bad reason. If someone had wanted to find a Raksuran colony tree, they might have decided to steal Delin and force him to show them the way. "Let's ask him."

Jade nodded for him to go ahead, and Moon tapped a claw on the crystal.

Delin looked up, startled, then waved enthusiastically. He scrambled to his feet and hurried to the window, turned the catch on the inside and swung it open. Voice low, he said, "I was hoping you would find me. I have much to tell you."

Jade drew back and motioned for Moon to go ahead. "I'll stay out here."

Moon climbed in through the window and dropped to the floor. He shifted to groundling; though Delin had never been afraid of Raksuran scales and claws, it seemed more polite in this confined space. In soft-skinned groundling form, Moon was tall and slender, with bronze skin, dark hair, and green eyes. His clothes were simple brown pants and shirt, dirty now that the mud and moss that had been on his scales had transferred to the cloth, and the only jewelry he wore was his red-gold consort's bracelet. The ability to make the shift and take objects with you from one form to the other was something fledglings learned very young; Moon had been lucky his foster mother Sorrow had taught him before she died.

The other reason for shifting was the number of groundling species who resembled some version of this form, though with varying colors, shapes, and textures. If someone else stepped into the cabin unexpectedly, Moon would pass for an ordinary groundling, and cause a moment of confusion that might buy him time to escape, rather than immediate terror and screams for help. Moon said, "Delin, did these people steal you?"

"Not exactly." Delin patted his arm. "But I am happy to see a friendly face."

The cabin was small but high-ceilinged, and the heavy rafters that supported the deck above crossed it lengthwise. They looked like the stems or stalks of a large plant. There was a bed space built into one wall and a basin for water, and various shelves for belongings, though Delin didn't seem to have brought many. There was only a small pack and a basket, and not much in the way of paper and writing materials. Knowing how many books Delin normally traveled with on his own wind-ship, that in itself was suspicious. The door was fan-folded, light enough that Delin could probably have battered through it. But this was a flying boat and there was nowhere for a groundling to escape to.

"How do you mean 'not exactly?'" Moon asked. Delin looked the same, though it had been more than two turns since Moon had seen him. He was elderly for a Yellow Sea groundling and his gold skin was weathered by turns of wind-ship travel, but he smelled like he was in good health. He wore the kind of clothes Golden Islanders usually wore on their ships or for outdoor work: a loose shirt and pants cut off at the knee, of a light fabric.

"The story is long and somewhat fraught." Delin sat down on the bed and Moon crouched on the floor. "The thing you must know immediately is that these people are of Kish-Jandera, one of the coastal territories of the Imperial Kish. They wish to find the Indigo Cloud court. I have said I would tell them the way, but after we entered the Reaches, I have willfully misremembered the route for these past few days, in the hope that I could warn you first."

"All right." If this was anybody but Delin, it would have been alarming and suspicious. It still was, but Moon had seen Delin navigate his way through some tricky situations. "Why do they want to talk to Raksura?"

"Not just Raksura, but you in particular." Delin leaned forward, his expression intent. "Moon, they have found an ancient city. I fear it may have been built by the forerunners, like the city you discovered on the northwestern coast."

Moon stared, and felt his back teeth start to itch from pure nervous reaction. "Where?"

A faint sound outside the door warned him, a footstep on the cork floor. Moon shifted and leapt for the ceiling, sinking his claws into the moss, curling his body up along one of the big stems that supported the structure. The door rattled and a voice said, "Delin?"

Delin stood and faced the door. "Yes?"

The folding door was pushed open and a groundling stepped through, passed under Moon as it crossed the cabin toward Delin.

The groundling was about Moon's height, with a dark cap of short, tightly curled hair and reddish brown skin that was rough and almost pebbly; it wasn't scaled, but it looked thick and tough. He was probably male. He wore a loose jacket of red-brown with figured designs in dull gold, open at the chest, and tight pants that went to the knees, with knee-high sandals with elaborately wrapped straps. The materials looked rich and carefully worked.

Moon dropped lightly to the deck, and shifted back to his groundling form by the time his bare feet touched the floorboards. He pushed the door shut.

The figure turned and fell back a startled step. His dark eyes opened wide, revealing a second lower eyelid.

Behind him, Delin said, "He is Moon of Indigo Cloud, a consort of the Raksura. So be very careful what you say and do." He added to Moon, "This is Callumkal, Master Scholar of the Conclave of the Janderan."

Callumkal eyed Moon. Moon knew he didn't look terribly impressive at the moment, standing barefoot on the deck in mud- and moss-stained work clothes. Callumkal glanced back at Delin and said, "I thought you might be delaying intentionally." He spoke Altanic, one of the more common eastern trade languages. He didn't sound angry, but it was always hard to read emotions accurately off strange groundlings.

He was wearing a leather harness under his open jacket, the straps hanging down below it. The dark leather was almost the same color as Callumkal's skin, and Moon hadn't noticed it at first, and had thought the buckles were jewelry. It looked utilitarian, and was worn in spots as if it had been used for hard work. Moon just couldn't figure out what sort of work. For riding some kind of grasseater, maybe. Except these groundlings had a flying boat; why would they need to bring riding grasseaters?

"It is better to speak here, away from the colony." Delin was undisturbed at being caught with a Raksura in his room. "Everyone will be more comfortable."

Callumkal inclined his head. "You could have explained that."

"Could I?" Delin shrugged. "Probably."

That Delin, one of the most straightforward groundlings of any race that Moon had ever met, felt the need to dissemble didn't bode well. Moon said in Raksuran, "And you said these people didn't steal you."

"They did not," Delin answered in the same language. He must have been practicing since the last time they met, though his accent was still terrible. "But they were determined on this course. It was better to let them think they were in command while I navigated from the stern."

Callumkal waited patiently for Delin to finish speaking. Then he looked at Moon. "You understand Altanic?"

"Yes." Moon stepped away from the door. If there was going to be a fight, he didn't want to start it. And moving put him closer to the window, where he knew Jade must be listening.

"Delin told us about your experience in the ancient underwater city. We only wish to speak to you about it." Callumkal glanced at Delin again, and his voice was tinged with what might be irony. "I'm sure he has told you by now, that we have located a place we believe to be similar, perhaps constructed by the same species, perhaps not. We intend to try to enter it, and wish to be as forearmed as possible."

"It might not matter how forearmed you are," Moon said. "There are some things you can't prepare for."

When some groundlings spoke with a Raksura for the first time, they seemed surprised. Moon could usually tell if it was surprise that

Raksura could speak a civilized language, or surprise that they could talk at all. It was ironic that the Fell rulers, the most dangerous and deadly predators of groundlings, were fluent in any number of languages, and that friendly races like the Kek had difficulty with everything but their own speech because of the structure of their vocal apparatus.

Callumkal was the kind of groundling who was surprised that a Raksura could sound so civilized. He got over it quickly, though, saying, "Delin has told us about what happened in the underwater city. I was hoping for a first-person account."

"Why?" Moon tilted his head. "You already know from Delin what we found. Would hearing it from me make you change your mind about what you plan to do?"

"Probably not," Callumkal admitted. "But if my party doesn't enter this city, I fear who else will."

Moon looked at Delin. Delin told him, "That was one of the things I wish to speak to you about." He added to Callumkal, "It is better if my friends and I speak in private. There are others I wish to consult." He started briskly toward the window.

In Raksuran, Moon said, "Jade, Delin's about to jump out. Be sure to catch him."

As Callumkal stared, uncomprehending, Delin boosted himself into the open window. Callumkal began, "You can't mean to—"

Delin heaved himself out head first. Moon heard the whish of Jade's wings an instant later. This let him approach the window at a leisurely pace. He was curious to see whether Callumkal would try to stop him.

Callumkal seemed too nonplussed to react. Moon said, "He'll send word to you in the morning." He caught hold of the sill and slipped out.

He dropped and shifted, and snapped his wings out. He heard someone cry out in alarm from above. He flapped into the cover of the tree canopy and landed on the branch where Jade stood with Delin and the warriors. Delin was looking up at Stone's large form and smiling. He said, "Friend Stone! It is good to see you again. It's good to see all of you."

"We like you too," Chime told him, bewildered, "but what are you doing here?"

"First, a warning." Delin turned to Moon. "You saw the harness Callumkal wore?"

Moon nodded, remembering that Delin wouldn't be able to read the flash of spines that meant assent. "I was wondering about that."

"It attaches to a device that holds a plant material, the same as in the construction of their sky-ship, that allows the wearer a simple, limited form of flight."

"Oh, that's great." Moon looked at the flying boat again. Figures moved on the deck, but none of the groundlings leapt into the air. Just the idea that they might was nerve-racking.

Above them, Stone rumbled in severe annoyance. Balm hissed and said, "As if we don't have enough to worry about."

Jade watched Delin intently. "That groundling said that he was afraid of who else would enter the city. Did he mean what I think he meant?"

"I fear so," Delin said. "It is the Fell, I am sorry to say. There are signs the Fell have found this strange ancient city. That is what we have to discuss."

CHAPTER THREE

Moon and the others flew back to the colony while Jade left Aura, Serene, and Vine to watch the flying boat from a careful distance.

Moon carried Delin, and so was able to plan his route to make the most of the moment when he flew out away from the overgrown platforms and concealing branches of the untamed mountain-trees. Delin had visited before but still murmured in appreciation.

The colony tree filled the huge clearing, the multiple branches that reached up to form the green canopy stretching out high overhead. The platforms extended out on the lower branches, many levels of them, some more than five hundred paces across. A waterfall fell out of the knothole entrance, which from outside was nearly big enough to sail a wind-ship through. The water plunged down to collect in a pool on one of the platforms, then fell to the next, and the next, until it disappeared into the shadows and mist far below.

When the court had first returned to take possession of the old colony tree, the platforms had held only overgrown gardens and the skeletons of irrigation systems and ornamental ponds. Now they were neatly planted with fruit orchards, root crops, tea plants and herbs, and the various fiber plants the Arbora used for making cloth and paper. It was obvious the colony was occupied now, with Arbora working or lounging out in the gardens and warriors circling the clearing on patrol.

Moon landed in the knothole and set Delin on his feet, while the others went ahead into the passage that led inside. The channel that fed the waterfall ran nearby, and decorative pieces of snail shell had been set into the smoothly polished wood. Moon lifted a wing to shield Delin from the whoosh of displaced air as Stone landed at the edge of the knothole. Stone shifted down to his groundling form, and Moon furled his wings and shifted too. To Delin, Moon said, "You never really said whether those other groundlings stole you or not."

"It's a hard question." Delin looked around, taking a deep breath. It was cool and damp in the cave-like knothole, and the water mist concentrated the sweet scent of the colony tree. "Your home is so beautiful."

"It's not a hard question," Stone countered. "Did they steal you or did you make them take you along? I know what you're like."

"You compliment me." Delin's tone was not ironic. Moon supposed that was answer enough. More seriously, Delin said, "I admit I want to see this city they have discovered, and study it. But I know enough to fear what might be there. I wanted to discuss this with others who also know that the answers the city might provide may not be worth the risk."

"How do you know they aren't lying to you about it?" Moon asked. "It could be a trick to get you to take them here, to us." If so it was an elaborate trick, but to some species it would make sense.

Delin cocked his head up at Moon. "They have an artifact. I have seen it. When I show you the drawing of it, it will become clear."

Moon exchanged a look with Stone. Stone sighed, and said, "There's something we need to tell you, too."

They started down the entrance passage, which was too narrow for Stone's winged form, and full of twists and turns meant to slow and trap attackers. As they walked, Moon told Delin about the shared dream. In the glow of the spell-lights, the furrows in Delin's face grew deeper as he listened. He said, finally, "A strange omen. I see why you are so disturbed."

They came out of the passage and into the cavernous greeting hall. It was more occupied than usual, with the warriors who had arrived back from the hunt still here and the Arbora and warriors who had stayed behind gathering to hear about everything that had happened.

Delin's arrival caused a minor sensation, and he flung his arms wide and headed for the Arbora. "Blossom, Rill, my friends! Niran sends you greetings!"

Stone glanced at the nearest warrior, who happened to be Band. "Go make sure Pearl knows Delin is here." Moon didn't think Jade would have forgotten to send someone to tell the reigning queen what had happened, but with Pearl it was always best to err on the safe side.

Band stared. "Me?"

Stone didn't have time to do more than tilt his head threateningly before Band realized his mistake and leapt for the nearest balcony.

"She's not going to like this," Moon said.

Stone gave him an ironic grimace. "That's putting it mildly."

Then Pearl dropped out of the upper levels and landed lightly on the hall floor.

It took a while to get Delin through the gauntlet of warriors and Arbora who wanted to greet him before they could hear the whole story. Finally Delin was settled in one of the small rooms behind the greeting hall, with water heating on the stones in the hearth bowl for tea.

Moon took his usual place next to Jade, across from Pearl. Other places were taken by Stone, Balm, Chime, and Heart, as well as Pearl's warrior Floret. For the past turn, Pearl had been giving Floret increasing responsibility among the warriors, which was a good thing as far as Moon was concerned. Though she was one of Pearl's favorites, Floret had always been able to get along with Jade's faction. Her increasing authority in the court seemed to be a sign from Pearl that there would be no more toleration of fighting between the two warrior factions.

Pearl had thrown out everyone else who had tried to subtly slide in.

Delin sat on a cushion with a cup of tea, looking around in appreciation at the carved Aeriat stretching up the walls. Pearl made a gesture with her claws. "So, tell us what this unwelcome visitation is all about."

Fortunately Delin had met Pearl before, and was also fairly impervious to attempts to insult him when he was focused on a goal. He leaned forward. "I was visiting in the city of Kedmar in Kish-Jandera, when

I was sent a message that a group of scholars wished to speak of long-dead cities. Naturally, I was intrigued."

Stone said, "How did they know you knew anything about dead cities?"

Moon was wondering that as well. As far as he knew, Delin's scholarship involved mostly other races of the Three Worlds.

"Yes," Jade added more pointedly, "Who have you been talking to?"

Delin said, "I took what you all had told me of the forerunner city on the northwest coast and the imprisoned being you found there and put it into a monograph, which had been copied and sent to the Scholars' Colloquium in Kish-Jandera, among other places."

There was a moment of startled and probably appalled silence. Moon knew he felt pretty appalled. He said, just to clarify, "Including the part that the species we call the forerunners is where the Raksura and the Fell came from."

Delin nodded. "That was one of the truly interesting parts. Scholars know of many vanished species, but there are many more, of much greater age, we know little to nothing of."

Moon exchanged a look with Jade. He had known Delin was a scholar, but somehow hadn't imagined him as being in contact with other scholars who weren't from the Golden Isles. Now that he thought about it, it had been a naive assumption.

Pearl's tail lashed slowly. Stone rubbed his eyes and said, "Was that really a good idea?"

Delin spread his hands. "It is what I do. What I did not do was speak of the young Raksura called Shade, of either his ancestry or how he was needed to open the creature's prison. That knowledge was far too dangerous to share."

That was a relief. Moon could almost hear tense muscles relax all around him. Only the right combination of Fell and Raksura could recreate a being close enough to a forerunner to easily open a passage into the hidden, abandoned city. Shade, Moon's half clutch-brother, rescued from the Fell as a fledgling, had been that right combination. Pearl and Jade settled their spines. "Good," Stone muttered. "That's something, anyway."

"My monograph did not include any illustrations." Delin reached into his shirt and retrieved a pouch that hung on a string around his neck. He opened it and drew out a folded square of thick paper. "Which was why this captured my attention."

He spread it on the floor and everyone leaned forward to look. It was a drawing of a block or a tile, with a figure carved into it. It looked like an Aeriat Raksura, but there were too many spines, and instead of a mane of spines and frills, there was a solid crest atop its head. A Fell ruler's crest. Floret, startled, said, "But that's Shade."

"No. This object was carved ages before that young consort was born. It came from a wall decoration below the city the Kishan have found. They cut it from the wall and took it away, and I have seen it and examined it myself." Delin watched them carefully, studying their reactions. "I am correct? This is a forerunner."

Pearl tilted her head at Jade, who sat back, her brow furrowed in worry. Jade said, "That's a forerunner."

Delin continued, "In the monograph, I explained that the account had been told to me by Raksura, but did not include anything such as specific locations of courts." He admitted, "That's probably why the Kishan scholars came to me first."

Jade flicked her claws, betraying a trace of impatience. "Then what happened?"

"We spoke of my monograph, and after some dissembling, they finally told me what they really wanted. Some months ago they had formed an expedition to follow an ancient map that had recently been uncovered, and had found the ruined city." He looked around. "You have no maps of the western coasts handy? I should have brought my own. I have not seen their map—they guard it jealously—but I think I have estimated its location."

"You can show us later," Moon said. "Just describe it."

Delin leaned forward. "The city was past the sel-Selatra, the seas off the far northwest coast of the Kishlands, that are separated by multiple archipelagos. If one goes far enough north, there are solitary sea-mounts, then the deeps of the open ocean. Those areas are not well-explored, at least as far as the Kish are aware. There are some sea kingdoms that were mapped at some point in the past, and there has been no word from them or anyone who has seen them for many turns. The map led the Kish to a city past the sea-mounts at the edge of the great deeps." He shook his head in annoyance. "They gave me some descriptions, but they have been withholding information. From what I can tell, the city is inside a formation akin to a sea-mount, but which is possibly not natural but a construction, and the top is protected by high walls. The Kishan party had with them a seagoing vessel, and a flying ship, the one they travel in now. The flying ship could not rise high enough to cross over the escarpment protecting the city, and neither could the lifting packs they use. And they could not locate an opening in the foot of the sea-mount itself. They were able to explore a small structure in the water near the base of the mount, and that is where they found this." He tapped the drawing. "But with no knowledge of how to enter the city, they had to look for alternate means. They left most of their party with the seagoing vessel, and took the flying craft back to Kedmar to seek assistance."

"But they aren't sure it's a forerunner city, are they?" Heart said. She leaned forward to touch the drawing. "All they have is this."

"Why would the city have that if they weren't forerunners?" Floret wondered. She had been with them when they found the forerunner city, but had been left on guard at the top of the shaft that had led to the entrance.

Moon knew she must be thinking of the Raksuran penchant for carving pictures of themselves into almost every available surface of the colony. "But the forerunner city we saw wasn't like that, there weren't any carved pictures, just flower and seaplant designs." A city nearly inaccessibly high in the air did make more sense for forerunners than the underwater city they had found. But they had thought at the time that it might have been constructed as a specific defense against or prison for the creature they had found trapped inside.

"This is a topic for much debate among the Kishan, as well," Delin said. "When they first began to look for this city, they believed it to be constructed by the foundation builders, another people of ancient times, perhaps far older than the flying island people. The foundation builders left many cities and roads in the lands of northern Kish, but only the barest bones and a few carved writings remain. Some races of the Kishan believe they must be descended from them. To discover if the foundation builders constructed this sea-mount city, they must get inside it." He added, "They came to me hoping not only that I could provide them with more information on how to accomplish this, but also hoping to commission my wind-ship to reach the top of the escarpment."

"Will that even work?" Chime asked. "How high is it?"

Golden Isles wind-ships traveled on invisible lines of force that crossed the Three Worlds, and their ability to move up and down depended a lot on the strength of those currents, which varied depending on the location. At least that was how Moon understood it. And the wind-ships weren't immune to storms and the vagaries of the wind, either. He started to ask, "And what about—"

Pearl interposed, "Both of you, quiet. Let him finish so we can get this over with."

Delin nodded to Pearl, and continued, "From what they described, I told them I did not think it was possible. The other problem—one of the other problems, I should say—came when they described certain deserted island settlements they had observed along the way."

"The Fell," Jade said, her voice grim.

"Yes. The remnants bore the characteristics of a Fell attack." Delin let his breath out in frustration. "You must understand first, the Fell are not as feared in the lands of the Kish as they are in the Abascene peninsula and the other eastern expanses. The Kish possess certain weapons and a command of magic that is effective against the Fell, and they share this knowledge with those under their Imperial trade agreements. It has made them poor targets for attack. I suspect, somewhere in the deep past, this was the reason for the formation of their trading Empire. I know there are several Kishlands settled by refugees who were driven there by Fell attacks. These scholars and explorers know of the Fell, but not the way we in the east who are their prey do. I fear they don't understand how much they should be afraid."

Stone sat back and growled under his breath. Moon felt it vibrate in his bones, and Chime stirred uneasily. Moon said, "And you think you know why the Fell are there. That they've been called by something."

"That is what I fear. What else would draw the Fell so far out to sea, with such distances between the islands, and no large settlements of sentient races to prey on?" Delin scratched under his beard thoughtfully. "Stone and Moon have told me of the strange portent you received, the dream all of you were drawn into. It seems an odd coincidence."

"More than a coincidence," Chime murmured. Pearl and Jade turned to regard him, and he said hastily, "I mean, it can't be a coincidence. Can it?"

"But if the Fell found the city, they must have someone like Shade," Balm said, with a glance at Jade. "Or there's no way they could get whatever was trapped inside out."

Chime frowned, absently running his fingers over a worn spot in the wood of the floor. "Maybe they don't have anyone like Shade. Maybe that's why they're hanging around out there, preying on the groundling settlements nearby."

"Why would they even go there then?" Floret asked.

Heart's brow was furrowed as she considered the problem. She said, "These Fell could have missed part of the instructions, somehow. They know to go to the city, but they don't know how to get in, or what to do once they're inside. Maybe they haven't spent turns and turns preparing, like the other Fell flight did."

Jade didn't seem happy with either of those explanations, and Moon had to admit he wasn't either. Jade said, "Is there any other reason the Fell might be there? Besides being drawn there by something inside the city."

Chime lifted his shoulders uneasily. "It's possible the flight that captured us in the west was able to share the knowledge of what they found in the underwater forerunner city." This was all too possible. Individual Fell flights didn't seem to join together or cooperate with each other much, but Fell rulers could share information within their flight and between flights without physically contacting each other, sometimes over great distances. "The Fell might realize now that there could be other ancient cities that have something valuable, and they've started to look for them. This might even be a foundation builder city, like the Kish think, and the Fell just mistook it for forerunner."

Jade shook her head. "I wouldn't like to count on that."

Stone looked like he clearly thought everything they had discussed was just making the situation worse. "And these 'scholars' don't think the Fell are a problem?"

Delin gestured in frustration. "They have read my monograph, and I have told them as plainly as possible about the danger and what the Fell sought in the forerunner city under the coastal island. They say their city may have been built by foundation builders, which is true. They say my tale is a secondhand account, and may be false. I don't know whose integrity they are impugning, if you are supposed to be liars or I just a fool for believing you." He sat back. "I admit my own desires are conflicted. I believe the city is more dangerous than the Kish think, but I also believe it could hold a great deal of knowledge about the past of at least this small part of the Three Worlds, whether it is forerunner or foundation builder. These coasts and islands of the sel-Selatra and beyond are very interesting places." He slumped a little and for the first time seemed tired. "I wish to have access to this knowledge. But I do not wish to die myself, or for others to die, or to set loose a powerful monstrous creature upon populated lands."

Moon didn't wish for those things either, and he didn't think the Kish scholars did. But not everyone was going to have Delin's perspective on the situation. "But the Fell might already be trying to do that."

His voice dry, Stone said, "And it's obvious these Kish want us to come help them get inside."

Everyone stared at him. Delin nodded grimly. "They have not spoken of it to me, but I think they do."

Pearl bared her teeth, possibly in pure irritation at the whole idea of helping meddlesome scholars she wanted nothing to do with in the first place. "And why was that so obvious?" she asked Stone.

Stone said, "They wanted Delin's flying boat, but then they realized it probably can't do what they need, any more than their own can." He met Delin's worried gaze. "But then they remembered Delin's descriptions of Raksura."

Delin spread his hands. "Just so. They have pretended they are following my advice, coming here to speak about your experience in the coastal forerunner city and ask for counsel. But it is more likely that they came all this way to ask for more than counsel."

Pearl snarled under her breath. "Idiot groundlings."

Chime gave Delin an apologetic wince. Moon stared at the carved Aeriat entwined overhead and set his jaw. It wasn't just fear of shapeshifters or the strong resemblance to Fell that caused groundlings to fear and hate Raksura. *It's also that Raksura can be such assheads*, he thought.

Jade forged on, saying, "So the question is, what do we do now, today? These groundlings want to talk, do we speak to them?"

"We could kill them," Stone suggested, not helpfully.

It would have been a tense moment, except Heart sighed impatiently and said, "Line-grandfather, not in front of company."

Delin lifted a hand. "I know Stone is merely stimulating discussion."

Pearl eyed Stone and lifted her spines. "Perhaps Stone could stop doing that."

Stone held Pearl's gaze. "Some of you were thinking it."

With the practiced ease of someone used to intervening when things got too tense between Pearl and Jade, Balm pointed out, "It wouldn't do any good, even if it was something we were willing to do. There's at least one other ship full of groundlings who know about this. And surely their people back at their home know where they've gone."

Everyone else was just clearly impatient to get past this and onto the real discussion. Which was exactly what Stone had wanted, Moon knew, even if he had had to take a swipe at Pearl to do it.

"So let's stop talking about it," Jade said, with a brief glare at Stone. "I think I should meet with these groundlings. I was at the forerunner city, and I can tell them what I saw with my own eyes. Maybe that will convince them to be cautious, at least." She rolled her spines to ease the tension in them. "And if you're right and they do want to ask us to come with them . . . We'll worry about it when it happens."

Pearl's spines were beginning to ease back down, mostly because she didn't like groundlings, so anything that kept her from having to talk to more of them was a relief for her. She said, grudgingly, "That's a possibility."

Moon hesitated, but they had to talk about this, and he might as well get it started now. He said, "What about the Fell? The shared dream?"

The room went silent. Pearl said, "The dream can't mean these Fell. If they encounter a creature like the one in the other forerunner city, it will destroy them, like it did the others."

Moon wasn't willing to bet anyone's life on that. "If this is a forerunner city, and there is something waiting in it, it might give these Fell what it promised the others. Weapons to let them destroy groundling cities and eat wherever they want." Moon was talking to Pearl but all his attention was on Jade. He couldn't tell what her reaction was. She had her opaque diplomatic face on, which was almost as hard to read as Stone's normal expression. "That may be what causes them to come here."

Heart stirred uneasily. Floret said, "We don't know that they'll come here. There's been nothing in the augury. The dream . . . It might have been a warning for the courts still in the east."

"Some of them were our allies," Chime put in. "We have to warn them."

"But we don't like them anymore." Stone's ironic tone was like acid.

"And the Fell would never come here," Moon said, "because there's nothing they've ever wanted from us."

Everyone heard the sarcasm in that.

Pearl's expression was withering. "I know what the risk is as well as you."

Moon just met her gaze. He knew she did, he just wanted her to say it aloud.

Breaking the tension, Jade said, "Let me speak to the groundlings. Maybe they can tell us more about what they saw."

Balm added, "We don't even know that this is a forerunner city yet. Maybe the Fell are mistaken, or it's only a coincidence that they're nearby."

Chime made a dubious noise and Balm elbowed him. Everyone else had recognized Jade and Balm's joint effort to stop the discussion before it got into an area which would end with a lot of yelling and hissing and growling.

Pearl stood and settled her wings. "Arrange the meeting with the groundlings for tomorrow. It's too late to do it tonight. And do not let them know where the court is—have it somewhere else."

Jade flicked her spines in agreement. "I will."

Pearl stood and in one bound reached the passage back to the greeting hall, the displaced air from her wing flick almost overturning the tea cups. Floret nodded to Jade and shifted to hurry after her.

Everyone except Stone let out a breath of relief.

Delin said, "I am sorry to cause this dissension among you."

Moon told him, "It was going to happen sooner or later."

As Jade turned to Balm, Stone said, "I need to talk to you," grabbed Moon's arm, and dragged him upright.

Moon followed him down a stairwell and through a twisting passage into someone's bower. No one was there at the moment, but Raksura didn't have strong feelings about privacy and Arbora and warriors slept in each other's bowers all the time. Whoever it belonged to probably wouldn't mind the line-grandfather and the first consort having a fight in it, as long as nobody broke anything.

As Stone turned to face him, Moon said, "If you hit me, I'll bite your face off."

Stone ignored the threat, probably because he didn't feel very threatened by it. "What do you think we're going to do? Follow the groundlings to this city and drive off the Fell?"

Moon hadn't been expecting Stone to cut through to the heart of the situation that way, and it silenced any retorts he had ready. He didn't want to go to some far-off place to fight Fell. He didn't want to leave his clutch. But that didn't change the situation. "We can't just ignore this." He didn't know what Jade would want, or how she felt about this. Or how angry she would be at the idea. "What if there is something in there that gives the Fell what the other one promised them?"

Stone groaned and rubbed his face tiredly. "Good question."

That was the point when Moon understood that Stone had dragged him down here not to yell at him, but so they could decide what to do. That wasn't reassuring, since he had been hoping Stone already knew what they should do. One thing Moon had figured out since joining the court was that being the one who pointed out what things were wrong was relatively easy compared to being the one who had to decide what to do about them.

Moon turned away, pacing absently until he reached the bowl hearth. The stones in it were only giving off a faint warmth and needed to be renewed. "If this isn't a forerunner city and the Fell just think it is for some reason, then . . . But how else would they know about it?"

The being in the other city had drawn the Fell to itself through turns of effort, with a mental call that Raksura couldn't hear.

"The Fell could have heard about the city in Kish," Stone said.

Moon turned to frown at him. "You mean, Fell rulers in Kish? I thought they couldn't get into the cities because of the Kish shamen." Like Delin had mentioned, Kish shamen had special magic that allowed them to spot Fell rulers, and it also made the shamen immune to the Fell's ability to confuse and deceive. Moon had always believed it was the main reason why the Fell avoided Kish territory, not fear of the Kishan weapons.

"Not rulers." Stone lifted his brows at Moon's expression. "What? You know they can make groundlings do whatever they want. You think they've never caught some groundlings and sent them into Kish to spy?"

That was a thought. Fell could plant suggestions in groundling minds, make them forget they had ever encountered Fell in the first place, make them remember events that had never happened. If they could send a groundling into a place to see and hear things, and come back to the Fell to report, it would avoid the shamen altogether. The groundlings wouldn't even know they were spies, and the Fell would probably eat them when they were done with them, destroying any evidence. "So if one of the scholars involved talked about this map where others could hear, and the Fell found out about it, they could find a groundling who could get close to the explorers—"

"Who could still be with them." Jade leaned in the bower's doorway.

Moon twitched in automatic guilt. He supposed it was unlikely that his and Stone's sudden exit had gone unnoticed. Jade spotted the guilt and demanded, "What? What are you planning?"

"Nothing," Moon said. He added honestly, "Yet."

She sighed and stepped into the bower. "I suppose you both realize we have to send someone to that city to see what's really going on."

It was a relief that Jade was willing to admit it, too. Moon felt some of the tension drain out of his chest. He didn't want to go against Jade on this.

Stone said pointedly, "We realize it, and you realize it. Will Pearl realize it?"

Jade didn't answer that. She eyed Moon critically. "You shouldn't have confronted her in front of Delin. You know how she is about groundlings."

She was probably right about that. But it had felt like everyone was ignoring the important point. And if you were going to challenge Pearl on something like this, it was better to get it over with as quickly as possible. He said, earnestly, "I thought she liked it when I confront her."

"Very funny." Jade's spines twitched in a combination of annoyance and amusement. Balm stepped into the doorway, and Chime cautiously leaned in after her.

"We have to send somebody." Chime grimaced in dismay. "I don't want to see one of those things again. But I'd rather see it still trapped in a forerunner city than see it in the Reaches."

There was a quiet moment where everyone was clearly thinking that over. *You can't wish Delin hadn't come to us,* Moon thought, *because if one of those things got loose and came looking for Raksura* . . . He said, "We could send to Opal Night for help. Malachite would realize how bad this could be—"

"I am not asking your mother for help," Jade cut him off. "Not until we know what we're dealing with."

Moon had no problem admitting that Malachite was a nerve-racking companion. He said, "But you think if we told her about this, she would believe it was serious enough to investigate."

Jade's mouth twisted as she thought it over. "Yes. I do."

Balm put in, "Maybe we should send her a message." Jade gave her a look and Balm held up her hands. "If worse comes to worst, we might need help. And you wouldn't have to convince her how dangerous this could be. She already knows."

"She's right," Stone said.

Jade shook her head in resignation. "I know, I know." Moon, Balm, and Stone all drew breath to speak, and Jade held up her hands to stop them. "We're getting ahead of ourselves. Let me talk to these groundlings of Delin's first and just see what they say."

Moon subsided, a little unwillingly. Then a female Arbora ducked under Chime's arm and stepped into the bower, looking around at them all in confusion. Jade asked, "What's wrong, Weave?"

"Ah, this is my bower?" Weave said uncertainly. "Do you need it? I don't mind."

"No, sorry." Jade sighed and squeezed Weave's shoulder. "We're just leaving."

Moon followed her and the others out, back to the meeting room. Delin was still sitting with Heart, having tea. Vine was there now too, in his groundling form, waiting impatiently. Before the meeting, Jade had sent five warriors back to the flying boat, to take over for Aura, Vine, and Serene.

Vine stood up. "Jade, we saw those pack things. Like Delin said, the groundlings are using them to fly around."

Jade's fangs showed briefly, a sign of strong annoyance. "Wonderful." She turned to Delin. "We're going to have to approach them and arrange a meeting."

Delin set his tea cup aside. "If you could return me to their ship, I can do this. You do not wish them to come here, but to meet at some neutral location?"

"You don't want to spend the night here?" Heart asked him.

"It would be better not to give them time to plan." Delin's tone was wry. "Or to argue amongst themselves."

Moon almost made a sarcastic comment about nobody here knowing what that was like, but managed to restrain himself.

Jade considered it. "We'll take you back. Balm will show you where we can have the meeting on the way, so you can guide the groundlings tomorrow."

So it was all settled. At least for tonight.

CHAPTER FOUR

It was nearing twilight and a light rain-mist was in the air when Moon went with Balm, Chime, and Floret to take Delin back to the groundlings' boat. They landed with him on a mountain-tree branch, heavily screened by leaves but with a view of the flying boat in its clearing. The warriors who were keeping an eye on it waited there.

As Moon helped Delin find a secure seat on a knob of wood, Balm told the warriors, "Jade wants you to come back to the court with us. She doesn't want anyone out here through the night."

"Are you sure?" Coil asked. He was a male warrior of Pearl's, though he had never been much involved in the infighting between the two factions. "We're not worried."

"She doesn't think it's worth the risk," Balm said. It was quiet at the moment, with treelings calling, and night birds and flying lizards coming out to hunt the clouds of evening insects. But a night without shelter in the suspended forest was always dangerous, and more so near a shaft clearing. Moon agreed with Jade that there wouldn't be much point in watching the boat when the warriors couldn't see it. Balm added, "And Delin says they won't move the boat tonight."

"There are lights, as with our wind-ships," Delin explained, wriggling to make sure he had a secure seat, "but they are not much use in deep forest like this."

Balm sent Coil and the others off toward the colony tree, and Moon told Delin, "We won't be far away. We'll make sure they've got you before we leave."

"I thank you for this," Delin said, "and I will see you tomorrow at the place you showed me."

"Just be careful," Moon said. Before they had left the colony, they had talked with Delin about the idea that the Fell might have an unwilling, or even willing, spy among the groundlings.

Delin had just said, "That is one of the many things in this situation to be worried about."

With Balm and Chime, Moon retired to a sheltered spot higher up in another mountain-tree, where they had a better view of the flying boat. Groundlings were moving around on the open deck now, the one divided by the wedge-shaped spine. Delin waited to give the Raksura enough time to get into concealment, then began to shout.

The groundlings heard him immediately and some ran through a doorway in the upper part of the boat. Worried, Chime said, "I hope they won't do anything to him because he's been with us."

"He didn't think they would." Moon didn't feel easy about it himself, but Delin had seemed confident. But then Delin always seemed confident. He was as bad as Stone that way.

A groundling came out onto the deck wearing a heavy backpack. He made some adjustment, tugged on something, then lifted smoothly off the deck into the air, with nothing to show how he had done it. "Some sort of spell?" Balm asked Chime.

He shrugged his spines. "Maybe. It's hard to tell. If it's the same thing that keeps the boat aloft, I wonder how they control it."

Moon watched until the flying groundling disappeared into the canopy, then several moments later reappeared carrying Delin. They were too far away to see exactly how the groundling was doing it, but it made Moon uneasy to watch. He just didn't trust groundlings to know how to carry someone while flying. But the pair landed safely on the flying boat's deck. Balm said, "We should go."

Moon flicked his spines in reluctant agreement. They turned away and dropped off the branch to fly back to the colony.

It had been a long day, and Balm and Chime were just as tired as Moon, so they all avoided the teachers' hall where the Arbora and the warriors gathered, and headed for their various bowers.

Moon climbed straight up the central well and over the ledge into the big queens' hall. It was all quiet now, except for the fall of water into the fountain. Pearl and Ember were probably in her bower, and Stone might be up in his bower or down with the Arbora or anywhere else in the colony. Moon went through the passage into the sister queen's bower.

At first he didn't think Jade was here, until he saw the pile of jewelry near the steaming bathing pool. The ready access to running water, and pools warmed by the mentors' heating stones, was one of the things Moon liked best about the colony tree. The system that took the excess water the tree drew up through its roots and channeled it for fountains, irrigation, bathing, and sluicing the latrines was complex and hadn't fared well during the long turns the colony had been empty. It had taken most of their time here to find all the blockages and get it working right again. Having lived most of his former life in places without that luxury, Moon never took it for granted.

He sat down on the cushions by the hearth. There was already a kettle on the warming stones and he found a cake of tea in the bowl and crumbled a few pieces off into the pot.

Jade rose up out of the pool, water dripping from her frills. "Everything all right?" She was in her softer, wingless Arbora form, and it was good to see her relaxed.

"Yes, the groundlings took Delin, and all the warriors are back."

Jade stepped out of the pool, took a cloth from the pile, and started to dry her scales. She said, "Well, this turned into another interesting day."

That was all too true. Moon turned back to the hearth. "I can't believe we might have to fight for this place again."

Jade sat on the fur blanket across from him. Her expression ironic, she said, "You mean it's not fair that we have to fight for this place again."

"Hah." Fairness was a concept taught to fledglings and babies so they would share their toys and food and not shred each other over trifles. It wasn't something that applied to real life, at least in Moon's experience.

Watching him, Jade said, "If I follow the groundlings to the city, will you go with me?"

Moon took the pot and swirled it absently, just to have something to do with his hands. He knew what a compliment it was that Jade trusted him enough, and trusted his abilities, to ask him to do something like this, so outside a normal consort's experience.

Being physically born a consort didn't convey any instinctive knowledge of how to be one, and Moon had struggled with it since coming to the court. This past turn, raising the Sky Copper fledglings and his own first clutch, it had seemed like he might have finally gotten past pretending to be a consort and started to edge into actually being one. Nobody had called him a feral solitary to his face in months. Now . . . He didn't want to leave his clutch while they were still so young. But he didn't want Jade to go off without him, either. And Chime would have to go too, as the only other one who had seen the inside of the forerunner city. He said, "I don't know yet. I know what I want to do. I want to stay here."

Jade's expression was hard to read. "I sometimes wonder if you've been bored. You're the one who's traveled all your life."

"Traveling is overrated," Moon said. Being hungry, cold, wet, lonely, stalked by predators, and hunted by groundlings hadn't exactly been a good time, though he had seen a lot of interesting things.

Jade said, "Sometimes I'm a little bored." She settled her spines and looked away.

Moon wasn't surprised, but he hadn't expected her to admit it. Jade had had more than a taste of travel herself, before the court had finally started to settle down. Because it was easier to make a joke, he said, "Queens aren't supposed to get bored."

Jade tilted her head. "Consorts aren't supposed to accidentally drown in bathing pools but I'm told it happens."

Moon tugged on one of her frills. If she wanted to drown him, he had given her much worse provocation than that. "Everyone's always telling me what I'm supposed to feel."

"Yes, and we both agreed how annoying that was." Jade absently turned her empty teacup upside down. She said, "I can't make the decision whether to go or not until after I speak to the groundlings." She smiled a little dryly. "Or that's when I'll tell everyone I've made the decision."

At least the court wouldn't just sit here and do nothing. That was worse than the alternatives. "Do you think Pearl will let you go?"

Jade let her breath out, considering. "I don't know. She didn't see that thing in the underwater forerunner city. I'm not sure she understands how bad this could be. But she had the dream too, and since we got here she's always been willing to do what was needed to protect the court." She flicked her claws through the fur mat. "I mean, she always was before, at the old colony. Now she's just willing to include the rest of us in her decisions. And listen to us." Her mouth twisted. "I don't want to ruin that."

If someone had told Moon, back when he had first arrived at Indigo Cloud, that Pearl would become someone whose good opinion he was actually concerned about keeping, he would have thought they were out of their minds. Now he didn't want to ruin the tentative progress he had made, either. He said, "You can talk to Pearl after we see what the groundlings have to say. There's no point in worrying about it now."

Jade made a derisive noise. "Just because there's no point in worrying has never stopped you from it before."

That was true. Moon leaned into her side and she wrapped an arm around his waist and tugged him closer. He said, "I thought of something we can do besides worrying."

Jade nipped his ear. "I thought of that too."

Afterward, Moon lay on the furs with Jade's warm weight curled around him, her breathing deepening as she slid into sleep. It had been a long anxious day and the sex should have left him relaxed, but he couldn't stop thinking, going over it all again until his head was about to split. Jade grumbled but didn't wake as he eased out from under her. He pulled on his clothes again and left the bower.

He walked out to the edge of the queens' hall to look down the central well. From what he could hear, the court was showing no signs of settling down the way it normally did at the end of the day. Every word that had been said during the conversation with Delin would have been repeated to everyone and would now be dissected by the Arbora, who would engage in increasingly fantastic speculation as the night wore on.

He turned back, shifted, and leapt up to the consorts' level.

Moon scented an outdoor draft, cool and damp, and knew Stone was up here. There was no central consorts' hall, but there were junctions between the bowers with hearth bowls set into the floor, meant as communal seating areas. The bowers in this section were just as finely decorated as the ones in the queens' level below, but mostly untenanted. Eventually Thorn and Bitter, the consorts of the Sky Copper clutch, would leave the nurseries and move up here, and later Cloud and Rain, the consorts of Moon's clutch. That would make the place livelier.

He found his way through the empty passages, to where a doorway in the outer trunk looked down on the garden platforms below. The door was open now, and Stone leaned in the opening, looking down.

Stone didn't acknowledge Moon's appearance, but Moon knew it hadn't gone unnoticed. He wasn't sure why he had sought Stone out, but found himself asking, "Would you go, if Pearl decides to let Jade follow the groundlings?"

Stone stepped away from the door, turning to face him. "I thought Jade already decided to go whether Pearl likes it or not."

Moon bared his teeth briefly. "No, she didn't decide that." Maybe he had come up here to have an argument. "Answer the question."

Stone's brow furrowed, just a little, but with dangerous intent. Moon said, "Or we could have a fight. But I'll still want you to answer the question."

Stone eyed him, and then turned to the doorway and looked out again. The night insects were singing, in chorus and singly. They would reach a crescendo as the night wore on and then gradually subside. Moon was so used to it now he had to make himself notice it, though to a newcomer to the Reaches it would probably be a terrible din.

Stone said, "You think I'd stay here, and let Jade and a few warriors go to this place?"

It was a good way to make Moon feel bad for asking, which he was sure was intentional. He said, "I wouldn't if this was last turn. But you've been gone so much."

Stone turned with a grimace of exasperation. "I was bored."

"Bored?" Moon stared. As a reason for Stone leaving the court, it seemed deeply inadequate. "I'm bored, Jade's bored, and we stuck it out and stayed here doing what we're supposed to do."

"I'm not supposed to be doing anything," Stone retorted. "I don't know if you noticed, but I'm old."

"That's never stopped you before," Moon countered. "We'd all be dead without you."

Stone snapped, "And now you don't need me."

Moon pounced on that. "Hah, that's it! You're not bored, you're just— Mad because you think we don't appreciate you!"

Stone snarled, "That's the most idiotic thing you've ever said, and we both know how tough the competition is."

Moon snarled back. It might have escalated even further, but from the passage, Ember said, "What are you arguing about?"

Moon glanced back. Pearl's young consort stood in the doorway, wrapped in a blanket, disheveled and beautiful and blinking like he had just woken up. Like Moon, Ember didn't often spend the night in his own bower, but he might just have been napping. Moon snapped, "We're arguing about—" He wasn't sure anymore. The point of the argument had evolved dramatically.

Ember scratched a hand through his hair. "You're arguing about whether Stone is bored or not?"

When you put it that way, it did sound stupid. He said, "Ember, why don't you go see what Pearl is doing?"

"Just don't hurt each other," Ember grumbled, proving he did know exactly what the argument was about after all, and retreated back down the passage.

As Ember left, they stood there in silence. Moon said finally, "You know how the court feels about you. You're—" These things were still horribly hard for him to say. He had spent most of his life watching every abortive attempt at a relationship fail. He knew how to start them and how to escape them, but he didn't know anything about maintaining them. It was easier when the other person did all the work. And maybe he had taken Stone for granted. "I don't want you to leave. Unless you're leaving with Jade."

Stone rubbed his face. "I am not leaving the court because I'm sulking over feeling unappreciated. That's something one of our many idiot warriors would do, not something I would do."

Moon shrugged. "Sure."

Stone glared at him. "The court is settling down. I'm not ready to settle down yet." He added, "And neither are you."

"I'm not going, I've already decided." Moon said it just to provoke Stone, but as soon as the words were out, he regretted it. He knew what a consort's duty was in this situation: to stay with the court and his clutch. But that had never been his duty, and it had never been what was best for the court.

Stone stared at him, as if trying to see inside Moon's skull. Stone finally said, "Because of the clutch? You think Blossom and the teachers won't take care of them if you're not here?"

Moon grimaced. Before he had become Jade's consort, he remembered thinking that he would never want to father children in the court and then leave them, that they might suffer without him to protect them. Now, he knew that wouldn't happen. That wasn't how Raksura treated any offspring, especially royal Aeriat offspring. But in his head, leaving the clutch felt like abandoning them. As if leaving them in the protection of all of Indigo Cloud for a few months, in the safety of the colony tree, was the same as leaving them to fend for themselves in a forest forever. "Of course not." He still didn't want to die somewhere in the wilds of the Three Worlds and miss the important moments, like teaching the new clutch how to fly and hunt and fight, and the all-important task of making sure they ended up with the right mates, or at least the mates they actually wanted, whether they were right or not.

Then Stone said, "You think you can protect them if the Fell come here, if they've got help from some monstrosity imprisoned in a forerunner city, and this time it fulfills its part of the bargain?"

Moon snarled. "I know—I know that. I know it's better to stop the Fell before they get anywhere near the Reaches—"

"If you know that, then why are you staying here?" Stone said. Then he turned and stepped out the doorway.

Moon let his breath out in a hiss. Now he knew why Stone was mad at him, at least. He went to the opening.

He heard one whoosh of big wings, and saw Stone's shadow cut down toward the knothole and the court's main entrance. He watched to make certain Stone was going in through the greeting hall entrance, then shoved the door shut and barred it.

The spot they had chosen for a meeting point was on the platform of a mountain-tree not far from where the flying ship was moored. It was a fairly large platform, with a pond and low mossy grass filled with the bright flicker of tiny flying lizards and the insects they fed on, and no heavy undergrowth or parasite trees that might provide cover for predators. The hunters used it occasionally as a resting spot during long trips. The dawn rain had ended and the green light filtering through the canopy was relatively bright; somewhere above the tree canopy, it was a clear day.

Moon and Stone accompanied Jade, who had also brought Chime, Balm, and Heart, as well as Root, Song, Floret, and Vine. Sage, with four other warriors, was positioned on an upper branch above them, in case anything went terribly wrong. They picked a patch of relatively clear ground near the pond, and the warriors took up positions around it. Root said, "Should we make a firepit? We didn't bring any tea, I guess."

"No." Jade paced, flicking her spines in a preoccupied way. "This isn't that kind of meeting."

Song, who had taken a seat between Moon and Stone, leaned close to Moon and whispered, "We give Delin and the Golden Islanders tea when they visit."

"They're different," Moon told her. "We know them." Stone was doing the annoying thing where he was pretending they hadn't had that conversation last night, so Moon was pretending too. He had the bad feeling he wasn't as good at it as Stone.

Jade paced to where Heart sat near Balm. She asked, "Anything?"

"Not yet," Heart told her. Sometimes mentors had visions at significant events, but it was rare.

The mentors had augured last night, but from what Moon had heard, nothing much had come of it. They usually had to be closer to the situation before they started to get genuinely useful visions. Merit was going to try while they were having this meeting, just to see if that influenced any answers. Hopefully the answers wouldn't involve the Fell swarming the Reaches.

Jade nodded and paced away. Moon didn't like to see her this edgy. But they were about to hear something that might make a huge difference to the fate of the court.

And their own fate. Moon shrugged uneasily, unconsciously settling his groundling form's non-existent spines.

Floret, standing near the edge of the platform, reported, "They're coming."

The pointed bow of the flying boat came into view through the mountain-trees, moving with slow caution. The colors of it blended in well with the suspended forest; it made Moon wonder what it looked like in its native environment, if the groundlings who had constructed it used the moss for their homes and other buildings as well.

As the ship drew closer, Floret asked Jade, "Uh, do you want us to do anything or sit anywhere in particular?" She glanced at Moon. When formally greeting another Raksuran court, consorts sat behind queens, and everyone was introduced in a specific order. Violations of this etiquette when not forced by circumstance generally opened one up to mockery and disdain by other courts.

Jade tilted her spines in a negative. "Just stay where you are."

The warriors looked at each other uncertainly, and Song crept back a discreet distance from Moon and Stone. Jade had told all the warriors except Chime to stay in their winged forms, though Moon, Heart, and Stone were in their groundling forms. Except for Stone, who didn't make an effort for anybody, they had dressed like they would to greet another court, in their better clothes and jewelry. Moon was wearing pants and a shirt of a dark silky material, with a red patterned sash Rill had made for him, and his consort's bracelet and the anklet that Jade had given him when the clutch was born. He should be wearing a lot more jewelry, but the groundlings wouldn't know that. Well, Delin would, but he didn't care.

Stone sighed. Jade glanced at him, brows lifted. "What?"

Stone said, "Nothing, that was me breathing. Why don't you sit down?"

Jade bared her teeth at him but at least moved to stand near Moon.

The ship drifted to a halt about a hundred paces away from the platform. Groundlings of different sizes moved on the deck, then four lifted off into the air. Moon could see one was Callumkal, and that another groundling carried Delin. Again, it made his skin itch watching it. He had carried plenty of Arbora and groundlings, but seeing someone who was not a natural flyer do it was nerve-racking. He said, "If that one drops Delin—"

"I'll catch him," Vine said, reassuringly confident. Spines signaling alert attention, he watched Delin and the groundling who carried him. "I'm sure I can get him before he hits the mist."

The packs that held the spell or device that allowed the groundlings to fly were bulky affairs, constructed of a rough brown material and attached to their wearers with harnesses. It explained the harness that Callumkal had worn under his clothing. The groundlings must rely on the packs a great deal if they wore the harnesses all the time. Moon didn't know why that bothered him. Did they lack confidence in their flying boat?

The groundlings reached the platform without anybody plunging to their death and landed at the edge. Moon saw Delin had actually been in a harness too, an extra one that attached to the side of the flying pack-wearer. That was something of a relief, but it still looked like a risky method. One of the groundlings stayed near the edge of the platform, while Delin and the other three came forward.

Callumkal was in the lead, and the groundling beside him was shorter and slighter but otherwise looked almost identical to him, with the same tightly curled hair and pebbly dark skin. His open jacket and pants were of the same rich materials in browns and golds. The third groundling was a different species, wide and muscular, and had silvery gray skin that was studded with round and oblong patches of a rougher hide that looked almost like craggy rock. These patches stretched up its long legs and arms, up to its neck and face. Its skull was covered with one large patch like a helmet. Moon couldn't tell if the patches were part of the groundling's body or were an armor that had somehow been attached directly to its skin. Though if it was, it seemed inefficient to leave bare patches in between. The groundling's eyes were wide and silver gray, and its nose was just a faint indentation above its mouth. It wore a light tunic and kilt of a soft material that seemed very at odds with the partially armored hide, and had a bag slung over its shoulder.

Before anyone else could speak, Delin stepped forward and said, "This is Jade, sister queen of the Indigo Cloud Court." He performed all the introductions, naming Moon, Stone, Heart, and all the warriors. He finished, "And this is Callumkal, Master Scholar of the Conclave of the Janderan." He gestured toward the smaller version of Callumkal. "His offspring, Kalam." He nodded to the silver armored person. "And Vendoin, she is Scholar of the Hia Iserae."

Jade jerked her chin toward the groundling who had hung back on the edge of the platform. Delin had been speaking Altanic, and Jade used the same language as she said, "Tell your companion she won't need that weapon."

"Ah." Delin turned to look, smiling a little. "That is Captain Rorra."

Captain Rorra was female, very slender, with pale green skin and thick gray hair braided tightly back from her face. There was something about her tall body and the proportions of her arms and legs that made her look a little like the groundlings of Aventera. Her clothes were practical, pants and a shirt of some tough dark brown fabric, with belts and a strap across one shoulder to hold various items, and she wore heavy boots instead of sandals like the others. An oblong canister with a tube running along the top was cradled in her arms. It had a trigger, and the tube looked not unlike the Aventeran projectile weapons Moon had seen, and Delin's device that was used to fire signal lights. He knew such weapons were more common in Kish. They shot a tiny projectile, coated with a substance that caused a stream of fire to shoot out of the weapon to strike whatever the projectile landed on. They were one of the reasons the Fell tended to avoid Kishan territories.

Delin added pointedly to Callumkal, "Captain Rorra should come and sit with us. She may have insights."

"Captain Rorra prefers to keep her distance," Callumkal said, with some irony in his voice. Moon got the impression that it had been decided ahead of time that Rorra would stay back and watch them with her weapon, and Delin clearly knew that and wanted to get it out in the open.

"Is she so afraid of us?" Jade asked.

Next to Moon, Stone breathed out, a near-silent hiss of annoyance. Moon didn't know why Jade was pushing this, but he thought it had the potential to disrupt everything before the meeting even got started. If Rorra fired her weapon, she could only get one of them, and the warriors waiting above would reach her before she could fire again. That was why the weapons were best used in groups, all firing at once. Rorra had to know that, and Moon didn't think Callumkal was a fool.

Callumkal hesitated. Kalam looked up at him, waiting, and Vendoin made a gesture with one hand, possibly signaling that it was Callumkal's decision. Callumkal said, "Very well." He turned. "Rorra, please join us."

It was Rorra's turn to hesitate, but then she walked forward, picking her way through the low grass. There was something tentative about the way she walked, as if her boots were awkward on the uneven ground. As she reached Callumkal, she said nothing, and just gave Delin a grimace. This close Moon could see her pale green skin was lightly scaled, her long-fingered hands had claws, though the tips had been filed down, and there were patches of loose skin on either side of her throat. *She's a sealing*, Moon thought, or at least she had been at one time. Groundlings who had sealing in their ancestry didn't tend to have the gills. Full-blooded sealings didn't stay out of the water for long periods, or come this far inland. He glanced down at her feet, noticing now how her boots were oddly bulky at the bottom and might be built up to account for fins. She caught him looking and frowned.

Delin said, "Now, show them the artifact."

Callumkal gave Delin a look that suggested he didn't appreciate being given instructions, but gestured to Vendoin. She pulled the bag off her shoulder and carefully drew out something wrapped in coarse cloth. She knelt and unwrapped it, then tilted it up to show them. It was a cracked stone tile, stained and weathered, with a forerunner carved on it, clearly the original of Delin's drawing.

Jade's spines moved in reaction, and she nodded grimly to Delin. "I see."

Vendoin glanced around, making sure everyone had gotten a look, then began to wrap it up again.

Callumkal said, "As Delin must have told you, some of us believe that the city this came from belonged to the species we call foundation builders, who lived in the Kishlands in the distant past. But some believe this object means it was a city of the people Delin calls forerunners. He told us you had discovered an ancient forerunner city, and that you had some words of caution."

Rorra interposed, "I wondered if you had any proof of this experience."

Delin gave Moon an ironic eyebrow lift and said in Raksuran, "Captain Rorra is very mistrustful. Apparently there are scholars who would have made the whole incident up, possibly with your help, for amusement or to gain attention."

Moon hissed under his breath. This meeting was already going badly, and he had no idea why. *At least nobody's actually dead yet.*

Chime made a derisive noise and said in Raksuran, "The incident wasn't what I would call amusing."

Annoyed, Heart added, "They don't want anything to come between them and their goal. They have their ideas, they don't want facts to bother them."

Rorra said, "Speak in Altanic, please."

Jade tilted her head, and said in Altanic, "We'll speak how we like."

Callumkal frowned, and said in Kedaic, "Captain, if this goes badly, you may need to return to the ship."

No one said anything, and Delin's expression remained pleasantly bland. The Kish obviously didn't realize that the Raksura could speak Kedaic. It was a common trade language throughout Kish, made up of words from all the various languages of the species who lived there, but Moon had heard it used in the east and the west, far past the Reaches.

Rorra's jaw went tight and she said nothing. Jade said, "We don't have any evidence because the city flooded and was destroyed when we escaped it. It was designed to flood, to kill the creature inside if it managed to get free of its prison."

Vendoin had tucked the tile away into the bag and stood, and now spoke for the first time. Her voice was light and high, and it made the

61

Altanic words sound almost melodic. "Was there some outward sign that the city held this creature? Some warning?" She gestured with an open hand. "I'm thinking of trading flags, and other such devices used by long-distance travelers."

That was a good question. Jade glanced at Moon to show she wanted him to answer. Jade apparently wanted to maintain an aggressive pose and leave the actual discussion to others. He wished he knew what had made her so angry all of a sudden. From Balm's worried expression, he knew he wasn't the only one wondering. He said, "If there was, we didn't recognize it as a warning. There were symbols we thought were just decoration, but nothing that stood out."

Vendoin and Callumkal seemed to absorb this information thoughtfully, while Kalam and Rorra both looked shocked that Moon could talk. *Why do groundlings do that?* Moon wondered, irritated.

Vendoin said, "You would think they would make it obvious that danger lay within, but there is no accounting for a strange species' reasoning." Her large eyes blinked, as she appeared to recall that the strange species was probably a Raksuran ancestor. She added, "No offense."

Moon shared a look with Chime, and decided the best course was just not to respond to that.

Stone, clearly fed up with how everyone else was wasting time, said, "The Fell were the only ones who knew that thing was there, because it told them."

Rorra said, "And they told you."

"Oh, here we go," Chime hissed under his breath in Raksuran. "This is like the Aventerans all over again."

"It's not an uncommon reaction," Moon said.

Stone gave him a nudge with his shoulder. It was meant to be comforting, but Moon was still too irritated with Stone to receive it in the spirit it was meant.

His expression perplexed, Delin added, also in Raksuran, "I noticed this too, with the Aventerans. Are people simply that blind to detail? I look much like Vendoin, in that we both have two arms, two legs, one head, and so on, but all else is different. It does not seem a survival trait to ignore these facts."

"What are you saying?" Rorra demanded.

Delin let a little impatience show, and answered in Kedaic, "We're speaking of your willful ignorance in confusing Raksura with Fell."

Also obviously nearing the end of her patience, Jade said, "This is entertaining, but you didn't come here for words of caution. Delin's given you those, and you've ignored them. And he's already asked, and knows the answers to, all these questions. What do you really want from us?"

CHAPTER FIVE

Callumkal glanced at Vendoin, and read something off the mask of her face that Moon couldn't see. Callumkal said, "Very well. Delin told us of your abilities. I think he must have told you that we want your help."

Vendoin turned to Delin. "Did you know we meant to ask this?"

Delin said, "It was a possibility that occurred to me, as a potential method of entering the city. But as I told you, I am undecided about the wisdom of attempting it in the first place." He eyed Callumkal. "I did wonder if your expedition would be too wary of the Raksura to make the suggestion, once you met them."

Callumkal inclined his head to Delin with an air of irony. "I'm glad I could surpass your low expectations."

Chime flicked a glance at Heart, and said, "Where is this city? Can you show us a map?"

Vendoin turned to Callumkal. "I think we must show them, before we continue."

Callumkal didn't answer immediately, clearly reluctant to take that step. Jade folded her arms, her spines taking on an irritated angle. "You can't ask us to go somewhere with you if you aren't even willing to trust us with the location."

"True," Callumkal conceded. Rorra drew breath as if to protest, but didn't speak as Callumkal reached into the flat pouch at his belt and drew out a square of waxed cloth. He stepped forward and knelt on the mossy ground. As he unfolded it, Rorra moved around him and stood close by. Kalam sat beside his father. Callumkal said, "This is a copy, of course. The original is carved into a stone that forms part of the support beneath the Archive Kedmar. We know nearly nothing of the species we call the foundation builders, who constructed it and carved the image. They left behind little else but some writings which are mostly poetry, the meanings of which are greatly disputed by various scholars, and the stone beneath the ruins of their cities."

"There should be more. I still believe something tried to destroy everything they left behind," Vendoin added, not reassuringly.

Callumkal made what Moon interpreted as an *I'm not going to argue with you in front of strangers* gesture. Callumkal added, "The annotations were made by the mapmakers who copied it."

The map was drawn on the cloth with a dark ink, the place names and directions neatly written out in Kedaic. Heart and Chime both leaned forward to look, Chime from one side and Heart from the other. One of the skills Chime had used as a mentor which he still had as a warrior was copying text and drawings, and Heart was expert at it as well. Arbora who copied books in the court's library tended to have excellent memories for writing and drawings, something that made the copying go much faster. Moon suspected this one long look would be enough for them to memorize the map and recreate it later.

Moon sat up on his knees to move closer. He reached for the edge of the map, meaning to tug out the wrinkles in it, and Rorra grabbed his shoulder.

Jade was suddenly between them. She slapped Rorra's hand away before Moon had a chance to draw breath. Rorra stepped back and instinctively jerked her weapon up. Delin stepped in front of her. He said, "It is always good to get permission before touching any stranger, but in a Raksuran court, one especially does not touch the consort."

Moon hissed in frustration. He knew he could have handled an aggressive, arrogant maybe-sealing without resorting to violence. He couldn't tell Jade in front of groundlings that she was overreacting, but he badly wanted to.

Rorra's gaze went to Jade. She said, "I don't like being threatened—"

"I'm not threatening you." Jade bared her teeth. "But if you want a fight, say so."

Vendoin said hastily, "No one wants a fight."

Callumkal shoved to his feet. "It was a misunderstanding."

Sounding bored, Stone added in Raksuran, "I came for the forerunners and the foundation builders and the groundling-eating monsters; if there's going to be a fight, I'm leaving."

In the same language, Jade hissed at him, "Promises, promises."

Speaking Raksuran too, Moon said, "She's not a queen, Jade. She doesn't even realize she's acting like one." He would have to save asking *what is wrong with you?* for later.

"Moon's right, Jade," Balm added, watching with concern.

Jade's spines quivered in irritation. "I know that."

Pointedly, Vendoin plopped down on the ground. "I'm showing everyone where the city is now. Those interested please look." She turned to Chime and Heart. "You see, these figures indicate seamounts. You are familiar with those formations?"

Chime and Heart leaned closer, and Heart said, "They're mountains?"

"Possibly natural formations, possibly constructed by former inhabitants of the region," Vendoin told her.

Rorra took a step back, still watching Jade warily. Callumkal looked from Rorra to Jade, and sat down again next to Vendoin. Moon found himself meeting Kalam's gaze. The boy was wide-eyed. Moon thought about trying to smile reassuringly, decided it was more likely to look like a threat, and eased back to sit beside Stone. Stone stared up at the tree canopy and shook his head in resignation at how stupid they all were. Moon muttered to him, "You're not helping."

Low-voiced, Stone replied, "If we can't get through looking at the map without a fight, how are we supposed to work with these people?"

Moon grimaced. Stone had a point. No one else heard except Delin, who rubbed his eyes wearily.

Trying to pick up the fallen threads of the conversation, Callumkal told Jade, "As Delin suspected, we hoped to ask some of you to travel with us to the city, to help us enter it." He looked around at the others, his expression conveying exasperation. "I hoped to work my way up to this request more gracefully, but there you have it."

Jade settled her spines deliberately. Sounding more reasonable, she said, "You haven't mentioned the signs of Fell presence."

At least none of the groundlings glared at Delin this time. Callum-kal said, "There is no proof that the Fell were in the area because of the ancient city, or that they were still there by the time we arrived. The settlements that were destroyed were travelers' outposts, as far as we could tell."

"Travelers' outposts?" Moon asked.

Vendoin answered, "We couldn't identify them from the . . . remains. It may have been a sea-going race who seeded the settlements as supply depots as they moved through the area. Some do this to extend their reach through the oceans or the empty seas, where there are no other ports or habitations, like stepping stones, you see?"

Moon did. It meant these people would return at some point and find their friends dead and no fresh supplies. It was a grim picture to imagine.

The scales of Jade's brow furrowed thoughtfully. Heart took up the questioning, asking, "Did you find the destroyed settlements on your way there, or the way back?"

Chime added, "And could you tell how long ago they had been destroyed?"

"The way back," Callumkal said.

Vendoin answered Chime, "We couldn't tell how long. The remains had been exposed to weather and carrion feeders." Anticipating the next question, she said, "We knew it was Fell because there were dead dakti, also partially eaten."

Moon exchanged a look with Stone. So the Fell could have followed the Kishan ships out to sea, and fed on the settlements while they waited for the groundlings to find the way into the city.

Sounding frustrated, Rorra said, "But if the Fell are there, and want the city, why haven't they entered it already? They are fliers like you, they could have made it through the winds at the top of the escarpment."

Jade managed not to sound too annoyed. "They might be in the city already. We don't know that any more than you do."

In Raksuran, Stone muttered, "Or they can't get in because they don't have a key."

A key. A forerunner or someone enough like one to open it for them. Also in Raksuran, Moon said, "Maybe they don't know what they need."

Chime turned to them. "In which case, if we go there, and can't get through the entrance, we'll know there's something terrible inside, and that we shouldn't keep trying."

Following the conversation closely, Delin waggled his hands. "That is a point. But I am not sure the logic follows completely."

Jade flicked a warning spine at them. Callumkal's expression was impatient. In Altanic, she told him, "They're discussing the idea that the Fell may not know how to enter, so are waiting for you to open it for them."

Callumkal clearly didn't think it worth discussing. "That's assuming the city is sealed in some way. The entrance may simply be hidden."

Jade tilted her head. "We're all making a great many assumptions."

Callumkal glanced at Vendoin. Moon had the idea they hadn't expected a Raksuran queen to be quite so interested in debating their conclusions and theories, at least during this discussion. Callumkal said, "I . . . assume you will want some time to make a decision. I hope you will not refuse us outright but will take some—"

"I'll return here to tell you our decision tomorrow morning." Jade twitched her spines, a signal to the warriors, who all immediately moved to the edges of the platform and leapt into flight. Chime and Heart shifted, and Chime stood and picked her up.

Jade nodded to Delin. "Are you coming with us or staying?"

"For tonight, I will stay with them." Delin got to his feet. "I will see you in the morning."

Vendoin hastily knelt down to pick up the map and fold it. Stone just got up and walked off the edge of the platform. Callumkal stared after him, but Stone didn't reappear; Moon guessed he had shifted lower down and didn't want the groundlings to see his other form right now.

Jade turned and strode for the edge of the platform. Moon followed with Chime and Heart, not wanting to spoil the abruptness of Jade's exit.

"So we're going," Chime said, low-voiced. "To the city, I mean."

Heart, her claws hooked around Chime's collar flange, said, "We were always going. There wasn't really another choice."

Moon said, "I hope Pearl knows that." He shifted, heard a startled gasp from someone behind him, and leapt into flight after Jade.

They flew back to the colony tree and went on through to the greeting hall, where many curious warriors and Arbora waited to hear what had happened at the meeting. Moon shifted back to his groundling form and stretched, trying to shed some of the tension while Jade and Balm answered the anxious questions.

Chime murmured to Moon, "Well, that was interesting. Why did Jade get so angry?"

"I don't know." Moon kept his voice low, watching Jade to make certain no spines pointed in his direction. "She wasn't when we got there." Thinking about it in retrospect, Jade had contributed almost as much hostility to the situation as Rorra had. Delin hadn't exactly been his usual even-tempered self, either.

Jade left the warriors and turned to Chime, motioning Heart to draw near. She asked them, "You can make a copy of that map?"

Heart nodded and glanced at Chime. "We should each do one separately, and then compare them to make sure we're accurate."

"We'll be accurate," Chime said, perfectly confident.

"When you're certain, make three copies," Jade told them. Then she turned to Moon, "Now, I'm going to talk to Pearl. After that, I want you to write a letter to your mother."

She didn't stay for an answer, immediately leaping straight up to catch the edge of a balcony. Moon let out a breath in annoyance, watching her start the climb up the well toward the queens' level.

Chime murmured, "I don't know which of those things is more frightening." Heart, apparently meaning to demonstrate how unfunny she found that remark, gave him a little punch in the ribs. Chime shied away from her and said, "Ow. Don't hit when I'm in groundling form."

Moon was betting on the encounter with Pearl being worse. He said, grimly, "I'll tell you later."

Chime and Heart started down to the lower level workrooms to make the maps. Knowing the talk with Pearl was going to take a while, Moon followed but turned off at the teachers' hall to visit the nurseries.

Moon spent some time playing with his own fledglings, as well as all the others who were awake. He ended up stretched out on the floor, watching Sapphire, Fern, Solace, Cloud, and Rain roll around trying to kill each other and their companions.

Over by the nearest pool, the teachers Bark and Bead were discussing who they wanted to clutch with. This involved a detailed examination of the good and bad traits of various bloodlines, and who was related too closely to whom. Within the court, breeding was serious business but sex was easy and friendly and casual, a welcome change from some of the places Moon had lived in the past. Warriors were all infertile, and queens and female Arbora could control their fertility at will, so there was no possibility of unwanted babies. Royal Aeriat took warrior lovers, and consorts were expected to have clutches with Arbora to encourage mentor births. Moon hadn't done that so far, mostly because Jade's clutching had been so nerve-racking that he couldn't bring himself to do another one yet.

Bitter and Thorn plopped down next to him, both in groundling form. The two consorts were a little too old now to play with quite such reckless abandon as the younger kids. Over the past season Moon had started to teach them and Frost the basics of fighting, and how to handle their claws, which was easier now that Bitter had actually admitted that he could fly. Moon said, "Where's Frost?"

Bitter made an elaborate shrug, as if indifferent to Frost's location. Thorn said, "The hunters are working on hides today and she wanted to watch."

Moon frowned. "She wants to learn how to tan hides?" He approved, but found it a little odd that Frost was interested.

Bitter gave him a wry look, clearly sad at how naive Moon was. Thorn said, patiently, "No, she wants to hear all about everything that's going on with the groundlings and the flying boat, and she knows that the hunters will be talking about it."

That made a lot more sense. "Oh. You know about that?"

Bitter sighed and rolled his eyes, and Thorn said, "Everyone knows. Part of it, anyway. Frost will come and tell us the rest when she finds out." Regarding Moon seriously, he said, "You're going off to fight some Fell, before they get into an old groundling city and then come here to attack us, like in the dream everyone had."

Moon shook his head. "I don't know yet if I'm going."

Thorn and Bitter stared. Then Bitter reached over and poked Moon in the head. Thorn said, "You have to go. What if something happens to Jade? Is Chime going?" Bitter leaned over and whispered in Thorn's ear. Thorn translated, "Bitter says the last time you let them go somewhere without you, something terrible happened."

Moon winced. "Thorn . . ." Thorn was gentle and perceptive and relentless, all good qualities for a consort, unless you didn't want to talk about something he wanted you to talk about.

"Are you worried about leaving us and your other clutch?" Thorn continued. "They're really too young to understand things like that yet. They'll miss you, but when you come back they won't be mad, and they won't really remember how long you were gone. That's how it was for us at that age."

"That's good to know," Moon said. *So if I get killed, it won't bother them too much.* That wasn't exactly an encouraging thought.

Bitter leaned in to whisper a remark, and Thorn said, "Bitter thinks you're worried about leaving us. We don't like it when you go away. But it's been a long time since you've had to go. So . . . I think it's all right with us."

Then Sapphire galloped over, flung a ragged doll at Bitter's chest, and galloped off again. Cloud slammed in to retrieve the doll, and then Bitter and Thorn were enveloped in a mass of fledglings and Arbora babies.

After a while, Moon reluctantly decided enough time had passed that Jade would have finished talking to Pearl, and started up to the queens' level.

He found Jade in her bower with the writing materials out, impatiently waiting for him. "How was Pearl?" he asked her, taking a seat by the hearth.

"Angry." Jade's expression indicated that she realized that was nothing new. "She didn't give me an answer yet. Ember is in there with her, to nod and say reasonable things, so that's the best we can hope for."

Ember was good at nodding and saying reasonable things to queens. It was a large part of a consort's duty, one Moon didn't feel he was particularly good at. But speaking of which, he asked Jade, "Why were you so angry with that Captain Rorra? Do you hate sealings for some reason?"

"Of course not. I've never seen a live sealing before." Jade bared her fangs briefly in exasperation. "I don't know, exactly. Something was just . . . odd . . . about her. I wanted to slam her off that platform before she even said anything."

Moon realized she was right, he had felt Rorra was aggressive and threatening before she had spoken. If he took the emotion out of it, all she had done at first was be cautious and watchful, which was presumably part of the job she did for Callumkal and the other scholars. "Huh."

Jade waved off the topic. "Now we need to write these letters. I'm going to write to Emerald Twilight and Sunset Water, but you should write to Malachite."

After a lot of practice, Moon could read Raksuran fairly well. But his handwriting was still terrible, so what Jade actually meant was that he would talk and she would write it down.

This was how Moon answered letters from Shade and his clutchmate Celadon, usually getting Chime to do the writing part. The letters were carried from court to court along the trade network, so it sometimes took them months to arrive. This letter would be taken directly to Opal Night by Indigo Cloud warriors. And for something this serious, Moon didn't think he should be involved. This seemed more like a queen thing. He said, "She's going to know you're the one writing it. You should just write it and tell her it's from you."

Jade put the pen down in exasperation. She had the pressed paper spread out on the floor and a cake of ink in a small bowl, all ready. "How would Malachite know that?"

Moon lifted a brow. It was always best to assume that Malachite knew everything. It was the only way to cope with her.

Jade growled under her breath and picked up the pen. "You're right, you're right."

He watched her write for a moment. "Are you telling her you're going?"

She stopped and scratched the pen through the ink again. "Yes."

"Without getting Pearl's permission?"

Jade's expression was dry. "I won't be able to send this for another day or so. By that time, I'll have her permission. Or not."

It would take that long for the warrior-messengers to get together supplies for their long trip. "Are you sending her one of the map copies?"

"Yes. Someone else needs to know where we're going, and what we think we'll find. Someone all the other courts will listen to. Someone with the resources to do something about it, if it turns out we're right." Moon drew breath and Jade said, "Do not ask me how long you think it will take Pearl to decide."

Moon let the breath out. Stone wandered in and sat down beside the hearth. He asked, "Any word yet?"

"No." Jade kept writing. "You weren't very much help."

"This is between you and her, and you know it." Stone picked up the teapot and studied the contents critically. "Me trying to put a claw in would have just turned her against you. She would have gotten over it, but we don't have the time to waste." He set the pot aside and scrubbed both hands through his gray hair. "I'm too old for this."

Moon managed not to hiss in exasperation. If Stone wasn't too old to go wandering off alone, he wasn't too old for this. And it was even more irritating that Moon couldn't tell if these complaints were based in reality or just more sulking because Stone was bored or whatever it was that was wrong with him. Moon found himself torn: he wanted Stone to go to protect the others on the trip, but he didn't want Stone to get hurt, either. What came out when he tried to articulate this was a pointed, "Do you even want to go?"

Stone's expression showed he did not take the question well. "What does that mean?"

"You don't have to go. What if something happens at the court while you're gone? Pearl could use your help."

Still writing, Jade said, "You're going to get hurt."

She wasn't talking to Stone. Moon tried again, "I'm just saying, you're not obligated to do this." Exasperated, he added, "I can't tell if you want to go or not."

The court had depended on Stone's stamina and speed over and over again. The line-grandfathers they had encountered at other courts weren't like him. Many of them traveled, and some had simply left and never come back. Others stayed at their courts, but didn't participate actively in court life. But then Stone was old enough to remember when this colony tree had been abandoned, the long journey out of the Reaches and all the hardships the court must have endured before they settled in the eastern colony. That had given him a different outlook on Raksuran life and the duties of consorts than most courts, including Indigo Cloud, were used to. Also, at the point in his life where Stone's winged form had grown large enough to do whatever he wanted, he hadn't exactly been reluctant to take advantage of it.

He probably hadn't been the best choice to teach Moon how to be a Raksura, but then there hadn't been any other option. And Moon was fairly pleased with how things had turned out. Most of the time.

Jade put the pen down and told Stone, "He doesn't want you to die, you big old idiot."

Stone snorted derisively. "We're all probably going to die because of these stupid groundlings."

Moon threw his hands in the air and gave up. "Fine, fly yourself to death, see if I care. As long as you're doing exactly what you want."

"What is wrong with you?" Stone asked him. "Do you want to go? You said you didn't."

"Nothing is wrong with me!" Moon snarled.

"I'm writing to Malachite," Jade told Stone. She wiped the ink off the pen. "It's making him uneasy."

Moon was pretty certain they were both attributing their own feelings to him. Or something like that. He pushed to his feet. "I'm going to talk to Chime. Tell my mother I said hello."

Moon found Chime down in the mentors' libraries. It was a long, high-ceilinged chamber, winding some distance into the depths of the colony tree, and the walls were lined with shelves. They were made of a green and white polished agate, and stretched all the way up the high walls. Some were filled with folded and rolled books, their leather covers brightly decorated, but there weren't nearly enough to fill the space. After generations of travel, Indigo Cloud had lost large portions of its library. Since they had arrived back in the Reaches, the mentors had been trading for copies of books from other courts with some success.

Chime sat on the floor in groundling form, under the biggest cluster of shell lights, various bowls with ink cakes and charcoal drawing sticks set around him. The big square of cloth that would be used to make the map was stretched tight on a board. It was covered with charcoal lines and writing, and Chime seemed to be just sitting there contemplating it. Moon asked, "Are you finished already?"

Chime glanced up. "I've got all the rough outlines in, I want to wait for Heart before I start inking them."

Moon sat on his heels for a closer look. From his own memory of the original map, it looked accurate. "So you're just sitting here."

"Thinking." Chime pointed upward. "Listening."

It probably didn't fall under the helpful category so much as the odd but harmless category, but one thing Chime's new senses had given him was the ability to sometimes hear a strange deep rumble, which the other mentors thought might be the voices of the mountain-trees. Listening harder, he had been able to hear the colony tree, something he had described as a noise like a great storm wind, filled with little murmurs like leaves brushing against each other.

"You're not upset about going on the trip, are you?" Moon asked. The danger aside, Chime had never liked traveling outside the court, the way Moon and Jade and many of the other Aeriat did.

"No," Chime assured him. "This is exactly the kind of situation where I might be helpful."

That was certainly true. Moon watched him, trying to gauge whether Chime was just being brave or if he really wanted to go. "What happened with the last forerunner city was pretty bad," he said, aware this was a big understatement.

Chime snorted. "No kidding." He twitched his shoulders uneasily. "But it was much worse for poor Shade. He was lucky to survive."

It had been worse than Chime or any of the others knew. Moon hadn't told anyone else what he had seen the Fell do to Shade. The fact that Shade had come through it at all just showed how strong he was.

Chime continued, "But we don't know we'll find the same thing in this city. If it even is a forerunner city, and not these Kish foundation builders. And really, it just seems unlikely that every one of these forerunner cities are prisons for terrible monsters, even if the Fell are hanging around this one."

"It seems unlikely," Moon agreed, "but . . ."

"But I'm terrified that it's true," Chime finished. "And I don't know what we're going to do about it." He turned to Moon. "You know I don't mind if you don't go. I mean, I wish you would. You . . . I don't want to be away from you that long. But I understand. Is that what you're worried about?"

"I'm not worried," Moon said. That wasn't the right way to say it. "No, I am worried, but . . ." But he didn't want to tell Chime to stay, or say anything that might be construed that way. He barely felt able to make his own decisions at the moment, let alone decisions for anyone else.

And it was becoming increasingly obvious that he needed to make a decision.

Chime eyed him closely. "You're doing that thing where you're really worried and you don't want to show anyone."

Moon buried his face in his hands. "I have a clutch now. Two clutches, with the Sky Copper clutch. My place is here. That's what consorts are supposed to do."

Chime was silent for a long moment. "I know, but . . . You're not a normal consort. I've never thought you should pretend you are, or make decisions based on that pretense."

Moon looked up at him and Chime waved his hands and said hastily, "But I don't mean to tell you what to do."

They stared at each other for a long moment. Then Moon leaned forward and nipped Chime on the ear. He didn't want to leave the clutch. But maybe what he really wanted was for this nightmare not to have happened, and for everything to go on as it had before. And that just wasn't possible.

Chime nipped Moon on the neck in return, still an intense sensation on groundling skin, no matter how many times Moon had felt it. Moon pulled him close and Chime slid a hand around his hip.

At that point a breathless Song whipped in through the library door. She saw them wound together and skidded to a halt, her claws scraping the floor. "Sorry, sorry!"

"What?" Chime demanded. "Can it wait?"

"No, there's been an augury," she gasped. "You two need to come hear it."

CHAPTER SIX

Moon and Chime followed Song to one of the workrooms in the lower levels, which the mentors used for making simples and storing materials. The scents of various herbs grew more intense the closer they got to the room, so it was almost overwhelming when Moon stepped inside.

It was a big round chamber and the bent sapling wood rack arching overhead held herbs stored in bundles and bags. Pots and jars holding more ingredients sat on the floor. The combination of scents was fascinating, but Moon didn't know how the mentors could stand working in here for long periods without going scent-blind.

There was a large sap-sealed jar in the corner that Moon knew contained the eastern plant that was called three-leafed purple bow. It was used for Fell poison, which was prepared by boiling down the plant over and over again into an odorless simple that tasted of nothing but grass or waterweeds and could be easily concealed in food or water. It affected both Fell and Raksura, preventing you from shifting and making you unconscious or too sick to move. Some Fell it killed outright. Moon had discovered it the hard way, by having some groundlings use it on him when they thought he was a Fell ruler.

Since encountering a Fell flight moving through the west on the far side of the Reaches, the mentors had taken the precaution of trying to grow the plant here. They hadn't been successful until two rain seasons ago. Moon had thought it was a good idea at the time; considering the shared dream, he thought it was an even better one.

Jade was already there, with Stone and Balm. They were sitting on the floor with Heart, Merit, and Thistle.

Heart's version of the map lay nearby, with ink cakes and pens beside it. Jade looked up as Moon and Chime came in, and said, "We're waiting for Pearl."

Moon nodded and sat on his heels to look at the map; he couldn't see any difference from Chime's version, except in the handwriting. Chime knelt to examine it more closely, and asked, "Who's going to make the copies?"

"Rill and Merry said they'd do it," Heart said. Moon glanced up at something in her tone and saw her expression was set, her jaw a hard line. Merit seemed edgy and Thistle bristled with fury. Jade and Balm watched them worriedly. Moon found himself meeting Stone's gaze, which was ironic and exasperated. *Right*, Moon thought. He was getting the impression that this augury had not gone well.

Pearl swept in with Floret behind her. She settled on the floor, curling her tail around her feet, and gestured impatiently to Heart. "Tell us."

"It was a very strong vision," Heart said. She glanced at Merit and Thistle. "All three of us shared it, and we agree it was clearly an augury and not a dream, like the way it happened before. We've asked the other mentors and they all shared it to a certain extent. Even Copper, who is too young to have gotten any serious training in augury yet." She turned to Chime. "Did you feel anything odd, or see or hear anything?"

Chime's expression was frustrated. "No, and I was down in the library, concentrating on the map before Moon came in. There was no way I could have missed it."

Pearl's tail twitched in impatience. "Well, what was it?"

Heart spread her hands. "It doesn't make any sense . . ."

"Neither did the shared nightmare," Jade encouraged her. "Go on."

Heart's expression was tight and tense. "We saw white water. Solid white water. Chunks of it floating in a cold sea. A city of stone floating almost in the clouds, surrounded by mist, but we couldn't tell if it was groundling or skyling or something else. We saw something waiting there, something powerful. Then the cold sea again and another city of metal, moving with the waves." She hesitated, biting her lip, and Thistle stirred uneasily. Merit now had his gaze locked on the floor. Heart said slowly, "Merit didn't think I should tell you the rest."

Merit winced. Pearl's irritated attention was transferred to him, and she said, "Why not?"

Heart watched Merit, brows lifted. After a moment, Merit looked up and said, "I don't think that part of it was a real vision."

Thistle pressed her lips together. "He thinks I imposed it on the augury, and that it means I caused the shared dream."

Merit glanced at her, exasperated. "Not intentionally!"

"Why me?" Thistle demanded, obviously angry and offended. Moon didn't get it either. He had mostly seen Thistle's skills demonstrated more in healing than visions, but he couldn't see why Merit suddenly thought she was bad at augury.

As if it was obvious, Merit said, "Because it didn't come from Heart and it wasn't me—"

Chime's expression said he was not particularly thrilled with any of them. "You should have figured this out before you called the queens in here, and not interrupted the interpretation with it. And you should be able to tell if anyone imposed it on an augury, it would be markedly different from a shared dream—"

Heart bared her teeth at him. "I know that, Chime, and I'm saying we couldn't tell—"

"Then it must have been part of the vision—"

Stone cut through it all with the words, "Argue about it later," spoken in a tone with an implied *or else*.

All the mentors and Chime subsided, glaring at each other. Pearl, whose spines had started to take on an alarming angle and tension, said grimly, "You're going to have to explain what this means."

Heart said, "If mentors are sharing a vision, it's possible for one of them to accidentally add something to it. A fear, a hope, a memory. It's not like the shared dream, but it's not an entirely conscious act, either."

Merit interposed, "It's because you can tell your own thoughts when they mingle with a vision, but if someone else's are carried in the joint seeing, then you can't tell where they come from—"

"I can tell!" Thistle snarled, her voice roughening toward the deeper tone of her shifted form. "I can tell my own thoughts, and that wasn't one of them!"

"Merit, why do you think this part of the vision isn't real?" Jade asked. She was controlling her own impatience pretty well but Moon could tell it was an effort.

Merit shook his head but didn't seem to be able to answer. Thistle said grimly, "Because he doesn't want it to be true."

That wasn't reassuring, but Moon would rather just hear it. "Just tell us what it is," he said. If he had been in scaled form, he would have been signaling just as much frustration as Pearl, but he tried to keep his voice even. "Just tell us and let us decide."

Heart took a deep breath. "We saw Fell in the Reaches."

For an instant no one breathed. Moon felt a cold trickle down his spine, the sensation of having to suppress his fight reflex. The sole comfort of the shared dream was that it hadn't been a vision, not a true augury, just a joint fear. Somebody made a faint noise of protest. Moon thought it was Floret. He thought it was a kneejerk "it can't happen here" reaction, or maybe an "it can't happen again" reaction. And Merit and Heart had been two of the Arbora carried away from the old colony by the retreating Fell. Maybe that explained Merit's reluctance to believe in the vision.

Pearl's spines snapped into a neutral position. Belatedly, Jade did the same. Her voice expressionless, Pearl said, "Explain exactly what you saw."

Heart kept her voice calm and even too, despite the tension in her body. "We saw major kethel flying in the suspended forest. We couldn't tell where they were. They carried sacs, and we knew they were full of dakti. We didn't see any rulers."

Sacs were tumor-like growths that the kethel secreted to carry the dakti swarms over long distances. They could also make giant ones, carried by multiple kethel, that the whole Fell flight could travel in.

Thistle looked away, her throat moving as she swallowed. "I don't think it was an intrusion. I think it was part of the vision. It doesn't mean it's true, or that it's going to happen, but it was part of the vision."

Moon realized Chime was pressing against his shoulder; his breathing was shaky, as if he was trying not to tremble. Moon leaned into him.

Chime took a deep breath and said, "Well, I'm glad I didn't see that after all. The nightmare was bad enough."

Pearl's eyes were hooded. "And Heart, what do you think?"

Heart lifted her chin. "I agree with Thistle."

Merit twitched in discomfort, but didn't object.

Jade's brow was furrowed. "The last part is a warning, obviously. If we do the wrong thing, the Fell will raise the strength to attack the Reaches."

Balm lifted her shoulders, uncertain. "But does it mean that this happens if we go to the city or if we don't go?"

Moon wanted to hiss in frustration. That was the key point. Both the nightmare and the vision were obviously warnings. The hard part was figuring out what they were warning them about.

Jade rubbed her brow, trying to conceal either fear or exasperation, and added, "Or does it happen if we don't stop the groundlings from getting inside?"

Stone said, "They can't get into the city without us. That means we have a chance to get in first, and see what's there."

"I did realize that," Pearl said, her voice a half-growl.

"I'm just making sure we're clear on what we're talking about here." Stone asked Heart, "The vision didn't say we shouldn't go?"

Heart touched her forehead, frowning in concentration, and Moon thought again what a lot of responsibility the mentors had. But their visions had kept the court alive, turned uncertain plans into triumphs, recovered the colony tree's stolen seed, and had once saved Jade and her warriors against impossible odds. That sometimes the visions were too obscure to understand until closer to the event, or didn't come to the mentors until it was too late, was frustrating, but you couldn't argue with the successes.

Heart said finally, "I felt that we should send someone with the groundlings. The source of the trouble, the power, is where the groundlings are going." She looked up, her expression more certain. "I think we should be there when they find it."

Pearl looked at Thistle. "And you?"

Thistle nodded. "There are things about the vision that are confusing, but I didn't feel any benefit to staying here. I felt we had to take action."

Pearl flicked a spine. "Merit?"

Merit grimaced and rubbed his face. "I . . . agree. I just . . ."

Jade finished softly, "Don't want it to be true?"

Merit nodded grudgingly. "Yes." He added, "I'm sorry, Thistle."

Thistle's stony expression softened, and she nudged Merit's shoulder in forgiveness.

Pearl sat back, her spines still held rigidly neutral. Jade watched her, keeping her own face blank. Stone was wearing his opaque expression and Moon stopped breathing. Pearl looked around at them all as if this was their fault, and said, "Apparently there is no decision to make after all." She uncoiled her tail and stood, and told Jade, "Choose who you want to take with you."

As they left the chamber, Moon told Jade, "I'm going."

She glanced at him, her expression grim. "I thought you might."

The argument over who else was going raged for most of the night. Moon gave up after realizing it had been a few hours and went up to his bower to sort out what he needed to take.

Besides the usual supplies for traveling like flints, a blanket, a waterskin, and a knife, he was debating whether to bring extra clothes. For trips with other Raksura, when they weren't going to another court, he usually didn't bother. But they were going to be traveling with the groundlings much of the time, and nudity taboos could make washing the ones he was wearing difficult.

He opened a wicker chest and paused as he saw what lay on top, wrapped in a fragment of dark silky cloth. It was the jewelry piece Malachite had given him that had belonged to his father. It was a small disk made of ivory, carved into waved lines, the pointed ends flowing to the left, in a way that symbolized the west wind. The dark rim of jade that had once framed it had snapped off halfway around and the yellow-white ivory was marred by a faint bloodstain.

His father Dusk had been captured and eventually killed by the Fell, as part of an attempt to breed Fell and Raksura together to produce a being able to open the hidden forerunner city. It was proof that being a good consort and sitting at home in your court was no guarantee of safety. Moon had always known it was better to die fighting.

Ember came in and sat by the bowl hearth to watch Moon sort through his belongings. He didn't say he didn't want Moon to go, but his dispirited body language suggested it. Ember and Moon got along well but they weren't good friends, the way Moon was with Chime, and Balm, and Blossom and some of the others. They didn't have much experience in common, and didn't understand each other particularly well. But Ember had been raised with lots of other consorts and he supported Moon whenever he could in the court, and obviously found Moon's presence comforting. Ember finally said, "I hope nothing happens."

He meant *I hope you don't all get killed.*

"It'll be all right," Moon told him.

As a good consort, Ember pretended to be reassured by that.

After Ember left, Frost came in and plopped down on the fur beside the hearth. She was in her Arbora form, and poked a claw at the cold warming stones. Moon wasn't up here often enough to worry about getting a mentor to renew them. She announced, "Merit and Thistle are fighting."

Moon rolled up a shirt and tucked it into the bag. "Still or again."

"Again," Frost reported.

"Really fighting or just arguing?"

"Thistle shoved him. But then she said she was sorry. She wants to go instead of him."

"Pearl is going to decide who goes."

"Yes, but Merit's been out of the court more often, so everyone thinks he should go. Thistle says that means it's her turn."

Moon considered going to Merit's rescue, then decided to just let the Arbora sort it out. Moon disliked the idea of taking a mentor at all, but every past experience said it was too dangerous to go without one. All their other abilities aside, a mentor could scry for them and help guide their way.

Then Frost said, "I think I should go."

Moon had been waiting for that. "I don't think so."

Frost showed just how far she had come in the past couple of turns. Instead of throwing a screaming tantrum, she lifted her spines and said, "I'm big enough to help. It's my duty as a queen."

Moon dropped the bag and sat down at the hearth. "If you're big enough to go, you're big enough to stay here and do your duty to help take care of the court." He tried not to let her comment sting. He should be doing his duty, except he had two duties, one with the court and one with Jade and the others outside it, and choosing between them hadn't been easy.

Frost countered, "The Arbora say I have to stay in the nurseries. They won't let me help take care of anything."

"That's your duty as a queen right now, to learn to listen to the Arbora."

Frost unconsciously bared her fangs. Her rationale for going along on the trip depended on doing her queenly duty, and this effectively stymied her. Mostly because she was old enough to know it was true. Her spines slumped. "I don't want you to go," she muttered. "Or Jade. Or Balm. Or Chime. Or Stone. Or—"

That sounded more like the old Frost. "Unless you go with us?"

She twitched unhappily, her tail flipping anxiously. "Well, yes."

"I know, it's hard," he told her. "But being a queen is hard."

Frost met his gaze, and she seemed to realize he did know exactly how hard it was. She slumped further.

Jade walked into the bower. Frost glared up at her and said, "If I was a warrior, I could do whatever I want."

Jade lifted her brows. "Besides going on patrols and guarding Arbora, and doing what you're told?"

Frost seemed to grudgingly give in on that point, but added, "That's not a hard job most of the time."

"That's why no warriors with any sense want to be queens." Jade ruffled the frills on Frost's head. "I need to talk to Moon alone."

Frost sighed and grumbled at this outrageous request, but got up and left the bower with some semblance of good manners. She had been better with Jade, too, which Moon found a huge relief. He could only do so much; Jade was the one who would have to teach Frost how to be a queen.

Jade took a seat beside the hearth. "I've spoken to Song and Root and Balm. They've all agreed to go. I wanted Floret too, since she was there on the island even if she didn't go down into the city with us, but Pearl wants her and Vine here."

Moon had thought that would happen. With Balm going with Jade, he could see why Pearl would want to keep Floret. "Chime says he'll go too."

Jade tapped her claws on the fur, considering that. "Are you sure Chime wants to go? I know we need him, but I've never had the impression he likes travel the way Balm and Root and Song do."

"He says he wants to go." Moon had been thinking uneasily about Chime's reaction to hearing the vision of the Fell. "I told him, after what happened the last time, if he didn't want to risk that again, I'd understand. But he knows we need him."

Jade said, "What about you?"

Moon stared at her, not understanding. "What about me?"

"What happened last time happened to you, too. And the time before that, and the time before that." She pretended to count on her fingers. "I think that's it. Unless there are some times you haven't told me about, which I sometimes suspect there are."

Moon considered a few different responses, and then said, "I'm fine. If I wasn't, I'd say so."

Claws carefully sheathed, Jade touched his cheek. "That would be a first."

Moon didn't pull back, but decided on a different defensive maneuver. "You don't want me with you?"

"I didn't say that." Jade sighed a little. "Before the augury, the dream was bad enough. If Fell are coming to the Reaches . . ."

Moon thought of the nurseries, an involuntary image he couldn't push away. "I'd rather stop them before they get here."

They sat there in silence for a moment, then Moon picked up his pack to look through it again, trying to distract himself. "Who's the fifth warrior?"

Jade settled her spines and smiled. "River volunteered."

It was Moon's turn to sigh. His relationship with River had been long and fraught, starting almost the instant he had first entered the Indigo Cloud court. River had been sleeping with Pearl, and the long absence of any young consort in the court had almost let him take that place with the warriors, causing a lot of conflict between Pearl's and Jade's factions. Moon's appearance had disrupted that, and later when

Pearl had taken Ember, River had lost his status in the court completely. It had taken him some time to get the respect or at least tolerance of the other warriors back since then. "I thought he got over having something to prove."

"He pointed out that he has almost as much experience outside the court as Root and Song, which is true." Jade eyed Moon, obviously trying to tell if he had any real objection. "I'm inclined to agree."

It was true, and Moon couldn't argue with it. He said, "But no Drift." Drift was River's more obnoxious companion. He had experience outside the court too, but Moon had to draw the line somewhere, even though the two were sincerely attached to each other.

"No Drift," Jade agreed. She moved closer and tugged on his wrist. "Since we have time—"

"Is Jade in here?" someone called out.

"I'm here." Jade let go of Moon, annoyed. Moon had the bad feeling they had just lost their last chance for private sex for quite a while.

Sage ducked into the doorway. "The Arbora are up here to talk to Pearl. They wanted you to come hear them too."

The four leaders of the Arbora castes, Bone for the hunters, Heart for the mentors, Knell for the soldiers, and Bell for the teachers, were in the queens' hall, sitting near the hearth. Pearl was already there, waiting impatiently. When Jade and Moon had taken seats, Bone said, "We've been speaking among ourselves—"

Pearl, without twitching a spine, said dryly, "You know I hate that."

Moon couldn't do anything but stare. Pearl had just made a joke. Bone, the only one who wasn't fazed, said, wryly, "Yes, I know. But we think at least one other Arbora should go in the group, along with the mentor."

Jade didn't react, but Pearl lifted a brow and said, "This is what comes of thinking."

Bell pointed out, "Arbora were helpful when Jade and the others went missing on the way to Ocean Winter. Moon knows that."

Pearl turned her ironic gaze on Moon. He said, "They were." She tilted her head, and Moon shrugged. This one was not his fault.

Bone said, "Bramble is the best tracker we have, and good at figuring things out."

Bell added, "We discussed it with her. She's already agreed to go, if you agree."

"A hunter." Pearl flexed her claws, a gesture of distraction. "You don't trust your sister queen?"

Bone didn't fall for that one. He said, "I think she should have the help of Arbora if she needs it."

Moon thought Bramble was a good choice. She was intelligent, clever, and level-headed. He just didn't want to see her hurt or killed.

Pearl was thinking it over, her tail tip moving slowly. Finally, she said, "If Jade agrees, I'll make no objection."

Jade sighed, flicking her claws to show she was giving in reluctantly. "I agree. I'm not happy, but I'll agree."

Bone was too experienced at dealing with queens to show any satisfaction. "All we ask is that you consider our advice."

Pearl wasn't fooled. "You're lucky you're old and can get away with this." She turned to Jade. "You'll need at least one more warrior, if you have to leave the groundlings' boat and travel on your own."

Jade flicked a spine in agreement. "Briar. If she agrees." Briar was one of the younger female warriors who had managed to stay out of the faction infighting.

Pearl stood, settling her spines. "Then go and tell everyone to make ready."

The night was spent in preparations and saying goodbye. Moon spent it in the nurseries, with his own clutch and the Sky Copper fledglings, and all the others. Like Thorn had said, his own fledglings were a little too young to understand the idea that he would be gone for a long period. He hoped they didn't notice for a while.

The next morning, Moon said goodbye to Blossom, Rill, Bark, and Bell and the other teachers, and forced himself to leave the nurseries and gather with the others in the greeting hall.

Moon took the back way, because this was hard enough and seemed to get harder every time he had to stop and say goodbye to someone.

Everyone was all too aware of the danger. As he passed through the series of smaller chambers behind the far end of the greeting hall, he heard voices.

It was River and Drift, a couple of chambers ahead. Moon stopped, and they were too intent on each other to notice him. It had been a long time since anyone in the court had plotted against him, but suspicious habit was hard to break. There was a sob in Drift's voice as he said, "Just promise me you'll be careful."

"I will," River said. "I've always come back before."

"This is different. Just . . . You don't have to prove yourself. You have friends who love you. The past doesn't matter to the others the way you think it does."

River was silent a long moment, then said, "It matters."

Moon turned and silently slipped away.

He took the other way around to the greeting hall and found the other warriors and the Arbora gathered there, ready to leave. Much of the court was on the hall floor and the balconies of the well to watch them go. The others were saying quiet or noisy goodbyes to their friends and clutchmates. Briar was clearly trying not to twitch with nerves. Balm had told Moon earlier that Briar was pleased to be asked to go but also terribly nervous, and saw herself as inexperienced compared to the others. Moon would rather have a warrior nervous and inclined to be extra careful because of it than an overconfident one.

Moon went to stand next to Jade, Stone, and Pearl. After a moment, River came in and joined the rest of the group.

Bramble bounced around saying her goodbyes, and seemed more excited than nervous, a personality trait that was probably one of the main reasons she had been chosen. Moon still wasn't sure about bringing her, but maybe Bone was right: she would help in ways no one could anticipate yet.

Everyone carried a pack, with the supplies needed to survive on their own if necessary, and Merit had an extra satchel slung over his shoulder, holding the materials he needed for making simples. The warriors who were to take the message and the third copy of the map to Malachite had already left, a group of five led by Aura.

As the group gathered around, Jade said, "Remember, they don't know that most of us speak Kedaic. Speak to them in Altanic only."

Everyone flicked spines in assent. Pearl told Jade, "I hope this trip is for nothing."

She hadn't phrased it particularly well, but Moon had the feeling that everyone knew what she meant. With wry acknowledgment, Jade said, "So do I."

Chime picked up Merit and Song lifted Bramble, and they took flight through the forest to where the groundling flying boat was waiting.

CHAPTER SEVEN

M oon already knew this was going to be an awkward trip.

They flew through damp morning air of the suspended forest and found the flying boat still waiting near the meeting spot. As they drew near, Jade called back, "Land on the tree and wait there. I want to make certain it's safe first."

Moon tilted his wings to change direction and dropped down to land on the platform near the pond. Chime, carrying Merit, landed beside him. The others took positions on the branches above. Moon glanced around, making sure everyone was with them. For a moment he couldn't spot Balm and Stone, but then saw them together on a branch further back in the tree. Stone had shifted to his groundling form, probably so they could talk.

"How different do you think this is going to be from traveling with the Golden Islanders?" Chime asked, his attention on the flying boat.

Jade circled above it once and landed on the deck. Several groundlings were visible, and she was speaking to Callumkal. With relief, Moon saw Delin step out of a doorway in the ridge that ran up the center of the deck. It wasn't that he thought this was all an elaborate trap, it was just that even after all this time, suspicion was still a way of life for him. It wasn't something that went away fast, or as far as he could tell, ever. He said, "Very different."

Bramble, hanging onto Song, reached over to thump Chime in the shoulder. "It's exciting." Neither of the Arbora had been on a flying boat since they had come to the Reaches.

"That's one word for it," Chime muttered.

Jade lifted a hand, signaling them to come ahead.

Moon launched himself off the platform. He flapped to get above the boat, then dropped down to the deck. As the warriors landed behind him, he saw Stone was still in his groundling form, being carried by Balm. *What's that about?* he wondered. But maybe Stone didn't trust the boat's deck to support his winged form. The warriors cast a few puzzled stares in Stone's direction as Balm set him on his feet, but no one commented.

There were more crew members on the deck, and from their resemblance to Callumkal and Kalam, they were probably all Janderan. Though their skin varied a little in coloring, from a dark almost pure black to a deep warm brown, it had the same hard texture, and they all had the same rangy build. They also all radiated the same air of wary displeasure.

Jade caught Moon's attention with a spine flick, and everyone shifted to groundling. Moon managed to do it in time with the others. It was a trick queens used when greeting other courts. Moon's ability to participate was an achievement he was sure was wasted on the groundlings.

Callumkal nodded to them all. "We welcome you aboard." He made a gesture. "Kalam will show you to your quarters."

Despite the welcome, the crew still seemed uneasy, and watched them with an intensity that seemed both worried and unfriendly. Never a good combination, in Moon's experience. Considering how the meeting had gone yesterday, it wasn't a surprise. He didn't expect the Raksura would have come off very well when the story of it was repeated to the rest of the Kishan.

Jade tilted her head to Callumkal in acknowledgment, and told Moon in Raksuran, "You take the others. Balm and Briar, stay with me."

"Right," Moon said, trying not to sound relieved. Standing out here under the weight of all this scrutiny made his nerves twitch and brought up uncomfortable memories. It had been a long time since he had been around any groundlings except the Kek and the other species who inhabited the floor of the Reaches. He was out of practice at being stared at.

As Kalam led the way through a door in the ridge along the deck, Delin fell in beside Moon and Chime. He said, "They asked if you and Jade should be put in a separate chamber, and I said that you would all prefer to be together. Was that right?"

Moon glanced back to make sure everyone who was supposed to be with him was actually following. Stone was tagging along at the back. "That's right." For safety while traveling, they always slept in groups.

The hatch had thick doors made out of layers of the moss material, with bars meant to fasten them against heavy weather. Inside the ridge was a broad hallway lit by large globes, glowing with light. They were mounted in the ceiling ridges, but were clearly made of something gelatinous. Delin saw Moon look up at them and he explained, "They are a luminescent fluid, harvested from a type of squid."

The scents of strange groundlings and strange cooking smells almost overwhelmed the heady green odor of the ship. Kalam led them down a spiral stair to two levels below, to a larger room that seemed to be a gathering area. There were padded benches along the walls and stools scattered around. Several groundlings sat there, all Janderan. One said, in Kedaic, "So that's them. I wonder why they brought the old man along."

They were talking about Stone. Moon bit his lip to control his expression. Chime, walking between Moon and Delin, made an involuntary noise in his throat. As they reached the doorway to another passage, Moon glanced casually back and saw everyone had very blank expressions, except for River, who looked sardonic. He could read faint amusement from Stone's normally opaque expression. *This is going to be interesting*, Moon thought.

The passage curved and twisted down, then opened into a winding corridor lined with doors. Kalam slid open the first. In carefully pronounced Altanic, he said, "These two are your rooms, next to Delin's quarters. There is a bathing and elimination room at the end of the corridor. Uh . . ." He hesitated. Feeling unhelpful, Moon just stared at him.

Delin told Kalam, "I will explain how to use the equipment."

Moon stepped in, and found a room much like the one Delin had, with beds built into the walls. There was an opening in the wall to the next room which doubled the available space. It looked as if it had been recently made; the edges were raw and the scent of the moss was more intense. More importantly, there were windows along the outer wall, set with crystal, but able to swing open and easily large enough to climb out of. Moon turned back to Merit and Bramble, who were peering through the doorway. He nodded, and they pushed in, followed by the warriors. Stone strolled in last.

Kalam stood uncertainly in the doorway. "If there is anything else you require . . ."

Moon told him, "We'll ask."

Kalam hesitated again, then retreated away down the corridor. Moon waited until the sound of his footsteps had faded, then checked the door. It was a light sliding panel with no lock, with no way anyone could seal them in.

Bramble looked at Stone and said, "Old man?"

Stone gave her a push to the head. "I am old."

Except by "old" the Janderan had meant "useless." Raksura just got stronger and usually larger as they grew older; most groundling species didn't.

Delin said charitably, "Kalam is a good young person. They are an interesting species, and do not choose their gender until they near maturity. Kalam has only recently chosen his, and is perhaps too sheltered by his father."

It made sense. Though Delin's opinion was possibly colored by the fact that all his children and grandchildren were crewing or captaining wind-ships.

Merit put his pack against the wall. He looked like he was finding the situation daunting. "Is that how groundlings act toward everyone? Besides Delin and the other Golden Islanders."

"They know what we are," Moon said. He was used to this, but the others weren't. "They're afraid."

Annoyed, Song tossed a pack onto one of the beds. "They always think we're Fell."

"It's because we're shapeshifters," Chime added, poking at the padding on the lowest bed. "Groundlings are just afraid of shapeshifters."

"Aren't there any good shapeshifters?" Bramble wondered. "Besides us?"

"Not really." Moon felt the deck move gently underfoot and went to a window. The ship was turning and lifting, starting the tricky job of navigating up past the mountain-tree branches and platforms. They must mean to travel above the tree canopy, which was somewhat safer. Hopefully Callumkal didn't mean to go high enough to get into cloud-walker territory. "Not that I've ever heard of."

"It is worth a monograph, perhaps." Delin came to the window too. "This fear and distrust, which persists in so many cultures that we know of. Even those like Kish, where the Fell are not as great a threat now as they were in the past."

Chime came to stand next to Moon, craning his neck to see out the window. "You think there's a reason for it? Not just groundlings hearing stories of the Fell, and passing them on?"

"It's intriguing to speculate," Delin said. "We will have plenty of time for it on the journey." He combed fingers through his beard thoughtfully. "You were able to duplicate the map from memory?"

Moon thought it was a good thing that it wasn't Delin they were trying to fool. Chime told him, "We thought it was best."

Delin nodded agreement. "It is a possibility that my grandchildren Niran and Diar have taken our wind-ship and crew to follow me here from Kish-Jandera. It would have taken them a little time to ascertain who I left with, and where we were bound. Once they do, they will follow me to Indigo Cloud to discover what happened. They will not wish to return to my daughter Elen-danar and inform her that they have lost me."

Moon turned to stare at him. "You just left them in Kish with no idea where you went?"

Delin shrugged. "The situation was serious, and I did not want to delay the journey here with family arguments." He admitted, "I hope that they will follow us to the sel-Selatra. It would be well to have the extra support."

Stone gave Delin a sideways glance. "You don't trust these people very much, do you?"

Delin watched the mountain-tree platforms drop past. "I don't think they mean to betray us. But as you said, the Fell may have ways of finding out what the Kishan plan. I am not willing to leave our fate to chance."

A faint vibration went through the deck, and a moment later the flying boat brushed past the leaves of a tree canopy as it moved up into increasingly brighter sunlight. They were on their way.

For a while, they just watched the Reaches from above, enjoying the breeze and the warm sun. When Moon was flying, the ground went by far too fast for much observation, and his attention was on the wind and keeping to the right direction. On a flying boat, there was endless time to see everything below you in detail.

Then Stone said, "We need to get the groundlings over the idea that we're going to stay shut up in this room the whole time."

Moon leaned against the window sill, reluctant. He wasn't happy about socializing with these particular groundlings, but Stone was right. It would be a good idea to get them used to the fact that the Raksura would be moving freely around the boat. "We need to be careful."

The look Stone threw him was not approving. "I know that."

Moon managed to keep his mutter of *I know you know that* subvocal.

Chime eyed Stone warily. "What are you going to do?"

"I'm going to get in a fight," Stone told him.

Moon stared in exasperation at the ceiling. Stone's mood hadn't improved any. Root said, "Really?" River made a snort of derision that seemed to be aimed at all of them. Chime protested, "It's only the first day."

Stone sighed, with that air that suggested he wished he had never mated in the first place. "That was a joke." He went to where Delin had retired to a cushion in a corner, making notes. He gave Delin a nudge and said, "Come and give us a tour of the boat."

Delin began to put up his writing materials. "Excellent idea."

"I'll stay here," Moon said. He wanted a chance to look over the map again, and he wasn't as interested in being stared at by groundlings as Stone was. To the others, he said, "Just remember, speak Altanic. Don't let them know you understand Kedaic. And be careful what you say."

He got dutiful murmurs of assent from the Arbora and Chime, Root, and Song, and a glance of contempt from River. They followed

Stone and Delin out into the corridor, a bemused Merit trailing along last. Moon rubbed his face and wondered if any of their efforts at subterfuge would last past the first day. For a race who had supposedly originally used their shapeshifting abilities to trap and prey on groundlings, Raksura were lousy liars.

He got the map out of Chime's pack and spread it across the bed. It didn't show their entire route, just the coast and a portion of the sel-Selatra, then the trail of islands and sea-mounts leading toward the site of the city. It didn't tell him much he didn't already know, but at least he had the directions of their route in his head now.

He was folding the cloth map when someone shook the sliding door. Moon stuffed the map into the pack, pulled out a packet of writing paper Chime had brought, and pretended to be reading the first sheet. "Come in." If the groundlings found out they had made one copy of the map, let alone three, the whole situation would be even more difficult than it already was.

The door slid open. Surprisingly, it was Captain Rorra. She said, "Am I allowed to speak to you?"

Moon kept his attention on the paper. "I don't know; are you?"

Rorra stepped into the room. Stiff as one of the cork floorboards, she said, "It was my understanding that you are the property of the queen."

Moon let his breath out in irritation, and looked up at her. "I understand the connotations of the word 'property' in Altanic and if you didn't mean it to be an insult, I don't think you would have used it."

Her face worked, as if she was struggling with different emotions and didn't want to show any of them. None of them appeared to be chagrin. "Isn't that the case? An insult to you is an insult to her."

It was hard to explain something that he didn't quite understand himself, at least not well enough to articulate it. Especially when he was being provoked. "I belong to the court, just like everybody else in it." He groped for the right words. "She protects me to show she can protect the court."

"So you're helpless, to be protected—"

Moon was on his feet in one smooth motion and looking down at her. "I'm really not," he said. He didn't shift, though the surge of pure anger at her words made it difficult.

A surge of anger. *That's odd*, Moon thought.

He stepped back. Rorra's expression went blank and her eyes hooded, a defensive response. Her voice trembled just a little as she said, "That's good. We don't need any dead weight in this expedition."

Moon knew he had a temper, but she hadn't been pushing him that hard. He had taken worse insults than that without threatening anybody. Something else had to be going on. "Hold it. Are you causing that?"

She took a step back. Now she was showing emotion. It was humiliation. Stiff, angry humiliation, but still humiliation. "I don't mean to."

Moon tasted the air, and caught just the faintest unfamiliar scent off her skin, almost too ephemeral to detect. He couldn't place it. "What is it? There's a scent. A pheromone?" He used the Raksuran word for it because he had no idea what it was in Altanic, or even if the idea existed in Altanic. "A scent that makes people react. That communicates."

That she understood. Her expression was grim. "Yes. It isn't intentional."

"I'm sorry I reacted like that." The fury had disappeared, overcome by a keen appreciation of just how awkward and embarrassing this was. At least it had happened in private. Moon fumbled for something to say. "That must be . . . hard to deal with." Or impossible to deal with. But it must not affect every species in the same way. He doubted she would have survived very long if it had. "Not everyone can scent it?"

"No, some species can't. Not the Kish-Jandera, like Callumkal and the others of this crew. They have little sense of smell." Rorra swallowed hard, flustered. "I should go."

It explained why Jade was so agitated around Rorra. As she turned to go, he said, "Tell me what it is. That might make it easier to ignore."

She hesitated, a little of her habitual glare returning. He said, "Raksura know a lot about scents." This was true. There were scent-markers that queens could produce and detect that no one else could, like the one that signaled to other queens that Moon was Jade's consort. As a consort Moon experienced some scents more clearly than the warriors and Arbora did, and Arbora could follow scents that the warriors could barely detect. Stone hadn't seemed to react to her at all, but then Stone was odd. Sitting here with her for a few moments would give Moon a chance to learn the scent so he could hopefully filter out the effect.

She grimaced, clearly reluctant, but she turned away from the door. "It's a characteristic of my species of sealing. In saltwater, it's a request for distance, a neutral signal. In the air . . . it is not neutral. I can't control it. I can make other scents but this one is . . . not voluntary."

Moon tried to imagine how difficult that would be to cope with in a tense situation. Anticipating it probably brought it on even more quickly. No wonder she radiated tension. He couldn't think of anything to say. "I'm sorry."

She looked away. "You've already apologized. I'm used to it." She made what was obviously a determined effort to change the subject. "I actually wanted to speak to you about the underwater city you found. The creature inside it. Delin told us about it but I wanted to hear it from one of you." She hesitated. "I wasn't sure if I should speak to you without the queen's permission, especially after what happened last time."

Moon sat down on the bed. "What did you want to know?" Since the first attempt at a conversation had gone astray rapidly even from something as innocuous as *can I talk to you?*, it would be best to keep this one as on target as possible. Rorra seemed to be naturally reticent, and the scent that made everything she did seem like a deliberate affront had to make it worse. He wondered why she had left the sea at all, to put up with this. Plus the fact that her feet didn't seem designed to walk on land and she needed the boots to compensate, she must have a powerful motivation. He felt asking what it was would just make the whole situation worse.

When Moon's survival had depended on pretending to be a groundling for turns at a time, he had avoided asking questions, since they usually opened him up to being asked questions in return, often very hard-to-answer questions. Old habits died hard, and now he tended to operate on the principle that if people wanted him to know things, they would tell him.

Rorra seemed relieved to be talking about something, anything else. "Delin said you first thought it was a shapeshifter?"

"It was pretending to be one, to keep the Fell there while its prison was opening. What it was really doing was making us see things. You've heard of how the Fell can do that?"

"Yes. I've never experienced it."

If she had, she would be dead, but there was no point in explaining that. "This was similar, but it was happening to all of us. A Fell ruler can do it to multiple groundlings, but it has to work on one person at a time. It has to get close to them and tell them what it wants them to see, or think, or remember. This thing made itself look like a forerunner. It made us all see that the city was filling up with water. It happened instantly. We could feel the water, but one of us was in groundling form and his clothes were dry. We realized it wasn't real, but the thing was still able to hide from us under the water. The water that wasn't really there." It was hard to get across in words just how terrifying the experience had been.

Rorra frowned, but now he could tell she was worried and not angry. Maybe knowing about her odd scent did help. "That's disturbing."

"That's one way to put it." They didn't know how many people the creature could fool at one time. It might be a handful of Raksura and Fell, it might be hundreds.

"And it attached a Fell to its own body?" Rorra appeared to fully realize just how horrible this was. "To consume it?"

"Maybe." Moon tried to think of a way to describe it. "We saw a predator once that attached parts of its prey to its own body, to be able to do things that they could do."

Rorra's frown deepened in confusion. "How did the predator do that?"

"We don't know. We had to kill it before we had a chance to ask." At her expression he added, "I don't think it would have told us anyway."

She hesitated. "I ask about this because I want the expedition to be prepared."

"That's good," Moon told her. He didn't think it was possible to be prepared for some things, but it was a good thought.

Rorra said, "You're different than I thought you'd be," and abruptly left the cabin.

Moon decided that if he had almost gotten into a fight with someone who wasn't even trying to argue with him, he had better check on the others.

He found his way to the common room without running into anyone. There were several Kishan inside, sitting on stools or benches. They had the same dark roughly-textured skin and curly dark hair as Callumkal and Kalam, but were all shorter and heavy-set. They weren't talking or moving, and after a moment he realized that was because Bramble was in the room.

She was studying the maps mounted on the walls. The Kishan kept glancing at her, then down at the floor, then at each other, then at her again.

In her groundling form, Bramble still didn't look harmless. She only came up to Moon's shoulder, but she was wearing her work clothes, a light sleeveless shirt and pants cut off at the knee, and her stocky build and the muscles in her shoulders and forearms were obvious. Despite the flower someone had stuck into her hair before they left the colony, she looked like she could pick up one of the Kishan and easily toss them across the room. In her scaled and clawed form, she could easily rip them limb from limb, but nobody needed to mention that.

Then Bramble turned to the Kishan, pointed at one of the maps, and, speaking Altanic, said, "Is this where you're from?"

The Kishan hesitated, but a brave one stood and said, "No, not exactly." The silver-trimmed dark blue coat was open and there were four protuberances on her chest that looked like breasts, so Moon assumed she was female. She went to the map and stood barely a pace away from Bramble, though Moon could tell she was nervous. She pointed to the map. "Most of us are from Kedmar-Jandera. That city is the nearest port and trade capital, Irev-Jandera."

Bramble bit her lip, studying the map. "All the cities are connected? You're all called Kishan?"

"Yes. Well, there are a lot of different groups, and species, in all the different cities." She indicated the others in the room. "Our species is called Janderi, and we're related to the Janderan. We're from the Jandera, which was where the Kish trade empire began. But in general, we're all called Kishan. Or Kish-Jandera, if you're just talking about us and the Janderan."

"So . . ." Bramble hesitated, then evidently decided to just ask. "How do you decide what to do? When you're all so spread out like that?"

Once it had turned into a general discussion and lecture about the history of the Kishan trade empire, and how groundlings governed themselves without queens or courts, Moon slipped away down the corridor. It was interesting, but he should probably find Jade.

He took the stairs up to the deck, and came out into bright sunlight and a steady breeze to see Jade still with Balm and Briar, talking to Callumkal and Vendoin. The two warriors had shifted to groundling, the wind catching at their curling hair. Moon saw Stone, Chime, Merit, and Delin up in the bow, leaning on the rail and looking down. It was tempting to join them, but Moon decided it was probably his duty to stand next to Jade and look decorative.

As he reached her, Callumkal turned to lead the way through a doorway in the ridge. Balm murmured to Moon, "He's going to show us how the ship works."

With the warriors, Moon followed Jade and Callumkal and Vendoin down a corridor and into the steering cabin in the bow. The long windows all around had top and bottom shutters angled to give some protection from the outside, and had reflective interior surfaces to allow a better view. The actual steering device was a long lever projecting out of the back wall, like the tiller of a small boat. A Janderi woman held it in position while Kalam consulted a small glass and metal directional device. There were benches around the walls, and a flat board that extended out from the wall for examining maps.

The only thing Moon couldn't figure out were the pottery jars with clear crystal windows on a shelf along the back wall. They might have been decorative, but somehow he didn't think so.

Callumkal spread the map out on the extendable board for Jade and Vendoin. Tactfully, no one mentioned the disagreement over it at their first meeting. Callumkal said, "Delin told us that the regions the forerunners must have occupied have not been mapped."

Jade shrugged her spines. "Delin knows more of the forerunners than we do. There are no Raksuran stories about them."

"That seems very odd," Vendoin said. "There are a great many stories throughout the Kishlands of the different species who lived there before us. Not so many of the foundation builders, granted, for they seem to have come before all the others."

After the discovery of the underwater city, the mentors at Opal Night had gone through their libraries looking for old forgotten legends. There had been nothing. The fact that the Raksura and the Fell had once been one species was referenced in many of the older stories, but there was nothing about what that species might have been like.

Chime and Delin had wondered if Opal Night was actually the first court, if the forerunners had come to the Opal Night mountain-tree when it was young, and had decided to camp there. If they had built the city that the roots of the tree had destroyed uncounted turns ago. If the fringe of the Reaches was where they had met the Arbora. There were no answers, though there were lots of questions.

And Moon might just be overly suspicious again, but he got the distinct feeling that Callumkal and Vendoin thought the Raksura were holding out on them. He noticed Kalam was staring at him, which didn't help any. Kalam seemed to notice he was staring, and looked hurriedly away. That didn't help either.

There wasn't much room left around the map, so Moon sat down to wait, knowing Jade would go over it all later for the others. Kalam hesitated, then moved around the cabin to sit next to Moon.

"What are those jars for?" Moon asked, since sitting in awkward silence was worse than awkward talking.

"Oh." Kalam looked around as if he had forgotten their existence. "They hold samples of the different growth materials of the ship, the ones that suspend it off the ground, the ones that protect it. In the jars, you can see if the samples need to be sprayed with water, or other fluids we can prepare. If they do, there's a good chance the materials of the ship need tending too."

It sounded like a wise precaution. "So this ship was grown in Kish?"

"Yes, by the Kish-Latre. That's what we call them. You can't say their name in Altanic or Kedaic or any of the other trade languages. They live under mounds of earth in the jungles, and they grow all sorts of plants and molds that can be used for a lot of different things." Kalam hesitated. "Will you tell me something about Raksura?"

Moon saw they were almost done with the map, so an escape would be available soon. Vendoin was explaining something to Jade about wind patterns affecting trade and habitation in the sel-Selatra islands and there was only so long Jade was going to listen to that. "Maybe."

Kalam ducked his head, a gesture that Moon wanted to read as shy, though he wasn't sure if it meant the same thing for Kalam's species. "Is it true you weren't always a consort? Scholar Delin mentions it in his book."

"I was always a consort, I just didn't know it, because I had never seen a Raksura before." Moon read Kalam's confused expression and explained, "I was an orphan. It's a long story."

Callumkal gently interrupted the wind-pattern lecture with, "I know you will want to see the growth chambers for the materials that keep the ship in flight."

As the others moved to the door, Moon stood to follow, and said, "You should ask Delin, he knows all about it." He noticed Balm looking at him with an expression he would have described as wry amusement. *Whatever that was*, Moon thought, and followed Jade out.

At sunset, when they had retired to their cabin with Delin, Moon explained to the others about Rorra's scent and what it meant. The breeze had died away and the room was warm and softly lit by the light globes mounted on the walls. Root hung from the ceiling by his foot claws, but the other warriors were getting ready to bed down on the floor.

Jade heard the story with a mix of relief and embarrassment, and said, "That explains a lot. I thought I was losing my mind, getting so angry because a sealing looked at me the wrong way." She turned to Stone, where he was stretched out on one of the shelf beds. "Didn't you scent it?"

Stone sat up on one elbow. "I scented something, but I filtered it out. It wasn't Fell, that's all I cared about."

Delin, seated on one of the stools with Bramble and Merit at his feet, admitted that he must have been affected too. "It's a very disturbing thought, that I have misjudged her because of it."

Moon asked him, "Do you know anything about her? Why is a sealing living inland?"

Delin said, "Kalam told me that she comes from an isolated deep-water sealing kingdom off the western coast of Vesselae, near the sea-trade route called the al-Denar. She lost her right set of fins, in the spot a foot would be on a groundling, to a predator, and she left the sea because of it. The sealing healer changed her body, so she may breathe air at all times, and she came inland and found work with Callumkal."

That explained the clunky boots. They must be built up on the inside to compensate both for the missing fins and the ones that were left.

"They could change the way she breathes but not just fix her fin?" Briar said, helping Song pull blankets out of the packs. "That's not very good healing."

Merit frowned, and said, mostly to himself, "That's terrible healing."

Delin said, "She has never spoken much of it but it was apparent that she faced great hardship at first."

Moon agreed. It sounded like an Aeriat having their wings removed. He wondered if it had been voluntary after all.

Disturbed, Bramble said, "Can we go talk to her about it?"

"No, because it's private. Don't bring it up unless she does first." Moon might not be an expert on groundling behavior, but some things were obvious even to him.

Bramble still looked doubtful. In their defense, the Arbora's concept of privacy was vague at best. It was probably difficult for them to imagine not living in a way where everyone around you knew everything about you at all times.

River was wrapped up in his blanket in the far corner, as if trying to stay as far removed from the rest of them as possible. He helpfully said, "Groundlings don't want to talk to us, haven't you noticed?"

"Talk to us, or talk to you?" Chime asked, also not helpfully, "because if it's the latter—"

Jade broke it up with, "This room is too small for an argument, unless someone wants to have an argument with me."

That stopped the discussion, and as Delin showed them how to dim the light globes with a little lever that caused the luminescent fluid to flow back into a pocket in the moss wall, everyone settled down to sleep, or try to sleep.

Moon was in one of the beds with Jade wrapped around him, the others in the beds or the floor according to inclination. Bramble and Merit had talked Delin into staying with them, and had used some bed cushions to make a pallet for all three of them on the floor.

Jade whispered in Moon's ear, "I still don't know if this trip is a good idea or not."

It wasn't something she was willing to admit to the others, and truthfully, Moon didn't know either. He wondered if their clutch had noticed he was gone yet, and buried his face in the warm scales of her neck.

The night was uneventful, and the next day even more so as they passed over the nearly impenetrable mountain-tree canopy of the Reaches. The crew seemed more than content to ignore the Raksura despite Bramble's determination to make friends and Stone's determination not to acknowledge that most of the Kishan didn't want them here.

Moon knew he needed to get a better idea of the whole situation. Vendoin was more gregarious than the others, so that evening he wandered over to where she stood at the railing and took up a position nearby. Not too close, but not so far away that it would make conversation difficult.

The breeze had died and the air was warm and damp, the sinking sun turning the limitless blue sky a gray-violet. The warriors had spent most of the day napping. Below, the great green sea of the Reaches was just starting to give way to sporadic pockets of smaller trees, or open meadow. One meadow contained giant lumpy gray things, at least forty paces tall and more than that wide, that might be sleeping grasseaters with large armor-like scales, some other sort of animal, or a hive or habitation for groundlings. Whatever it was didn't show any interest in the flying boat passing over it.

The Kish weren't much worried about anything on the ground. Callumkal had shown them the boat's weapons earlier in the day, two larger versions of the fire weapon that Rorra had carried at their first meeting. One was concealed in a compartment up in the bow, the other in the stern. Moon thought they would be very helpful as long as you had enough warning to use them.

Vendoin didn't speak immediately, and Moon was considering what to say for an opening remark, when he felt someone staring at him. He twisted around, scanned the windows in the ridge that ran down the center of the boat, then up to the upper cabin level. He saw Kalam leaning in a window there, not looking out toward the view, but down at Moon. Their gazes met and Kalam withdrew in confusion.

Moon snorted, and turned back to the railing.

Vendoin had noticed. She said, "He's only curious. Please don't take offense."

Moon lifted his shoulders, and then not sure she would understand the gesture, said, "I'm used to being stared at."

"Are you?" Vendoin turned to regard him more seriously. "I thought Raksuran fertile males lived a secluded life."

The other Kishan didn't seem to know much about Raksura, but it sounded like Vendoin at least had bothered to question Delin, even if she hadn't read his book, like Kalam. "They do, but I wasn't with a court until a few turns ago."

Vendoin waited a moment, then said, "Now, you've aroused my curiosity. Where were you if not with a court?"

"The court I was born into was destroyed by Fell, when I was too young to remember." That wasn't quite true, but the bits and pieces of fragmented memories he had weren't worth mentioning.

"We have that in common," Vendoin said, looking out toward the distance again. "My people were driven out of their original home by the Fell three generations ago, and took refuge in the Kishlands." She turned to him again. "How did you escape?"

At least Vendoin might have a better grasp on how dangerous the Fell were than the other Kish. "A warrior escaped with me and a few Arbora children. They were all killed later, and I was alone, until Stone found me and brought me to Indigo Cloud."

The rough patches on Vendoin's face moved. It might be inquiry, puzzlement, or even concern. Moon couldn't tell. Vendoin said, "But that was the vital time of your development, was it not? From before adolescence to adulthood?"

Moon felt compelled to point out, "It wasn't by choice."

"Of course. But did it not make everything . . . very difficult?"

"It did," Moon admitted. So Vendoin didn't think he had spent the entire time huddled alone in a forest somewhere, he added, "I traveled, lived in different groundling cities and settlements."

Vendoin cocked her head, maybe as a gesture of understanding, or maybe of curiosity, it was hard to tell. "As a Raksura?"

"As a groundling. It was in the east, where they're more afraid of Fell, so I couldn't show anyone what I was."

"I see." Moon wasn't sure she did, but he wasn't going to argue. And he thought all her questions gave him an opening to ask some in return. "Have you worked with Callumkal for a long time?"

"Oh, not so long." Vendoin didn't appear to mind the question. "My people are called the Hians, and I am a visitor from the Hia Iserae, which is to the north along the Imperial Edge, near the basin of Saminrel. I was with the archives there, and studied in particular the foundation builders. During the season of spring rain, Callumkal invited me to come to Kedmar and work with him on the map."

"So you don't know what the foundation builders looked like?" Moon was wondering if their ruins were just less well-preserved forerunner remains.

"We don't even know if they were one species, or a collective." Vendoin sighed. "But they left very little behind, whoever they were. We have fragments of carvings and images and one method of writing that seems to be mainly poetry, and which we are not sure we have deciphered correctly. We have a great deal of speculation, and legends that may be handed down from some dim past, or that may have been constructed by later generations to explain things they did not understand."

"So do you think the sea-mount city is foundation builder or forerunner?"

"There is great debate over that, such great debate, one would call it arguing and shouting." Vendoin sounded weary. "The map is on the stones of the foundation builders for a reason. That is all I will admit to." She made a dismissive gesture. "Others construct what I can only think are fanciful stories about it."

Moon said, "Does Callumkal think the city was made by the foundation builders?"

"No, he inclines to the theory that it was the forerunners, but I'm not sure he thought so before he encountered Delin's work." Vendoin hesitated. "The two others with you, the Arbora. Delin says they are the same species as Raksura, as odd as it seems, and that you come from the same family groups."

"That's right." The Arbora had been a different species once, but had joined with the Aeriat at some point in a past so distant that no record of why it had happened had survived. And Moon didn't know how the family groups of Vendoin's species worked, but Raksuran court bloodlines were a complicated tangle. Since Merit was a mentor he was probably closely related to a consort. Considering Merit's age, it might have been Rain, Pearl's consort, or Dust or Burn, who had been sent away to other courts when Rain died. Moon didn't know about Bramble. "The Arbora used to be a separate species, a long time ago. Then something happened and . . ." Moon made a vague gesture he wasn't sure was very helpful. "It's in Delin's book."

Vendoin politely pretended that what Moon had said made sense. "Is it true that the Fell and the Raksura come from the forerunners? That is also in Delin's book."

Moon felt himself go still. He found it very hard to read Vendoin. Some groundlings were better at communicating with different species than others, and he wasn't sure if Vendoin wasn't one of them, or if Moon just wasn't interpreting her body language correctly. He said, "Yes."

Vendoin's head tilted as she studied him. "So. I think it may be inferred. From the physical resemblance."

Moon made himself shrug, though he wasn't sure how Vendoin would interpret the gesture. "It's not something we know anything about. There aren't any stories from that time."

Vendoin was quiet a long moment, then said, "I see. Perhaps if this city is forerunner, and we can discover its secrets, it will shed some light on this myth."

Moon leaned on the railing and looked into the distance. Light was the last thing the "myth" needed.

Chapter Eight

For the first handful of days on the flying boat they were still traveling over the forests and meadows that bordered this fringe of the Reaches, and there wasn't much new to see. Moon spent most of his time leaning over the railing watching the ground, or watching the crew cut back the plants that occasionally sprouted in the boat's moss, or talking with Jade and Chime and the others, or watching Delin sketch, or trying not to be irritated by bored warriors. Napping on the sun-warmed deck quickly became a favorite pastime.

There was no good safe place for basking anywhere on or near the colony tree, and Moon had missed it. The cabin roofs and the ridge up the flying boat's center were particularly good spots, as the mossy material seemed even warmer up there. Callumkal had explained that it was part of the process that kept the boat aloft on the lines of force that crossed the Three Worlds. It had to do with the moss and the way plants in general took in the sun to feed themselves and make themselves grow, and Moon hadn't understood the explanation past that point, but it amounted to the fact that the moss produced excess heat which had to be released along the upper parts of the boat.

It made the deck pleasant for sleeping even in the evening, though Jade decided it was safer to keep to the cabin after full dark. Moon agreed, not liking the feeling of being exposed in the night, with the low deck lights to draw attention. The flying boat had what were called in Altanic "distance-lights." They were big moss-lights that used reflective surfaces to direct the light for long distances. Rorra explained that they used them at night only to make sure they weren't about to hit something, it not being a good idea to direct them toward the ground and antagonize anything they might be passing over.

Bramble kept trying to make friends with the Kishan, with little success. Merit made an augury every day, but got nothing besides some visions of an empty calm sea. He explained, "I think we're just too far away from whatever it is, yet. Maybe when we get closer."

Finally, Jade decided they needed to hunt. The Kishan were sharing their own supplies, but they weren't big meat eaters. Raksura could last quite a while on fruit and grains and roots, but it was making the warriors cranky. Cranky warriors made queens and Arbora annoyed and made consorts, especially line-grandfathers, homicidal, at least in Moon's experience.

Callumkal told them they could bring their kills up onto the deck at the flying boat's stern, so Jade and Moon took the warriors hunting, and after a while managed to flush out a large variety of bando-hoppers. Moon had been taking short flights with the others every day just for exercise, but it was a relief to really stretch his wings and hunt.

It was twilight by the time they finished eating. Despite Callumkal giving permission, the crew was clearly disturbed by it. They avoided the area, except to gather in small groups at the windows, peer out quickly, and withdraw in horror. It was getting on Moon's nerves, and everybody else's.

"They could draw a picture, if they're so interested," the normally good-natured and oblivious Root muttered.

Delin had come out while they were eating and sat on the deck so he could continue a conversation with Chime, and had appeared completely undisturbed. That helped a little, but the warriors and Arbora were still self-conscious. Moon was used to being self-conscious, around both groundlings and Raksura, but he knew how unpleasant it was to feel as if your normal habits were somehow an affront.

"Now I know what you mean when you say you hate to be stared at," Balm told Moon quietly, rippling her spines to release tension. "Do you feel like this all the time?"

"Yes," Moon told her. Briar, crouched on Balm's other side, looked horrified.

Root and Song tossed the bones and guts and other leftovers over the railing, and Bramble glanced uneasily up at the windows. "Maybe I should go down with the warriors next time. I could clean the kills and dress them on the ground before we bring them up."

Moon wasn't sure that would help. Jade said, "It's dangerous, and unnecessary. We don't know this area at all."

Stone ruffled Bramble's frills. He had been the only one who hadn't shifted to eat, but fortunately he didn't really seem to need to. "The groundlings will get used to it." He paused to give Delin a hand up, and wandered down to the hatchway with him and Chime. Chime was saying, "That was just what Ocean Winter's library had about it." He had been so involved in the conversation with Delin that he hadn't much noticed all the scrutiny.

"Yes, but it does align well with your findings at Opal Night," Delin replied as they moved inside.

The others were standing on the deck, looking at Jade, somewhat dispirited. Moon knew part of it was boredom. This terrain just hadn't been that interesting to look at, and the Kishan's nervousness of them was beginning to wear. Jade's expression was sympathetic. "Stone's right, they'll get used to it. In the meantime—"

A thump from below shook the flying boat. Jade spun, scanning the sky, and Moon tasted the air. The offal that was still staining the deck was all he could detect. No, maybe that wasn't offal.

Further down the deck, a heavyset Janderi dropped the bucket he carried and stared around, startled. Briar and Song started toward the railing and Jade snapped, "Stay where you are."

The Janderi took a step toward the railing to look down. Then something loomed up beside the flying boat.

It was big, with a green mottled hide, and it fastened tendrils around the railing. One tendril snatched up the Janderi and lifted him into the air. The hide split into a mouth a good ten paces wide, lined with writhing feelers.

Moon didn't have a chance to do more than hiss when Jade launched herself off the deck. She hit the base of the tendril and closed her foot claws around it. Green fluid spurted and the creature flung the Janderi away. Balm bounced straight up in the air, caught him, and landed on the deck again.

More tendrils shot up from all around to grab at the railing. Moon heard a terrified yell from the bow. He looked and saw more tendrils wrapped around the steering cabin. He bounded down the deck, leapt and landed on the wall next to one of the windows.

Inside he saw the tendril had broken through the window on the opposite side and wrapped around a tall Janderan. It tried to drag him out the narrow opening, a process that would surely tear him apart. Rorra held on to him while frantically stabbing at the tendril with a pointed navigation instrument. Moon shoved the window open, slithered inside, and slammed past Rorra. He jammed himself in between the desperate Janderan and the broken window, and bit into the tendril. It tasted terrible, but he jerked and twisted, ripping into it.

Rorra wrapped her arms around the Janderan and yanked backward. Moon braced his legs against the frame of the broken window and pushed.

The tendril gave way and they all fell away from the window to land on the cabin floor. Rorra, still holding on to the gasping Janderan, scrambled back, dragging him with her. More tendrils shoved into the room, waving angrily, blocking the way to the door. Moon pushed Rorra and the Janderan back into a corner and braced himself in front of them.

Then the tendrils all flinched in unison, a sudden sharp movement. They jerked backward out of the window and disappeared from view. Moon waited tensely, but they didn't reappear. "What happened?" Rorra whispered hoarsely.

Moon figured that Stone had happened. He eased to his feet cautiously and looked out the window. Below on the deck, a few confused Kishan ran around with their fire weapons, but no one was shooting at anything. The warriors and Jade perched up on the railing looking down. Moon spotted Stone, in his groundling form, casually sling himself back over the railing. Jade turned, saw Moon, and waved an all-clear.

"It's gone now." Moon waved back and crouched down to help the Janderan sit up.

"It?" Rorra got her boots under her and rolled into a sitting position. "There was only one?"

"I think so. I think most of it was on the bottom of the boat," Moon told her. He was worried about the Janderan. There were light gray circles under his eyes and around his mouth, standing out against the dark brown of his skin. It wasn't normal and it couldn't mean anything good. Moon untangled the tendril fragment still around the man's waist and helped Rorra hold him upright. He was gasping for air and it was usually easier to breathe while sitting up. Rorra asked him anxiously, "Magrim, are you hurt badly? Your ribs, your chest?"

Magrim moved his head uncertainly. "I'm— Ribs feel broken . . ." He grabbed Moon's arm and said in Altanic, "Thank you, thank you."

Rorra said, "Yes, thank you." She added, a little wryly, "Now I know why your queen brought you."

Her communication scent was strong, but knowing what it was and that it was there made it much easier to ignore. And some groundlings would have found a way to interpret the whole thing as Moon helping the creature try to eat them, so he appreciated Rorra and Magrim's clear-headed view of the situation. He said, "You're welcome."

Callumkal burst through the door, exclaiming in alarm, and Moon moved away so he could get to Magrim.

Kalam stood in the doorway, asking breathlessly, "Is everyone all right in here?"

"Magrim might need a healer," Moon told him.

"I'll get help," Kalam said, and ducked back out the doorway.

Moon followed him down the interior passage and out to the deck. Toward the stern, the warriors gathered around Jade, and the Kishan were at the rail now, aiming their weapons toward the ground. The man that Jade and Balm had rescued was on his feet, being helped to a hatchway by a Janderi woman. Chime and Delin had come out of the hatchway further down, and looked bewildered by the confusion. The wind held a fading trace of the creature's predator musk, the rotted-flesh scent that had been masked by the offal of their kills. Moon asked, "Was anyone else hurt?"

"Not badly," Kalam said, waving to a woman midway down the deck. "We're doing a count now, to make sure everyone's still . . . here."

The Janderan woman strode toward them, a heavy bag over her shoulder that Moon assumed carried her healing simples and supplies. Kalam told her hurriedly, "Serlam, it's Magrim, in the steering cabin. He may be injured."

"It squeezed him around here," Moon added, motioning to his rib cage.

As Serlam headed inside, Vendoin reached them. She said, "We saw Stone— How did he do that? Can you all do that?"

It sounded like the emergency had caused Stone to give up his effort to keep the size of his winged form a secret. "You mean . . ." Moon prompted, just in case he was wrong.

"With wings he's almost as large as a small major kethel," Vendoin said. He couldn't read her expression but she seemed more awed than agitated.

"It was amazing," Kalam said, turning to Moon. "The predator was all around us, reaching for us, and he leapt up, and changed, and tore it right from the ship—"

Vendoin persisted, "The rest of you, can you do that?"

"No, it's because he's so old," Moon told her. "Our other forms get larger as we get older. No one else here is anywhere near as old as he is. Delin knows all about it."

"Ah." Vendoin seemed unsatisfied with the explanation. She hesitated, but someone shouted for Kalam, and Moon took the opportunity to escape, following him down the deck and heading over to where Jade and Stone waited near the rail.

Looking down, Moon spotted the remnants of the predator, scattered on the tall grasses of the wetlands they were passing over. There was a broad river visible through the trees some small distance away, and the flying boat's course paralleled it. He didn't see any groundling bodies, so hopefully Kalam was right and no one had been flung overboard. "Do we know what that was?" he asked them.

Stone shrugged. "There was a small shallow lake bed below us, a little too round, no streams feeding it. I think that was its burrow."

"It must have felt the boat's shadow pass over it." Jade's spines and tail still moved restlessly. "Callumkal said he'd tell them to fly higher until we get past this area." Her voice lower, she added, "And from now

114

on I'm going to have the warriors fly the offal away from the boat before they drop it."

Moon admitted it was probably a good idea.

Chime moved to the railing beside Moon and peered down. "I'm glad I missed that."

Jade sent Song and River up to the top of the boat to keep watch, and Moon and the others stayed out on deck, waiting for the flying boat to clear this stretch of country and move over the sparse forests closer to the river.

Soon, Callumkal came out on deck to tell Jade, "I wish to thank you. No one aboard was killed or badly injured and this is solely due to your intervention."

Jade clearly hadn't expected such fervent gratitude. Moon figured she was probably still thinking about the offal and the possibility that it had attracted the creature's attention. She managed, "I'm glad none of you were badly hurt."

Callumkal turned to Moon. "Rorra told me what you did for Magrim. He would have been torn to pieces without your help."

It was Moon's turn to feel uncomfortable, but Callumkal had already turned to stride off down the deck.

Over the next few days, things grew steadily better between the Raksura and the crew. Moon and the others kept careful watch and spotted a couple more possible nesting sites for large ground predators, and directed the boat to steer wide of them. They were also able to help when it came time to refill the boat's large water tanks. Bramble and Stone managed to have conversations with various Kishan, and Rorra and the recovering Magrim spoke easily to them. And, oddly, Kalam, who seemed too shy to talk much himself, made sure to invite the Raksura to sit in the common room or to share meals with them or to see how various parts of the flying boat worked. He even demonstrated the flying packs for them, which were powered by the same moss that provided the lift for the boat.

There were no more horrified or fearful looks, and Moon noticed there was no more reluctance to get close when he passed crew members in a corridor. Moon felt the Kishan had at least gone from thinking of them as "those Raksura" to "our Raksura."

The fourth day after the attack, Moon was lying out on the stern deck with Stone. Song, Root, and Chime were back against the nearest cabin wall, napping, and Jade and the others were inside. The terrain below was flattening out as they neared the coast, grassy plains with the occasional lake or stream or rocky outcrop, and a few stretches of low forest.

Moon heard steps through the soft material of the deck and sat up and stretched, thinking it was Jade. But it was Bramble, with Kalam, Magrim, and the other navigator, Esankel, who was one of the Janderi.

"Won't we be bothering them?" Esankel was asking Bramble cautiously.

"Oh no, it's fine, come and sit down." Bramble plopped down on the deck next to Moon.

Kalam hesitated a little, then leaned on the railing nearby. Magrim, who still had a wrap around his cracked ribs, settled down on the deck with Esankel's help, and she sat next to him.

"Are you going to be a scholar too?" Bramble asked Kalam, apparently continuing a conversation. "Is that why you're here with your father?"

"I don't know." Kalam looked out into the distance. "I've been studying the foundation builders, and the water builders, and some of the others, since I was very young, and it's interesting."

Moon thought that was the least enthusiastic response possible. That opinion seemed to be shared, because Bramble asked, "What about your mother?"

"Jandera only have one primary parent," Kalam explained. "I have several secondary parents, and they're all scholars too."

Esankel said, "You could be a navigator. You're good with the maps."

"Or an explorer, like Scholar Delin," Magrim added.

"I could," Kalam agreed, clearly being polite. He asked Bramble, "Was your job decided for you by your parent?"

His eyes still closed, Stone snorted. "Bramble does what she wants."

"I do not." Bramble nudged his ankle. She told Kalam, "It's not really like that with us. When you have a clutch, you're very happy about it, and you're close to them, of course. But the teachers raise them, and you don't tell them what to do once they're out of the nurseries. The queens do that."

Kalam took all this in like it wasn't a way of living that he had ever considered. Esankel and Magrim were listening closely as well. Kalam asked, "Then how do you decide what role to play in your society?"

"If you're an Arbora, you just decide." Bramble shrugged. "You can try being a teacher or a hunter or a soldier, and change your mind if you don't like it. For Arbora, the only caste you have to be born into is mentor, like Merit. And you don't have to be a mentor if you really don't want to, though I think it's pretty rare for someone to not want to be one."

Kalam turned to Moon. "Is it like that with you?"

"No, not for consorts, or queens. Or warriors," Moon told him.

"If you could be anything you wanted, what would you be?" Kalam asked.

Moon thought it over for a moment, watching a flock of brightly colored birds swerve away from the flying boat. "A hunter." All of the Arbora hunters but Bramble were home with their clutches, and not traveling on flying boats having to make hard decisions.

Bramble gave him a sympathetic nudge. Stone muttered, "Ingrate."

Ignoring that, Moon asked Kalam, "What do you want to be?"

Kalam hesitated again, then smiled down at Moon. "I would like to stay in Kedmar and build places for people to live. Finding new ways to use the shape-moss, and maybe ways to build out onto the old water platforms in Kedmar bay."

"That's a good job," Magrim said, wincing a little as he stretched. "Surely your father would approve."

"I'd have to ask him first," Kalam said, but it sounded noncommittal, as if he was hoping everyone dropped the subject as fast as possible.

Moon did, and was glad when the conversation wandered into a comparison of various Kishan family structures, and Bramble trying to explain how she was related to Jade via a long list of clutchmates and half-clutchmates and cross-clutchmates.

That night, Kalam invited them to sit in the common room after the Kishan had eaten, and Moon ended up in a corner with a few of the others, listening to Vendoin and Callumkal argue politely about the city.

Jade sat on the padded bench next to Stone, her tail curled up around her legs. Moon was on the floor, leaning against the bench, Chime next to him with Bramble sprawled on her stomach. Delin, Kalam, and Rorra sat nearby, listening too, though most of Delin's attention was on the sketch he was making. Rorra's scent wasn't noticeable, and Moon suspected that the more relaxed she became around them, the less it would appear.

They were all drinking the clear liquid the Kishan preferred in the evening. It was supposed to be an intoxicant, but the only groundling drug Moon had encountered that had any effect on Raksura was Fell poison, and no one would ever consider drinking it for fun. But the Kishan liquor did have a pleasant taste, vaguely reminiscent of the big pomegranates that grew in the upper Abascene.

"I appreciate all your arguments but I still think we will find it is the foundation builders," Vendoin was saying to Callumkal.

"If you would share your reasons for that, perhaps I would agree with you." Callumkal's tone was wry.

Vendoin made a throwaway gesture. "It is in the same style as the other ruins we have found. Even the tile with the image of the forerunner is similar."

"Why do you want it to be forerunner?" Moon had to ask Callumkal. "What are you hoping to find?"

"Well. I hope not to find a tremendously dangerous trapped predator, as you did." Callumkal paused to gather his thoughts. "There are many other species who have lived where we live now, over thousands of turns. This is clear to anyone who steps outside their own doorway. Many of them surely earned their own destruction, like the flying island races who destroyed each other in their wars, the Tsargaren tower people, and the Varirath to the west, or the island builders to the south. Many others have left behind little or nothing to tell us who they were or why they fought. Others are still here, in some other guise, with their origins forgotten. There are others who should still be here. Why are they gone? How could they fade away and leave no sign of the cause? Will their fate befall us? Those questions occupy me."

"Those questions are why I study the present," Delin said, not looking up from his drawing. "I hope to leave the knowledge to be passed down to others."

Callumkal made a gesture of agreement. "This city may be a sign that the forerunners and the foundation builders existed at the same time, that they knew of each other and interacted. Which could provide clues to why each one disappeared." He said to Moon, "If the forerunners truly are your ancestors, then perhaps the foundation builders have descendants as well. There are many who believe the Janderan and Janderi are descended from them."

"Even with our flying ships, distances defeat us." Vendoin stared absently at the floor, lost in thought. "There may be gatherings of scholars to the far west, or far around the ocean, who have these answers already."

Chime had been listening intently, leaning forward to follow the discussion. "Or who have the missing pieces to answer your questions, and you have theirs," he said.

"Just so," Callumkal agreed. "Perhaps this city will provide some answers, perhaps it won't. But I also feel it is worth seeing the interior for its own sake." He eyed Vendoin. "To settle our debate about its origins, for one thing."

Vendoin shook off her reverie and signaled agreement, her mouth folding up into an approximation of the Janderan's smile.

Her head propped on her hand, Bramble said thoughtfully, "I think we need to carve our history into the colony tree, to make sure it's still there even if something happens to the books. There are a lot of empty walls in the lower levels. I'll get started on that when I get back."

"And how long will the project take you?" Vendoin asked, intrigued.

Bramble shrugged. "If the others help, maybe about a month."

"She isn't joking," Jade said, probably to stave off any comments that they might have to take offense to. "The Arbora are very . . . efficient."

She was right. Moon thought the enthusiasm for a new major carving project would already be high; once Bramble explained why she wanted to do it, it would probably take over all the castes.

Stone, obviously thinking along the same lines as Moon, sighed. "It'll be the damn drains all over again."

Eyes narrowed as she planned the carving, Bramble said, "I'll include a Raksuran-Altanic translation."

Callumkal told Bramble seriously, "You should do this. Future generations of scholars will praise your name."

The Court of Opal Night, in the Western Reaches

Lithe sat bolt upright, her heart ice inside her chest and a scream trapped in her throat. She knew she was in her bower, that her body lay in the comforting shell of the hanging bed, the chamber softly lit by the flowers she had spelled to glow. But her mind was trapped in a battle with a Fell flight as it attacked the Reaches.

It wasn't real, she told herself, her heart pounding. Curled next to her, eyes still closed, Reed's throat worked as if she struggled to speak. Lithe pressed her hand to Reed's forehead and concentrated briefly, the method used to rouse someone from a too-deep healing sleep. Reed snapped awake and blurted, "Fell. There were Fell—"

"You saw it?" Lithe demanded. "It wasn't just me?"

"Fell attacking the Reaches." Reed struggled to untangle herself from the blanket. "Where— Not here. The east?"

"I think so." Lithe slung herself over the side of the bed and landed on the floor as Reed flung cushions aside. She found her shirt by tripping on it in her lunge to the doorway, stopped to drag it on, and ran out into the passage.

Sounds of disturbance echoed off the polished wood walls, worried voices and someone's startled outcry. Lithe's bower was deep in the old section of the colony tree, on a wide corridor with one end leading down into a spiral of teachers' bowers and the other with an open balcony onto the central garden well. There was no Fell stench in the cool night air, no screams, no sound of fighting. Lithe's heart unclenched a little. "It wasn't an augury. It was a dream."

The auguries within the past month had been frightening enough. All the portents hinted that Fell were moving somewhere, though nothing indicated that they were near the Western Reaches. The reigning queen Malachite had sent messages to their nearest allied courts, but their mentors had seen nothing similar yet. But this had been more painfully real than any augury.

"But we both had it," Reed said, stepping out of the bower behind her. She tilted her head, listening to the voices echoing down the corridor, from the bowers above and below them. She met Lithe's gaze, startled. "Everyone had it."

Then Auburn ran past them down the passage, calling, "Come on!"

They bolted after the older mentor, following him through the winding passages, past the teachers' and hunters' bowers and down toward the main greeting hall. The large domed chamber was carved with warriors in flight, swirling around the image of a queen in the center, her body curled to follow the curve of the dome. It was already crowded with anxious warriors and Arbora, but one figure instantly commanded all the attention.

Malachite stood in the center of the room under that image, her scales so dark they didn't show green until the light struck them, the gray tracery of her scars like silver gilt. She was a cold still presence, as formidable as the mountain-tree itself, and just seeing her calmed the frantic pounding of Lithe's heart.

The sister queen Onyx stalked around Malachite as warriors and the Arbora soldiers came forward to report to them. Her dark copper scales flashed angrily as her tail lashed. Malachite's daughter queen Celadon stood beside her, while Onyx's daughter queens waited nearby, along with Umber, Onyx's consort.

The only other consort here was Shade, sitting to one side with his warrior Flicker and a worried group of teachers. Lithe hoped he hadn't had the dream too. She glanced at him, but he smiled reassuringly at her. She and Shade might have Fell blood themselves, but they had never seen a real one until last turn. The thought of a Fell attack on the colony made Lithe's skin turn to ice. Looking around the chamber, it struck her how many of the court were scarred by the Fell, on their bodies or their minds, even those who had been born later, or whose bloodlines had never left the Reaches. *It can't happen again*, Lithe told herself. *Not here. Please not here.*

Tail lashing as she paced, Onyx spotted Lithe and said, "Perhaps Lithe has insights the other mentors lack."

Lithe pressed her lips together. Most of the time no one commented or much thought about the fact that she was half Fell. Lithe never thought much about it herself, and was fairly sure Shade and the others didn't either. When Malachite had brought them to the court, she had said they were a sign that the Fell had taken nothing from them that couldn't be taken back, and everyone had accepted that. But Onyx had a sharp temper and liked to poke at Malachite through others, as poking directly at Malachite was a game too dangerous for even another queen to play. Still, when Lithe stepped forward to answer, she was relieved when Reed and Auburn stepped with her. She said, "We think it was a shared dream."

There was a puzzled murmur from the watching Arbora and warriors. "But what caused it?" Malachite asked. Her voice was neutral and colorless, as if they were discussing a minor crop blight.

"The same cause as the auguries," Onyx said, with another tail lash.

Celadon betrayed some impatience in the angle of her spines. "Probably, but we still don't know what caused the auguries—"

Moth, one of the warriors on guard patrol, burst in from the opposite passage and scrambled to a halt in front of Malachite. He said, "A group of warriors are at the entrance platform. They say they have an important message from Indigo Cloud."

"Indigo Cloud, in the east Reaches." Lithe didn't realize she had said the words aloud until Reed turned to her and said, "Whatever sparked the dream, it's coming from the east."

Onyx lashed her tail again and said to Malachite, "Of course, it would be something to do with your offspring."

Malachite didn't flick a spine. She told Moth, "Tell the Indigo Cloud party that I'll hear their message in the queens' hall now."

A few days later, Moon woke during the night to the faint scent of smoke in the air. He nudged Jade gently until she rolled off him, and sat up. The light and his internal sense of the sun's position said early pre-dawn; the window crystal was open and the air was just barely tinted with wood smoke.

They had seen some small settlements in the distance, mostly too far away to discern any detail, and once a structure stretching between two low hills, a little like a Dwei hive. The skylings who lived in it had fled the flying boat and hid inside before they could get a close look at them. But now the complexity of the scent on the wind told Moon they were approaching a much larger habitation.

He slid out of the narrow bed and picked his way over sleeping bodies to the nearest window. Briar, sitting by the door on watch, whispered, "What is it?"

"I think we're coming up on a groundling city," Moon whispered back. He paused and did a quick body count. "Where's Stone? And Bramble?"

"They stayed with Delin."

Stone had probably needed a break from the warriors. Moon reached the window and leaned out, but the sky was still dark enough to show stars, and he couldn't make out anything in the distance. He knew he wasn't going to be able to sleep anymore. He told Briar, "I'm going up on deck." He shifted, and climbed out the window.

He scaled the hull easily, pausing to peer cautiously over the railing to make sure none of the crew were in eyeshot. They were more used to Raksura now, but still easily startled. The deck on this side of the ship's spine was empty, so he slung himself over the railing and shifted back to groundling. He stretched and rolled his neck. The air was cooler, the steady breeze tugged at his clothes. He went toward the bow, tasting the air. He could scent the salt of the sea now, part of the complicated blend of odors.

He went forward, the deck still warm under his feet. Two crew members spoke in Kedaic on the other side of the spine, an idle conversation about someone's relative's prospects. There was a lamp hanging outside the hatch in the spine, one of the bright fluid lights, and Moon circled around the pool of illumination.

He reached the bow and leaned against the railing. Trying not to think about the clutch, the court, and what might be going on at the colony was easier up here than while lying in bed staring sleeplessly at the ceiling.

The sky was lightening, and soon he could see that they were traveling over coastal plain, with tall grass and stretches of marsh. The great dark expanse ahead started to show flickers of light. Trying to decide which sparks were in the port, which were on islands, and which were ships occupied him until he heard a step on the deck behind him.

He leaned back into the railing and watched Callumkal approach. He didn't think Callumkal realized there was a Raksura standing in the shadows. To test the theory, he said, "We're nearly there."

Callumkal flinched and fell back a step. Then he made a rueful huffing noise. "I hope you were concealing yourself with some power of invisibility."

At least Callumkal wasn't taking it badly. Rorra would probably have never forgiven herself. "No, I was just standing here."

"Well, it's early." Callumkal leaned on the railing. "You can see it from here?"

"Just some of the lights."

"Hmm." Callumkal squinted into the darkness. Most groundlings couldn't see that well at extreme distances. "We'll reach it by full dawn. It's than-Serest, the largest trading port along this stretch of the western coast. We didn't come this way before, of course. We went through the smaller port of Yukali, on the sel-Selatra. We'll stop here briefly and purchase supplies."

"Have you ever been here before?" Moon asked.

"No. Have you?"

"No." Moon had never come this far north on his own. "Stone might have, but he hasn't said anything."

Callumkal considered the view for a moment. "We shouldn't be there long."

"You're not worried about taking a bunch of Raksura into a groundling city?" Moon asked. Even if they all stayed on the boat, the idea made him uneasy. They had no idea if the people in than-Serest knew about Fell, and someone catching a glimpse of a shifted Raksura might prove awkward. Or worse than awkward.

Callumkal gave him a sideways glance. "Perhaps I wasn't until just now." He looked back toward the clusters of buildings along the coast, slowly forming out of the dark horizon, that he probably couldn't see yet. "We won't be staying long. And you don't have to leave the ship, if you don't care to."

Moon appreciated the fact that Callumkal hadn't attempted to make that an order. Jade, who probably didn't want any of them, especially the Arbora and the more inexperienced warriors, leaving the boat anyway, would not have taken it well. "What kind of people live there?"

"Many kinds; it's a very active trading port. I can't pronounce the name of the main race, but they are from a group of species called Coastals. They run most of the ports along here and populate the closer islands. They come from an older groundling species that interbred with the shallow and deepwater sealings." He added, "It is an interesting place. The port is still closely allied with the shallow-water sealing colonies just beyond the islands, and there is actually a great deal of interaction between them, with special trading areas in the docks."

It did sound interesting. Moon asked, "Are you going there?"

Callumkal lifted a hand, making a negative gesture. "I'll be occupied with obtaining supplies, and local maps."

Moon turned that over thoughtfully. Sealings should have contacts all along the coast, and out into the archipelagos, and maybe beyond. It might be useful to see if they had heard anything about Fell.

By dawn the port city was fully visible. There were a great many spiral stone towers of different sizes—or at least Moon thought they were stone. The surfaces caught the light in a way that showed they were oddly smooth and polished, and might be treated with some other material. Between the towers were small dwellings and winding streets, leading up to the curve of the shoreline. Islands studded the harbor, and beyond them lay the limitless sea, the sun glinting off the white-capped waves, even as high clouds threw shadows across the gray-blue water.

The shore toward the north end was open beach, dotted with small houses or buildings. The other end was all docks, extending out far into the harbor, some turning into bridges reaching to the nearest islands. And there were boats and ships of every size and shape imaginable. Moon spotted a couple of flying bladder-boats tied up to a smaller tower, but didn't see any Golden Islander craft, or anything else similar. He wondered where Niran and Diar were, if they had been able to follow as Delin hoped.

Earlier Callumkal had gone into the steering cabin, and Jade had come up to the bow to watch the city appear on the horizon, trailed later by a still sleep-bleary Chime. The others had followed them, Merit and Bramble lining up along the railing with Delin and Stone, and the other warriors perched up on the center ridge. Jade stirred now and said, "Did Callumkal say where he was planning to put this thing?"

"He said we're going to dock on one of those, with the bladder boats." Moon jerked his chin to indicate the smaller towers that seemed to work as air-docks.

"We're leaving by dark, right?" Chime asked. He watched the approach of than-Serest uneasily. "The last time we went to a groundling city like this, they tried to give us to the Fell."

"And Delin was with us then, too," Moon pointed out.

Chime glared at him, not appreciating the humor. Moon nudged his shoulder in apology. "You don't have to get off the boat if you don't want to."

"None of us have to get off the boat." Jade eyed him. "Do we?"

Moon hesitated, considering his half-formed plan. "I'd like to hear if there's any news, especially any news of Fell. Or things happening that might mean Fell are somewhere around. And I'm not sure if the Kishan know how to ask for it."

Jade made an annoyed noise in her throat. "Where would this news be?"

"Callumkal said there were trading places where you can talk to the sealings that live in the shallows. They may have heard something from the sealings further out in the sel-Selatra."

"That . . . doesn't sound like a bad idea." Jade's brow furrowed thoughtfully.

"Would they have contact with sealings so far away?" Chime asked.

"I don't know, but we can ask." Moon didn't know much about the sea kingdoms, but a city where groundlings and sealings were allies seemed like a good way to find out. And it wouldn't seem odd for a flying boat heading toward the sel-Selatra to ask if anyone had heard about any trouble out there. Or at least it wouldn't have seemed odd back in the Abascene, where Moon had done most of his traveling.

Chime nodded slowly. "I suppose asking Rorra for help would be out of the question."

Moon winced at the thought. "Right, no." They had been getting along with Rorra fairly well, getting used to her scent and learning to treat it as just part of the scents associated with the flying boat. But Rorra was still a difficult person in her own right, and it was obvious her past as a sealing was a subject to be avoided.

Jade was still doubtful. "Have you ever talked to sealings before?"

"No, but someone you're related to has." Moon turned to look back along the deck where Stone leaned against the railing with Delin. Stone saw them all staring and narrowed his eyes.

Chapter Nine

Despite the strong wind from the sea, the flying boat managed to lower itself down enough to tie off at the upper level of the smaller docking tower. Like all the towers it formed an open spiral, stretching up from a broad base and narrowing at the top. The flying craft were docked by securing their ropes around the outer rim of the spiral, and then a plank bridge was connected to the ship so the crew could disembark.

Watching this process with Jade, Stone, Chime, and Delin, Moon asked, "Is that going to hold?" The bladder-boats docked here seemed to be secure, but the Kishan flying boat was considerably larger and probably stronger.

Delin told him, "The material is not stone, not metal. No one knows what it is. Vendoin says these towers were all here long before the port was built or the Coastals settled here." He made an impatient gesture. "Another mystery."

The breeze was fresh and strong, scented of salt and the sea and groundling city. The warriors and the Arbora were on the far side of the boat, staring at this closer view, with Balm to keep an eye on them and make sure none of them shifted.

The groundlings who helped with the docking must be Coastals. They were tall and slender, their skin covered with pale gray scales that seemed flexible and soft in texture, almost like feathers. Their heads were a long narrow shape, eyes oblong slits, noses long and pointed, jaws long and mouths small, as if originally meant for eating small shellfish. They wore loose-fitting clothing, mostly brief wraps around the waist, and their hair looked a little like water grass, curving back from the crests of their heads. There was variation in colors and shapes between some of them, which might indicate different races. The differences were probably terribly important to them, though like Moon, most other species probably found them barely noticeable. Like the way most other species confused Raksura, especially Raksuran consorts, and Fell rulers.

They watched Callumkal, Vendoin, Kalam, and two crew members go down the plank onto the tower. Callumkal stopped to speak to the Coastals who had helped with the docking, then he and the others started down the ramp. Moon looked down the deck for Rorra, and saw her just vanishing into the passage to the steering cabin. She clearly had no intention of visiting even the groundling portion of the city.

As Callumkal's group took the first turn down and disappeared from view, Jade said, "Are you sure you want to do this?"

Moon faced her. She was serious, and, from the furrow of her brow and the angle of her spines, very worried. He said, "It's how I lived most of my life."

"I know, but . . ." Jade sighed. "You weren't very good at it sometimes."

Moon decided to let that go. Besides, she wasn't entirely wrong. "I was good at this part."

Jade seemed to find this less than reassuring. Stone said, "Hey, I'll be there."

Jade's expression made it clear that she didn't see this as a benefit. "Just be careful."

Callumkal had told his own crew that if they left the boat, they must stay in the vicinity of the market around the base of the tower. Moon had heard a few complaints about this, but the fact that the boat was meant to leave by late afternoon had reconciled most of them.

Several Kishan left after Callumkal's group, and Moon and Stone gave them a chance to get a little way ahead, and then followed.

Walking down the tower's ramp, they had a good view of the city. Moon had spotted grasseater-drawn carts from the air, but at this distance he could see that the grasseaters weren't the big furred or armored mammals he was used to seeing used as draught animals, but big flightless birds. They towered over the groundlings, easily twenty to thirty paces high, and their feathers looked more like shells or plates. Tall crests of that hard metallic plumage obscured the shape of their heads, but their beaks looked long and sharp. "Are the groundlings here out of their minds?" Moon muttered.

Stone said, "They might not be meat-eaters."

Moon snorted. Flightless birds that size were usually meat-eaters.

The buildings between the towers were constructed of combinations of stone blocks and sun-bleached wood, with shells embedded as decorations. They had large windows and doorways, slatted shutters open to catch the breeze, and most of them seemed to be part of a market complex that stretched between the docking towers and this end of the harbor. The roads were white, and from the other port cities along the Crescent Sea that Moon had been to, he knew they would be shells crushed into fine powder and packed down so tightly that they didn't move much underfoot. It would be smooth enough for easy walking and for the wagons and hideous bird-things.

The groundlings, at least the ones Moon could spot from here, were enough of a mix of different species so that Moon and Stone, and the Kish-Jandera for that matter, shouldn't draw much attention. Near the base of the tower, Moon spotted short green-skinned groundlings with round bodies and lumps for heads, tall skinny dark-skinned ones with long manes of white hair extending down their backs, and gray-skinned ones with long heads and weirdly-jointed limbs.

As they came around the last curve it was obvious that the nearest buildings all seemed to be selling food, and the smell of frying oil and grilled fish and sugar hung in the air. Moon's stomach grumbled, even though he wasn't hungry; groundling food tended to affect him that way. Callumkal and the others went past the food stalls and Moon stopped by a pillar at the base of the ramp to watch them.

The tower was on higher ground and the slight elevation let him see that the Kishan were taking a turn off the main road into a compound of larger, more substantial buildings. From the wrapped bundles, bags, and crates piled up in the yard, it was a trading factor and was probably where Callumkal meant to buy supplies. Moon turned to say that to Stone, and found Stone had disappeared.

Moon gritted his teeth to suppress an annoyed hiss. *This went wrong fast*. But a moment later, Stone stepped out of a food stall across from the end of the ramp. Relieved, Moon went to meet him.

Stone had a paper wrap filled with fried lumps of something that smelled so good it made Moon's prey reflex twitch. Stone said, "Want some?"

"No." Moon was still mad about that moment of worry Stone had given him. "How did you buy it?"

"Traded an opal." At Moon's incredulous expression, he said, exasperated, "They change currency for trade too. They gave me a sack of metal bits that are good in most of the trading ports around here."

Moon grimaced in annoyance. "You don't go to the first place. They'll charge more than the others further away."

Stone sighed with weary patience. None of the Raksura understood trading or barter the way groundlings did it, and none of them understood why Moon cared. None of them had ever been stuck in a groundling city where they had to trade for food or not eat. Stone said, "So? If we need more metal bits, we'll get more." He held out the paper again and this time Moon gave in and took one. They were fried lumps of sweet dough, crunchy on the outside and soft on the inside.

Chewing, Moon said, "Callumkal and the others went to a trading factor over there." He turned in time to see Kalam walk out of the compound's entrance and head down the road toward the docks.

"Now where's he going?" Stone said, eyes narrowed thoughtfully.

Moon took another piece of fried dough. They had speculated that one of the Kishan close to the expedition might have been infected by the Fell, might be spying for a ruler without knowing it. "Let's see."

They set off at an easy pace, following Kalam at a distance.

Fortunately there were just enough groundlings out on the street to blend in with, but not so many that it was hard to keep track of Kalam. Most of the groundlings were going in and out of the market stalls, or occupied with moving cargo toward the port on the giant bird-thing carts. The gray people with the weirdly-jointed limbs were even stranger close up, with bulging eyes that were set wide apart.

No one seemed unduly interested in Moon and Stone, or Kalam for that matter, beyond the occasional curious glance. Moon had always preferred this type of groundling city, where everyone was occupied with their own business and expected to see different species. He hated any place where he was stared at, hated to be singled out for scrutiny that might lead to suspicion that might lead to fleeing for his life.

The ground sloped slightly as it curved down toward the harbor. Over the low rooftops, Moon spotted the masts of the larger ships and the jungle-covered peaks of the closer islands. They circled a group of groundlings unloading a wagon, the bird-thing turning its head to glare as they passed. The road curved around another large cargo yard and opened out into the harbor front, a maze of walkways built atop the piled-up rocks covering the beach.

The wind was stronger here and heavier with the scents of salt and dead fish and sea wrack. At a set of docks a little way down, groundlings loaded or unloaded big sailing vessels, and several shallow-draft barges floated further out. Down toward the other end of the harbor, the walkways curved back from the beach and naked groundlings were playing in the waves. It was too bad they couldn't bring the Arbora and the warriors down here, but there was no time, and they would want to shift and swim in their scaled forms. Even in a place like this, shifting would cause a riot.

One of the broader walkways led out to several interlinked docks built of the same material as the towers. They extended out away from the shallow area into the deeper water, and Moon thought at first that they led to low-lying barges. But a closer look showed that they were structures sitting in the water.

And Kalam was heading for the walkway. Moon said, "I think he's going where we were going."

"To see the sealings?" Stone leaned on a piling. "If he was meaning to follow us, he did a bad job of it."

Kalam went along the walkway, pausing to watch a large vessel lowering its butterfly-shaped sails as it angled in toward the next set of docks. The boy didn't look like he was doing anything surreptitious, and he didn't look like he was being compelled to go to a Fell ruler, either. "I don't think so. Callumkal told me about the sealing traders, I bet he told Kalam, too. Maybe he just came down here to see them."

Stone made an annoyed noise. Kalam was moving again, out onto the docks with the trading station. Stone said, "Come on. If he's sightseeing, we're sightseeing, too."

Moon followed, only a little reluctantly. If Kalam saw them he was sure to tell Callumkal, and Moon didn't want the whole crew to know their business. Because Kalam wasn't speaking to Fell didn't mean no one else was.

They went down the walkway and out onto the first dock. Moon saw he was right; this was the same metallic stone as the towers. And the structures standing only a few paces above the waves were built of the same material. So whoever had built the towers had built the trading station for the sealings. Or for whatever had lived in the water back then.

Moon was prepared to wave and look innocent if Kalam glanced back and saw them, but Kalam headed for the outer dock, slipping past the other parties of groundlings. There were five structures partially above the water, and at least two further out that sat lower, their roofs just below the waves. The largest had heavy clear crystals set into windows along the sides, and two entrances, where stone steps led down into wells in the sides of the building. It also looked the most crowded, as both entrances were temporarily blocked, one by groundlings trying to carry large pottery jars down into the structure, the other by a Coastal who had a twisted leg joint and was being helped up the stairs by a companion.

The other groundlings on that part of the dock just milled around, waiting for the entrances to clear, but Kalam hesitated, then started for the smaller structures further down. "No," Moon muttered, "he's going to the wrong one."

"What?" Stone squinted against the salt spray in the air.

"That's the trading station." Moon jerked his chin toward the large structure. "The one those groundlings are waiting to get into. I don't know what those are."

Those blocky structures were smaller, further underwater, and didn't have any sky-lights. A few groundlings were going down into their stairwells, or making their way toward them along the dock. Moon's instincts for navigating groundling cities had all been gained the hard way, and they told him that while the trading station looked like a relatively safe prospect, those places didn't.

"Huh," Stone commented, and strolled after Kalam.

Kalam picked the first structure he came to and started down the steps into the entrance well, which again didn't bode well for the theory that he had been unconsciously compelled to meet a Fell ruler and wasn't just exploring a strange city. Moon was half-inclined to give up on Kalam and just go to the trading station where they were more likely to hear news of the sel-Selatra. But Stone was already following Kalam down the stairs, so Moon suppressed an annoyed hiss and went after him.

It was dark inside after the bright morning sun, but Moon's eyes adjusted quickly. It was a big oblong room, the walls light-colored, and there were long crystal windows, all below the surface so the light was dim and constantly changing as the waves crashed over the roof above. The artificial light came from glass lamps, placed on small shelves randomly studding the walls. Moon couldn't tell what was inside the lamps, if it was magical illumination or just a glowing mineral or plant material, but the light was white and not strong. The air was intensely damp and the place was also bigger than it looked on the outside. This was only the first level, and Moon spotted Kalam's head going down the circular stairwell in the middle of the floor.

There were only a few groundlings here, standing in groups and talking, and no one who looked like a sealing of any kind. A Coastal with patchy scales was selling cups of various caustic-scented liquids from a set of pottery urns in the far corner of the room, and that was the only activity taking place. Stone barely bothered to glance around and followed Kalam.

The stairs curved down into a bigger lower level, where the dim white light was even more murky and the view through the windows was darker, except for the occasional silver flicker of a fish, or little blue shellfish clinging to the crystal. There were more groundlings here, standing and talking or sitting on cushions on the floor. And finally there were sealings.

There were a dozen round pools cut into the floor that must have some passage outside, because the water scent was fresh and salty. The sealings swam or lounged on the edges of the pools, speaking to the groundlings gathered around. These were shallow-water sealings, able to breathe both above and below the surface. They had green scaled skin and long, dark green hair that looked like heavy lengths of water weed. Their hands and feet were heavily webbed and they had long prominent claws, and filmy fins along their arms and legs. Most were wearing jewelry, unpolished lumps of pearl and jasper in nets of braided cord. "Finally," Stone muttered, and wandered into the crowd, headed for the pools.

There were Coastals selling various things, mostly more caustic drinks and little glass cups that emitted vapor and were meant to be held under the nose. It competed with the more attractive scents of the water and the sealings themselves.

Moon looked for Kalam and spotted him partway across the room. Most of the crowd was dressed in lighter fabrics, and Kalam's reddish brown skin and dark hair stood out among all the grays and greens. He was trying to circle around a group to get closer to the pools, but suddenly the group circled him.

It had occurred to Moon that if Kalam had been compelled by the Fell, the rulers might have sent another infected groundling into the port to talk to him. He moved closer, trying to see what was happening. One of the groundlings, a tall gray male with a long head and limbs that made him look as if he might be related to the Aventerans, stooped over Kalam.

But as Moon stepped closer, Kalam tried to back away. Kalam, clearly uncomfortable, said in careful Altanic, "I'm just here to look around. I'm not interested in company."

Moon hissed under his breath, annoyed. Kalam had picked the wrong place, all right; this structure must be mainly for getting intoxicated and meeting people to have sex with. Moon pushed forward and elbowed aside the groundling blocking Kalam's retreat. He said, "He said he's not interested."

The group edged back a little. The one Moon had elbowed fell back against the wall clutching his middle. Moon had gotten used to elbowing warriors and had lost the habit for being more careful with groundlings. The maybe-Aventeran jerked back a little, startled. In badly slurred Altanic, he demanded, "Who are you?"

Moon showed his teeth in an expression that was not a smile. "I'm a friend of his father's."

The maybe-Aventeran's companions and the other groundlings who had been gathering to see the fight immediately started to back away.

"How should I know that?" the maybe-Aventeran demanded again, hesitated in confusion as his support retreated, then hurriedly followed them across the room.

"Thank you." Kalam turned to Moon, a little breathlessly. "I didn't know what to do."

"Why are you here?" Moon hoped Kalam wouldn't ask why Moon was here.

Kalam, being young and flustered, didn't think to question Moon's sudden appearance. "I wanted to see the trading station. My father gave me permission. The people at the supply factor said it was safe."

Moon drew on the ability he had cultivated while raising fledglings to be patient in the face of the most willfully ignorant behavior. "Yes, but this isn't the trading station."

"I know, but it was crowded, and I thought this would be quicker. I'm not supposed to be gone too long."

Kids, Moon thought, exasperated. Kalam was probably old enough to be let out alone in a Kishan academic enclave, but maybe not old enough to wander a busy port city. "The next time you tell your father you're going to the trading station, you go to the trading station. You have to be careful in strange places."

"I know." Kalam's expression was a convincing combination of embarrassed and miserable. "I will."

Moon said, "Just stay with us." He looked for Stone and saw him sitting by a pool toward the center of the room, with a couple of other groundlings and a Coastal. A sealing floated in the pool, speaking to the Coastal.

Moon made his way through the sparse crowd, aware Kalam was sticking obediently close. He sat next to Stone as the Coastal and the other groundlings left. Kalam took a seat on the opposite side of the pool.

The sealing, a young female, stared at Moon in what was probably supposed to be a provocative way. Moon was still irritated from the encounter with the maybe-Aventeran, and it just made him want to bite through someone's neck artery.

Apparently this was obvious. The sealing turned to Stone and said in Altanic, "What's wrong with him?"

"He's in a bad mood," Stone explained, "he was born that way. Does the one who's down there with you want to talk too?"

The sealing sank into the water a little, swishing her fins in exasperation. "I take it you're not here for the usual."

Stone said, "I don't know what that is. I want to know if you've had any news from the waters in the direction of the place the groundlings call sel-Selatra."

Scaled brows drew down in thought. "Toward the wind passage? The land of the sea-mounts?"

"That's it."

"There was some—" The sealing's whole body jerked, as if something had grabbed her from below and tugged. Moon's instinct said *predator* and he almost shifted, catching himself just in time. The sealing said, "Ah, someone else wants to talk to you," and sank below the surface and out of sight.

Stone gritted his teeth and gazed up at the damp ceiling. He said in Raksuran, "I hate talking to sealings. Everything's a damn bargain."

"You hate talking to everybody," Moon said, in the same language. It didn't help, but Moon felt he had to point it out.

"Shut up. Why is he here?" Stone jerked his head toward Kalam.

Moon said, through gritted teeth, "So I don't have to shift and kill everybody in this stupid stinking place."

Stone sighed. Another sealing broke the surface, and water lapped up over the edge of the pool. This was an older female, or at least the faint dull sheen at the edge of her scales made her look older.

She studied them both thoughtfully, with an edge of contempt in her expression, then said in Altanic, "We sell isteen. If you want to buy that, stay. If you don't, get out before you regret it." She bared fangs. "We don't sell information."

Moon didn't know what isteen was and he didn't care. Considering the other groundlings in here, it was probably a simple that made you stupid. Stone just said, "That's good, because I wasn't planning to pay you."

She swayed in the water, as if considering. "Buy isteen, and perhaps I'll give you the information you want."

Stone said, "I don't want isteen, and I'm not giving you anything."

"If I give you information, I need to be paid." She nodded toward Moon. "I'll take that one."

After having to rescue Kalam from drunken groundlings who couldn't control their own genitals, this was too much. Moon said, "Try."

The sealing focused on him, really looking at him for the first time. Whatever she saw made her scales ripple. Whether it was aggressive or defensive, Moon didn't know, but it nearly set off his prey reflex. Stone tilted a sideways look at him and made a noise in his throat, just a faint growl, not enough to vibrate through the floor. "Moon. No."

The message was clear. Moon hissed at him, and laid down on the damp floor, head propped on his hand, as if prepared to wait as long as it took.

The sealing relaxed a little, the water splashing toward Kalam's side of the pool as she flexed her fins. She said, "I had to ask. What else have you got to pay me with?"

Stone smiled. Most groundlings wouldn't have recognized what was behind that expression but it would have made the warriors scatter like startled lizards. "You want me to come down there and ask?" he said.

The sealing stared hard at him, eyes narrowed, as if trying see past his skin. "What are you?"

Moon swallowed an annoyed snarl and said, "She wants to scare us. Why don't you just act scared?"

Kalam kept looking from Moon to Stone to the sealing, wide-eyed and deeply fascinated. At least somebody was having fun.

Still smiling easily, not betraying any impatience, Stone said, "I'm terrified. Want me to come down there and be terrified?"

The sealing looked from Stone to Moon to Kalam. Then she kicked once to glide to the far side of the pool. She leaned back against the edge and stretched her arms along it, claws displayed but relaxed. "Most of the groundling traders who come here defer to us. They're afraid of sealing females."

No one said *we're not groundlings* though Moon felt it hang in the air. He said, "Our females would have pulled you out of there and ripped your skin off by now."

"And that's why we can't be friends," Stone said. "Now do you know anything about the waters in the sel-Selatra or do I need to go to the next pool and start over?"

She exhaled, a salty breath that made Moon wince. "We speak to the Viar, who live mostly on the surface, in floating colonies. They say they've seen an island that should have groundlings that is now empty. It was on the edge of the first sea-mount. The Viar are not . . ." She made an elegant gesture with her claws. "Like us. They have no limbs or ears, they see in different ways, they care about different things. But these groundlings gave them powdered grain they like in exchange for driving fish into their nets during a certain season, so the Viar noticed when they went there and found them gone. There is no taste of them in the water anymore. It was a strange story to hear, so it was passed on through our nets of speech."

Moon thought that it meshed unpleasantly well with what they had already heard. Stone took it in thoughtfully. "Where did this happen?"

It took some time to figure out the location, as the directions and landmarks the sealings referenced were completely different from those used by water or air vessels, and were often seen only from below the surface. Both Stone and Moon had to ask a lot of questions, and Moon just hoped Kalam didn't realize that they had a suspiciously accurate picture of the sel-Selatra considering they were only supposed to have seen the map once and briefly. But Kalam seemed more interested in the sealing's descriptions of the sea bottom.

Finally they were able to leave, and climbing back up the stairs into the sunlight and clean wind and the crash of waves against the dock felt like stepping into a completely different world. It made Moon feel like they might just escape the port without anyone being murdered.

On the dock, Kalam hesitated. "Can we go to the trading station too? We're so close and I hate to miss it—"

Moon started to say no but just then a groundling walked up from the station's nearest stairwell carrying a paper wrap of something that smelled of sweet grease and salt. Stone shrugged and turned toward the station. "Sure."

Moon was about to protest, but inspiration struck. He caught up with them and said, "If the Arbora find out we took Kalam to the trading station and not them, they'll be furious." This had the virtue of being completely true.

Stone paused, catching on immediately. He told Kalam, "You have to promise not to tell anybody we were here with you."

Kalam, wisely realizing this would mean his father wouldn't hear about his adventure in the sealing drug bar, said, "I won't say anything to anyone."

Moon didn't expect their absence would go unnoticed, and when they had walked back up the tower's ramp to the flying boat, Callumkal was waiting for them on the deck. His expression of relief on seeing Kalam was obvious. He said, "I was beginning to worry."

"Sorry, it was so interesting, I stayed longer than I meant to," Kalam said as they crossed the plank to the flying boat. He nodded to Moon and Stone. "I met them at the base of the tower."

Moon hoped Callumkal hadn't noticed that Kalam had delivered that information a little too readily. Callumkal said, "I'm glad it was interesting." He looked at Moon and Stone and started to speak. Then Jade stepped forward and demanded, "What were you eating?" She looked appalled.

"Just the things from the food places down there," Moon said. He walked down the deck with her, noting out of the corner of his eye that Stone had wandered in the opposite direction toward the bow. Callumkal was speaking to Kalam, but from the boy's expansive gestures, Moon bet he was describing the trading station.

Jade said in Raksuran, "We're waiting for the supplies to be ready. He's going to let all the crew who are willing to help carry them up go to that market down there, but he wants to leave after that. He didn't seem suspicious. I told them you wanted to see the market and Stone was keeping an eye on you, and he seemed to accept it. And really, what were you eating?"

"It's like fried bread batter with boiled sugar cane," Moon said. Jade winced. "We talked to a sealing, and they've heard of at least one disappearance of groundlings from an island in the sel-Selatra. It's not anywhere near the places where Callumkal said they found signs of what could be Fell attack. It sounds like the Fell were wandering around out there for a while."

Jade leaned on the railing and growled under her breath. "They're looking for prey."

Moon agreed. And he was afraid it meant that the Fell hadn't followed the Kishan expedition, that they might have already been out there, scouting the city, for some time.

They wouldn't know until they reached their goal.

The wind eased in the late afternoon, and the flying boat took advantage of it to cast off and head out to sea. The bladder boats still anchored to the tower must not be as powerful as the Kishan boat, and their crews watched enviously as it departed.

Callumkal had told them that the sealing city might be partially visible from the air, so all the Raksura and Delin were lined up at the railing of the main deck to look for it. Every crew member not occupied was out there too, though they took up places a little distance away. Only Kalam and Magrim had come over to stand next to Delin. Rorra was nowhere to be seen, but then somebody had to be steering the flying boat.

Chime, leaning on the rail next to Moon, said, "So the sealings were hard to talk to?"

"I think it's just the way they act with other species." Getting back here successfully with some more confirmation on the situation in the sel-Selatra had noticeably improved Moon's mood. Or maybe it was just all the boiled dumplings and fried sugar dough eaten while walking around the trading station. Its multiple windows had allowed visitors to watch the waves crash against it on the upper level, and to look at underwater life on the lower. There had been raw material and goods trading going on with the sealings, but most of the groundlings had been there to see the place. "Or maybe just other species that want to buy their simples."

"Well, I'm glad you and Stone got out of there safely." Chime twitched his shoulders, unconsciously trying to convey his mood with the spines of his other form.

Moon thought about pointing out that as groundling cities go, the port was definitely one he would have classified as "safe." If he had ever gotten this far northwest on his own and run across it, he would have planned to stay for a while.

The boat had already reached the shoreline and moved out over the docks and the bridges that connected the nearest islands. "There it is!" Balm said suddenly, pointing. "Past that island!"

The warriors climbed up on the railing and the two Arbora pressed against it. The islands were covered with heavy greenery, but around them the waves moved in an odd pattern, disrupted by whatever was just under the surface. Moon pulled himself up onto the railing and perched one hip on it.

As the boat drew closer, the outlines of walls, tops of towers, and other structures less easy to understand became visible just below the surface. The water was clear enough that in the intervals between waves Moon could see bodies swimming, flickering in and out among a forest of water plants. The sealing city lay between and around the six major islands in the bay, far larger than Moon had been expecting. "I wonder . . ." Chime muttered, staring intently. "I wonder if they made the islands too."

Moon shrugged. He wondered if the sealings would have answered that question if asked. Maybe; it was probably more interesting than talking about drugs.

Down the deck, most of the Kishan crew were all straining to see. The boat was much closer before the crew started to exclaim at the wonders below the waves. Delin, who had been waiting more patiently, now started to sketch the outline of the city.

Jade moved over beside Moon, leaning on the railing to look down. "It's five days to the edge of the sel-Selatra from here."

Moon felt a stab of unease. By tomorrow they would be too far from the coast to fly back without help. Stone might be able to, but the further they went, the less likely it would be for him, too. Moon hadn't felt much sense of inevitable commitment to this plan when they first boarded the flying boat, but soon it really would be too late to turn back. He thought about the clutch again, and wondered if they were upset about his prolonged absence or too busy playing to notice, as Thorn had predicted. At least the Sky Copper fledglings were old enough to understand the situation.

But there really had been no opportunity to turn back. The shared dream and the mentors' augury had made the consequences of failure clear.

The flying boat sailed on over the islands, and the sealing city, until they were out of sight.

CHAPTER TEN

"I t's not going well," Ember whispered.

He was crouched on the balcony of Rill's bower, shielded from the sight of anyone in the greeting hall by the angle of the doorway.

Below, Malachite and Pearl confronted each other, loosely surrounded by an uneasy group of warriors and Arbora. Floret spoke for Pearl, and an older female warrior spoke for Malachite. So far they appeared to be making extremely awkward small talk, while Floret occasionally threw beseeching glances at Pearl, hoping for some sign that it was all right to invite the newcomers into the colony.

It wasn't the first unexpected visit since the groundling flying boat had left. Niran and Diar from the Golden Isles had arrived in their wind-ship only six days later. The court had hosted them for the night, given them a copy of the Kish map and all the information they had, and sent them on their way. It had been a relief all around. At least Jade and the others would have friendly groundling allies whenever the Golden Isles wind-ship caught up with them.

Behind him, Rill asked Aura, "The same visions? All their mentors?"

"That's what it sounded like from their descriptions." Aura had led the warriors who had carried the message to Opal Night. "Malachite barely gave us time to eat and rest before we started back here."

The thought that another court had experienced the same augury made Ember's skin creep. Given the seriousness of the visions, it wasn't a surprise that Malachite had come here. The problem was that along with a group of warriors, Malachite had brought Opal Night's half-Fell consort and half-Fell mentor.

They were with her now, standing with the Opal Night warriors. The warriors seemed relaxed and confident, but the half-Fell consort, now in his groundling form, looked nervous. The mentor was nearly hiding behind one of the larger female warriors.

Ember could tell the situation was becoming increasingly tense. Watching Pearl, studying the subtle nuances of her body language, Ember thought it was indecision she was wrestling with more than disgust or anger. In a way he understood. Indigo Cloud had been nearly destroyed by a deliberately crossbred Fell-Raksuran queen who had taken over her Fell flight. The court of Sky Copper had been entirely destroyed except for one royal clutch. The same thing had happened to Opal Night's eastern colony, turns and turns ago, and it must have been easy for Pearl to sympathize, even if she didn't understand Malachite's impulse to retrieve her consort's half-Fell issue.

All of Indigo Cloud had known about them, and heard the story of what had happened when Moon had been taken to Opal Night a couple of turns ago. But seeing half-Fell in the Indigo Cloud colony was something else altogether. Ember didn't know what to think or feel about it and he was certain not many of the others did either.

"It's wrong," Rill muttered, moving forward to crouch beside Ember. "Pearl should welcome them, too. They're part of our first consort's bloodline. That little consort is Moon's half clutch-brother."

"Did you see what that little consort's scaled form looks like?" Aura's spines moved uneasily. Ember hadn't seen it. He had been down in the nurseries when the Opal Night party had arrived. Then she admitted, "But when we traveled with them, he was fine. They both were. It just took a while to get used to the idea."

Rill glanced at Ember, her expression deeply concerned. "Not letting them in is . . . wrong. If we don't accept them, the other courts will take it as an excuse not to accept them either."

"I don't think they're going to do much visiting—" Aura began.

"What if there are others?" Rill's concern turned to borderline fury. "Lost out there, like Moon was, but part Fell, and not knowing what to do, except look for a court to belong to. And if they're turned away, or worse, killed, because—"

Ember squeezed her wrist, and she subsided, saying, "I'm just . . . What happened to the consorts and Arbora who were forced to make them is not their fault. We owe it to them to help."

Aura groaned. "All right, fine, but . . . Malachite should have sent someone ahead with us, so they could talk to Pearl first. So she would have time to think about it before they got here."

Aura was dead right about that, Ember knew. Pearl hated surprises, hated having her hand forced. He also knew that he would have been the one to have that conversation, and he didn't know if he felt the way Rill did. Maybe in principle, but in reality, he was afraid.

Opal Night had great power and influence, but other courts didn't know about the half-Fell fledglings Malachite had taken in. When they learned of it, they would have to make a decision whether to accept it or not. If Indigo Cloud accepted it, it wouldn't obligate any other court to follow suit, but it would be a powerful pull on all the interconnected strings of alliance.

Just one step. Somebody had to take it. Ember knew whose job it was, and it made his stomach sour with nerves. *This is what consorts are for.* He said, aloud, "I know what I should do."

Rill looked at him, holding her breath.

Ember stared at the half-Fell consort with the oddly pale groundling skin. The tension in his shoulders was clearly fear. Conflicting impulses said *he's half-Fell* and *but he's a consort.* Then *he's not only a consort, he's your first consort's half clutch-brother, just think about it that way.* Failing to welcome Moon's half clutch-brother would be offensive, a clear violation of etiquette, a terrible insult. But against that was . . . fear. The only thing holding him back was fear.

It couldn't be any worse than being dragged off to a strange court in turmoil where it had been immediately obvious that no one wanted him. "All right," Ember muttered to himself. "So then."

He stood. "Aura, please go up and get the seating area outside my bower ready to receive someone. Use my best tea set."

"Uh." Aura blinked, the implications hitting her. "Uh, yes, I'll do that."

She climbed down from the railing to head for the bower's doorway. Rill followed her, saying, "I'll help. You won't do it right."

"I will do it right," Aura protested and they disappeared down the passage.

Ember took a deep breath, and before he could talk himself out of it, shifted and leapt down to the greeting hall floor.

He landed and furled his wings, and the hall fell silent, all murmuring and whispering ceasing instantly. He walked toward the group at the center, managing not to look at Pearl and Malachite.

It was second nature to make it look graceful, though with every eye in the court on him and his insides roiling, it wasn't easy. Whether this was a good idea or not, he had no idea. But Shadow, the first consort of Emerald Twilight, had told him that Raksuran courts had strict rules of etiquette so they wouldn't kill each other. Now it seemed doubly important to follow those rules.

Close-up, the consort looked even more like someone who had frozen in place in terror and self-consciousness. Ember reached him, shifted to his groundling form, and said, "I'm Ember, consort to Pearl, the reigning queen."

The consort stared, wide-eyed. The fact that he was just as afraid as Ember somehow made the situation easier. Ember prompted gently, "This is where you tell me your name."

"Uh, yes," the consort whispered. "I'm Shade, of Opal Night."

Ember nodded. "Would you like to come up to the consorts' quarters?"

In a bare whisper, Shade managed, "Yes."

"Good." Ember took a breath to steady his pounding heart. "Follow me."

Shade said, "But I'll have to shift."

Ember hesitated. He didn't have time to consider all the implications, and found himself falling back again on common politeness. Suggesting that anything about Shade was out of the ordinary or unwelcome would be something only done to challenge or deliberately offend another court. Against a court that was not only an ally but whose bloodline was now mingled with Indigo Cloud's royal Aeriat, it was unthinkable. He said, "Yes, you'll have to shift. But it's all right."

Shade met his gaze, clearly forced his shoulders to relax, and shifted in time with Ember.

Ember blinked. He had heard the descriptions, but it was still a shock to see the reality. Shade's shifted form was big and muscular, though the proportions were clearly a consort's. His scales were a reflective black, with no contrasting color undersheen and no banding on his claws. He had a smaller, less prominent Fell ruler's armored crest and a mane of spines and frills sprouting from the base. He did look like the drawing of the forerunner from the ancient city that Delin had brought to show them. Heart had made a copy of it for the mentors' library and most of the court had studied it curiously. Ember managed to say, "Follow me," and he and Shade leapt up to the nearest balcony.

Ember took them far enough up the central well to make the point, then swung over a balcony and into a passage that led to a back stairwell. He shifted to his groundling form and explained, "I want to give them time to get the seating area ready."

Shade shifted as well. "Oh, right." Following Ember up the steps, he added, "I've never been to another court before."

"I hadn't either, before I came here," Ember told him. "I'm from Emerald Twilight."

"Oh." Shade hesitated again, then asked, "The warriors said Moon and the others went off with groundlings because your mentors think Fell will come here."

"Yes, that's what happened." They reached the top of the landing, the one with the life-sized carving of warriors in flight, twisting up the wall to the next level, but Ember was too distracted to point it out. "Aura said your mentors saw the same thing, Fell attacking the Reaches?"

"Yes," Shade said. "And right before your warriors arrived, we had a shared dream, just like the one described in Jade's letter. Except the Fell weren't at Opal Night, they were coming from the east, attacking all the courts on this side of the Reaches."

Ember stopped, turning to stare at him. "Really?"

Shade nodded. His brow creased in worry, and his oddly pale skin was flushed. Their gazes met for a long moment. Ember felt a chill wind its way up his spine. He was suddenly glad Malachite had come here. He said, "We haven't heard from our other allies yet, but . . ."

"We can't be the only courts this has happened to," Shade said. "There must be others. Lithe—she's the mentor with us—said the visions might be spreading slowly, because the other courts aren't as close to what's happening as we are."

Ember turned and started up the stairs again, considering it. "Lithe needs to talk to Heart, and our other mentors." As they walked, he told Shade about the Kishan flying boat and what Delin had said, which carried them up to the consorts' level and to the now carefully arranged seating area outside his bower, and through the first cup of tea. Having something substantive to talk about made the whole situation less awkward. After the second cup, Shade paused as if to gather his courage, and asked, "Did Pearl not want to let us in?"

"Pearl . . ." Ember tried to think of a way to explain it. Pearl was always gentle with him, though with the rest of the court she had good days and bad days. He didn't think she had ever really recovered from her consort Rain's premature death, and it had seemed to make a lot of things hard for her. "Pearl often thinks things are difficult, and you have to show her that they really aren't."

Shade seemed to understand. "So you made the decision to let us in for her. Is she going to mind?"

"No," Ember confessed. "If I handle it right, she'll think it was her idea, sort of." It was hard to explain. Pearl could make decisions all day when lives were at stake; it was only when they weren't that she had trouble. This complicated question of etiquette and the future of part-Fell Raksura in the Reaches was absolutely the kind of decision she hated. But now that it was made, he thought Pearl would find it much easier to go along on the path Ember had nudged her toward.

By the time Floret came down the passage, Shade seemed at ease and Ember was certain he had made the right decision. It was a relief to have another consort to talk all this over with.

Floret said, "Ember, Pearl wants you to come to the queens' hall now." She smiled at Shade, and Ember remembered they had actually met before, that she was one of the warriors who had been at Opal Night with Jade and Moon. "Malachite's there too."

"How is it— Are they—?" Shade tried to ask.

"It's going pretty well," Floret assured him. "Much better than before."

Ember led the way to the steps down to the passage that led through to the queens' hall, and he and Shade made what Ember considered to be a very decorous and correct entrance. Ember liked and admired Moon a great deal, but he wasn't very good at entrances. He entered formal meetings looking either like a captive dragged there against his will or like he was coming to murder someone.

Pearl and Malachite were now seated, facing each other over the court's best blue glazed tea set, a few warriors arrayed around them. Malachite had the mentor Lithe with her, and someone had had the forethought to summon Heart and Bone to sit with Pearl. Arbora tended to be a calming presence anyway, and Bone disliked conflict almost as much as Pearl, but he was much better at defusing it.

As Ember and Shade took seats on the cushions left for them, and the introductions were made, Ember had a chance to get a close look at Malachite.

She was bigger than Pearl, clearly more physically powerful, and her scales were a green so dark it was almost black. There was light gray scarring across her scales, concealing what should be the second color of her webbing. Her only jewelry was silver and crystal sheaths on her claws. Ember thought she looked like a very fine ceramic bowl that had been broken and repaired with silver in the cracks, to make it stronger.

Continuing the conversation, Pearl said to Malachite, "Staying the night would be more sensible. It's almost twilight and you'll have to stop and camp anyway."

As opaque as the queen carved into the wall above Pearl's head, Malachite said, "Perhaps you're right."

It was ridiculous to embark on another long flight now when you had the chance to leave rested and fed in the morning. Malachite and Pearl both knew that; they were just doing an elaborate dance of politeness and respect.

Malachite twitched one spine. It wasn't a nervous gesture, but Ember couldn't read it. He could see Heart and some of the warriors betraying little twitches of anxiety. Ember understood; Malachite was by far the most intimidating queen he had ever seen, and at close range the effect was even more daunting. He had no trouble believing she was

Moon's birthqueen. She said, "And it will give me the chance to see the new royal clutch."

Pearl tilted her head slightly, obviously trying to think of a way to deny or postpone this perfectly reasonable request. Ember sighed. Maybe it wasn't so much of a dance as it was a fight. Finally Pearl said, grudgingly, "Of course."

Then Bone intervened with, "Do you plan to try to join the Golden Islanders? Niran and Diar are Delin's descendants, and I think they would welcome you."

Malachite turned her attention to him. One of the others might have quailed a little under that intense regard, but Bone weathered it without a twitch. It was impossible to tell if Malachite was aware of the effect of her presence. She said, "It's the best solution. The map shows a route from island to island, presumably the way the Fell managed it, but going directly will be faster."

Ember looked at Shade, startled. The mention of the Fell was a reminder of how dangerous this trip would be. "Surely you're not going— Are you returning to your court after this? Or you could stay here until Malachite returns."

Ember knew Pearl would have words with him for issuing the invitation without speaking to her first, but half-Fell or not, Shade was a consort, a young inexperienced one, as unlike Moon as Ember was, and he should not be taken into such a situation.

Malachite's attention fell on Ember. His skin twitched involuntarily, his mouth went dry, and he dropped his gaze to the teapot. Then she said, "Shade, it's your decision."

Shade seemed pleased by the invitation, but he said, "No, thank you, I have to go. It's something I have to make myself do."

Malachite tilted her head back toward Pearl. "The augury suggests that none of us have a choice in this."

"That has not escaped me," Pearl said, dryly, her spines conveying disgruntled resignation. "Now I assume your mentor will wish to consult with ours about the possibility of Fell attack."

Malachite set her tea cup aside, her claws clinking on the delicate ceramic. "First I want to speak of precautions."

Pearl's spines tilted suspiciously. "What sort of precautions?"

Malachite said, "I have two hundred warriors I can spare for the defense of the Reaches. I'd like to bring them here."

The flying boat traveled over open sea for the next stretch of days, passing only the occasional uninhabited island, and only a few flying island fragments. Callumkal had explained that the winds tended to blow them inland.

Moon passed the time by teaching the warriors how to fish on the wing. Then they came within sight of a set of sandbars where the skeleton of a sea creature so large it could have eaten the flying boat whole lay scattered. The water was clear and shallow enough that they saw the ribs and vertebrae and jaw hinge on the sea floor. It made Moon think of the giant waterlings of the freshwater sea. A small group of sealings played among the bones and paused to watch the flying boat pass overhead with no alarm.

Callumkal said that according to the map, the shelf of land the sea was on curved inward here, and they were skirting the edge of the ocean. That if they went straight into the wind they would eventually reach it and see the spot where the shallows dropped away into the deeps. The creature must have died there and been pushed up into the sea by the current. Moon found it tempting to fly in that direction, just to see what the ocean looked like. But they were going to see it anyway, when they got past the archipelagos.

The weather had been good for flying, another temptation. They passed through a light rain shower one day, but the rest of the time it was sunny with clouds forming ever-changing white mountains in the distance. Moon, Jade, Stone, and the warriors took flights off the deck to stretch their wings and scout ahead a little. Stone had spent enough time on Golden Islander flying boats to be adept at the trick of jumping off before shifting, and of shifting back to groundling some distance above the deck as he came in to land.

Interactions with the crew had been quiet, but there had been no hostility. Moon saw Stone and Magrim, still recovering from his broken ribs, sitting and talking near the bow. Vendoin came to sit with the Raksura and Delin in the evenings, and often Callumkal appeared.

Kalam was there every night, obviously feeling more comfortable with them now after his outing with Moon and Stone.

One night, everyone was thinking of the approaching sel-Selatra and the first sight of the ocean. They were sitting on the floor of the common room on their deck, listening to Delin tell a story of the Golden Islanders' explorations, drinking tea made on one of the ship's hearths. These were square boxes with a layer of thin stone in the bottom that never got hot, with a block of plant material in it that emitted heat, and a metal frame above it where pots could be placed. It wasn't that different from a Raksuran hearth with heating stones.

Delin was seated on a cushion, taking notes as he talked, with the Arbora and Kalam gathered around him and warriors sprawled on the floor in whatever position seemed comfortable. Moon leaned against Jade, with Chime on one side and Balm on the other. Except for the green walls and the faint sense of movement, they might have been back in the teachers' hall at Indigo Cloud.

Then Bramble asked, "Does anything live in the ocean? Anything different than in the sea? Besides fish and giant sea creatures, I mean. Are there ocean sealings?"

Still writing, Delin said, "I don't know. We know of ships that cross it, or have crossed it, but I have never traveled quite so far. Our ships are more vulnerable to weather than this one." He looked up at Stone, sitting across from the hearth. "Have you?"

Kalam, and Vendoin, who sat at the outer edge of the group, looked at Stone in surprise. Stone said, "Once or twice."

Jade sighed. "What were you doing at the ocean?"

"I got curious," Stone told her. Moon could understand that. If he had Stone's wingspan and stamina, he might go visit some interesting places too.

"What was it like?" Bramble persisted.

"Empty, mostly." Stone's expression was thoughtful. "Just wind and water in every direction. The scent is different from these seas. You can't smell land at all."

Chime leaned forward, propping an elbow on Moon's hip. "Was anything living there? That you could see?"

"Skylings, mostly," Stone said. "Like the upper air skylings we see over the Reaches, and over mountain ranges. But the swarms that these skylings feed on sometimes fly down and land on the water, and the skylings follow them and dip down and scoop them off the surface."

"Are there sealings?" Merit asked.

"I didn't see any. I did see shapes in the water. Big shapes."

"How big? As big as that skeleton we saw?" Root asked.

"Bigger than that," Stone said. "Shadows longer and wider than skylings, moving below the surface."

Everyone absorbed that in silence for a moment. Past Stone, Moon saw Rorra, standing in the doorway, listening. She caught his eye and stepped away to vanish down the corridor, the faint thump of her heavy boots on the soft material fading slowly.

Then Vendoin said, "Well, you shall all see for yourselves soon."

Later that night, Moon woke with Bramble leaning over him. "Jade, River thought he heard something."

"Like what?" Jade asked, instantly awake. Moon felt her shift to her winged form, the change in the heat and shape of her body as she uncoiled from around him.

"Something big, moving through the air outside."

Moon sat up. "Is it—" He had started to ask if it was Stone, taking advantage of a clear night to stretch his wings, but Stone stood beside the window, head tilted to listen. River still crouched by the door for his turn at guard, and the others were stirring. Balm stepped over Merit to stand beside the bed.

"Can anyone hear it now? Stone?" Jade asked.

After a moment, Stone nodded. "He's right."

Moon saw River's tense posture relax a little. If anyone else had mistaken a wind shear for a wingbeat in the middle of the night, it would have been cause for some teasing and complaint and forgotten by the time everyone fell back asleep. Moon wasn't sure if River making that mistake would have been any different, but River evidently thought so.

Jade climbed over Moon and out of the bed. Moon rolled out after her and grabbed his clothes from the shelf overhead. Even if he had to shift, he wanted to have them with him. Jade said, "Chime, Merit?"

Merit replied first, "I'm not having a vision." Somewhat testily, he added, "And yes, before anyone mentions it, I know that's not unusual." Merit's augury had continued to be uninformative, and it was bothering him more than it was anyone else.

Chime hesitated. "I don't hear anything. Not just with my ears, I mean—"

"I know what you mean," Jade told him.

That's a relief, Moon thought, rapidly tying the drawstring on his pants. Though it could still be Fell, since with the strong wind the Fell stench would be hard to scent. Or it could just be a gigantic predator.

Everyone was awake now, scrambling out of the way as Jade stepped across to the doorway. She said, "Balm, Moon, Chime, Stone, with me. The rest of you stay here for now."

Bramble said, urgently, "Jade, Delin went back to his room."

Jade paused in the doorway. "I want a warrior within arm's reach of each Arbora. And Delin."

Moon followed her down the corridor. She was already thinking ahead to what they would do if something attacked the flying boat. Moon hoped that wouldn't happen. And he hoped Callumkal had those flying packs for all the groundlings on the crew.

Jade reached the stairwell and started up. Moon shifted to follow her, flowing up the steps. He scented Rorra before he saw her, and heard her say, "What—"

As he reached the top of the stairs Rorra stood in the open common area there. She was dressed in a loose sleeping robe and her boots, wide-eyed and startled. Jade paused to tell her, "Something big flew past the boat."

"Something—" she repeated blankly, then comprehension dawned. She turned and strode down the passage toward the steering cabin.

Moon came out onto the deck behind Jade. The lamps were set low to protect the look-outs' vision, but to Raksuran eyes it still made the boat a bubble of light surrounded by walls of solid darkness. Moon leapt up, caught hold of the center ridge, and climbed to the top.

After a moment, his vision cleared and he saw the sweep of stars overhead, the blend of indigo and violet in the sky, blotted out in a few places by clouds. And one of the clouds was moving. He whispered, "There it is."

Chime, clinging to the ridge below him, said, "Oh, it is big."

Below, Stone went to the railing and Jade and Merit toward the bow. Balm scaled the lower end of the ridge, heading for the other side of the boat. Moon tasted the air deeply, sorting out the scents of saltwater, sand, the flying boat, a trace of rotting fish from some distant island or sandbar. He caught the scent of the intruder then, musky and metallic and strange. He tracked the shape as it circled the boat. It curved downwind, then abruptly veered away. It dipped to pass under the boat and then shot out toward the sea.

Moon watched it streak away into the night, until the dark shape vanished into the horizon. He waited, his spines tense, but it didn't reappear. The night felt empty again, untenanted except for the boat itself.

Jade stood on the bow railing. She hopped lightly down and started down the deck with Merit. Balm climbed up to join Moon, asking, "Did you see it?"

Moon said, "I saw it, I couldn't tell what it was. Could you?"

She dropped her spines in a negative. "I thought it was shaped like a cloudwalker. But that could have been my imagination."

Clearly annoyed, Chime said, "I didn't hear a thing. This is one of those times my useless ability is even more useless than usual."

"It's not useless," Moon said. "You're just mad because you got woken up for nothing."

Chime's irritated spine flick showed that was accurate. Balm said, "Maybe you didn't hear anything because it didn't mean us any harm."

"No, that's not it." Chime looked up at the sky. "You have to remember, it's not like what a mentor can do. Mentors can scry things that pertain to us, that are going to affect us at some point. The things I hear are usually useless."

Balm nudged him. "Except when they're not."

Rorra and Callumkal came out of the doorway below. They flinched when Chime swung down to land on the deck near them, and he said, "Sorry."

Moon climbed down after him, Balm following. As Jade approached, Callumkal said, "What was it?"

"I couldn't tell." She looked at Balm and Moon.

Balm lifted her spines in a helpless shrug. "Maybe a cloudwalker, but I'm really not certain."

Merit was equally baffled. "There was nothing I could recognize."

Stone came strolling back from the rail. They all looked hopefully at him and he said, "I have no idea."

"Not a cloudwalker?" Moon asked.

Stone shook his head, turning to look toward the horizon again. "Cloudwalkers don't come down this far just to look at a groundling flying boat, especially in the dark. At night they drift on the upper currents and sleep."

Chime said, "Maybe we woke it up and it was curious."

Exasperated, Stone said, "It went straight away, not up. And it went because it scented us. That's not a cloudwalker or any other kind of upper air skyling."

Callumkal said, reluctantly, "Well, it did no harm. Whatever it was, perhaps it was just curious."

Jade moved her spines, then, remembering Callumkal couldn't read that as agreement, said, "Probably."

Callumkal stepped back inside, though Rorra stayed on the deck and walked out to the railing to look into the dark, the wind pulling at her robe. Jade asked Merit, "Can you scry about this?"

Merit nodded. "I'll do it tonight."

By dawn, Callumkal reported that they were within the boundaries of the sel-Selatra, and should be drawing near a sea-mount soon. Moon, Chime, and Delin went up into the bow for the first glimpse of it, though the clouds had come in and mist obscured much of the view.

Delin was cranky because no one had woken him to not see the nighttime visitor. "Next time, you must tell me," he insisted. "It could have been an entirely new species, or new to our studies, glimpsed for the first time."

"It might have smashed the boat and eaten us all," Chime pointed out. "Or it might have just been a cloudwalker. Merit's augury wasn't much help."

Merit had reported the results of his efforts earlier that morning. "I saw a hive floating on the water," he had told Jade.

Waiting for the results in their cabin, Moon had fallen asleep again and was still lying curled on the bunk next to Jade. For a moment, he thought he was still asleep, but everyone else seemed to have heard it, too. Jade said, "You saw a what?"

Merit thumped down on the deck and sighed, and rubbed his face. "I know. It doesn't make any sense. I'm beginning to think you should have brought Thistle instead. I haven't gotten anything since we started."

Bramble gave him a shove to the shoulder. "We have a ways to go yet. You still have time to try."

"Just tell me about the hive," Jade said patiently.

Merit shook his head, resigned. "It was big, and it was floating on the water. This sea, somewhere. That's all I saw."

Moon sat up on one elbow. Stone, sitting on the floor with Balm and Bramble, was staring thoughtfully at a wall. Moon asked, "Have you ever seen anything like that?"

"That's what I was trying to remember." Stone grimaced. "No, I don't think so. That doesn't mean it doesn't exist."

Jade tapped her claws. "Maybe it will make sense later." She told Merit, "It's all right, Merit. Try to get some rest."

Merit had wandered off with Bramble, a little reassured. Later, Moon had talked to Chime about it, who had offered the opinion that a hive floating on the sea was too odd an image to be entirely random. But there was no telling what it meant.

Now, standing out on the bow, Moon spotted something in the distance. It was a long straight shape rising out of the mist. "I think that's it."

"What?" Chime squinted into the distance. "Oh, there."

Moon pointed for Delin, who wouldn't be able to see it yet. "Keep looking that way."

After a time, the shape sharpened and Moon could make out that it looked like a tower, unbelievably tall. The top would be some distance above the flying boat when it passed by. But not so tall that Raksura couldn't fly up to it, unless the wind up there was much worse than at this level. After a time, Delin said, "Ah, I see it."

As the day went by and the boat drew closer, Moon made out more detail. The sides weren't smooth as they had looked from a distance, but rough and craggy. Vegetation clung to pockets and ledges, and it looked like there might be some on top, though it was hard to see from this angle. He couldn't see the base, since the mist was obscuring the surface of the sea at its feet.

He felt Jade behind him and looked to see her and Balm walking up the deck. He asked her, "Are you thinking what I'm thinking?"

Jade's spines lifted, her gaze on the sea-mount. "Let's take a look."

"Are you sure you will be safe?" Vendoin asked, standing at the rail and worriedly regarding the sea-mount. Callumkal had confirmed that the top of the sea-mount was too high for the flying boat or the Kishan's flying packs.

"If the wind is too strong, we'll come back down," Jade told her.

Moon was already shifted and perched on the railing, ready to go with the warriors. The Arbora and Delin were lined up to watch, Jade having told them that they had to stay behind, at least until she decided how dangerous it was. All three of them had protested this decision and there was a general air of disgruntlement hanging over the deck. Even some of the Kishan crew seemed envious. Esankel the navigator said, "See if you can make out any islands to the south. I want to verify our maps."

Stone was staying behind as well, leaning on the rail with the others. It was Jade's order that they never left the Arbora alone on the boat, if there was any way to avoid it.

Moon asked him, "You sure you don't want to see it? We could send the warriors back and then you could come up."

Stone shrugged one shoulder. "I've seen one before. And somebody has to stay down here and keep an eye on the boat."

"So you're just tired?" Moon said.

Stone pushed him off the railing. Moon let himself fall past the boat and then spread his wings, catching the air and testing the wind as he circled. Above him, Jade leapt off the boat and snapped her wings out, the warriors falling into the air after her.

Moon flapped to catch up and they flew toward the sea-mount. Jade led them in a broad circle around it, partly to examine the sides at closer range, partly feeling out the winds.

It helped that the currents weren't particularly strong today, though Moon wouldn't have wanted to try to land on the side of the sea-mount. Or he wouldn't have wanted one of the smaller warriors to try it. He thought he and Jade, and certainly Stone, might be strong enough to ride the current up to the wall of rock and catch hold without losing control. Taking off, however, might be tricky.

The rocky walls were covered with random blue and gray streaks, probably mineral veins uncovered by years of wind and rain. The rock was also riddled with little holes, which might possibly be signs of some form of life, though Moon didn't see any movement and couldn't scent anything but the sea wind. The mist had cleared somewhat and he could see the bottom now, or at least the point where the rocky tower plunged into the sea. There were tumbled rocks around it and what looked like the meandering lines of reefs, visible through the clear shallow water. There was nowhere for a water boat to land, and nothing that looked like it had been intentionally constructed.

Jade started to spiral upward toward the top, and he tilted his wings to follow her.

They went up and up, until Moon could glance back and look down at the flying boat, small in the distance. Finally they reached the top and circled above it. The space was flat and a few hundred paces across, with a small jungle of vegetation, mostly ferny plants and grasses, low bushes, and some fruit vines. Moon couldn't see or scent anything besides plant life. The wind was strong across the top but there was nothing to smash into, so Jade curved around and dropped down to land.

Moon dropped onto the soft grass beside her and folded his wings. A cloud of startled insects with glassy, brightly-colored wings shot out of the bushes and streamed away into the undergrowth. The warriors all landed around them, though Chime stumbled forward in the high wind. He was a much better flier now than when Moon had first met him, but not being born with wings had its disadvantages.

Then River, so distracted he forgot to sound sullen, said, "Oh, look!"

He was staring toward the west. Moon followed his gaze, and saw the ocean.

It was still some distance away, but the line where the crystal blue of the shallow sea suddenly turned deep indigo was clear to see. That dark water stretched forever, until it met the clouds on the horizon.

There was silence while everyone absorbed the sight. Then Root said, "I don't see any giant sealings."

Since Stone wasn't here, Moon gave Root a shove to the head. Root grinned and ducked.

Jade settled her spines, and turned away from the view with some reluctance. "Everyone take a look around the sea-mount now. Be careful."

"Uh, what are we looking for?" Song asked.

Jade lifted her spines in a shrug. "Forerunners. Foundation builders. Fell. Anything that makes us think this is something other than a strange skinny mountain."

The others spread out, and Moon started on a circuit around, poking into the undergrowth and brush. After a short time they met back in the middle, and Jade asked, not hopefully, "Anything?"

Everyone moved their spines in a negative. Moon hadn't raised anything but insects; he felt lucky he wasn't wearing his groundling skin.

"There's no sign anyone built it." Chime sounded disappointed. He kicked absently at a clump of grass. "Or used it for anything."

"Esankel was right about the islands to the south," Song put in, "but that's all there is to see."

There might be some sign of occupation under the plants but most of them seemed to be growing right out of cracks in the rock. Moon had to agree; if there had been anything here it was long gone, or buried in the stone where they couldn't find it.

"Why would anyone want to build something like this?" Briar asked, turning to look around again. "What would it be for?"

"Same reasons groundlings build towers on land," Moon said.

Briar had very little prior experience with groundlings, except for the Kishan on this boat and meeting Delin's wind-ship crew. "What are those reasons?"

"As a resting spot, for long flights across the sea?" Balm suggested.

"That's a thought," Jade agreed.

"Or for signaling, maybe." Moon was thinking of signal lights for groundling ships, or the flares that the Golden Islanders used. "If there was a light up here, flying boats and water boats could use it to help navigate."

"Why do they need help navigating?" Briar clearly found the notion baffling.

"Groundlings don't always know where south is, like we do," Chime told her. "At least the Golden Islanders don't."

Briar took in that information with a startled expression. Balm said to Jade, "Should we get back?"

"Might as well." Jade hissed out a sigh. "At least it broke up the day."

Catching the wind from the top was easy, and they managed to get into the air without incident. They cleared the tower and dropped down to land on the deck of the flying boat. A hopeful group of Arbora, Kishan, and one Golden Islander immediately surrounded them. Stone was there too, but he was leaning back against the railing, not looking particularly hopeful. The Kish-Jandera must have been staring into the wind, trying to see the Raksura, because their milky inner eyelids were all half-closed.

"Nothing," Jade said, before anyone could demand information. "Just plants and bugs."

"Well," Callumkal said, trying to conceal disappointment. "It was worth a try. And still, now we know what the top of a sea-mount looks like, or at least this variety of sea-mount. If you would be good enough to give me an exact description—"

"Chime can do that," Jade told him. "He can write it for you in Altanic, then you can ask us questions."

Delin took out his drawing book. "I can make a sketch from your descriptions. Here, Balm and Briar, while your memories are fresh . . ."

This seemed to improve Callumkal's mood a great deal. He said, "That would be excellent. I'll go and get my writing materials."

As Callumkal went to the hatchway and the other Kishan dispersed in disappointment, Jade said, "I was really hoping we'd find something."

Moon wasn't sure what that something would be, but Chime said, "Something to prove we're right about the city or wrong about it. So we can stop wondering."

"It won't be long now." Delin shielded his eyes to look into the distance. "Soon I think we will know."

By late the next day, they had seen six more similar sea-mounts in the distance, and according to the map were nearing another area of sparse islands. Moon was sunning himself on the flat top of the flying boat's ridge, near the bow. Chime was a little further up the ridge from him, though at some point he had drifted off to sleep.

Moon was aware a few of the warriors were lying on the bow deck below, but he hadn't paid much attention to them until he heard River say, "Did Jade say if we were going to check out any of the other sea-mounts? These should have even better views of the ocean."

It was such an innocuous question, it took several moments for Moon to realize no one had answered it. He sat up on one elbow and looked down.

River lay a short distance from Balm and Briar. All three were in groundling form, the sun bringing out bronze and copper highlights in the brown of their skin, glinting off the bright colors of their clothes. They had all been bathing and washing clothing in the sea to save the boat's stored water, with Stone to make sure no predators swam near, so they all still looked fairly presentable. River said, "Is it a secret, then?"

Still no response. Then River snarled to himself, flung himself to his feet, and stamped off down the deck.

Groaning under his breath, Moon rolled off the ridge and landed on the deck. Balm and Briar both twitched around to stare at him. Moon said, "Balm, can I talk to you?"

Balm exchanged a puzzled look with Briar, but got to her feet. Moon stepped back behind the cistern fastened to the side of the ridge, out of Briar's earshot. He said, "What was that about with River?"

Balm sighed. She would obviously have preferred to say it was none of Moon's business, but since he was the first consort, theoretically everything in the court was his business up until Pearl or Jade said it wasn't. She said, "I don't speak to River. He knows that."

Moon frowned. "When did you stop speaking to him?"

"Since the Fell made me almost get everyone killed." Balm's brow furrowed, and she looked away. It was obviously still a painful memory. Especially since all Balm had ever been able to recall properly was the moment when Flower had discovered the Fell influence on her. She had never been sure when or where it had happened. "Since before we came to the Reaches."

"Balm—" Moon tried to remember if he had ever seen Balm speak directly to River in a way that wasn't hostile, or not a general command to a group of warriors. "Does Jade know this?"

Balm bit her lip, considering it. "Probably . . . not."

Moon controlled an exasperated hiss. "Why didn't I know this?"

Balm's expression said the answer was obvious. "Because you'd do this, talk to me about it. Or get angry. You're just as bad as Stone, except you still care what we do."

"I have to care because the others are following your lead."

Balm bared her teeth briefly in frustration.

Bramble came down the deck, spotted them, and leaned in around the cistern, brows lifted in curiosity. "What are you doing?"

Hoping for rational help, Moon asked her, "Did you know Balm hasn't spoken to River since before we got to the Reaches?"

Bramble regarded Balm in surprise, then rolled her eyes. "Warriors," she said in disgust, and unhelpfully withdrew.

"Balm—" Moon wanted to say, *you're supposed to be the sensible one*, but it didn't seem entirely fair. Balm was the sensible one, but she was also entitled to her feelings about River. There was a reason so many warriors in the court had turned against him when Pearl had rejected him. River had even bullied Chime once, which Moon had dealt with by beating River nearly unconscious. After that River's conflicts with Chime had all been verbal, and Chime usually won. "If you want to play those games in the court, I can't stop you." Moon could, probably, but it would start far more trouble than it would stop. "But you can't do it here."

"I'm not a fledgling, I know we can't fight while we're doing this." She folded her arms uncomfortably. "I'll be more polite." At Moon's expression, she added, "It's not like I'm going to let him die, or anything."

It was grudging, but Moon suspected that was as much as he was going to get. "I'd appreciate that."

Balm hesitated. "Are you going to tell Jade?"

"Jade doesn't want to know this." Moon was pretty certain Jade already had enough to worry about. And if Jade had noticed and hadn't already talked to Balm about it herself, it meant she didn't want to discuss it and was hoping no one else had noticed. "I'll ask Bramble not to say anything."

Balm smiled a little. "Bramble won't. She knows how we are."

As Balm went back to Briar, Moon rubbed his face and sighed.

Chime climbed down from the ridge above, asking softly, "What happened?"

"Nothing," Moon told him. "Warriors being warriors."

"I know," Chime said with a groan. "We're irrational. It's so exasperating. It's one of the things I hate most about changing."

CHAPTER ELEVEN

Niran lay in his narrow bunk in the steering cabin of the *Koltera*, face buried in a too-thin pillow, and was not much amused when Tlar opened the door and stood over him. "What is it?" he groaned. He had taken the last night watch and it was Diar's turn for the morning. They were passing over wetlands and the dampness in the air clung to the bedding and made sleeping uncomfortable, but he was determined to do it.

"Some Raksura arrived," Tlar said.

"Raksura?" Niran heaved himself up on one elbow and squinted blearily up at Tlar. "From Indigo Cloud?" If they had heard from Delin, received some message . . .

Niran was furious with Delin. He was well acquainted with the fact that his grandfather did as he pleased, indifferent to danger. Delin was a scholar and an explorer, and it didn't matter how many others had died while pursuing his vocation, he was determined to continue it. "We're lucky he didn't choose to study the Fell," Diar had said once, unsympathetically. His sister was always unsympathetic toward Niran's attempts to keep grandfather close to home; she felt that if they allowed Delin to do as he pleased he would include them in his plans and make it easier to watch over him.

This had not worked in the Kish-Jandera city, when they had come back from a day of trade meetings to find a note saying Delin was not at the library of Kedmar but had left for the Reaches with an expedition of Kishan scholars.

"Did he say he was kidnapped?" Diar had asked Blossom and Heart and Bell and the others who had received them at the Indigo Cloud colony. "We couldn't tell from his note, but he left most of his things behind, as if he was given no time to pack."

"Or did he trick them into taking him?" Niran had added. "You know what he's like."

The Arbora had all demurred, until Blossom reluctantly admitted, "I don't think he ever said."

Niran knew Blossom well from his own long journey with the court, and he couldn't fault her for refusing to betray the old man. But the Raksura did not age as the Islanders did, and had little idea how fragile a man grandfather's age could be.

Now Tlar said, "No, from the other settlement, the one further west that grandfather wrote about. The queen is here. She's . . . large." She made an expansive gesture. "And she brought the consort and the mentor who are partly Fell."

"I'll be right there." Considerably more awake, Niran flung off the blanket. Tlar stepped out of the cabin as he hurriedly dressed.

He stepped outside to see Diar seated on the deck, facing a Raksuran queen even larger than the intimidating Pearl. Delin had described Malachite of Opal Night, but seeing her with one's own eyes was a whole different experience. Even this crew, used to Raksura enough to be at ease with them, stared uneasily.

Belin was serving a pot of grain water with slightly trembling hands, but Diar had the map spread out and appeared to be explaining their route as if nothing was out of the ordinary. A dozen brightly-colored warriors were perched around on the railing, as well as one dark creature with an armored crest that after a startled moment Niran identified as the half-Fell consort.

An Arbora in her soft-skinned form sat on the deck behind Malachite. That should be the half-Fell mentor, though she looked like an ordinary Raksura to Niran. She was smaller than the others, her skin a dark red-brown, and her dark hair cut short and standing out in a halo around her face. She was dressed in simple clothes like a wind-sailor would wear, a longer tunic with a light shirt over it and pants cut off at the knee. She wouldn't have gotten more than a second look at any

Yellow Sea port; there was nothing to show she was Raksura, much less part Fell.

With an impenetrable calm born of much experience exploring the Three Worlds, Diar said, "Malachite, reigning queen of Opal Night, this is my brother Niran."

Speaking in Altanic, Malachite said, "We want to travel with you. You have no objection?"

Adjusting to months of living alone with Raksura while Indigo Cloud had returned to its ancestral home in the Reaches had been difficult; this was nothing. And considering the evidence of Fell attack that the Kishan had reported, and Delin's own worries about what might be inside the sea-mount city, it would be madness to refuse a Raksuran escort. No matter how harrowing the queen was. Niran said, "None at all."

The next day, it was made plain to everyone just how useful it was to have Raksura aboard.

It was midafternoon and Niran was out on deck with Diar, consulting over the map. "There's no way we'll catch them in flight," Diar said. "We're faster, but we have no idea if they're going through the archipelago or straight across."

It was frustrating that the Kish hadn't marked any route on the map the Raksura had managed to obtain. "Or if they're planning to stop on the way," Niran agreed. "I just hope grandfather hasn't managed to get himself killed in the meantime."

"You should have more confidence in him." Diar jerked her head toward the stern, where the Raksura had settled in, the warriors draping themselves all over the deck and the cabin roof. Malachite was nowhere to be seen, but then Niran hadn't seen her all day. She seemed able to vanish at will. Diar continued, "He has friends with him now, at least."

Niran wasn't sure that was any better, since the Raksura just gave grandfather more mobility and opportunities to find something that might kill him. He was about to say so when the consort Shade wandered up and asked, "When will we get to the sea?"

At first, Niran had had no idea what to say to someone who was half-Fell. But Shade had proved unexpectedly easy to speak to, mostly because he wasn't hesitant to ask questions. "This is much faster than Delin's wind-ship," Shade had said on the first day, while leaning precariously far out over the rail. The Aeriat Raksura's complete lack of concern for heights was one thing Niran had never gotten used to. "But it's so much bigger."

"This ship has a more powerful sustainer," Niran had told him. The *Koltera* was the largest wind-ship the family owned, and meant for exploration rather than trade. Her cargo space was given over to water containers and food supplies, and she was meant to travel long distances without needing to stop. "Most of our wind-ships only need one or two chips of flying island heart to support them on the lines of force. This one has seven."

This had turned into an explanation of how exactly the sustainer worked and how the size of the rock chips dictated the configuration of the wind-ship and how the *Koltera* was this length in order to balance the force contained in each, and then a tour of the ship's steering cabin. Lithe, the mentor, had followed along, shy but interested in everything as well.

"Perhaps by morning," Diar said to Shade now, turning the map so he could see it. "I think we're—"

The lookout called a warning an instant before three shapes dropped out of the sky and landed on the ship's rail.

Diar drew in a startled breath. Niran stared, astonished both at the temerity and the stupidity. The creatures had rounded bodies and broad, nearly translucent wings. Their arms and legs were long and stick-like, and whatever features were on their round heads were buried in a multi-layered, brightly-colored shell. It was like being confronted by something with a flower for a head. An instant later Niran realized they wore tool belts fastened to their bodies, with various grass-woven pouches suspended from them.

Diar demanded, "What do you want?"

The largest one spoke in rough Altanic, "You're in our air. We demand payment."

Niran snorted in annoyance. "We don't pay tribute."

The nearest female warrior, a large muscular person called Saffron, was suddenly between Shade and the interlopers. She snarled, "You're on the wrong boat."

The lead flower-head hesitated, perhaps taking in the fact that there were six Raksura sunning themselves nearby on the deck, now awake and watching with the intense focused interest of predators. One of the other flower-heads fell backward off the railing.

Shade turned toward them, shifted, and half-lifted his wings. He said, in his deeper raspy voice, "Don't make me wake my mother."

The last two flower-heads finally seemed to realize they had made a terrible mistake. They dropped off the railing and flew away, fleeing rapidly back toward the hills just visible past a stand of tall plane trees.

A male warrior strolled up, baring his fangs so he could pick his teeth with a twig. "Should we chase them?"

"No." Shade rippled and changed back into his smaller self. "Just watch to make sure they don't follow us." He turned back to Diar and the map. "Were we going through these islands? Or straight across this way?"

Niran exchanged a look with Diar. Possibly it was madness to associate with Raksura; Niran had thought so once and there were undoubtedly those who thought so now. But then everyone aboard was related to Delin, so madness ran in the family. Turning her attention back to Shade, Diar said, "Yes, we take the direct route."

Over the next few days, Moon couldn't tell if talking to Balm had helped or not. He had the feeling that it hadn't, that it had just made the warriors more careful how they behaved when he could see them.

They were out on deck, watching the sea as the sun set. The wind was down and the gentle swells were full of tiny sparks of blue light, either plant or animal or both. It was fascinating, and all the Raksura, Delin, and most of the crew had found a spot to watch it. Moon was on top of the steering cabin with Jade, Balm, Chime, and Briar, taking advantage of the heat that the soft material was radiating. They were all in groundling form, and Jade in her Arbora form, to enjoy it better. Lying on his side with Jade's arm around his waist, watching the flickering water, Moon wished they could have taken this trip for no other reason than just to see things like this. Then Chime said, "There's something out there."

Jade sat up and Moon rolled over to face Chime. He crouched on the edge of the cabin, staring toward the south. Chime pointed. "See the outline in the water?"

There were murmurs of assent from the others as they twisted around to look. A black shape was outlined against the blue flickers of light that rode the constant movement of the water. It was still some distance away. Jade said, "An island?"

Chime shook his head. "It's drifting."

Balm said slowly, "It's not . . . Merit said a hive, didn't he? Floating on the water?"

Moon tasted the air deeply. It occurred to him suddenly that a hive floating on the water might actually be a giant Fell sac, used like a portable island. But there was no Fell stench in the wind.

Jade shifted to her winged form. "That's what he said. Briar, go tell Stone, ask him if he can see it any better than we can."

Moon rolled back over and hung down to look into the steering cabin's window. It was softly lit, and he could see Magrim holding the steering lever. He had been judged recovered enough to be allowed back on duty a few days ago. Moon tapped on the crystal. Magrim glanced over, startled, then stepped to the window to open the catch. "What is it?"

"There's something to the south, something big, drifting on the surface."

Magrim turned immediately to call to someone, "Find Callumkal!"

Jade made the decision to investigate immediately, but Callumkal was out on deck by then and tried to convince her to wait until morning. "Surely it is too dangerous now," he said.

The Kishan had covered the deck lights and they were standing in the dark. It made the shape of the hive easier to see, floating on the sparkling water. Moon kept his gaze on it; it made his spines prickle nervously.

Jade replied, "There's no movement. Whoever they are, or whatever it is, they don't know we're here."

They were unconsciously keeping their voices low, though they were too far away for any potential inhabitants of the hive to hear them. They hoped. Moon sympathized with Callumkal's concern, but they still needed to do this.

"Probably don't know we're here," Delin corrected. "This may be a trap." Bramble and Merit stood in mutinous silence, though it wasn't quite as mutinous as Briar, Root, and Song, who had been ordered to stay behind with them.

"We'll be fine," Jade said. She swung up onto the railing. "Just don't bring the boat any closer."

She dropped over the railing and Moon, Chime, Balm, and River followed.

Moon tilted his wings to ride the wind down and circle above the structure. He heard the whoosh of air behind him, the distinctive sound of Stone's wings. Stone had jumped off the stern of the boat and shifted in midair.

There was still no stench of Fell, but no scent of anyone else, either. The light was just enough for Raksuran eyes to make out the domed shapes of multiple hives, though Moon couldn't see anything in detail. Then they flew over a structure like a flat open cup that stood out from the side of the larger hive.

They came around for another pass, and Jade said, "I'm going to try to land on that flat spot."

Behind them, Stone made a noise between a snort and a growl. Moon said, "Jade, no. That could be the mouth," but she was already diving down.

As Moon landed beside her, she said, "It's not the mouth."

The platform, whatever it was, crackled underfoot. Its scent was more plant than animal but plants could be predators too. Moon said, "It could still be the mouth."

"This is dried seaweed." Jade moved cautiously forward. "And that's a door."

Moon was tempted to argue that it was a throat, but managed not to. He was starting to think she was right. There were faint crunches behind him as the warriors landed. Something dark loomed over them, vanished abruptly, then Stone dropped down onto the platform in his groundling form. Startled, the warriors flinched away and Moon hissed.

Jade snapped, "Stop that. Who has a light?"

Chime dug a lighted object out of the bag around his neck and handed it to Moon. It was one of the metal cups from the flying boat, spelled for light. Merit must have been in a hurry. He passed it to Jade, and she stepped into the opening and held it up.

The glow showed them walls made of dark seaweed, the long fronds woven and braided together. Jade furled her wings and moved further in. Moon followed, with the others behind him.

The opening led to a passage spiraling down into the structure. Moon started to scent other odors. Rotting fruit, rotting vegetation. Jade said, "Something with hands made this. It wasn't . . ."

"Extruded," Chime supplied, from behind Moon. "That's what I was thinking."

Stone said, "Jade, hold the light up higher."

Jade stopped and lifted the cup. Looking up, Moon realized the roof was high and net bags hung from it. His mind still on Fell, for a moment he tried to see their contents as dead groundling bodies. But while he was looking at a larder, it wasn't for the Fell. The bags held various water plants, ropey vines, the kind of melons that grew under the sand of both fresh and saltwater beaches. There were crustacean shells also, and pieces of driftwood. "Their supplies," Balm said softly. "They must be sealings, or some kind of waterlings."

It was reassuring, but . . . *Where are they?* Moon thought. This place felt empty.

Jade moved on. After two more spirals down, she stopped. "I hear something. Breathing?"

Stone said, "It's below us. There's a little movement, too."

Moon felt prickles of unease crawl up his back under his scales and spines. Chime twitched nervously.

They continued on, following those faint traces of sound through the maze of the structure. Then Jade said, "There's something ahead." She raised her voice a little and added, "We apologize for entering your craft, or dwelling."

Moon stepped up beside her, head tilted to catch any faint sound. Just past the edge of the light was a doorway. Past it something was breathing. Or a lot of somethings were breathing. It was a muted rushing sound, like a hundred little puffs of wind.

There was a long pause, and then a faint vibration through the woven floor as something moved in the room ahead. Moon twitched a little, realizing Stone was standing at his other shoulder, having stepped up from behind in complete silence.

Then a hesitant, raspy voice spoke. It was clearly a language, but Moon couldn't pick out individual words. It sounded like modulated rushes of air. More voices joined in.

Jade said, "I can't understand you," and stepped into the doorway. Her spines twitched in surprise. Behind her, Moon angled for a view, and stared. *All right, that's new.*

The inside of the room was filled with niches, and more than half of them were occupied with different beings. They were all small, the biggest no more than a pace high, and all translucent, with various arrays of tentacles, pincers, or fins. Some had bulbous heads, some had no head at all. Some toward the top of the room began to glow, gradually lighting the room with a faint blue illumination. A large group tumbled out of their niches, but instead of coming toward the Raksura invading their domain, they gathered in a tight clump in the center of the room.

They clung to each other in a heap, then stood up.

Jade hissed in wonder. "Have you ever seen—"

"No." Moon had never seen anything like this.

Behind him, Chime whispered, "What is it?"

Moon said, "There was a bunch of them, and they got together and made a person."

"It's not as disgusting as some things we've seen," River pointed out. He was right about that.

The sturdier beings had formed three legs, others clung to each other atop them to form the torso, and two longer ones hung off it to make arms, the short tentacles at the ends of their bodies acting as fingers. A bulbous one at the top seemed to be the head. It spoke again, from a mouth that opened in the center of the torso, and this time Moon could hear individual words, though he still didn't understand them.

Stone said, "That's a sea-trade language." He moved Moon out of the way by the shoulders and stepped into the room. He spoke a few words. "I told it—them—we're travelers."

The tentacle-hands, glowing faintly, the fingers connected by translucent wisps of skin, moved in an open-handed gesture. It spoke for a time. Stone said, "It's asking us if we've seen others like them."

"That's an easy answer," Balm said softly.

Stone spoke again. The other beings came closer to listen, several fluttering down from the upper portions of the room on filmy wings. Stone frowned, glancing back at Jade. "I told it we hadn't seen any others. It asked me how long we've been traveling in the air."

"That thing that came near the flying boat—" Moon began.

Jade finished, "Was it them?"

Stone waved a hand. "It was them. Now quiet, I'm trying to get them to tell me why they're looking for these others."

Moon looked around the room at all the little beings watching from their niches, or from the floor. If they could form a flying creature of that size, what else could they do? He wondered if they had only formed an upright shape because they were imitating the Raksura.

Balm had moved a little distance down the corridor. "If some of them are missing, that would explain why this place feels so empty."

"And why there are so many supplies," Chime added.

Moon turned back as Stone said, "A large group—I have no idea how many, I can't understand that part—went out gleaning some time ago and didn't return. They've been searching for them."

Moon bit back a hiss. "Another disappearance in this area." The sealings at the trading port had heard of one and they had randomly encountered another. How many had there been?

He could tell Jade was trying to keep the growl out of her voice as she said, "Have they seen signs of Fell?"

It didn't seem a difficult question, but the problem was this strange colony of beings perceived the world in an entirely different way than Raksura, or groundlings, or sealings, or anybody else Moon had ever encountered. They didn't seem to understand scent, at least not as Raksura did. They could describe things the group as a whole saw, but not in terms Stone could translate.

Moon muttered to Chime, "We've talked with plants that were better at communicating with other species."

"Plants make sense," Chime said. "Maybe they all got together because no one else understands them."

After a time of fruitless back and forth, Jade twitched her spines in resignation and said, "Tell them we'll watch for their missing companions in our travels, but we must go."

Stone spoke again, and the beings answered. Stone sighed and rubbed his face wearily. "They just asked me if I thought their friends were dead."

Moon looked away. Just because the beings were nearly impossible to communicate with didn't mean they didn't have the capacity to care for each other. And their way of living was so intimate, if they did care, they probably cared a great deal.

Jade winced. "Tell them yes."

Stone said something in the trade language, and the shape collapsed, all the little beings flowing away back to the walls. Their self-generated light started to fade. Stone stepped out of the room. "Let's get out of here and leave them alone."

They found their way up through the structure and out to the open platform. The cool wind lifted Moon's frills and took away the heavy scents of dried sea wrack and rotting vegetation. It was a relief to take to the air again, and leave the silence of the hive behind.

They returned and gathered in the common room of the flying boat, where Jade told Callumkal and Rorra and the others what had happened. Moon was standing back against the wall with Chime when he heard Vendoin ask Merit, "You can actually see the future, then?" She seemed completely astonished. "It isn't superstition?"

Chime exchanged a look with Moon and gritted his teeth. Moon shrugged. Vendoin had been polite and had seemed to readily accept them, but he had long since decided he liked the others better. There were some indications that Vendoin found them amusingly primitive. The other Kish might have had their fears about traveling with Raksura, but at least they had been honest about it.

Merit kept his temper and said, "It's not really seeing the future. The future isn't there yet, so you can't see it. We see things that might happen, as images, based on what we're doing or about to do. It's easier to scry when you're looking for something that has happened, and trying to see what effect it has on what you should do next."

Vendoin took this explanation in with blank surprise. Fortunately Callumkal got the room's attention and said, "From now on, all crew on deck will go armed, and will take turns standing ready at the bow and stern weapons. Keeping them replenished and ready to fire simply isn't enough."

It was a wise precaution, though Moon felt they should have already been doing it.

As the group around Callumkal broke up, Rorra and Kalam came over to join them. Rorra was frowning in worry. Kalam said, "It would be so much easier if Avagram hadn't died."

Chime asked, "Who?"

"He was the arcanist for the expedition, but it turned out he was ill, and he died while we were on the way to the city for the first time," Rorra explained.

"That's unfortunate," Chime said, and flicked a look at Moon.

Moon agreed. It was also convenient, if the Fell were involved, and didn't want a Kishan sorcerer around. But after so many days on board, he couldn't imagine any of these people as being under Fell influence. He knew that didn't mean anything, but it was hard not to be lulled into a sense of false security, even for him.

CHAPTER TWELVE

Finally one morning, as the sun rose, the dim shape in the distance slowly became the escarpment where the Kish said the ancient city lay. It was taller than the sea-mounts they had passed on the way here, and it stretched for some distance across the water, bigger than any other island they had seen. The gray cliffs had vertical ridges like a curtain, with greenery growing in the cracks. Above them the top of the escarpment was lost in mist.

Leaning on the railing, Chime said, "How did the Kishan even know there was anything up on top?"

"You can see the walls when the mist clears, I am told," Delin said. He made an ironic gesture. "They said it is tantalizing."

Deliberately? Moon wondered. He knew he could be overly suspicious—some people would say it was much worse than "overly"—but if this place was a trap . . . *If it was a trap, it should be easier for groundlings to get into.* The forerunner city under the island hadn't been tantalizing; it had been a fortress turned prison, well hidden, difficult to get into, and impossible for its single inmate to escape. That made much more sense.

Moon asked Delin, "Are you still conflicted about what we should do?"

"My conflict has only increased, with every step we go toward this place." Delin watched the distant shape of the formation with a grimace of distaste.

It was the next morning when they drew close enough to see the narrow rocky strip of land at the cliff's foot, not a place a sailing boat would want to try to tie up, and no room for a flying boat of any kind to dock without the wind smashing it into the cliff wall. Several hundred paces from the escarpment lay a much smaller island, with a narrow beach around it, covered with ferns and broadleaf trees and flowering brush; it was suspiciously rounded, as if it might have been shaped by intention and not random nature. Scattered around it were several smaller islands, or maybe miniature sea-mounts: rounded rock formations standing up above the water, covered with greenery, each no more than a few hundred paces across.

As the flying boat curved around the island, Moon spotted a large sailing ship anchored off the beach. This was the Kishan vessel occupied by the other half of Callumkal's expedition.

It was longer than their flying boat, with four masts with what looked like vertical expanding sails, not unlike those on a Golden Islander wind-ship, except there were many of them and the arrangement seemed far more complicated. The stern was wide and there were three levels of deck cabins stacked like stairs. "It's called a sunsailer," Kalam explained. "It's made of metal, but uses the moss like this ship does, to generate power for the motivator."

"A metal ship," Jade said in Raksuran. She looked at Merit, one spine lifted inquiringly.

Merit stared at the sunsailer for a long moment, then said reluctantly, "No, it's not the metal ship from the vision."

"Really?" Root said, "because—"

"No." Merit was certain.

Moon leaned on the railing. This sea was far too warm to be the one the mentors had described in the vision, and metal ships weren't uncommon. He wasn't sure if they should be relieved by that or not.

Two much smaller boats were anchored closer in, but they only had one mast each and looked as if they were meant for short trips away from the larger boat, and not long voyages. There was another flying boat too, Moon realized. It was a small one, not much larger than the one-masted ships, anchored on the island and drawn down by cables until it was at the level of the ferny treetops. It was constructed of green moss, like their boat, and he had mistaken it for a particularly large tree canopy.

At least there was no sign of Fell attack. Groundlings stood on the deck of the sunsailer, watching their approach.

"I'm ready to get this over with," Jade said. "Where's Stone?"

Stone stood up from behind the rain cistern at the base of the ridge and stretched. Why he had been sleeping back there, Moon had no idea, but Stone liked sleeping in odd and what would appear to be uncomfortable places. "You want to go up there now?" he asked. "Or wait for the mist to burn off?"

"Are we going to be able to see to land?" Balm frowned up at the top of the escarpment.

"We don't even know if we want to land yet," Chime pointed out.

Moon agreed. Jade flicked her spines impatiently, but seemed to be listening. She said, "I just want to stop wondering about this stupid place." She looked at Moon. "Well?"

He shrugged one shoulder. He thought they should give the wind a chance to die down, and talk to the Kish here first. "I'd wait."

She hissed out an annoyed breath.

Callumkal came out of the hatch near the end of the ridge, shielding his eyes to look toward the escarpment. "Not much to see at the moment. It should be visible by later this morning."

Jade told him, "We're talking of going up to take a look now." It was hard to tell whether she was hoping he would try to talk her into it or out of it. Moon knew that unless it was one or the other, Jade wouldn't have said anything.

Callumkal said, "Ah, I would prefer you wait, until I speak with the members of the expedition here."

Jade's spines lifted in a way that combined slightly offended surprise with inquiry. "Why is that?"

Callumkal appeared to understand her perfectly without being able to read her spines. "My colleagues are . . . not expecting you. The decision to ask for your assistance was something I didn't make until after I had spoken to Delin, and there was no way to send a message."

Chime muttered in Raksuran, "Oh, good."

Delin was frowning now too. He said, "That I understood, but I also thought that it was your decision to make. You are not the one in command of this venture?"

Callumkal said, "It isn't a question of being in command of it—"

Stone folded his arms, sighed, and wearily shook his head at the sky. Moon knew how he felt. He leaned on the railing and rubbed his face. *This can't go wrong now. Not now that we've come all this way.* Chime nudged his shoulder sympathetically.

Callumkal was still talking. "—we are a collective of scholars. I need to inform the others of my decision to ask for your help first." He looked around at them all and said with a little exasperation, "I assure you, there will be no difficulty. They will understand why your help is necessary. Haven't I proved myself to you yet? I feel we are working together very well."

"We are working with you very well, so far," Jade said pointedly. "It's your companions I'm worried about."

"I promise you, there is no need for concern." Callumkal seemed sincere. *And he probably is*, Moon thought sourly. Altogether, Callumkal was a fairly reasonable person. Fairly reasonable people often expected everyone they knew to be fairly reasonable too, and were shocked when this proved not to be the case.

The flying boat was circling in toward the island, and the crew came out on deck to start breaking out the cables to prepare to anchor it. There were some makeshift structures just above the beach and opposite the sunsailer's anchorage. These had clearly been constructed recently by the Kishan, and were mostly elaborate tent structures made of blue and white cloth, supplemented by the fern-topped saplings and branches from the island. Groundlings, mostly dark-skinned, tall Janderan like Callumkal and Kalam, and a few shorter, wider Janderi, stood on the beach, waving at the flying boat.

"They look happy," Chime said hopefully.

Moon grimaced. "I hope they're happy after they see us."

It took some time to lower the flying boat down toward the upper part of the beach, above the tide line. The crew dropped several anchor disks that didn't seem heavy at all, until one of the groundlings on the beach ran forward to twist something in the top of each one. Then they suddenly sank into the sand like heavy metal weights. The crew used them to winch the boat down until it was only about thirty paces above the sand, then opened a section of the deck and dropped a boarding ladder.

While this was going on, Jade had sent Balm to warn the rest of the warriors and the Arbora, and tell them to get their packs together, just as a precaution. She told Moon and Chime, "I told them to stay in the cabin for now. If they hear me call out, they're to go out the windows. I just want to be prepared if we have to leave in a hurry."

Moon approved the precaution, but he hoped they wouldn't need it.

Stone asked Delin, "Want to come with us?"

Delin shook his head. "If you have to leave, I will stay here, and try to bring Callumkal's companions around."

Rorra came out of the door, her boots clumping on the soft material of the deck. She frowned at the Raksura gathered at the far end of the deck, and then at Callumkal, Kalam, and Vendoin waiting with some of the crew near the ladder. She seemed undecided about which group to join, so Moon pushed away from the railing and went to her. He said, "We're worried the Kishan here won't like the fact that Callumkal brought Raksura."

Her frown turned to an irritated grimace. "Surely not. It would be ridiculous to turn away help."

It was somewhat reassuring that she hadn't anticipated any problems. Someone was climbing up the ladder, and Callumkal went to give him a hand onto the deck. This groundling was a different race, similar in build to the tall Janderan, and dressed like them, but his skin was light blue and softer in texture, and his hair was white and straight. "Who's that?" Moon asked Rorra.

"Kellimdar," she said, "A head scholar, about the same rank as Callumkal."

The groundlings spoke among themselves for a moment, probably greeting each other, then Kellimdar glanced around and saw Jade. Then he registered Stone, Delin, and Chime, then spotted Moon with Rorra. He turned back to Callumkal and his expression was not reassuring. Unless he was like Rorra, and the thunderous frown was normal for his face.

Moon watched Callumkal obviously explaining the presence of the strangers. Kellimdar's expression of deep concern, uncertainty, and mild horror meant Callumkal must be explaining exactly what the strangers were. The Raksura must have looked like odd figures to him, most of them like ordinary soft-skinned groundlings dressed in light clothing a little the worse for travel and saltwater, but with no boots, no weapons except for a couple of belt knives, none of the things groundlings usually had to carry. It would be unsettling, to know how deceptive that appearance was.

As Callumkal drew Kellimdar toward Jade and Delin, Moon went over to stand with Stone. Rorra trailed after him.

Callumkal introduced Jade, whose expression was neutral though her spines were set at a skeptical angle. Kellimdar acknowledged the introduction with a bowing motion, then turned to Callumkal and said in Kedaic, "I'll have to speak to the others. You were meant to return with more supplies, and more scholars if you could persuade any to come. That you have returned with—I feel this is ill-advised, and—"

Jade interrupted in Altanic, "I've told Callumkal, we'll attempt to reach the top of the escarpment as soon as the mist burns away."

Kellimdar hesitated, obviously caught between suspicion and pure greed at the chance to find a way into the city. "You can do this?"

Jade tilted her head. "We won't know until we try."

Callumkal said, "They had no trouble investigating the top of a seamount. And I assure you, we can use their assistance if any predators appear. And we found another indication of possible Fell presence on the way here—"

Kellimdar wasn't impressed. "We haven't had any trouble—"

"Nevertheless, you must speak of it and prepare," Vendoin interrupted. "I wish to show the Raksura the glyphs and carved images in the structure along the foot of the escarpment. May one of the small boats be prepared?" She turned to Jade. "It isn't a dangerous undertaking, only tricky, with the currents. The morning is the best time to attempt it."

Delin rubbed his hands together briskly. "Yes, I would very much like to see these images."

"Of course," Callumkal said hastily. "Rorra, would you?"

Rorra started toward the ladder. Vendoin asked Jade, "Who would like to come? Delin, perhaps, and the young one, Merit?"

Jade turned to Moon and said in Raksuran, "I'll stay here. You, Stone, Balm, and Chime take Merit and Delin. See if it looks anything like what we saw in the forerunner city."

It was a relief to have something to do, and Moon was anxious to see the carvings himself.

From the railing, Moon watched Rorra and Vendoin climb down to the beach and secure the use of one of the two smaller sailing boats, then wade out to it with a couple of the Janderi expedition members. He didn't know what explanations Vendoin was giving about the Raksura, though from the body language the Janderi were asking lots of questions. It was good of Vendoin to do this. Even if she could be a little condescending, she obviously wasn't afraid of them, and she was doing a good job of smoothing their way with the others.

Rorra brought the little boat around, and Moon and Chime shifted and carried Merit and Delin down to the deck. Balm carried Stone so he didn't have to shift and risk sinking the small boat. Moon lit on the soft material of the deck and set Merit down, then furled his wings and shifted to give the others room. Rorra, standing under the boat's canopy and holding the rod that steered it, didn't react, but the two Janderi stared in wide-eyed dismay.

Merit sat on his heels to peer down through the hatch in the deck, where Vendoin was banging around. "What's down there?"

"Supplies and storage." Vendoin's armored head and shoulders appeared above the hatch, and she handed Merit a wooden tube. "That's a distance glass."

Chime landed and set Delin down, then shifted to his groundling form. He muttered in Raksuran, "I hope they don't think we're going to eat them. I hate that."

Delin immediately went to the two Janderi. "I am the scholar Delin-Evran-lindel. What are your names?"

Both were women, one called Rasal and the older one Sarandel. Neither looked terribly reassured by Delin's courtesy or Rorra's stoicism.

Balm landed with Stone, who tugged his shirt back into place as Balm shifted to her groundling form.

Rorra called, "Ready?"

"Ready," Moon confirmed. Rorra did something with another lever, and the boat started forward.

The small boat had a light metallic hull, much like the larger sunsailer, and was about twenty-five paces long. The sail seemed just for extra speed, and Rorra and the Janderi crew hadn't bothered to unfurl it. The thing powering it was in the stern, a cross between a fungus and something Moon had heard called various names, most often a glass fish because it looked like a downturned crystal cup. Whatever it was drew the water in from the surface and expelled it below on command. They found this out because Chime immediately went to the stern to hang off the side and examine it. "Do you have to feed it?" he asked Rorra.

She shook her head. "It's a plant, lives off the sun and the saltwater." Leaning on the steering lever, she jerked her chin toward the escarpment. "The images are on a stone island right at the base."

The boat glided steadily toward the escarpment, and Moon started to feel the disruption in the wind as it dashed itself against the rock. Even down here at the base, it was bad, making choppy waves as they neared the wall's rocky feet. To reach the top, they might have to wait for a calm day. That wouldn't make the flying any easier, but it would be safer. He tasted the air deeply, but there was nothing but salt and water and the sea wrack on the rocks.

Moon moved up toward the bow with the others, Chime with him. As he stepped past the two Janderi, Rasal moved uneasily aside. Stone, Balm, and Merit all looked toward the wall at the base of the escarpment, while Delin and Vendoin both used distance glasses. Delin swayed and Moon put his hands on his shoulders to steady him. "What do you see?"

Delin snorted. "Not as much as you, I suspect."

Moon thought they were looking at the remains of a harbor, or at least a dock of some kind. From here he could see the cliff wall had been carved out, that the deep grooves and furrows were straight lines, vertical and angled in an abstract design. A short distance from the wall, pylons stood in the water, perhaps thirty paces above the surface, in a roughly rectangular arrangement with platforms between them.

Stone turned away and went over the railing, water splashing the deck as he vanished below the choppy waves. There were startled exclamations from the Janderi, and Vendoin lowered the distance glass to stare at Moon. Moon sighed. "He's fine."

From the stern, Rorra called, "How close are we?"

Sarandel told her, "About two boat lengths to the shallow. And careful, a rock shifted a few days ago and changed the currents."

Rorra muttered a curse in Kedaic that probably no one but the Raksura heard. The boat bumped against something that bounced off the hull; the groundlings swayed, but Moon was fairly certain it wasn't a rock. Balm muttered, "I hope that wasn't his head."

Moon called, "Rorra, can you stop?"

She worked the lever and the boat slowed. Something tugged gently on it to bring it nearly to a halt. Moon stepped to the side as Stone popped up out of the waves, back in his groundling form. He hooked an arm around the railing and said in Altanic, "There's a lot of stuff down there."

Delin stepped closer and Vendoin almost flung herself over the railing, demanding, "What?"

Stone shoved the wet hair out of his eyes and pointed toward the pylons. "There's a set of steps coming down from the platform at the base of the pillars on the right. It goes down about thirty paces and stops, still above the bottom. Though it's pretty shallow here."

Everyone was leaning over to listen now, even Rasal and Sarandel. Stone continued, "There are a lot of broken pylons below the surface. This was a big docking area, probably."

Chime asked, "Could you see an opening? Any way inside?"

Stone sank down a little in the water. "No, but I'm wondering about those stairs."

Merit said in Raksuran, "Can you get me something to scry with? A chip of carved rock, maybe?"

"Sure." Stone let go of the rail and sank below the waves.

A moment later Stone surfaced with a splash and handed up a fragment of tile, mud and a weed still clinging to it. Merit took it carefully, wrapped it up in a cloth, and stored it away in his bag.

Rorra called, "Are you done? I need to start the motivator again so we don't smash into those rocks."

Stone grabbed the railing and hauled himself back aboard, his clothes dripping onto the deck. Wringing out the tail of his shirt, he said, "Done."

Rorra worked the starting lever and steering bar, and the boat swayed underfoot as it turned away from the rocks. She said, "I don't think we can get much closer, not with the water so choppy."

Moon pointed toward the wall beyond the pylons. Waves washed the ledge at its base, and he could just make out the shapes carved on its surface. "Is that it?"

"Yes." Vendoin confirmed. She appeared to remember she was speaking to Raksura. "Ah, can you reach it? Without the boat?"

Moon knew he and Balm could. He glanced at Chime. "Can you do it? If not, one of us can carry you."

"Uh . . ." Chime hesitated, studying the situation. "I can get there. Don't tease me if you have to carry me back."

Balm nudged his shoulder. "We won't."

Delin was already holding his arms up for someone to carry him. Moon shifted and picked him up, and Balm shifted to lift Merit. Before Moon could ask Stone if he wanted to come, Stone went backwards over the rail again. Moon sighed. He asked Vendoin, "Do you want someone to come back for you?" He didn't want Chime to have to carry anyone, just in case.

"Thank you, no," Vendoin said, bemused. "I saw the images several times on our previous trip."

Moon crouched and leapt, snapped his wings out to catch the wind, and rode a gust to one of the pylons. He landed and had to furl his wings and clamp his claws on the wet stone surface to steady himself. Glancing down, he saw Stone's big dark shape move through the water below, weave in between the bases of the pylons, and then sink out of sight. "Exhilarating," Delin commented.

Balm landed with Merit on the next pylon. Chime overshot but curved around well before the wall and managed the landing on his second pass. He crouched, breathing hard, clinging to the top of his pylon. Balm and Merit watched worriedly.

"You did good," Moon told Chime, thinking, *I'm definitely carrying him back.*

Chime nodded, his spines flicking anxiously. "Right, yes. That was fun."

Balm took the long jump across to the ledge and set Merit on his feet. It was a wider space than it looked, about six paces, but half of it was awash. Moon went next and set Delin down. His foot claws were washed by cool seawater, and the wind pulled a little at his spines and frills, but it wasn't a bad perch. They all watched as Chime made the leap, and landed without a stumble. "That part was easy," he told them, clearly a little annoyed at their concern.

Merit thumped him in the arm. "It didn't look easy."

Delin turned to the wall to examine the images. The water churned, then Stone popped up in groundling form. He sat on the ledge, squinting at the wall. Moon turned to look and found himself staring at the carved figure of a forerunner.

The images were scattered along the wall, along with symbols and figures he couldn't guess the meaning of. Delin, Chime, and Merit moved up and down the ledge, examining everything in detail. Chime touched the cut-out section where the tile they had seen on the boat had been removed.

To get out of the way, Moon withdrew to the edge where Stone sat, and Balm joined them. "Were there images like this in the forerunner city?" Balm asked.

"No." Moon frowned at the wall. "It didn't look like this." He remembered Vendoin asking if the images at the forerunner city had at all resembled trading flags or other methods for displaying information for travelers. "I think this was done by someone else, for someone else."

Stone nodded toward the water. "This was a docking area for surface ships, so that makes sense."

"But wouldn't they already know they were going to a forerunner city?" Balm pointed out, her brow furrowed.

"It might not be saying that." Moon settled his spines, aware they wanted to convey unease. He wasn't even sure why, though he could see Balm reacting the same way. "It might be saying, 'if you aren't a forerunner, leave.'"

"Or," Chime said, "'If you don't have a forerunner with you, leave.' Or 'Wait here till a forerunner comes to get you.' Or anything." He sat on his heels beside Balm. "The good thing is, I'm not hearing or feeling anything. Nothing odd, I mean. No voices."

That was good news. Moon hoped the place was just an empty shell, either forerunner or foundation builder. Then the Kishan could poke at it to their hearts' content without fear of releasing anything horrible. As long as the Fell stayed away.

"But then where's the door?" Balm flicked water off her claws. "You don't put up a message like that—if that's what it is—unless it's on or near an entrance to something."

Delin, leaning so close to the wall his nose was almost resting on it, pointed at her without turning around and made a waving gesture. Chime said, "I think he agrees with you."

"The Kish took that tile out because they were looking for the door, not because they wanted the image on it," Moon said.

Stone made a "hmph" noise. "They want into this place bad. Even before they sat there on that island for the last couple of months staring at it."

That wasn't encouraging. Merit came over to them, shifting to his Arbora form so he could sit in the water on the ledge without getting his pants wet. He held another fragment of rock. "Maybe I can scry something about the door. I took this from the edge around the missing image."

Delin turned away from the wall. "Intriguing." He asked Stone, "There was no sign of an underwater door?"

Stone shook his head. "Not that I saw, not below this wall. If it's there, it's hidden well." He looked back toward the boat. "And if it's there, I don't think we want to find it. At least not until we know what we're dealing with."

Delin frowned at the boat too. "We should get back."

The wind had calmed a little and they reached the boat again without too much trouble, though Moon took two trips, one with Delin and one with Chime. Chime objected, but not too strenuously, saying, "You don't have to. I could probably make it."

This was no time to force the issue of the tricky flying that Chime had always been slow to master. Moon told him, "It's the probably part that worries me."

Once they had shifted back to their groundling forms, Rorra guided the boat back toward the island. Shielding his eyes from the glare, Moon could see Jade and the other warriors and Bramble on the beach, talking with two figures that were probably Callumkal and Kalam. Or Jade was talking to them; Bramble played in the surf with Root, and Briar and Song wandered on the beach just above, looking as if they wanted to play in the surf. The other Kishan had gone back to their camp.

It was a peaceful scene and Moon hoped it meant Kellimdar and the other scholars had agreed to accept the Raksura's presence.

Rorra took the boat back to its spot near the beach and Rasal and Sarandel dropped the anchors to keep it in position. Chime offered to fly Delin to the shore, so Moon shifted and jumped into the water.

He arrived, dripping, at Jade's side, with Chime and Delin already there, and Stone wandering up the beach behind him. Rorra was walking with Balm and Merit, while the two Janderi women headed up toward the camp.

Jade regarded him with cocked spines, and Moon said in Raksuran, "Nobody got eaten."

She snorted, and said in Altanic, "The others say the clouds generally burn off by later in the day. Callumkal says they'll give us a tent." She added in Raksuran, "The Kish here are 'uncomfortable' with the idea of sharing their camp with us, but other than that, they don't seem openly hostile."

Stone muttered, "Hmm," and wandered off toward the trees.

"Will he be all right by himself?" Kalam asked Moon, worried. "I know his other form is very large, but . . ."

"He's fine," Moon said. "Just try to ignore him."

Callumkal turned to Delin. "Did you get a good look at the images on the structure?"

Delin nodded. "Yes. We agree it is the remains of a docking point for the city. Stone was able to see steps and some continuation of the docking structure below the surface."

Callumkal stared after Stone, startled. "Below the surface. Like the underwater city the Raksura discovered?"

Delin eyed him. "Possibly. Possibly also this sea was more shallow, or entirely absent, in the time of the city's occupation and what we think is a dock is actually for land-going craft." He frowned at the escarpment. "There is no evidence to draw conclusions at this point."

Moon looked toward the escarpment again, the summit still wrapped in clouds. There was so little evidence that they couldn't draw the conclusion that there was a city there at all, except for the Kishan's word for it.

CHAPTER THIRTEEN

As predicted, it was mid-morning when the wind changed, and the clouds began to dissolve into shreds. Moon and the others went down to the beach for a better view.

They had spent the remainder of the morning setting up their camp. The tent the Kish had given them was at the edge of the main camp, and looked like it had just been pitched. Bramble and Merit had immediately taken it down, dug trenches to give it better drainage, and put it back up again in a different configuration. The warriors' attempts to assist them with this process were not appreciated. Chime dodged a swipe from Bramble for trying to help her hold a pole, and retreated over to Moon. He called back to her, exasperated, "Fine, you do it! I'll never help you with anything again!"

"Is that a promise?" Bramble called back.

Moon had just stood there, arms folded. To the Kishan watching from a distance, it would just sound like growls and hisses. If it was Moon's decision, he would have been a great deal more circumspect around strange groundlings. But it wasn't his decision.

Stone had flown out from the island, but hadn't been able to detect any Fell stench. If the Fell were nearby, they had retreated to whatever island they were using as a nest, and weren't in the air. Kalam had said that while the Kishan here had waited for Callum-kal to return, they had spent the time searching this island, and all the others surrounding it, for signs of the foundation builders. They had found a few fragments of stone platforms and support pillars, but that was all.

Now, as the clouds dissipated, Moon saw the top of the escarpment. It was a flat plateau that curved up into a sharp pointed peak at the western end. The peak formed a graceful curve, like a horn. The edge of the city was visible as a partial line of conical towers along the top of the cliff. Still obscured by shreds of cloud, they were hard to make out even with Raksuran eyes, but the shapes of the pointed rooftops were distinctive. They didn't line the entire escarpment, just the portion of it directly above the docking structure.

"It's not centered," Chime said. "That's kind of odd."

"It ruins the effect," Bramble agreed, tilting her head as she stared at the escarpment. "That peak doesn't look natural, either."

Now that they had pointed out the tilted effect, Moon noticed it too. The escarpment itself was roughly square, like the sea-mounts, and faced the island. But while the ruined docks at the foot and the towers along the top were aligned with each other, both were set closer to the western end of the escarpment than the eastern, clearly off-center and leaning toward the peak. He had seen some natural rock formations that were almost as odd as the peak, though he had to admit that the elegant curve of it above the plateau did look artificial.

Jade turned to them. "I'll go up, with Moon and Stone. I want the warriors to stay behind for now."

Chime and Balm exchanged frustrated expressions. River looked insulted, and the others disappointed. Bramble sighed and kicked at a lump in the sand. Moon knew they were all considering the angle of Jade's spines, and deciding not to voice any objections.

"Do we take Merit?" Moon asked Jade. He wasn't sure if it was a good idea or not. It would be good to have a mentor's opinion of whatever they found up there, but the flying was going to be dangerous already.

"Stone can carry me," Merit said, bouncing anxiously. "If he has to let go to climb, I'll hold onto him."

Jade's brow furrowed. Moon had the feeling she was contemplating Merit losing his hold and falling some untold number of paces to his death. Depending on how bad the wind was, they might not hear a scream for help.

Balm suggested, "What if the warriors follow you, but stop about halfway up. That way if something happens, we can help." She clearly meant, *catch Merit if he falls*.

Jade nodded a reluctant agreement, but said, "That won't do much good once we're over the city."

"Getting over the edge of the escarpment should be the hard part," Balm countered. "It'll be less tricky once you get past it."

We hope, Moon thought.

Jade eyed all the warriors again. "All right, we'll take Merit. Root and Chime will stay here with Bramble. The others will follow Balm, and stop at the halfway point."

Merit slung his bag over his shoulder and shifted to his scaled form. Bramble gave him a nudge to the shoulder. "Careful."

Callumkal and Delin slogged through the sand toward them from the camp. Callumkal called, "Are you going to try for the city?"

Delin called, "You will take me?"

"Not this time," Jade said. She nodded to Stone, and he stepped back and shifted to his winged form. Callumkal slid to a halt, startled. Apparently seeing Stone do it in midair a couple of times didn't prepare you for a sudden close-up view. Delin continued to trudge through the sand and stopped beside Bramble.

Stone extended an arm and Merit scrambled up to tuck himself in under Stone's collarbone. Stone curled a protective hand around him, then leapt into the air. Moon, Jade, and the others followed.

The farther up they went, the worse the wind got, and riding it up the cliff without smashing into the side became increasingly difficult. Soon Moon was breathing hard and concentrating so intently on playing the wind on his wings that he had no time to look at their surroundings.

A little after the halfway point, Jade signaled the three warriors to stop and they all dropped back. Moon kept flying, though his wing joins hurt, his head was pounding from the constant wind pressure, and his lungs ached. An interminable time later, Moon realized they had reached the edge of the escarpment, that weather-stained white towers were dropping away below them. With Jade and Stone, he let the wind carry him forward.

Reflected light blinded him. The next instant he thought the city was gone, or had never been here. The top of the escarpment was empty, just a huge open space.

He didn't realize what he was looking at until Jade landed on it and furled her wings, and he saw her reflection. Moon lit on the crystal surface beside her, staggering with the sudden cessation of wind. The peak and the towers were acting as a windbreak. Behind him Stone slipped sideways out of the wind current and dropped down to land.

A heavy crystal roof covered the city, much of it cloudy and stained from uncounted turns of weather. Moon crouched and ran his hand over it. His scales weren't as sensitive as his groundling skin, but he could feel the smooth crystal, and the tiny pits where the material was damaged. It was warm from the sun and condensation formed just beneath the surface. He leaned close, trying to see down into it, and glimpsed a long shadow that might be a column, and the narrow canyon of a street or walkway.

He looked up at Jade. Her tail lashed, and she said, tiredly, "Well, this is typical."

Merit scrambled down from Stone's shoulder and stared around, frowning. He waved his arms, a gesture of pure frustration. Moon stood as Stone paced away to investigate more of the crystal surface. He shielded his eyes, the fitful wind buffeting his spines and furled wings, trying to gauge the size of the transparent slab. It didn't stretch over the whole top of the escarpment, but covered an area that he judged as roughly the size of the colony-tree's circumference. Parts of the crystal shield were covered with patches of what looked like rock. Moon went to the nearest and poked at it with his claws. It was actually windblown sand, packed and crusted until it was nearly as hard as sandstone.

He turned to look toward the towers. They were huge, rounded, each one swelling out into a bulbous shape, then tapering up to a sharp point. They were made of a light-colored stone, now heavily weathered by wind and rain. There were no openings from this side, at least not that he could see. "That has to be the way in, those towers," he said, but he felt a sinking sensation. It was possible they had been built as a windbreak and nothing else. "It can't be completely sealed off."

"Can't it," Jade said, her voice flat. She squinted to look up at the peak. The light surface of the stone was smooth, except for pitting from the weather. From this angle, it was clearly made of the same material as the towers.

Jade and Merit continued to examine the crystal, Merit bounding and Jade making short flights, looking for any break in it, or anything like a door, or just a spot where they could get a clear view down into the city. While Moon went for a closer look at the towers, Stone flew toward the far end of the escarpment to examine the other side.

Moon found each tower had been carved from solid rock, all in a piece, and there was no way in that he could see. He examined the bases from the inner side, then climbed out to get slammed by the wind and investigate the outer. He was frustrated, cold, and mad by the time he gave up and climbed back over.

He went to join Jade and Merit in their fruitless search. They were at the far edge of the crystal barrier, where it flowed smoothly into the shaped rock of the escarpment. "Any luck?" Merit asked hopefully.

Moon explained what he had found, which was pretty much nothing. "I didn't even see any carving," he told them, shaking ice crystals out of his frills.

Jade scuffed her disemboweling claw against the crystal surface. "If the towers and the horn were built to be a windbreak, then this must have been open at one point."

Merit scraped at some sand on top of the crystal. "Keep looking?"

Jade's tail lashed in tired irritation. "Keep looking."

As the sun moved into late afternoon, Stone returned from his investigation, an annoyed growl rumbling in his chest. He shifted down to his groundling form to say, "I went all along the far edge. Past the crystal, it's just solid rock. There's no way in."

Merit sat on his heels, his spines drooping tiredly. "They had to have an entrance lower down. There's that dock, for one thing."

Stone rubbed his forehead. "I'm wondering if the Kish fire weapons could break this."

"Maybe. I'd hate to carry a groundling up here through that wind," Jade said.

Moon agreed. The Janderan and the Janderi had tough skin, but not as tough as scales. He wasn't sure they could take the cold.

And then we have to decide if we really want to find the way in, Moon thought. Because this city was sealed off, impenetrable, like the one under the island. And it might be for the same reason.

So they had come back down, uneasily riding the punishing wind, to report failure. The warriors had been watching for them and came up to meet them partway down, and Moon was so exhausted he was glad for the escort.

About thirty strange Kish-Jandera were waiting on the beach with Callumkal, Vendoin, and Kellimdar. A short distance away, Delin sat on the sand with Chime, Root, and Bramble. The warriors, and Stone with Merit, landed further away down the beach, but Jade spiraled down to land close to the Kishan, and Moon landed with her.

The crowd parted as Delin and the others slogged through the wet sand toward them. Moon was tired, damp, the skin under his scales chilled from the wind at the top of the escarpment. He hated standing there under what felt like an array of hostile stares. He knew it was his imagination, that the groundlings were just anxious for word of what the Raksura had seen, but knowing that never helped.

"We couldn't get in," Jade said, as Callumkal was drawing breath to speak. She described the crystal shield and the towers, to growing expressions of dismay from Callumkal and Kellimdar, agitation from Vendoin, and grim worry from Delin.

Moon shifted to his groundling form. It was a miscalculation; the aching muscles and exhaustion could be borne with his winged form. In groundling form it made him stagger. The warriors shifted too, and Song and Briar both sat down in the sand. River wavered, as if he wanted to but meant to use sheer willpower to stay on his feet.

Jade caught Moon's arm to steady him and said, "We need to rest. Follow me to our tent, and I'll answer all your questions."

The discussion moved to the Raksuran camp, where Bramble had made a hearth and started heating some tea. Moon had a cup and then retreated into the tent to sleep. Chime curled up with him, with Song and Root settling nearby.

Moon slept deeply for a short time, then woke and found the tent empty. He stretched to ease the lingering ache in his back muscles. He had heard a little of the discussion with Callumkal and Delin and the others, as they had talked about the crystal shield, and what weapon might penetrate it, and how best to get it to the top of the escarpment. Callumkal and Vendoin were both against breaking the crystal unless it was absolutely necessary. Kellimdar was more impatient, but Delin also wanted to wait, saying that there must be an entrance lower down. Moon knew Delin was playing for time, hoping they would find some definitive sign that the city had been built by the foundation builders and not forerunners. Chime had said Delin had been going over all the notes and drawings Kellimdar and the others had made while waiting for Callumkal to return, but had so far gleaned no more from it than the Kishan scholars had.

Now Moon rolled to his feet and stepped outside. It was nearly dark, and the wind had eased somewhat. Jade was down at the beach, watching the warriors and the Arbora, who were either playing in the waves or looking for shellfish and lizards in the tidal pools. Chime and Delin sat in the sparse grass only a little distance from the tent. Delin had his writing materials spread out, the paper pinned down to keep it from blowing away in the wind.

Moon couldn't see Stone for a moment, then finally spotted him. He was in his groundling form, half-buried in the warm sand above the waterline. *Groundlings are right; Raksura are strange*, Moon thought, not for the first time.

He looked toward the Kishan camp and saw it was quiet. Only a few people were out, cleaning up after the remains of a meal at the center of the camp. Several more headed down to the small boats on the beach, probably about to return to the larger sunsailer.

And Callumkal, Kellimdar, and Rorra were just stepping into one of the larger tents near the back of the camp, at the edge of the trees.

On impulse, Moon turned and walked into the jungle. He shifted to his winged form as soon as he was past the cover of some flowering brush, and leapt up to climb the nearest tree.

There were only a few large branches, but the broad leaves offered just enough concealment. He climbed from tree to tree, until he reached one just behind the Kishan tent. He could hear voices. He wrapped his tail around a heavy branch and hung upside down to listen.

Kellimdar was saying, "That's what they said they found. How do you know you can trust them?"

"Delin trusts them." Callumkal sounded as if he was uninterested in arguing the point. Or at least that he didn't want to discuss it with Kellimdar.

"Delin? Who doesn't believe we should be trying to enter this city at all?" Kellimdar was skeptical. "Hasn't he hampered us more than he's helped?"

"He's helped a great deal." Callumkal's voice took on more heat. "His work—"

"From what you've said, Delin offered to take you to the Raksura, then got you lost in a dangerous wilderness and refused to show you the way to their settlement."

There was a pause. Rorra's voice said, "That's not a fair description. We were uninvited, we had no permission to approach the Raksuran settlement, and Delin didn't think we should. We weren't lost, and he knew they would find us quickly."

Kellimdar persisted, "But they don't want us to enter the city. They're the reason why Delin believes as he does."

He was right, and if Moon had been part of the conversation, he couldn't have argued that point. But it was disturbing that Kellimdar thought they were lying to the Kishan. And Callumkal probably did too, he just wasn't willing to say so to Kellimdar and undermine his own authority. Rorra sounded like she had an open mind, but Moon wasn't sure how much the others listened to her.

It all meant that if they did find something that showed it was dangerous to open the city, the Kishan weren't going to believe it.

Callumkal said, "We've barely been here one day. I understand your concern, but can we please have some time to evaluate the situation, and actually see what everyone says and does before becoming angry about it?"

Kellimdar was silent a moment, then said, "Very well. I'm sorry if I've overreacted—"

Callumkal said, "No, I understand your frustration. We worked very hard to get here. And if this is a forerunner city, and there is something inside, still a danger after all this time . . . I can't think leaving it there as a danger to future explorers who may have no warning of its existence is much better than taking the chance of accidentally releasing it."

Well, he's right about that, Moon thought, his own frustration growing. It wouldn't be much of a victory to save the Reaches from some powerful Fell attack now, only to have it happen a generation or so later because a less wary or less intelligent set of groundlings stumbled on a way to open the city.

Practical as ever, Rorra said, "So we don't know what to do."

"Correct." Callumkal sounded resigned.

Moon hung there a while, thinking, even after they left the tent. He didn't know what to do, either.

By the time Moon returned to the Raksuran tent, the sun had set, turning the blue of the sky to deep indigo, and the wind dropped to a light steady breeze. Bramble had made more tea, and the warriors had brought in some fish and swimming lizards for dinner. All the Raksura were sprawled around in the sand in relative comfort, except for Briar and River, who were on watch. Moon took Jade aside and told her about the conversation he had overheard, and she buried her face in her hands and groaned. He felt the same way.

The Kishan camp had also quieted as the few remaining inhabitants retreated to the sunsailer or went back to the flying boat as the night settled in. Then Callumkal walked over with Rorra, Kellimdar, and Kalam to invite them to sleep on the sunsailer, but Jade said they would stay here. She told Callumkal, "If the Fell are watching you, and waiting for you to open the city, they might come closer in during the night to spy on you. We'll be better able to detect them out here."

This sparked a little argument about the Fell, with Kellimdar going over all the reasons the Kishan who had remained here thought the Fell were gone, and Jade countering with all the reasons the Raksura thought they must be here, and Callumkal acting as arbitrator.

Kellimdar said, "I believe they came here only to hunt the inhabited, unprotected islands to the west, and then left."

Jade managed to hold on to her patience. "We told you the signs we encountered on the way here. It can't be a coincidence that the Fell are out this far."

"But you don't know that those signs were caused by the Fell," Kellimdar protested. He claimed to understand their concerns but he kept circling back around to the idea that there was nothing to worry about. In some ways Moon understood; the Kishan had been chasing the idea of this city for a long time, and all the speculation about it had been proved right so far. Turning your back on all that and just leaving would be terribly hard.

And what Callumkal had said earlier was right; leaving wouldn't solve the problem either. Not until they knew if the Fell knew a way inside, or were waiting for the groundlings to find one. Or knew what was in there. If anything was. Moon rubbed his face in frustration and held back a growl.

Jade said, with an edge to her voice, "Perhaps we've had enough speculation for tonight."

Callumkal said wearily, "I agree."

Rorra, who had accepted a cup of tea from Bramble while Kellimdar was arguing, pushed decisively to her feet, took Kalam's arm, and hauled him up after her. She said, "Callumkal, if you want to stay on the sunsailer tonight, it will be tricky to bring the tender alongside in this current."

That got Callumkal and Kellimdar moving. Chime asked Delin, "Aren't you going with them?" He added in Raksuran, "You know, you could listen to what they say."

Delin shook his head wearily. "I've heard it all already."

When the Kishan had all trekked down the beach, and the sound of the efforts to get the small boat into the water had faded, Delin took a seat beside the hearth and said, "So. The underwater stairs that Stone found. I know it has occurred to all of us that they may be underwater for a reason."

Moon had an instant of intense memory, of the moment of realization that the creature in the forerunner city had followed them up through the doorway. He felt a ripple of nerves run down his shoulders, where his absent spines wanted to twitch. The creature trapped under the island had been killed by saltwater, one of the reasons they thought the prison had been chosen for it. Chime said, "But like you said, it could also be that the steps were built when the sea wasn't here, and the dock built on top of them later."

"It's a possibility," Delin said, "but we must ascertain the age of the stairs, and the docking structure above it, to be sure." He threaded his fingers through his beard. "I am not sure how to do this, but I think the Kishan perhaps know methods."

Stone stretched and lay back in the sand. "I'm having a lot of trouble with the idea of leaving this place without knowing if there's something dangerous inside it or not."

"Yes. Callumkal said that too." Jade's spines drooped in resignation. "I'm not happy about the idea of living the rest of our lives in the Reaches waiting for the Fell to show up, and knowing we could have avoided it if we had tried harder."

Root said, "So either we can't find a way into the city and have to leave, and not know if the Fell are going to get something from it and use it to come after the Reaches. Or we get into the city and maybe that sets loose the thing that the Fell get and use to come after the Reaches. Or we leave, and somebody else gets into the city later and the Fell—"

Song shoved him in the shoulder. Root fell over into the sand and protested, "I'm not wrong."

"We know you aren't," Chime said, "That's the problem." There was a moment of glum contemplation.

Then Song said, "Why can't we use the thing the Fell are going to get against the Fell?"

There was an uncomfortable moment of silence. Moon was struck by a deep gut-and-bone-level instinct for how bad an idea that was, but he didn't know how to put it into words. Then Jade said, "You didn't see it."

Moon expected Song to drop the subject. She hadn't seen it because she and Root had been almost killed while trying to fight off the Fell. Song still had the scars on her throat. But instead she said, "There were only a few of you there. Stone wasn't even there. If there were more, we could control it. Or kill it."

The warriors all looked at Jade, except Balm, who stared at Song, her expression suggesting that someone was about to get a slap to the head. Song hadn't exactly made a direct challenge to Jade, but the tension of the moment made the comment more pointed than Song had perhaps intended. Her voice tight, Jade said, "As I said, you didn't see it."

Song leaned forward. "But it could be our chance to fight the Fell, really fight them, maybe kill a lot of them at once. If this thing is going to be powerful enough for them to use it to attack and overwhelm the Reaches, then it's powerful enough for us to use it to attack them."

Jade tilted her head.

Sitting up on his elbows, Stone muttered, "Uh oh," under his breath. Chime glanced at Moon worriedly, and Delin sat very still. Balm had unconsciously bared her teeth at Song. Root had frozen in place. Moon sat up a little, trying to think of something to say to disarm the situation.

Then Bramble snorted. "Song, did you get hit on the head?"

Bramble and Merit had been so quiet, Moon had forgotten they were there.

Merit was going through his simple bag, and without looking up, said dryly, "You know, I may be young and not the most powerful mentor the court has ever had, but if I had scryed something like that, I'd mention it."

"There were only a 'few of you' there. Let's see." Bramble ticked the list off on her fingers. "Jade, our sister queen. Moon, our consort who fights Fell. Malachite, a reigning queen who killed a whole Fell flight. A half-fell consort. A half-fell mentor. And Chime, our mentor who turned into a warrior who has strange abilities that no one understands yet. Even without Stone there, that's as strong and powerful a group as most courts could put together." Bramble leaned toward Song. "Exactly how do you expect to control this thing? Have a bunch of warriors there for it to kill as a distraction?"

Merit added, "If we gave it a hundred warriors to kill, maybe it would get tired—"

Song curled her arms around her legs, physically withdrawing from the battle. "All right, all right! You don't have to rip my face off."

Bramble grinned. "If someone needs to rip your face off, I'll do it."

"Bramble, Merit, enough. You made your point, you don't have to enjoy it," Jade said, but her voice wasn't tight anymore. She rippled her spines to release tension and stood. "We'll take this up tomorrow. We need some rest."

Bramble and Merit put on contrite expressions and didn't argue, having gotten exactly the reactions that they had been aiming for. Stone flicked a fish bone at Bramble's head.

As Jade started toward the tent, Bramble turned to clean up around the hearth and the warriors all got to their feet. Moon scrambled up to follow Jade.

Everyone got settled, with Delin bedding down on one side with the Arbora and Chime, Moon and Jade on the other. Stone stayed outside in the sand.

Root and Song were supposed to be changing guard places with Briar and River. Through the tent wall, Moon heard Balm stop Root and say, "Go back into the tent. I'm taking your place." Then a moment later River whispered, "What's going on?" and Root hissed at him to be quiet.

Jade bunched up the blanket and gave it a punch, muttering, "Idiots."

Moon rescued the blanket from her and spread it out over the cool sand. Briar and River slipped inside the tent and settled down to at least pretend to sleep. Moon hoped Balm had talking more in mind than fighting, and knowing her she probably did. He was irritated with Song on several points, but mainly the fact that she had interrupted the ongoing discussion of whether they should try to get inside the city or not right at the moment when they might have come to a decision. He thought they were probably going to have to try, just because Jade and Callumkal and everyone else who had brought it up was right: it would be impossible to leave this place knowing it might at some point be used against them by the Fell. Of course, the others were right about the possible consequences, too.

He curled up next to Jade on the blanket, and she tucked an arm around his waist. *In the morning*, he told himself. *Worry about it in the morning.*

Moon woke with Stone leaning over him. Stone whispered, "Get up. There's Fell stench in the wind."

Jade whipped to her feet. Moon rolled to a crouch, shifting in mid-motion, and tasted the air. He couldn't detect anything yet, but Stone's senses were far more acute at long distances.

Around the tent, the others scrambled to their feet. Jade said, "Which way?"

"The southeast, from across the island," Stone answered, and stepped back outside.

"Where do we go?" Delin whispered, helping Bramble stuff blankets into her pack.

Not the right question, Moon thought. Carrying the Arbora and Delin, they could fly downwind and outrun the Fell, if the wind didn't drive them into the side of the escarpment or out over the ocean. But it would leave all the other groundlings to die, leave the city and its secrets to the Fell. He said, "Fight or run?"

Jade snarled. "Fight." She jerked her head at the Arbora. "Dig in and hide. Take Delin with you."

"They'll never find us," Bramble said it with absolute conviction.

Merit said, "Are you sure you don't want me with you?" His voice shook a little. He had to be thinking of the time he had been captured by the Fell, at the old eastern colony.

Jade said, "No, stay with Bramble. Wait until we're in the air, then go." She flung herself out of the tent and Moon darted after her.

Stone stood on the beach, looking up at the night sky. Balm and Song flanked him, their spines flared in agitation. The other warriors shot out of the tent and formed a tight group around Jade. Chime bumped into Moon's shoulder, radiating nervous fear.

They had left no mentors' lights or fires lit outside, and the untenanted Kishan camp was also dark. The obvious target was Callumkal's flying boat tethered sixty paces or so down the beach, with the soft lights along its ridge and on its stern and bow. The other, smaller flying boat was dark, lost among the treetops, but the Fell might have marked its location during daylight. The sunsailer lay at anchor several hundred paces from the shore, deceptively vulnerable, lights shining out of cabin windows. Jade said, "River, warn the Kishan on the flying boat. Don't fly; run to it and go up the ladder. Then come back to me."

River bounded off, his movements soundless on the sand.

Moon said, "We can warn the ship without the Fell knowing. Some-one can swim out to it."

All Jade's attention was on the sky. "Chime, do it. Stay there."

She had chosen the warrior least likely to be an effective fighter. Both situations were dangerous, as the ship would surely be a prime target, but Chime would be close to the water, able to stay under far longer than a groundling, and it was unlikely the Fell would detect him. Moon nudged Chime. "Swim out to the ship and climb the hull. Find Callumkal."

Chime hesitated. "But— You should—"

Moon gave him a push toward the shore. "Swim fast, stay under as long as you can."

Chime flicked his spines in assent and bolted down the slope of the beach. Moon caught a faint reflection on his scales as he dove into the waves and disappeared.

Jade said, "Stone, from above or below?" She sounded tense and it worried Moon a little that she was asking for advice.

As calm as if they were planning a grasseater hunt, Stone said, "Doesn't matter, they'll expect us from either."

Balm snapped, "Kethel!" and pointed.

The big dark shape moved across the faint starlight. The ground-lings in the east called kethel harbingers, because they were so often the first sign that a Fell flight was nearby. Their armor-like scales were matte black and they had a halo of horns protecting their heads. They were the least intelligent of the Fell, and totally under the control of the rulers. Kethel never traveled alone, and this one's presence meant the rest of the flight wasn't far behind.

Between the distance and the darkness it was hard to tell the size. Moon thought it might be three times Stone's wingspan. *Good, not a big one*, he thought. Jade said, "Wait, wait."

"Another kethel," Briar said from behind Moon.

Moon said, "They'll hold the third back." A flight wouldn't nor-mally send more than three kethel until it was time to feed. The rulers would want to keep some with their progenitor. It was especially likely with a flight in this position, traveling from island to island over water, with probably only one secure place to retreat to. The progenitor might not even be anywhere nearby, but be waiting with the rest of the flight on the mainland, which meant there would be fewer reinforcements.

Jade said, "Stone, you take that one. Moon, with me. The rest of you keep the dakti off us."

Stone's shape flowed into darkness, already lifting off of the beach as if insubstantial. A heartbeat later his great wings beat once and Moon staggered from the displaced air. The shape gained weight and substance as it shot upward toward the closest kethel.

Jade leapt after Stone, and Moon followed her. He felt the warriors in the air behind him as Jade crossed under Stone's path and headed for the second kethel.

Moon flapped his wings hard, angling to get a boost from the wind, focused on Jade and the dark shape of the kethel above them. They had to get to it while it was distracted, before the dakti that were in the air somewhere could swarm them. From behind and further up a noise broke the silence, like a strangled growl. It echoed off the face of the escarpment, distorted by the wind. Moon thought it was Stone seizing a startled kethel by the throat and hoped it confused the rulers and dakti.

He sensed movement swoop toward them and Balm flashed by and slammed into a shape about her own size. *That was a ruler*, Moon thought. It took everything he had to keep flying after Jade, to not drop back to engage it. Root broke off and twisted after Balm, following her and the ruler down.

He heard River snarl, "Briar, on your right!" and the rest of the warriors broke off. Moon risked a glance back and saw distance-lights glowing from the flying boat, crossing back and forth in the sky.

The kethel above them reacted, but slowly, turning away from its course and back toward where Stone had attacked the first one.

Then Jade struck it in the throat. Moon struck it further down on the chest and gripped with his claws to hold on. It probably couldn't feel him through its coat of heavy plate scales, but it could feel Jade. Kethel usually wore an armored collar, decorated with the bones of groundling victims. The kethel jerked its head and roared as Jade dug her claws in. Knowing he only had a few moments before a dakti swarm came to its aid, Moon scrambled up its body, around its shoulder, and onto its armored head. Then he stabbed his claws into its right eye.

It shrieked in agony and slammed its clawed hand up to swat him. Moon ripped its eyelid off to give it something else to worry about and jumped away.

He was facing toward the island and saw the moment when something big and dark flashed through the searching lights and struck the flying boat's deck. Moon thought, *We found the third kethel.*

The roar of fire weapons sounded and a kethel bellowed in pain. Then something cracked inside the flying boat's body and it suddenly bent double, with a terrible ripping sound and several loud metallic bangs. Moon tried to think who had said they would be staying on the flying boat, if Rorra might have gone back to it. Big wings flapped above the shape of the ridge, fire from the bow weapon ripped across the dark scales. The flying boat was going down but the kethel was going with it. *That kethel had to know . . . It killed itself to wreck the boat . . .*

Then he sensed something diving toward him and twisted away. A ruler missed him by so little it brushed his spines. Moon flapped to recover his balance and a dakti struck him in the side. He ripped it in two and twisted again to meet the ruler rushing toward him. It grabbed for his throat and he caught its arms. Before it could pull him close, he brought both feet up and used his disemboweling claws for what they were meant for. The ruler made a strangled keening noise and Moon felt hot blood and guts wash over his feet. He jerked his claws free and dropped the ruler.

Moon turned and flew right into a swarm of dakti. They screamed in alarm as he tore through them, then they scattered, too disorganized to attack effectively. He couldn't see Jade, couldn't see the kethel he had partially blinded, couldn't see the warriors. Then he realized one reason for the complete darkness was that the lights on the sunsailer had gone out. *Chime got there*, he thought in relief.

Then fire blossomed on the vessel's deck. It illuminated a dozen groundling shapes standing near it. As they dodged away, the light shot upward, trailing sparks. High in the air it burst into pieces, erupting into a fountain of fire. It lit the sky, the ship, the beach and the water around them. Like one of the signal devices that the Golden Islanders used on their wind-ships, except far more powerful.

Dakti scattered away from the light, and Moon banked, trying to see the other kethel. Only one was visible, the smaller one that Moon and Jade had attacked. It curved around to dive at the sunsailer, just as another bundle of fire burst up off the deck.

This fire was smaller and faster and arrow-thin, and it arced up to hit the kethel right in the chest. It jerked and floundered in the air, its roar baffled and pain-filled.

Then a heavy body hit Moon from behind. He flared his spines and told himself *this is what you get for not paying attention.* He struck back with his feet and grabbed the arms that wrapped around him. Teeth scraped across his shoulder, his collar flanges preventing them from sinking in. Moon twisted and rolled, trying to dislodge the ruler, and on the second roll got a glimpse of a shape streaking toward him, the light from the first fire-blossom glinting off blue scales. He rolled again so his back and the ruler's back were toward it.

The impact jolted his breath, and an instant later the ruler was snatched away. Moon twisted, flapped to get some height, and saw Jade in the process of tearing the ruler's head off. Another ruler dove on her and Moon shot upward and ripped at his wing.

The ruler turned on him with a snarl. They struck at each other, grappled, broke apart, and struck again. This ruler was considerably older and smarter than the one Moon had ripped open. He was careful not to let Moon get too close, trying to wear him down. It was a good strategy; Moon was dangerously close to being worn down.

They were also both dropping rapidly toward the waves just off the beach. The last time Moon had fallen into water with a ruler it hadn't gone well. He ducked a swipe to the head, twisted in and grabbed the ruler. Claws tore at his side but he managed one flap to push them further out and into the right position. Then he rolled to get on top and pulled his wings in.

They fell faster, the ruler unable to catch the wind from this angle. It released its grip on Moon, frantic to get away, and Moon held on harder. Just as they started to roll, Moon let go and shot his wings out, curving them to slow his fall. The ruler slammed into the deck of the sunsailer. Moon landed on top of him a moment later and used the instant of dazed distraction to rip the ruler's throat out.

CHAPTER FOURTEEN

Moon straightened up out of a crouch, dripping with his own blood and the ruler's, and saw he had an audience. The fire-blossom device pointed at the sky, illuminating the space above the sunsailer. In its reflected light, several Kish-Jandera, all holding the bulky tubes of the fire weapons, stood on the deck staring at him. They were all strangers, no one he recognized from the flying boat crew. No one shot at him, which was good.

The deck was littered with dead dakti, and Chime perched on the roof of a cabin, breathing hard from exertion. He called anxiously, "Are you all right?"

"Sure." Moon lifted his right arm and hissed at the pain where the ruler's claws had pierced his scales. Chime started to jump down to the deck, and Moon said, "No, stay up there. Can you see the others?"

Chime said, "Jade's killing a ruler over by the wrecked flying boat. River and Song and Balm were fighting off a bunch of dakti toward the groundling camp, or that's the last place I saw them. The last kethel flew away, and Stone went after it. I lost track of Root and Briar."

Moon flicked his spines to show he had heard. He turned, trying to look up without using any muscles on the right side of his body. He couldn't see much from this position, the glare of the light obscuring what moved in the darkness beyond it. Then a door behind him banged open and Kalam stepped out. One of the others called a warning to him but he ignored it and ran up to Moon. He said breathlessly, "Rorra's on the upper deck. She saw you come down and said you were hurt."

"No, well yes, but—" Ignoring Moon, Kalam pushed a folded cloth against the worst wound, pressing hard to stop the bleeding. Moon admitted, "All right, that's actually a good idea. But if I tell you to run—"

"I will," Kalam promised.

"I can't see any more rulers or dakti in the air," Chime reported from the cabin roof. "They might— Oh, Jade's coming!"

Moon swayed, partly with relief. Careful to sheathe his claws, he put a hand on Kalam's shoulder to steady himself. One of the Janderan stepped closer and said, "Kalam, you should back away—"

Kalam said, "Tell the physician to get down here. There must be other wounded out there, and on the airship."

The Janderan hesitated, but then turned back to give the order. Jade banked overhead and spiraled down, the light glinting off her blue scales. Moon was starting to realize how lucky he was the Kishan hadn't shot a fire weapon at him. They would have seen two nearly identical dark figures hurtling toward them.

Jade landed on the deck. She took in the dripping blood and the dead ruler. "Are you all right?"

"Yes," Moon said. "Did you see Root and Briar?"

"They're on the beach with Stone." She leaned in to look and Kalam moved the pad so she could see the wound. She grimaced. "How many were aboard your flying boat? Do you know?"

Kalam answered, "There were five aboard. Is it destroyed?" He looked up at Jade, wincing in anticipation of the answer.

She shook her head. "It's on the ground, but I didn't get much of a look at it."

Chime reported, "I see Balm coming this way."

The cabin door banged open again, and Callumkal came out, followed by another Janderan. As they drew closer, Moon saw she was the healer, Serlam. Callumkal said, "On the beach— Were there survivors? We were lucky that most of the crew decided to sleep here tonight but there were five left on duty aboard—"

"Stone is there now and I'm about to go join him," Jade said. "Tell your people not to shoot anything in that direction. The Fell are gone and Stone may have to lift the upper portion of the flying boat to look under it. If we find anyone, we'll bring them here. Will you help Moon?"

"Yes, of course." Callumkal hesitated, frowning, but apparently was only trying to consider the logistics of helping a person with spines on his back. "Can he change?"

Kalam peeked under the pad again. "He's still bleeding, but not as badly."

Jade's gaze was worried, but Moon didn't want to delay her. He said, "Kalam, step back." He didn't want to fall on him.

Kalam moved away, and Moon shifted. And then things got vague and dim, and his knees started to fold. Callumkal caught him and held him up, and Moon managed to at least look like he was still alert and conscious. "Go on," he told Jade.

She stepped back, then took a running leap off the deck. Callumkal and Kalam guided Moon through the doorway and then down a wide corridor. Unlike the flying boat, the deck was wood and the walls a dull copper metal. The liquid light bubbles were built into the ceiling and nested in patches of moss.

They half-carried Moon into a cabin with wide padded benches built against the walls, and a braided grass rug on the deck. Callumkal lowered Moon down to the nearest bench. "Are you going to be all right?" he asked.

Gripping the bench, Moon managed a nod. Callumkal took him at his word and left, hopefully to go back out on deck. Moon wanted him out there, keeping any of the nervous Kishan from overreacting and shooting a Raksura. Kalam reappeared, urging Moon to lie down, and stuffing a cushion under his head when he did. Moon pulled up his blood-soaked shirt to see the wound. Kalam made a noise of dismay.

"It looks worse than it is," Moon tried to croak. He wasn't in danger; it was just going to be painful until his body could heal it.

Serlam pulled Kalam away and sat down on the bench next to Moon. He hadn't spoken much to her aboard the flying boat. She was one of the Janderan who had kept her distance. She said, "I don't suppose you're going to bite me."

"Not unless you ask nicely," Moon told her.

She blinked, then made a huffing noise he assumed was a laugh, and opened her satchel. "I've never treated one of you before. Can you tell me what I should do?"

"Just clean it." She took a wad of folded cloth out of her satchel that smelled astringent. Moon set his jaw and didn't flinch when she wiped away the blood. Her touch wasn't rough, but she wasn't as deft as Merit.

She finished cleaning the wounds, her expression still uncertain. "Are you sure I shouldn't sew this up?"

Moon was pretty damn sure. "It's not bleeding anymore because underlayers of skin have already started closing up. It'll be fine if I don't rip it open again." It wasn't the explanation Merit would have given; Moon had made up the word underlayers himself to describe what he had noted about the way his deeper cuts and slashes healed.

She leaned close, frowning. "Hmm. All right, but I'm going to strap it, just to make sure."

He let her bandage the bigger wounds, and endured questions like "is your skin supposed to be this hot?" when he had no idea if it was or not. It didn't feel hot to him and no one else had ever seemed to think it was odd.

Then heavy steps and bumping in the corridor signaled the arrival of Kishan crew members carrying more wounded. "Are they from the flying boat?" Moon asked.

Serlam said, "I don't know. I have to go. Try to rest, and I'll check on you later," collected her bag, and strode out.

Gritting his teeth, Moon levered himself up in time to see three Kish-Jandera carried past, one on a makeshift stretcher. From what he could see, their condition wasn't good.

"He's in here," someone said, and Stone stepped into the cabin.

"What—" Moon grimaced as the slashes and punctures in his side stretched. "The Arbora and Delin?"

"They're fine." Stone sat on the bench next to Moon. "Bramble dug in under the tent, literally. There were three paces of sand on top of them. They were still digging out when I left."

Moon sank back down onto the bench again, too relieved to comment. Whether it was fear or the Arbora talent for doing things thoroughly that had led them to dig so deep, he was glad Bramble hadn't underestimated the Fell. "What happened at the flying boat?"

"It's in pieces, and two Kishan were killed, Berkal and Lilan. They were running the big fire weapon that took out the kethel. Esankel was a little banged up, but the other two are in bad shape. The Fell got that smaller flying boat too, the one that was anchored on the island, but there was no one aboard it." Frowning, Stone looked under the bandage. He tasted the air, possibly looking for scents of poison or infection. He didn't look like he had been in battle with two kethel, except that maybe his skin was a little grayer than usual. "You need Merit?"

"No." Moon levered himself up on his elbows again, ignoring the painful pull at his ribcage. He couldn't talk while he was lying flat on his back. "Did you—" He took a closer look at Stone's expression. "What?"

Stone sighed. "The Kishan caught a dakti with that projectile weapon they have. They took it off the beach in one of the small boats and are bringing it up on deck now."

"Caught . . . It's still alive?" Moon had trouble understanding. "What's the point of that?"

Stone's expression was sour. "They want to talk to it."

Moon hissed, but he knew the Kishan scholars well enough by now to not be entirely surprised. "They realize what they'll actually be talking to, right?" Individual dakti had feelings and apparently personalities of their own, but they acted as conduits for their rulers, and probably for their progenitors, too. Something else would be seeing and speaking through the dakti's body.

Stone grimaced. "There's realizing it, and there's understanding what it means." He threw a wary glance toward the doorway. "I wish your birthqueen were here."

Moon suddenly found himself defensive and he had no idea why. Maybe because he had been wishing Malachite was here too, and didn't like to hear Stone articulate that hidden thought. "Why? Even Malachite can't kill a ruler by talking to it through a dakti."

"I wouldn't count on that," Stone said.

Stone started to stand, and Moon held out a hand. "Help me up, I want to hear this." Stone's expression was not encouraging. Moon glared. "Come on, we know more about Fell than anybody here. And it's not like the rulers didn't see us already."

Stone said, "Don't think you're fooling anybody with that 'we' bit. You think you know more about the Fell than anybody here," but took Moon's arm and hauled him to his feet.

Stone helped Moon out to the corridor. Moon scented Fell, but the door was open onto the deck and the whole island and the sea between here and the escarpment stank of Fell right now. "How did they breathe under three paces of sand?" Moon asked suddenly, remembering the Arbora's hiding spot. "And how did they keep Delin breathing?"

"I don't know," Stone admitted. "Sometimes I wonder about the Arbora."

Sometimes Moon did too. They limped out onto the deck where the wind had died and the hanging fluid-lights glowed steadily. The fire blossom in the sky had faded but distance-lights on the upper decks swept the air and the beach. Jade was out there, with Balm and Chime, still in their winged forms. Balm had long scrapes and scratches on her arms, but didn't look wounded anywhere else. Moon was beginning to think his decision to grapple with a Fell ruler all the way down to the sunsailer was possibly not the best choice. Calumkal, Kellimdar, and Vendoin stood with half a dozen of the Kishan crew. The mast of one of the smaller boats was just visible above the railing.

Moon heard Kellimdar say, "I feel we should apologize, but we truly saw no sign the Fell were still in this area." He sounded genuinely regretful.

Callumkal said, "They were waiting for our return, clearly. But how did they know?"

Jade said, "That's a good question. You know they could have put one of your people, a Kish-Jandera, under their influence and set them to spy on you."

"That should have been impossible," Kellimdar told her. "Our arcanist, Avagram, was alert for such deceptions when we were on our way here. He died before we arrived, but there was no chance of the Fell abducting anyone and returning them while we were underway."

"It could have happened before we left Kedmar," Callumkal said before Jade could. "We weren't as careful then, not suspecting the Fell might be interested in our actions."

"Perhaps the Fell were attracted by the Raksura," Vendoin said. There was a pause as Callumkal and even Kellimdar stared at her, startled by the suggestion. Jade's spines started to lift.

Vendoin raised her hands. "I did not mean deliberately attracted! I meant, perhaps the Fell thought we sought out the Raksura because they knew the way into the city, and acted because of that."

Jade, having spent a good portion of the night saving groundlings from Fell, managed to lower her spines with difficulty. "It's possible," she said, an edge to her tone that could have cut bone.

"Since I was the one who invited the Raksura to come here," Callumkal pointed out, grimly, "I ask that we put this discussion off until later."

"Perhaps after my consort's blood is washed off the deck," Jade added, still eyeing Vendoin.

"I meant no offense," Vendoin said.

Moon sighed. For someone who didn't mean any offense, Vendoin had picked the worst time to cause it.

Chime glanced back, saw them, and stepped over to Moon with a relieved wince. "Are you all right? You don't look all right."

"If I move around, it'll heal faster," Moon said. It sounded right.

Chime's concerned expression turned exasperated. "No, not really."

Moon didn't want to argue so he didn't reply. Balm threw a worried glance at them and nudged Jade's arm. Jade looked over her shoulder, did a double-take, and glared at Moon. He glared back.

Jade wasn't able to take any action because the winch extending off the upper deck creaked as two crew members turned the wheel at its base. It hauled something in a net up off the small boat, and Moon caught the scent of burned dakti. All the attention shifted to the rail.

The net swung over and was lowered to the deck. Wary armed Kishan surrounded it and the dakti trapped inside snarled at them. It was still in its winged form, small compared to an adult warrior. It had armored plates on its back and shoulders instead of scales, and it had a long jaw and a double row of fangs. Moon had seen dakti in their groundling form, which was not particularly prepossessing either. It moved like it was injured, but wasn't showing any emotion except anger and what was probably a thwarted desire to eat groundlings.

Jade stepped forward with Callumkal. Balm moved a step sideways, putting herself between the dakti and Moon, Chime, and Stone.

Callumkal asked Jade, "How do we begin?" He sounded a little uncertain and Moon thought, *Good*. Overconfidence wasn't going to help anything.

The angle of Jade's spines suggested that if they had to do this, they might as well do it thoroughly. She said, "Just wait. There's no point speaking to the dakti itself."

Watching uneasily, Kellimdar said, "Does it understand us? If the rulers won't speak through it, perhaps we could offer to release it to carry a message to them."

Jade flicked her spines in a negative. "It's hard to explain, but that wouldn't work."

The dakti would know the rulers would probably kill it for showing that much initiative. Moon figured all the dakti who were capable of thinking for themselves and resisting a ruler's commands were either dead, or had slipped away from their flights and were living happy though lonely lives in a forest somewhere.

Callumkal said, "I've heard speculation that they are a group mind, incapable of individual thought. Delin said it was a theory, but nothing was known for certain."

Jade's spines relaxed a little at these signs of understanding. "He's right, we don't know, for certain. They act as a group mind much of the time, share memories with each other. But sometimes the rulers act as individuals, so we don't know who has the control, if it's a group of the rulers or the progenitor or . . . something else. But the dakti and kethel have been bred to be obedient."

Moon heard Rorra's boots on the deck behind them and a moment later she stepped up beside Chime. She must not have heard about the dakti, because her expression was wide-eyed and incredulous. She muttered something in a language Moon didn't know. It sounded exasperated.

Then the dakti stirred and stretched its head up.

Everyone went still. The dakti's mouth opened and its throat worked. A voice, grating and hollow, said, "So here we are."

Moon's skin prickled as if he had just been dipped into freezing water. No matter how many times he had seen a ruler do this, it never got easier. Maybe because the dakti clearly had no choice, no identity once the ruler took over. Maybe because it seemed so easy for the Fell to give up that identity.

Callumkal said, "And who are you?"

The voice said, "A friend. You seem sorely in need of friends." It would have been a chilling moment, but Stone made a disparaging noise in his throat clearly audible to everyone on the deck.

The Fell spoke in Altanic. Fell always spoke their prey's language, which meant this flight might come from the eastern peninsula, where that was the most common trade language among groundlings. It also might mean it came from closer to Kish, and just didn't want to reveal that by speaking Kedaic. Or possibly Moon was overthinking this.

Jade leaned toward Callumkal and said, keeping her voice low, "They always speak that way to groundlings, at first. They always call themselves friends."

Callumkal made a gesture of assent. "So I've heard."

Kellimdar whispered, "It's disturbing to see it in practice."

Moon felt the tension in his chest ease a little. Chime, who had apparently been holding his breath this entire time, gasped.

Callumkal raised his voice to say, "We are in need of friends. We've just been attacked by Fell."

The ruler who spoke through the hapless dakti said, "We attacked the Raksura."

Rorra, standing with her arms folded, snorted in derision. Callumkal said, "The flying craft did not belong to the Raksura."

Moon sensed the mood on the deck turn from uncertainty and fear to something more grimly angry. All the Kishan were focused on the dakti, and no one looked at the Raksura. Moon suspected the loss of the flying boat and the dead and injured crew aboard it was not going to be easily excused by any of them. It was a relief.

"So what did they want, then?" Chime whispered. "They could have approached the Kishan like they normally do, tried to trick them. Why attack openly?"

It was a good question. Moon noticed Rorra leaning close to listen. He said, "Maybe because they're Kishan. Maybe the Fell thought it wouldn't do any good to try to trick them."

Stone muttered, "It's not going to be that simple."

The fact that the ruler hadn't answered immediately was telling. Though what it was telling, Moon wasn't sure. Then it said, "It can't be discussed in this manner. We must meet with you."

Callumkal didn't appear convinced by that argument. "I'm having no trouble discussing it in this manner. Just tell me what you want from us."

There was a pause. "We want to help you enter the city."

Callumkal's whole body went tense. He looked at Kellimdar, who shook his head and muttered in Kedaic, "Playing with us like toys."

Callumkal said to the dakti, "You have an odd way of helping us, destroying our flying craft, killing our people."

The Fell said, "That was the Raksura. They attacked us."

Moon wanted to growl and managed not to. Fortunately, Callumkal and Kellimdar, whatever his doubts, didn't appear to believe any of it. Callumkal said, "We don't want your help."

The Fell said, "But you want to enter the city."

Jade flicked her spines impatiently. "If you want to help, tell them where the door of the city is. On top of the escarpment? Somewhere on a cliff? Around the base where the water meets the rock? Tell us."

The dakti made a choking noise, coughed up a dark gout of blood, then collapsed. Most of the Kishan flinched back. After the dakti lay still for a moment, a Janderan approached cautiously and poked it with the butt of a fishing spear. It didn't move. She said, "It's not breathing."

The other Kishan cautiously moved closer. Stone tasted the air, and said in Raksuran, "It's dead, all right."

"Abrupt way to end a conversation," Callumkal said sourly. He turned to Jade. "Will they be back tonight?"

"I don't know." She glanced at the sky. "But they will be back."

"So why did they bother to talk?" Moon asked Stone. Chime leaned over to listen to the answer. "To see if we were still allies with the Kishan?"

"Maybe," Stone said. "Maybe they just wanted to see how badly we wanted to get into the city."

Jade had managed to sound skeptical and indifferent about the prospect, and Callumkal had made it clear he wasn't interested in help from the Fell. But that didn't tell them when the Fell would attack next, or how.

"They want to keep us here. That's why they destroyed the flying boat," Chime said, keeping his voice low. "We could have put all the groundlings on it and taken off downwind, and the Fell couldn't have tracked us. Now, they have us trapped."

Balm glanced back, her expression grim. "Hush."

"They were testing us," Callumkal was telling the Kishan crew. "Testing our weapons, testing the Raksura."

Someone said, "But was that all of them? If it was, we can hold them off here."

Everyone looked at Jade. Her spines tried to rise and she forced them back into a neutral position. She said, "I don't know. They might have held back part of the flight."

Balm said, "We need to know where they've nested. If it's nearby, I don't know, maybe we could get close enough to see how many there actually are."

"That's a big maybe," Stone said. He added, under his breath to Moon, "But it's a good idea."

It was a good idea. Moon wondered if Callumkal had a map showing nearby islands, or if there were any flying islands in this area.

Chime muttered, "It's a good idea but I don't like it."

"But why would the Fell attack now?" Callumkal said. "I thought if they were truly here watching, they must be waiting to see if we could open the city."

Jade said, "That's a good question." After a moment of thoughtful silence, it was apparent no one had an answer.

They did this for a reason, Moon thought. The Fell had been tracking this expedition for a long time, watching it, waiting until the flying boat returned. They hadn't just gotten hungry and taken off to see how many groundlings they could grab. *They have a plan. Or they had a plan, and something went wrong.*

Moon heard a disturbance in the water, but Stone said, "It's the other small boat."

A Kishan posted on the upper deck called out and swung a light around. Rorra hurried to the rail, calling, "Lower the boarding ladder!"

River, Briar, and Song climbed up over the railing without waiting for help. River glanced around the deck, then went to Jade. "The Arbora and Delin are with the groundlings in the boat. Bramble wouldn't let us fly, she said the Kishan would shoot us." Fortunately for their relationship with Callumkal and Kellimdar, he said this in Raksuran.

Jade just said, "Good."

At the rail, Rorra gave Delin a hand up, as Merit and Bramble scrambled over. Both Arbora were in their groundling forms; probably Bramble being cautious again. Magrim and two more Janderan followed Delin up the boarding ladder. Callumkal asked them, "Is anything salvageable?"

"Some of the supplies that were on board, yes, and we were able to find all the levitation packs," Magrim reported. He looked weary, and his pants and the sleeves of his shirt were dusted with sand, as if he had been digging in the wreckage. "But the ship itself, no. The motivators were torn loose from the hull. That's what caused it to fall."

Merit spotted Moon's injuries immediately and hurried across the deck toward him. "What happened? Let me see." Bramble followed him, making worried exclamations.

Moon fended Merit off. "No, it's fine." Delin had joined Jade, Callumkal, and Kellimdar and was speaking urgently and Moon wanted to hear.

At that point Balm came up and took Moon's arm firmly. "Jade said to go back inside and let Merit look at you or she won't let you help anymore. She says to take Bramble with you."

That was just unfair. Moon said, "That isn't—"

Callumkal was telling Jade, "Let's go inside and speak of this. We need the chief navigator and the maps before we can come to any decision." He turned to Kellimdar. "Will you make sure the crew is prepared for another attack?"

Stone tugged Moon along, and Moon relented, since the action seemed to be moving inside anyway. Maybe he would feel better if he sat down. As they reached the hatchway, Delin caught up with them and said in Raksuran, "I had an idea, while we were under the sand. I think that may be where the entrance is."

Confused, Chime said, "Under the— You mean the sand underwater, at the base of the cliffs? Where the stairs were?"

"Yes. Stone could see no indication of a door or opening, but perhaps it was even lower." Delin lifted his brows. "Could Stone dig underwater?"

Stone's sigh was more than half growl, causing the Kishan waiting in the corridor to edge uneasily away. He said, "Stone thinks Delin needs to make up his mind whether he wants to get into this city or stay out of it."

Resigned, Delin said, "Stone is right."

Kalam waited in the corridor, and told them they could have the cabin where the healer had treated Moon. The choice was good for the Raksura, since it was close to the hatchway and the open deck. Moon was about to point that out when he got dumped onto a bench, half-smothered with cushions, and told to stay put while Merit examined his wound.

Delin and Callumkal and the other Kishan headed on down the corridor, but Jade turned to the warriors. "Does anyone need Merit to look at their injuries? Do you need to rest, or can you go outside on guard?"

Everyone flicked their spines in a negative. They were all keeping to their winged forms so whatever cuts and bruises they had would heal faster. Briar said, "I don't think I could sleep if I tried."

Root added, "I'm kind of hungry."

Bramble, stowing their packs under a bench, said, "That I can do something about."

Jade smiled and gave Root's shoulder an affectionate shake. "I want Briar, River, and Song on watch outside, on the upper decks. Balm, come with me, and Chime, stay here with Moon and Stone. Root, stay out on that lower deck for now, in front of that hatchway."

The warriors went out and Jade turned to Stone. "You're staying here?"

"For now." Stone dropped down on another bench. "I'm going to take a nap."

Jade turned to Moon and he said, "I'm staying here too."

"You'd better." She stepped close to look over Merit's shoulder.

Merit had pulled up the bandage and spread a sweet-smelling simple on the slashes that immediately dulled and eased the pain. He asked Jade, "Do you think they'd let me help with the groundling wounded?"

"Maybe. We can ask." Jade brushed her hand against Moon's cheek, and then left with Balm. Merit hastily gathered his satchel and hurried after them.

Bramble watched her go, frowning. "She's worried."

Chime folded his arms, and his spines flicked nervously. "Should I go out on watch too?"

"No, you should do what Jade told you and stay with Moon," Bramble said. She stood and went to Kalam, who still waited uncertainly beside the door. The conversation had been in Raksuran, so he would have understood none of it. She said in Altanic, "Can you find us some food? The warriors will need to eat soon."

Kalam looked relieved to be able to help. "Yes, I'll show you."

As they left, Moon's tense muscles relaxed. His eyelids felt heavy and he had a distinct feeling that it had something to do with whatever Merit had put on his wound. If it made it heal faster, he was all for it. Stone was lying on the bench across the room, asleep or just resting. Chime was still standing there, and Moon patted the bench beside him.

Chime hesitated, then shifted to groundling, and came over to sit on the bench. He slumped a little, his clothes still damp from the swim across the cove. In his groundling form, it was easy to see his eyes were a little too bright and he was trembling. Moon knew then why Jade had wanted Chime to stay in here. He had been all right out on deck, but the reaction was setting in and Jade had seen it.

Moon managed to heave his almost inert body over a little, and said, "Lie down, there's room."

Chime winced and rubbed his eyes. "I'm supposed to be on watch."

"Root's on watch." Moon tugged on the back of Chime's shirt. Chime gave in and lay down on the bench, his back to Moon's side, but pressing close. Moon settled in and let his mind drift. After a long moment, Chime took a deep breath and relaxed. The corridor was noisy, with Kishan going back and forth, but it was a reassuring sound. Not long after Chime stopped trembling, Moon slid into sleep.

CHAPTER FIFTEEN

"Something's changed," Lithe said aloud. She opened her eyes and found herself facing Malachite.

They sat on the floor of the long cabin in the hull of the wind-ship, where the groundlings took their evening meals. Shade crouched nearby, with some of the warriors, the groundling crew, and Niran and Diar gathered around. The food the groundlings had been about to eat still sat forgotten on the low table. Everyone stared worriedly at her, except for Malachite, who just looked thoughtful. Lithe remembered following the others into the room, but not what had happened after that. "I had a vision."

"It came on you suddenly," Malachite told her. "What did you see?"

Lithe closed her eyes to capture the images that wanted to slip away. "Something wants them to go inside. Something old. There's another mentor there and it clouds his sight, he can't see to warn them. It doesn't mean to. It's old and powerful and not like us."

She opened her eyes. Diar glanced at Malachite, and asked Lithe, "You said something changed."

Lithe hesitated, trying to sort through the thoughts that were hers and those the vision had brought. Sudden visions like this tended to fade fast. Then she had it. "Something has forced their hand. Will force their hand." She took a sharp breath, the urgency that came with that fading image like a sudden punch in the chest. "The Fell are there."

Malachite tapped a claw and Flicker leapt to obey. He brought Lithe a cup of tea and sat beside her. Lithe drank, the warm liquid soothing her throat, and Flicker patted her knee sympathetically.

Niran grimaced in frustration. "We can't get there any faster."

"I'm not sure it would help," Lithe said. She concentrated, trying to tease out the last threads of true meaning. The images were blended with her own thoughts now, obscured with the color of her emotions. "The Fell are near them, watching. That's all I have. I'm sorry."

"It's enough," Malachite said.

Niran and Diar and all the others looked at her. "It is?" Diar said. She was asking the question the warriors and the other groundlings wanted to ask, but didn't quite dare.

Malachite stood in one smooth motion. "It tells us they're still alive."

The others seemed a little reassured, and Lithe tried to be. But the vision had left a strong aftertaste of saltwater and death, and she was afraid.

Moon woke gradually, listening to familiar voices. He could tell from his sense of the sun's passing that it was still a few hours until dawn. He blinked and rubbed his eyes, struggling back to consciousness. It took him a moment of staring at the copper-colored ceiling to remember where he was. Chime sat in front of the bench, watching Jade, Balm, and Rorra, who was spreading a fabric map out on the floor. Stone was gone and Delin was asleep on the opposite bench.

Rorra sat beside the map, having to tug her booted feet into a comfortable position. She propped an elbow on one of her knees and said, "Callumkal said he doesn't wish to put you in danger."

"I don't want to be put in danger either, but we have to find the Fell, regardless of what we decide to do next," Jade said.

Balm seconded, "Even if we decide to run, we have to know where they are. If they have a resting spot downwind of us, or anywhere between us and the ocean, they're going to overtake us."

"And if we see how many there are . . ." Jade flicked her spines uncertainly. "I don't know. If this is a small flight, and they attacked with all their strength . . ."

Balm finished, "It still doesn't make sense."

"No," Rorra agreed wearily.

Moon cautiously sat up on one elbow. The claw slash in his side was a dull ache. He could feel under the bandage that the cut was forming scar tissue. He could also smell dried fish. He sniffed the air, and Chime handed him a bowl of something that looked like chips of gray and white rock. "What is it?"

"Food," Chime said. "Sort of."

Moon took the bowl and bit into a chip. It tasted like fish. Terrible fish, but still fish. "Where is everybody?"

"Bramble is taking food to the warriors, and Stone went out on deck," Chime said.

Rorra marked points on the map with a charcoal stick. "We're here, and there are three islands nearby, that we know of."

Moon leaned over to look. The islands were upwind of the escarpment, but to the southeast, and the wind had been strong and coming directly from the south since they had gotten here. He didn't think they would detect much Fell stench from those islands, not unless the wind changed.

Rorra said, "This area is not inhabited or traveled by any species Kish has contact with. This map was made by the first scouts for the expedition, trying to locate the escarpment. But they weren't trying to make accurate maps, they were just looking for the best routes, if you see what I mean. They only mapped what they could see from their air vessel."

Jade tapped her claws on either side of the islands. "So there could be more small islands out here."

"There could be anything out there." Rorra's expression was glum.

Jade exchanged a frustrated look with Balm. "This is going to be even more fun than I thought."

Chime sat up suddenly. "Oh. The gleaners. Or whatever they were called."

Moon frowned, remembering their night visit to the floating hive. "The ones who disappeared?"

"Yes, them." Chime moved around Balm for a look at the map. "We thought the Fell took them to eat them."

"Right." Jade's brow furrowed. "Why else would they take them?"

"Because they can make floating platforms," Chime said.

Everyone stared at him. "Hmm," Rorra said, and studied the map again. Jade nodded slowly, her spines lifting. Balm said, "That might be it."

The more Moon thought about it, the more sense it made. He said, "The Fell would know that the Kishan would have maps of the islands."

"Yes," Jade said. "And they would want something they could move around in. Like that giant sac the flight looking for the other forerunner city had."

Rorra's brows lifted. "Giant what?"

"The kethel can make sacs, to carry dakti. This one was . . ." Balm made a gesture, indicating something round and by her expression horrible. Moon had to admit that was about as close as he could come, too. "Hard to describe."

Chime's attention was all on the map. "The hive platform we saw looked like it was just drifting on the current. The kethel could push it, but they would want to keep it out here somewhere." He tapped the circle of small islands.

"If it was on the other side of the escarpment, the currents are too strong. It would be carried out into the ocean." Rorra traced a path through the islands. "I think it must be along here. This current makes a circular motion, you can tell by the pattern of the islands. If their platform drifted too far toward the open sea, they could easily turn it back."

Jade said, "We should check this area first."

"How can you do this without the Fell being aware of you?" Rorra asked. "If you can see them, surely they can see you."

"To us, Fell have a distinctive . . . scent." Jade's hesitation was probably due to remembering that Rorra had a distinctive scent too. It was an awkward subject. "Stone will be able to tell they're in the area from a much longer distance."

Rorra nodded understanding. "So the wind patterns will let you eliminate a large territory with minimal effort."

That would be the easy part, Moon thought. The difficult part was going to be getting close enough to see anything without getting eaten.

Late the next morning, Moon sat on one of the small boats with Chime and River. Rorra was at the steering lever and Kalam and Magrim were acting as crew. The sky was clear with only a scatter of white clouds, the air warm, the breeze cool and steady, and Moon had nothing to do except worry. It was just as tiring as being in the air searching for Fell, with none of the sense of accomplishment.

They had taken the boat around to the point on Rorra's map where the current turned, and the islands were only distant smudges on the waterline. Stone had flown ahead to scout, and Jade and Balm had split off to skirt the islands. Moon and the others were to meet them here. There were so many questions that still needed answering, but at least they could find out where the Fell were nesting.

River, in his groundling form and sitting on the bench next to the rail, looked sour and bored and kept glaring at Moon like this was his fault. Moon had refused to stay out of the search, and Jade had refused to let him come with her or go with Stone, and going on the boat was the compromise they had reached. Chime and River were, in River's words, "stuck guarding the stupid consort." So far it had been an uneventful trip, with no sightings of Fell. Mostly Rorra and Magrim had guided the boat, listening and commenting occasionally while Kalam talked to Chime and Moon.

The Arbora, Delin, and the other warriors had been left back on the sunsailer, with orders to help the Kishan salvage the remains of the large flying boat. The small flying boat that had been tethered on the island for emergencies had been destroyed almost completely, leaving behind only a few chunks of moss from its railings and cabin walls.

Moon, sitting on the side railing, yawned. It was tempting to nap on the sun-warmed deck, but he was making himself stay awake. Last night, Jade had made sure all the warriors had a chance to sleep, but always left at least two on watch. Not that the Kishan weren't watching too, but the Raksura were watching harder.

River sighed exaggeratedly and said, "So if they aren't back by this afternoon, should we hunt?"

Moon said, "I'm the stupid consort, I can't tell you to do anything." River had spoken in Raksuran, but Moon answered in Altanic, not wanting to exclude the groundlings. Kalam snorted in amusement, Rorra lifted a brow, and Magrim, who was used to them by now, controlled a smile. River glared.

"That aside," Chime said, leaning on the pole that supported the canopy over the steering mechanism. "There's not a lot of food out here, just a few fish and lizards."

"That's probably why there aren't any sealings around here," Kalam said.

Chime nodded. "Right, but what are the Fell eating? There aren't any groundlings."

"They're probably eating the dakti," Moon said.

"Ugh," Kalam said succinctly.

Moon felt the boat move, just a little push against the current. He stood and shifted. "Something's in the water."

River and Chime both flowed rapidly into their other forms. Rorra gripped the steering lever, Kalam turned to survey the water, and Magrim reached for the small fire weapon tucked under the bench.

Chime pointed suddenly. "Right there. Something under the surf—"

A dark shape broke the surface only a few paces from the rail. Water sprayed and the boat rocked. Moon caught the scent and flung out his arms. "Stop! It's Stone!"

Magrim whistled in relief and lowered the fire weapon. "Can he give some warning next time?"

River sat down on the bench and pinched the bridge of his nose. Chime turned to Moon. "If I'd been in groundling form I would have pissed myself."

"Some of us were in groundling form," Rorra muttered sourly, taking the weapon from Magrim and stowing it back under the bench.

The water churned as Stone shifted out of his winged form, then he surfaced and caught hold of the rail. He looked up at Moon's expression, then glanced around at the others. "Too close to the boat?"

"Too close," Moon said, giving him a hand up.

"Sorry." Stone heaved himself over the side and stood on the deck, dripping. "There's a lot of sand in the current down here and it's hard to see."

"It's fine," Moon said. "Did you find anything?"

"They're here, all right." Stone jerked his chin toward the southeast. "Chime was right."

"I was?" Chime looked gratified. "They're using the gleaners?"

"They were. I found pieces of dead gleaners floating all through here." Stone took a seat on the bench, his wet clothes forming a pool of saltwater. "As soon as I got close, I caught Fell stench, so I had a general direction. I went into the water to try to get a better idea of where they are, and their stench is in the current too. I followed it about as close as I could without them knowing I was there."

Moon let his breath out. It was a relief that they were right. He gave Chime a nudge to the shoulder. "You saved us a lot of time searching."

Chime's spines flicked in pleasure. "Now we just need to figure out a way to get close and see how many there are."

"That's not going to be easy," River said.

That was a vast understatement. Moon had no idea how they could do it out here on the open sea without being seen. But the Fell already knew they were here. He wasn't sure how revealing that the Raksura knew where the flight was located would be giving away any vital information. He was about to say so, when Rorra said, "Can the Fell detect scent in the water, the way you can?"

"It's not scent in the water," Stone said. "It's carried in the air just above the water. But Fell aren't great scent-hunters, no."

Rorra hesitated. "I could do it."

Moon stared at her. *Right. Rorra's a sealing.* He had almost forgotten. "You can still breathe underwater?" Delin had said that she had been altered to allow her to stay on land, and Moon had assumed it would make her unable to breathe water.

"I can't go down to the depths anymore," Rorra said, "and I'm slower than I used to be. But I could handle this."

The faint wrinkles on Magrim's brow deepened in worry. "Rorra . . . Are you sure?"

Kalam added, "You don't have to. Just because you're a sealing . . ." He hesitated, clearly not sure what to say. "Well, you don't have to."

She made a faint amused noise. "No. But I can get close enough to see them, without them seeing me."

"Unless there's a kethel in the water," River pointed out.

Rorra didn't appear concerned, though Moon was fairly sure she was. She said, "I came from a sea that has many large predators. I'm good at avoiding them."

"You sure you want to do this?" Moon said. He didn't want Rorra to die and he especially didn't want to be the one to get her killed. He could imagine too many things that might go wrong.

She let out a gusty breath. "Someone will have to do it. It's safer from the sea than the air."

"There's Jade and Balm," River said suddenly, pointing.

Moon turned to look, and spotted two shapes flying toward them from the direction of the islands.

"Not Fell?" Magram said uneasily, shading his eyes to look.

Rorra and the Kishan probably couldn't see anything yet. "Not Fell. I can see the color of their scales," Moon told them.

Chime waved.

Jade and Balm approached rapidly. As they neared the boat, they banked and circled above it. First Balm, then Jade, dropped down to light on the railing, then stepped down onto the deck.

"Good news," Jade told them as she furled her wings. "We found the Fell."

"So did we," Moon told her. He didn't understand why Jade and Balm had changed their plan to search, or why they had gone so far to the south.

"In the sea, that way?" Stone pointed.

Jade frowned, and Balm looked baffled. "No," Jade said, "on the second island, that way." She pointed at a right angle to the direction Stone was pointing.

Chime turned to Rorra. "Could the current do that? Make it seem like the Fell were in the open water when they were actually on an island?"

Moon remembered the map, the way Rorra had drawn the current's path with her hand, and he didn't think so. Rorra confirmed it, saying, "No, not this current, not from the second island."

"Then there's two of them," River said, turning to Jade. "Two flights."

Moon let out his breath. He hated to say it, but River was right.

Stone rubbed his face. "Of course there are."

Jade hissed in exasperation. "That's all we need."

Moon asked Jade, "Did you get close enough to see them?"

"Yes. They probably spotted us, but they didn't try to come after us. They were dug in under an old ruin and we only saw two kethel."

"Did the ruin look like it might have been part of the city, made by the same people?" Kalam asked.

Balm glanced at Jade, and spread her hands. "It was a structure made out of coral, looked fairly old."

"How many were in the flight you saw?" Jade asked.

"We didn't see them yet." Moon looked at Rorra, wondering if she was still willing to carry out their plan. "Stone picked up their stench in the current."

"I'm going to go take a look now." Rorra sat down on the bench and started to unlace her boots. "And yes, I'm sure."

Moon saw Jade's confusion, then her expression cleared as she remembered what Rorra was. She said, "If we get you killed, Callumkal isn't going to like it."

Rorra glanced up, her smile thin. "Callumkal knows me too well." She pulled her first boot off, and Moon saw her fins for the first time, folded and pinched together to make a rough foot-shape to fill the boot. They were dark with bruises and scar-tissue. It looked so painful it made Moon's spines twitch in distress.

Kalam said, "Rorra's careful. She won't get hurt." It sounded like a combination of loyal support and fervent hope to Moon.

Moon was trying to think of all the possibilities. Rorra's scent wouldn't matter in the water. The Fell wouldn't be able to detect it there like a sealing would. "How fast can you swim?"

Rorra pulled off her other boot. On that leg the fins were missing, the limb ending in a rounded stump of scar tissue. "Not as fast as you can fly, so don't expect me back immediately."

Moon turned to Jade. "We need to get her closer to where Stone scented the Fell. Otherwise she'll have to search for them and it will give them more time to find her first."

Rorra stripped off her shirt and started to unbuckle her pants. The skin of her torso had only faintly visible scale patterns, but there were wide gill slits on either side of her chest. Magrim and Kalam both looked away. The Kishan, at least the Kish-Jandera, appeared to have a mild nudity taboo. That was probably another reason they had so much trouble getting used to Raksura.

Jade glanced at Stone. "Can you take her?"

"Sure." Stone saw Rorra's dubious expression, and said, "I won't drop you from too high."

"Lovely." Rorra grimaced. She glanced around, saw Kalam and Magrim were still studiously looking away, and held out a hand to Moon. "I need help standing."

He shifted to his groundling form to keep from accidentally poking her, stepped in and put an arm around her to help her stand. She looked at Stone. "How do we do this?"

Stone eyed her appraisingly, then smiled just a little. "Jump in, but stay on the surface. I'll scoop you up."

"What a comforting thought," Rorra said, and jerked her head toward the rail.

Moon helped her limp over to it. Balm stepped up to take her hand and steady her from the other side. Rorra breathed, "Thank you." Then she leaned forward and flipped over the rail and into the water.

Her body slipped through the low waves, fast and sleek, even with the missing fins. Stone waited until she was about fifty paces away, then he stepped up onto the rail and dove off the boat. He shifted before he hit the water and slid smoothly under the surface.

Confused, Kalam said, "I thought he was going to fly."

Watching with narrowed eyes, Jade said, "He's building up speed."

Moon could see it too, the rapidly moving line of ripples just below the surface, angling away from the boat and Rorra. Then the ripples disappeared. Chime said, "I think he's going to—"

The big dark body broke the surface with a powerful flap of wings and launched itself upward. Kalam and Magrim gasped. Stone caught the wind with the second flap and lifted smoothly into the air. Spray showered the boat.

"That was impressive," Balm admitted.

It was. Moon wasn't sure he would be able to do it.

Stone gained some height, water still sliding off his wings, then banked around. "I can't see him," Kalam said, rubbing his eyes in frustration. "I mean, I can see him, but I can't make out detail." He nodded toward the other Raksura. "I can see all of you fine."

"I can't see him either," Moon said. He had always just considered it something that happened to line-grandfathers. No one else had ever remarked on it. He asked Chime, "Why is that?"

"I don't know." Chime shrugged his spines. "There isn't a lot of mentor lore on line-grandfathers. For one thing, they're rare, and for another . . ." He gestured toward Stone. "They don't like to answer questions."

Stone lined up for a dive toward Rorra. He flew low over the water, one clawed hand reaching down for her. It had to be frightening from Rorra's perspective, even though she knew what was about to happen. Stone's hand folded gently around her and pulled her out of the water. He tucked her against his chest, tilted up again, and banked around toward the direction where he had detected the Fell stench.

Jade sighed, and glanced around the little boat. "Well, we have a wait."

They waited most of the afternoon. Moon had flown a little distance away and gone fishing, both because he needed to stretch his wings after the injury and because the dried fish from the sunsailer's stores hadn't been very satisfying. Magrim had admitted that the settlement he came from in Kish liked their fish raw, too. He got involved with showing Kalam how to slice one up and pick out the best bits. After they ate, the Raksura took turns napping, curling up on the warm deck. By unspoken consensus, they were getting ready for what could be another violent night.

At one point, while the others were resting, Jade told Moon, "Song apologized to me."

"That's good." Moon could tell she meant a real apology, where she and Song had actually talked it over, and not just that Song had stopped arguing because Jade was the queen. "Was something bothering her?"

Jade shrugged her spines a little. "She's been more aggressive, lately. It's just a sign she's growing up, wanting a more important place in the court. She'll settle down." Jade flicked a fish scale at Balm, sleeping nearby. "Balm was like that."

Balm opened her eyes, glared sleepily, and brushed the scale off her nose.

When the light started to shade into evening, Magrim began to make worried comments about trying to sail back in the dark. "We can wait longer," Moon told Jade. They were curled up in a corner together, Chime sitting nearby, and River napping beneath the bench on the opposite side of the deck. Balm was taking a turn at watch, sitting on the railing. "If we have to go back after dark, we can tell him which direction to sail in." Raksura, with an inborn knowledge of where south was, didn't need compasses.

"Yes, but there are rocky patches and reefs through here," Jade said. "We could see them as we were flying over. It might be more than tricky if—"

Then Balm said, "I see Stone."

Stone slung himself up onto the rail, and held down a hand for Rorra. He said, "Help her, she's not in good shape."

"Is she hurt?" Jade said, moving Moon aside. She leaned over the rail, caught Rorra around the waist, and heaved her up and onto the boat. Rorra slid down to a sitting position on the deck. Her face was drawn and gray with exhaustion and her body was wracked with hard shivers.

"Just tired and cold." Stone swung himself onto the deck.

Moon knew being carried by Stone at high speed in a strong wind was not a pleasant experience. He said, "Kalam, is there something to dry her off with?"

Kalam opened one of the supply boxes and dug out a drying cloth that might be used to clean the deck, but it was good enough for an emergency. Moon took it and crouched in front of Rorra, holding it up. She nodded, her teeth still chattering, and Moon started to dry her arms and legs.

Above his head, Stone said, "We have a problem."

"An additional problem?" Jade said. "Because if it's two different flights of Fell—"

"Rorra saw a half-Raksuran Fell. A queen."

Everyone went silent. Moon froze for an instant, then Rorra shivered again under his hands and he went back to drying her legs. "Get her clothes," he said.

Kalam moved first, bringing Rorra's shirt, jacket, and pants.

Jade said, finally, "You're sure? You saw it too?"

Stone said, "No, just Rorra. But she described it, and it can't be anything else."

Jade hissed out a curse. Balm said, "Did she see any others? If there's mentor-dakti—"

"That was the only one she saw," Stone said. Moon thought, *one's enough.* Especially if it was a female Fell ruler with the abilities of a Raksuran queen. Stone continued, "Like we thought, the Fell were on a floating platform thing, like the hive the gleaners built. Most of them were inside and she didn't get a chance to count them, or see if there were any others that didn't look like Fell."

Moon guided Rorra's arms into her shirt, then put the rest of her clothes over her legs like a blanket. Rorra said in a choked voice, "Apparently sealings don't fly well."

"I don't know, it sounds like you did great," Moon told her. "Chime, River, come here and sit on either side of her." Raksuran bodies were the best heat source on the boat right now.

Chime moved over to sit by the rail, squeezing in next to Rorra. River, startled by Stone's revelation, didn't argue, just shifted to his groundling form and moved to crouch down on her other side.

Kalam and Magrim had been hovering nearby, watching Rorra worriedly. Kalam said, "We should start back now. We need to get around the islands before dark."

Jade told him, "Yes, as fast as the boat can go."

Balm asked, "Should I scout ahead?"

Stone still sat on the rail, scanning the horizon. "I didn't see anything up there. And if they followed us, we don't want anybody in the air to give away our location."

Jade told Balm, "Wait till we get past the islands."

Magrim turned to go to the steering lever and get the boat moving. Chime, chafing Rorra's wrist, said, "I wish we had some tea to give her."

"I'm all right." Rorra's voice was still a harsh croak, but she was only shivering a little now, and her color was better. "I need to tell you what I saw. Stone says it's important."

Jade stepped over and sat down on the deck next to Moon. "Tell us."

The boat swayed as Magrim turned it. Rorra took a deep breath. "Stone put me down in the water some distance from where we believed the Fell were. I swam for perhaps two hours before I found them. As we thought, they had forced the gleaners to build a platform for them. It was large, nearly as big as our ship, with the dome shelters atop it. There was a great deal of floating debris around it, some plant matter and also pieces of what I thought must be gleaners' corpses, and bits of the platform itself, as if parts of it had collapsed at some point." She pulled her shirt more tightly around her. "They didn't see me. I can see through water to the surface, better than most beings. My eyes are designed for it. I floated just slightly under the surface with the flotsam and watched them. Dakti were perched on top, perhaps keeping watch, about thirty or so of them. I saw one kethel, sleeping on an open section of the platform. Perhaps smaller than those that attacked last night."

She coughed and Kalam handed her a water flask. After a drink, she continued, "I watched for some time. I was hoping to see more kethel, or something to tell me how many there were. Then finally three Fell came out onto the platform where the kethel slept. I described them to Stone later and he said two were rulers in groundling form." She looked at Moon. "They looked like you, but their skin was very pale, with no color to it at all. And their hair was . . ." She made a helpless gesture. "Different. I might have mistaken them for Raksura, if I hadn't seen Raksura before."

Moon nodded grimly. Chime muttered, "We get that a lot."

Rorra continued, "I didn't have a good angle of view, but they seemed smaller, about Root's size. The third being was larger, female, with scales that were dark like yours, and wings, but the textures were different. Her head had a heavy crest like the rulers, but she also had those things." She pointed to Jade's back. "She spoke to the rulers, though of course I could hear nothing. Several dakti came out to listen too. She . . . patted one on the head."

River made a noise of disgust.

"Then the kethel woke, and slid into the water suddenly. I was afraid . . ." She hesitated. "Terrified, actually, that they had sensed me somehow and sent it after me. I stopped resisting the current and let it carry me away from the platform, until I thought I was far enough away. Then I swam back to where Stone was waiting for me."

There was silence for a moment. Moon bit his lip, and said finally, "It could have been a half-Fell, half-Raksuran warrior."

"Would the rulers have listened to a warrior?" Jade sat back and shook her head. "And why keep a crossbreed warrior? It would just be an inferior kind of ruler, to them."

Stone said, "That's what I thought. It's got to be a ruler-queen." Moon met his gaze and Stone looked away toward the sky again. *What might be in the city was bad enough*, Moon thought. *This is worse.*

Kalam had been quiet, listening carefully all through Rorra's description. He said now, "You're saying that Raksura and Fell can interbreed. Is that because you are both descended from forerunners?"

"Probably," Moon said.

"Does Delin know about this?" Kalam asked.

"Uh . . ." Moon looked at Jade. If someone had to make the decision whether or not to reveal to the Kishan that a crossbreed Raksura might be able to open a sealed forerunner city, it wasn't going to be him.

Jade looked tired. She said, "Yes. But I want to wait to talk about this until we return to the others."

In Raksuran, River said, "If it's a queen, we're in trouble."

It was a vast understatement. The last half-Fell half-Raksuran queen they had encountered had a queen's ability to keep Raksura from shifting. It had taken both Jade and Pearl to kill her. Her voice dry, Jade replied in Raksuran, "Really? You think so?"

River snarled, "Somebody had to say the obvious and Root isn't here."

Balm snorted a laugh, and tried to turn it into a cough. Kalam said, uncertainly, "What are you saying?"

"We're talking about how much trouble we're in," Moon said.

Chime's expression was drawn in thought. "So are these two different flights then? And not one flight nesting in two places? And if they are, which one attacked us last night?"

"Good questions," Jade said. She pushed to her feet and faced the bow, every line of her body radiating impatience. "We need to get back."

CHAPTER SIXTEEN

The wind had changed slightly so it took longer to get back than Moon had hoped. It was full dark by the time they spotted the lights of the sunsailer. The stench of dead kethel, coming from the corpse left on the beach after last night's battle, tainted the air.

There hadn't been much to do on the way back, except take turns scouting and listen to Chime, Jade, Balm, and even River speculate about the Fell's plans and purpose. It wasn't as bad as listening to the Arbora do it, but Moon found it annoying enough. Stone must have too, because he retired to the back of the boat to talk with Magrim.

Rorra felt well enough to stand up and finish dressing, and to get her boots back on. Then she fell asleep. Moon mostly answered Kalam's worried questions and tried not to overthink everything. The fact that this flight had at least one Raksuran crossbreed with them was just more confirmation that their and Delin's speculation had been right all along. The Fell must be certain it was a forerunner city, even if the Kishan weren't.

Though the Fell who had managed to open the underwater forerunner city had specifically needed a half-Fell half-Raksuran consort, as close to what a forerunner looked like as they could come. The question that Moon most wanted the answer to was whether the reason the Fell hadn't managed to get into this city yet was because they couldn't find the doorway, or because the crossbreed queen wasn't close enough to a forerunner to make it open.

"I wonder what court she's related to," Jade had said, frowning into the distance as the sky and sea darkened around them.

"Some eastern colony that was overwhelmed and destroyed." Balm's shoulders twitched in an involuntary shudder.

That thought was too close to home for Moon. But unlike Opal Night's eastern court, there hadn't been a Malachite to search for survivors and retrieve their half-Fell children. Moon didn't want to think what life would have been like for Shade and Lithe and the others if they hadn't been found and brought to the Reaches.

"You think there's a progenitor, still? Back in that hive somewhere?" Chime asked uneasily.

"A progenitor voluntarily sharing power over the rulers with a part-Raksuran queen?" Stone snorted. "I doubt it."

It was a relief when they came within range of the sunsailer, and one of its distance-lights crossed the bow. Rorra waved, and the Kishan on guard on the deck waved back. "Doesn't look like there's been another attack," Balm said. She was in groundling form, and the cool wind lifted the curling strands of her hair. "They must be waiting until tonight."

Chime said, "Merit said he was going to try scrying again, but I guess Bramble wouldn't have much to do, unless the Kishan let her help with something."

Stone made a "humpf" noise.

"What?" Jade asked him. "She didn't have much to do on the flying boat, either."

Stone said, "There's a lot more trouble to get into here than there was on the flying boat."

Magrim maneuvered their craft alongside the sunsailer's hull, and Moon and the others caught the lines tossed down by the crew and tied them off at Rorra's direction. Two ladders dropped down and everyone started to scramble up the side. Callumkal waited on deck, saying, "Were you successful? We've made a great discovery here."

"A discovery?" Kalam asked, eyes alight with excitement. "The city?"

Moon swung over the railing, realizing Callumkal looked, and sounded, more excited than Moon had ever seen him. He hadn't seemed this agitated when the Fell had attacked. Beside him, Chime muttered, "Uh oh."

Callumkal said, "Delin discovered the location of the doorway!"

"Oh," Jade managed, after what Moon was sure was a moment of stunned dismay, because that was what he was feeling. She added, "How?"

"Delin was able to interpret some clues, but it was Bramble who really made the breakthrough." Callumkal was obviously proud to deliver this good news. "We couldn't have done it without her."

Balm, River, and Chime all looked at Jade, wide-eyed. Jade somehow kept her spines from lifting, and said, "I'm sure you couldn't."

Of course not, Moon thought. Stone said, "I told you so."

"We didn't mean to find it." Bramble sat on the floor in the cabin they had been given. "Things . . . just got out of hand."

Delin had been absently combing his beard. "It is not their fault. I had no idea we were so close. I meant to delay—"

Both Arbora looked tired, and Bramble in particular smelled strongly of saltwater and sea wrack. "He said to stop digging, but I had water in my ears, and I didn't hear—"

Merit, who had withdrawn across the room and was pointedly sitting near Jade, said, "I told her not to do it."

Moon buried his face in his hands. Briar, Root, and Song perched on the bench, all being very quiet. Balm and River had been told to go out on the top deck to watch for Fell and had seemed glad to do it.

Moon didn't even think Jade was angry at the warriors. Warriors just weren't used to telling Arbora what to do. Especially younger warriors like Briar, Root, and Song, when faced with a mature Arbora like Bramble. Moon would have been happy to tell her what to do, along with Stone, and also Balm, who was used to relaying Jade's orders and anticipating what those orders were going to be. River probably wouldn't have been bad at it either, and Chime, having been an Arbora himself, would have been even more effective. But none of them had been here.

Bramble, glaring at Merit, said, "That's not helpful."

Jade flicked her spines in a way that signaled everyone really needed to shut up now. She said, "Delin, tell us what happened."

Delin sighed. "I had been thinking about the possibility that the entrance was underwater, placed there either as a protective measure, or because the sea did not yet reach the foot of the escarpment when it was built. This morning I proposed to Callumkal that I take a rowing boat back over to the ancient dock and look at the carvings again. Bramble was bored with idleness and Merit's help was not needed with those wounded last night, so they came with me, along with two Kishan to manage the boat."

Jade looked at the warriors. Song said, "We were guarding the boat, and we took turns flying over to the dock, to keep watch on them." Briar and Root nodded, and Root added plaintively, "It's the way we keep watch on the Arbora at home."

Jade just gestured for Delin to continue.

He said, "As we examined the carvings at the base of the escarpment, the wind had died, and the water was much calmer. Bramble decided to try to explore the steps and the area below the dock that Stone had briefly examined." He spread his hands. "I suggested it might be dangerous, but she was confident of her abilities."

"I imagine she was," Jade said, her voice dry. Bramble was finding something absolutely absorbing in the loose threads on the tail of her shirt.

"So she began to dive down to the sand at the base of the dock structure." Delin added, "She can hold her breath for an inordinate amount of time. I knew her capabilities by that point, so I was unsurprised, but the Kishan were impressed."

"And what did Merit do?" Moon had to ask. He didn't want Bramble taking all the blame.

Merit bit his lip and squinched his eyes nearly shut, as if trying to recall. Delin said, "He took clumps of sea wrack and made them glow, to illuminate the area underwater where Bramble was searching." He gestured to Bramble. "You should explain the rest."

"It was these symbols in the carvings on four of the pillars," Bramble said. "They weren't anywhere else we had seen so far. They looked decorative, but maybe they weren't. Maybe they were a symbol for 'opening' or 'pathway.'

"I looked underwater, in the sand between each of those four pillars, and I found broken rock, like there was a causeway," Bramble continued. "But whatever that causeway led to isn't there anymore. But then I went back up onto the docks and I started to look on the wall of the escarpment, above the carvings the Kishan had already found. I saw a spot fairly far up, where just the shape of the rock looked curved. It looked like a larger version of that symbol was there, and that the rock was on top of it, somehow. So we swam over to the escarpment and climbed up about twenty paces toward the spot I saw— And then part of the rock came off in my hand."

"It turns out it's not rock, not on that section of the cliff, it just looks like it," Merit put in. "It's like coral, it's all drilled through with tiny little worm tunnels. Some plant or animal or plant-animal grew up the wall of the escarpment at some point, and then died, and it left this coating that weathered to look just like rock. It's still very hard down at the bottom, where the Kishan were searching. But it was more break-able further up the wall."

"And we kept knocking it off," Bramble finished, "and we found the symbols, and a seam."

Jade was leaning forward now, absorbed in the story. "A seam for an opening?"

"A big one." Bramble waved her arms. "There's a huge door in the cliff. We didn't mean to find it, and it wasn't Delin's fault. He started yelling and waving at us, but we were so interested we didn't hear him."

"I thought he was cheering us on," Merit said with another wince. "The Kishan on our boat saw it, and then a big section fell off and every-body saw it. It's a really big door. Big enough to sail this boat through."

"They stopped, then, so the door is not completely exposed," Delin said, "and we still are not certain of how to open it. But—"

"But now there's a door," Jade concluded. "And all the Kishan know about it."

Delin conceded, "Yes."

Chime said, "And the Fell will know, as soon as they see it in day-light." He turned and gave Merit a shove to the shoulder.

"Ow," Merit protested.

Jade said, "Merit, I thought you were going to scry while we were gone."

Merit looked at the floor, lifting one shoulder in a not-quite-shrug. He suddenly looked very young. "I tried, but I didn't get anything," he admitted reluctantly. "I thought maybe if I stopped for a while and helped Bramble and Delin . . . I don't know what's wrong. I should be seeing something about what the Fell are doing now, or the city, but I just get images of water."

There was an uncomfortable silence. *Maybe he's trying too hard*, Moon thought. But Merit usually did his best work when he was trying too hard. Frowning, Chime said slowly, "Maybe there's just too much going on right now."

Stone groaned, leaning his head back against the wall. Watching Jade anxiously, Bramble said, "I'm sorry we found the door. Is it really that bad?"

They didn't know about today's discovery yet. Moon glanced at Jade, and got a nod. He told them, "We found the Fell, nesting in two different places. Rorra got close to one group and saw a crossbreed queen."

Bramble's mouth dropped open. Merit made a choking noise. Even the usually unflappable Delin looked alarmed. He said, "You think they will attack again tonight?"

"We're sure of it," Stone said. He pushed to his feet. "We need to get out there."

Jade was up and sweeping out the door before anyone else moved. As the warriors followed, Bramble leaned forward and caught Moon's arm. "Tell her we're sorry, Moon." She looked miserable, and Merit didn't look much better.

"She knows you are. It's all right," Moon told her, trying to sound reassuring. Jade was under a terrible amount of pressure, and she probably blamed herself for this; she needed a little time to just be angry. Moon didn't think it was necessarily anybody's fault for Arbora acting like Arbora and doing a thorough job of anything they put their minds to.

"You're all idiots," Stone said, gave Bramble a shove to the head, and walked out.

Bramble slumped and sighed in relief. "Stone still loves us."

"Just get some rest," Moon told them, and followed Stone out.

Stone and Chime were waiting for him down the corridor by the door to the deck. Chime whispered, "How much trouble do you think we're in?"

"A lot," Moon said honestly.

Stone growled under his breath and stepped outside.

Moon sat up on the roof of the cabin on the topmost deck, the metal still warm from the day's heat. The thin sliver of moonlight slid in and out of the clouds, casting an occasional silver illumination on the waves washing up onto the beach, or the tops of the broadleaf trees. The wind tugged at his spines and frills, and danced across his scales.

Chime, sitting behind him and facing the west, said, "Jade's right, you should be inside."

As a consort, Moon was a prime target for a Fell flight who had successfully produced crossbreed Fell-Raksura. He was also tired of being reminded of it every other heartbeat. If there was anybody here supremely conscious of that fact, it was him. He said, "Can we stop talking about that?"

He heard Chime twitch uneasily, scales scraping on the cabin roof. "Sorry. It's just . . . I'm worried. All right, I'm not worried, I'm terrified."

"Everyone's terrified. If anyone on this boat isn't terrified right now, there's something wrong with them," Moon said. Two of the Kishan distance-lights pointed up at the sky and moved in slow patterns, watching for Fell. There were more lights, but Vendoin had said they lasted only for a limited time before they needed to be rested, and their use had to be rationed.

"I don't know." Chime sounded weary. "The Kishan think their weapons are going to hold off the Fell because they did last night. I wish I thought so."

It was far more likely that last night had been a test of the Kishan's defenses, and a successful attempt to destroy the flying boats and cripple the Kishan's ability to escape quickly. Moon said, "I don't wish I thought so. It's better not to be surprised."

"If you're trying to reassure me, it's not—" Chime began.

At that moment, Stone said from the deck below, "Do you smell that?"

Moon stood and tasted the air. It held saltwater and sand, the green scent of the trees and the heavy groundcover that cloaked the dunes on the other side of the island. And something else, just a trace that smelled of the sea bottom brought to the surface, decaying mud and dead shellfish. He said, "Something came up off the bottom. Something big."

Stone said, "That's what I was afraid of. They're driving something toward us."

Chime groaned in dismay, and Moon hissed under his breath. It was a trick they had seen before, where an attacker would take control of some large being that was normally harmless, and use it as a battering ram. Moon said, "Chime, go warn the others."

Chime jumped down to the deck. His voice drifted back as he hurried away, "I didn't think there was anything that big out here!"

Moon hadn't either. The sea all through this area was shallow and he hadn't seen anything bigger than an Arbora swimming through it. "Can you tell the direction?" Moon knew it was coming toward them from downwind, but that was it.

Stone swung up on top of the cabin. "It's behind the island."

Moon listened, trying to separate out the wind, the waves washing against the beach, the running footsteps and growing agitation on the ship below. They didn't know how the Fell could control other beings, but they knew it would have to be a ruler, and that ruler would have to be in physical contact to do it. The instance Moon had seen from far too close had been a ruler mounted on a cloud-walker's back, protected by a sac made from a kethel's secretions.

The wind carried the sound of a rushing torrent, the sound of something large moving through water. Moon said, "Do you hear that?"

Stone said, "I'm going to take a look. Stay here." He stepped to the edge of the cabin and leapt out into the wind. Moon ducked as Stone's large form flowed into being. Stone fell toward the water, then caught the wind and soared upward.

The distance-lights pointed toward the island now, moving along its shore, past the abandoned camp and the wrecked pieces of the flying boat, already coated with windblown sand. There was no movement there. Moon went to the opposite edge of the cabin and crouched down. One of the distance-lights was mounted on the lower deck, a big barrel with the light pouring out the fluted end. It steamed in the damp air and made ominous clicking noises. All the lights were lit now and Moon hoped they lasted through the night. He called down to the Janderi standing beside it, "Hey, can you point it east of the island, at the open water?"

The Janderi glanced around, clearly not sure who had called to her, but seized the big lever and swung the light to the east.

Moon stood again to look, but the light only revealed an empty stretch of water.

"Moon!" It was Jade's voice.

Moon jumped down to the deck below. Jade stood there with Callumkal and Rorra. Jade said, "Stone couldn't tell what it was?"

Moon moved his spines in a negative. "It's behind the island, in the water, coming this way." He turned to Rorra. "Can you move the boat?"

Rorra nodded and looked at Callumkal. Callumkal said, "You think they mean to trap us against the rocks of the—"

Then Jade snarled. She was facing out toward the sea and Moon whipped around. Caught in the glow from the distance-light were two dark shapes, each almost as tall as the ship itself. They were rounded at the top, and Moon had the impression that something moved along the sides, like tendrils or feelers. More shapes formed out of the darkness. Moon's spines prickled with fear and dismay. There were three more, five more . . .

Callumkal swung around to Rorra, "Tell the captain, get us underway—"

Rorra waved an assent, already limping rapidly toward the hatchway that led to the nearest stairwell.

"Do you know what those are?" Jade asked tightly.

Callumkal shook his head, his horrified gaze on the approaching sealings. "There should be little in the way of large sea life in this area, especially carnivorous sea life. I don't—"

"They don't have to be carnivorous, they just have to be able to swamp the boat," Moon said. From the stern, someone bellowed orders to release the anchor lines.

Jade said to Callumkal, "Can you—"

The hull moved under Moon's feet, then it suddenly jerked upward. His claws slipped on the wood as water and wet sand flooded over the rail. He slid down the deck toward the opposite side.

The distance-lights swung crazily, groundlings screamed. Moon slammed into the rail and held on despite the torrent of water, realized the tight grip around his waist was Jade's arm. He shook his soaked frills out of his face and saw Jade gripped Callumkal's arm, keeping him from being washed over the side; Moon was the only one with a free hand to hold onto the rail.

Looming over the deck was a dark shape, rounded on top, a long flowing fin along its edge. There was no sign of eyes, but a narrow lip across its belly poured out seawater. *At least it's not a carnivore*, Moon thought, not reassured. It must be something that normally lay flat on the seafloor, drawing in water and sand through some other orifice and pushing it out through this one, filtering out everything that had fallen to the bottom.

Something metallic screeched from the stern. Callumkal, shielding his face against Jade's shoulder, sputtered and gasped, "The anchor lines! They're holding us—"

Keeping this thing from turning the boat over, Moon thought, struggling to push himself off the rail. When the other sealings got here, the lines wouldn't be enough. Or this one would pour enough water into the sunsailer to sink it in place. He tried to plant his claws in the deck and push himself upright.

Then another dark shape loomed up over the sealing; Moon's heart stuttered for an instant because he thought it was a kethel. Then it buried jaws and claws in the top of the sealing and he realized it was Stone.

The torrent of water stopped, and Jade choked and spit out a mouthful. "Finally," she gasped, then yelled, "Balm, Briar! Where the shit are you?"

From the stern, Balm yelled, "Jade!"

Moon braced himself as Stone reared back, dragging the sealing with him. The hull swung back to rock toward the sealing, and Moon tightened his grip, holding on to the railing to keep all three of them from falling into the creature's maw.

With a crunch, Stone ripped the sealing away from the boat, taking a chunk of the opposite railing with it. Jade let go of Moon and Callumkal and they staggered on the rocking deck.

Callumkal recovered and ran down the deck toward the stern, shouting for the crew. Jade said, "We need to keep them off until the boat can move," and leapt to the top of the cabin.

Moon followed her to the cabin roof and jumped from it to the upper section. He caught a glimpse through the large windows of the steering cabin, saw the flying boat navigator Esankel and two Janderan pulling levers and turning wheels and shouting at each other. Callumkal was just climbing up the stairs from below.

Moon leapt down to the stern deck where Jade had found Balm, Briar, and River. There were Kishan on the overhanging deck working the distance-lights and the weapons, and another group huddling over the winch attached to the anchor line. But there was one person Moon didn't see. *Chime was heading here*, he thought, sudden fear tightening his chest. *Where is he?* But then Chime, with Song and Root behind him, slammed out of the nearest hatch.

Chime staggered on a buckled deck plate and said, "Sorry, we got stuck inside when the ship went sideways. What happened?"

Moon turned him around to face the island, where the shapes of the sealings were visible in the shafts of the distance-lights. Chime made a strangled noise.

Jade said, "Balm, Briar, Song, get in the air and try to see where the Fell are. River, Root, and Chime, get back up on the cabins, watch this deck. Don't let anything get inside."

The warriors took flight from the deck. Moon started to follow and Jade grabbed his frills and jerked him to a halt. "You stay with me," she said.

Moon bounced impatiently, thought about protesting, and decided it would make him sound too much like Root. Then he saw Stone bank through the air and come in low over the top cabin roof. "There's Stone," he said.

Jade hissed, "Come on," and went up the wall onto the next deck. Stone shifted, dropped down to the cabin roof, and landed on his feet in his groundling form. He swung down to their deck and said, "Where's Callumkal?"

"This way." Moon turned to the nearest hatchway.

It opened into a corridor with two stairwells, one up and one down. From the watery rushing noises and yelling, the down one led to something important, probably the motivator. Moon took the upper one and climbed rapidly, rounded a corner, and up again into the steering cabin. It was a wide cabin with windows all around, like the steering cabin of the Kishan flying boat. The wall below the front window had a number of levers and wheels and long tubes with horns on the end, which, from how Esankel and the other two were using them, were apparently for yelling at people in other parts of the sunsailer. Vendoin was there with Callumkal, and Kellimdar clutched one of the fabric maps. Rorra held the steering lever, her weight braced against it to keep it in place. They looked up as Moon stepped aside to let Jade and Stone get into the room.

Callumkal started to speak and Stone interrupted, "They're coming in from the east and the west. There's no way to go."

Rorra swore in another language. Callumkal and Vendoin just stared. Kellimdar said, "But—" and stopped, as if he had no idea how to finish that sentence.

"The sacs." Jade turned to Stone. "If we can rip open the sacs on some of the sealings, maybe just enough for the sunsailer to get past the others—"

Stone said, "I couldn't see any sacs, and no rulers. The Fell are controlling the sealings some other way."

Moon hissed in disbelief. He felt unexpected sympathy with Kellimdar. He wanted to say *but that's impossible*. He heard footsteps on the stairs behind them and saw Delin climbing up. He looked a little shaky and Moon stepped out to give him a hand up. Moon had forgotten he was in scaled form, but Delin closed his soft-skinned hand around Moon's scaled palm and claws with no hesitation. His face etched into worried lines, Delin said, "Oh, this has not turned out so well."

Moon steadied him on the landing. Figuring he might as well get the worst out of the way, he told Delin, "They've got us trapped between the island and the escarpment."

Delin nodded grimly as he stepped into the steering cabin. "I thought as much."

Callumkal was saying, "We'll fight them. We still have our weapons."

Jade's tail flicked continuously, a sign of her racing thoughts. "How long? Do your weapons run out?"

"Yes," Kellimdar said, his voice thready. "They will function for some hours, but the mosses need to rejuvenate. They need sunlight . . ."

Then Delin said, "We must try to open the city."

Moon, and everyone else, turned to stare. Delin said, "We can retreat to it, take shelter. If we can open it."

Jade recovered first. Speaking Raksuran, she said, "I thought it would take a crossbreed Fell-Raksura to open it, someone who looks like a forerunner. We saw the Fell have a half-Raksuran queen."

"That was our theory and may be what the Fell believe," Delin replied in the same language, "but we do not know if that is so. There may be another way. If it is a foundation builder city and not forerunner at all, there is certainly another way."

Callumkal found his voice. "Please speak Altanic. Do you know how to open it?"

Delin spread his hands. "Bramble, Merit, and I accomplished much today. We found the door, we can find the way to open it."

"Can you do it in time?" Vendoin asked.

"That is a good question," Delin said. "Perhaps the Fell and their sealing battering rams will be driven away by our weapons and it won't matter."

Stone made a skeptical noise, and Delin added, "I agree."

Callumkal looked at Vendoin and Kellimdar, then Jade. He said, "He's right, we have to try. Even if the city holds some danger, there is no other option. We can send Delin and the others over in the small boat, if your people will guard them—"

Rorra gestured toward the railing. "Both the small boats were hulled when that thing tried to overturn us."

She was right; the mast of the boat that had been tied off there was still visible above the rail. But it sat at an acute angle that didn't bode well for the rest of it. The Kishan had those little rowing boats, but they would take too long. "We can fly them over," Moon said. He thought it was a bad idea. He also thought it was the only idea.

Jade's tail lashed in frustration but she snarled, "We don't have a choice." She turned and flung herself out the door and down the steps.

Stone caught Moon before he could follow. Stone said, "Tell Jade I'm going to try to hold them off as long as I can."

"Right," Moon said. He wanted to say a lot of other things, but there was no time right now, and no real point.

Delin tapped his arm. "Your assistance?"

"Sure." Moon lifted Delin up and carried him down the stairs, then outside and over the rail down to the lower deck.

There, River and Chime waited with Jade. She must have told them how bad things were. River looked the way he usually did, except maybe less sullen, but Chime's spines and tail twitched nervously. As Moon landed, Root came out of the hatch with Bramble and Merit. Moon sat Delin on his feet and told Jade, "Stone's going to try to hold them off."

Jade flicked her spines in assent. She said, "The Arbora will go with Delin to try to open the city, Root, River, Chime, and Moon will fly them over. I'm going to join the others."

Overhead, Stone launched into the air, his shifted form skirting the distance-lights and diving toward the oncoming sealings.

Bramble nodded tensely. She and Merit were in their scaled forms, spines and tails twitching in anticipation and nerves. She said, "We could use Chime's help."

Merit seconded that. "He's done this before."

"Sort of," Chime corrected, but he didn't object.

"Whatever you have to do to get that door open," Jade hesitated, then grabbed Moon's shoulder and nipped his ear. "Be careful," she whispered. "And take care of them."

Moon's throat went tight; she didn't mean just the Arbora. He thought of their clutch again. But he said, "I will. Just come back."

Jade stepped away, jumped to the railing, and then into the air.

Moon took a deep breath. "Everybody grab someone," he told the warriors. "I'll take Delin."

Root obligingly picked up Bramble. "What are we doing?" he said, "because I missed that part."

"We're going to open the city," Moon said, lifting Delin up. It sounded far too optimistic.

"Oh." Root's spines drooped. "I was hoping it wasn't that."

Moon asked Chime, "Are you going to be all right?"

Chime moved his spines in an assent that wasn't quite as confident as Moon would have liked. "The wind's better than it was before. I can do it."

River snarled, "Let's just get it over with," and picked up Merit. Moon decided to let that go and leapt off the deck into the wind.

He caught the strong current and banked to turn back toward the escarpment. As the others followed, Delin gripped his collar flange and gasped, "One of the creatures nears the ship!"

Behind Moon, Kishan yelled warnings and he heard something strike the ship's metal hull. Moon hissed and concentrated on his flying. The wind had died down a little when the sun had set earlier, but this was still going to be tricky.

He let the wind carry him toward the escarpment, then pulled up at the last instant and let it shove him toward the wall. He caught hold of the rock with his free hand and his foot claws. Delin, whose head was a handsbreadth from the stone, whistled in admiration.

Moon twisted to look over his shoulder. Chime hit the wall several paces below him and slid a little. River and Root landed with less velocity, Bramble freeing one hand to help Root hold on.

But the sunsailer wasn't doing so well.

Moon couldn't see the sealings, but there must be at least one or more, possibly underwater or just above the surface. They were pushing the sunsailer slowly toward the escarpment. The wind carried the sound of a straining rumble: the motivator that drove the sunsailer, fighting the pressure.

"The ship?" Delin gasped.

"You need to hurry. Hold on, I'm going to climb down." Delin gripped his collar flange so Moon could use both hands to climb down to the ledge. Bramble and Merit had already spread out over the wall, pounding and clawing the obscuring coral-rock off the surface.

Moon set Delin down in front of the carvings at the base. He started to say, "Do you need any help?" when River shouted, "Dakti!"

Moon twisted around, spotted the shapes outlined against the sunsailer's lights. He snarled, "Chime, stay here, River, Root, get in the air!"

Moon launched himself off the wall, veered away as River did the same. Root went too low and almost ended up in the water, then flapped his way to an unsteady recovery at the last moment.

Moon flapped upward. The first group of dakti shot toward River and Root. Their night vision must be dazzled by the distance-lights, and they hadn't seen Moon, his dark scales fading into the night. He waited until they bunched up, nearly on top of River, and then hit them from above.

Dakti shrieked and tried to scatter as Moon tore through them and slashed their wings, slapping them out of the air. River slammed through a knot of survivors who tried to regroup and Root came up from below to tear through three stragglers.

Chasing stray dakti, keeping them away from the escarpment, Moon rapidly lost track of time. Suddenly he was circling, looking for prey and finding none in sight. The sunsailer still held its own, closer to the escarpment than it had been but not impaled on any rocks. The Kishan had managed to turn one of their weapons to point down over the side. The fire bundles thumped down into the water, glowed under the waves like some strange sea creature, then went out, but it was working. The huge sealings who had managed to get close stayed back from the hull, thrashing angrily in the water.

Moon gained some more altitude, trying to get a look at the situation further out. He saw Jade and the female warriors circling, driving off or killing the dakti who darted at them.

A small number of dakti were the only ones trying to get to the sunsailer, because most of the other Fell were attacking each other.

Moon stared, trying to make sense of it. He saw distinct swarms of dakti, striking at each other and falling back. Rulers flicked back and forth, darting at each other. Near the beach, three kethel fought in a confusing mass of wings and tails. Another dead one lay in the waves, next to the one that had been killed last night. Taking advantage of the situation, Stone dove on one of the sealings, snatched it up in his claws, and flung it away across the water. *What the shit is going on?* Moon thought.

Movement in the water caught his eye and he swung around, but it was Bramble, just pulling herself up onto the docking platform. She ran over to the pillars, studying them in the light of a glowing sea-weed clump Merit must have made for her. Moon growled under his breath at the danger she was putting herself in. But he realized that while Delin and Chime and Merit had all made extensive drawings of the symbols, it was all sitting back on the ship, because Moon and Jade hadn't given them any time to go get it. Bramble must have needed to check on what exactly was carved into the pillars.

A group of dakti came in low over the water, past the bow of the sunsailer, and River and Root dove for them. Moon hung back, waiting to see if it was a distraction. But the Fell fighting with each other near the island couldn't be a distraction. Not unless it was the dumbest distraction anyone had ever thought of in the long and varied history of the Three Worlds.

Then Moon saw a dark shape swoop on Bramble. He dove, pulled in his wings and arrowed down. Closer, he saw it was a ruler, and it had her pinned to the dock platform. Moon had never been blind with rage, the way he had heard some groundlings describe it. He had been so consumed with killing that it blotted out all rational thought, and that was what he was now.

He snapped out his wings at the last moment to retain control over the strike and slammed into the ruler. He knocked the ruler away from Bramble and down onto the stone dock. They slid a good twenty paces, the ruler on the bottom. Moon reached to tear the stunned ruler's throat out. Then a voice behind him called, "Let him go!"

He twisted around. Another ruler gripped Bramble's shoulders. Then he saw it wasn't a ruler; it was the half-Fell queen.

She had the Fell crest and the Raksuran spines like Shade, Moon's half-Fell half-clutchmate, and her scales were matte black, like a ruler, like a Raksuran consort. The light from the ship caught a reflection off a web pattern of contrasting scales, like a queen's. Her voice harsh, speaking Altanic, she said, "You let him go, I let her go."

Moon, now terrified as well as enraged, was paralyzed for an instant. *If I let him go, he'll kill me and she'll kill Bramble.* You couldn't bargain like this with Fell, you couldn't. Fell lied like it was breathing, they didn't see any other living thing as sentient.

Then the Fell queen pushed Bramble away. Bramble staggered, then scrambled out of reach, toward Moon.

Moon, almost by reflex, dragged the ruler upright and shoved him away. The ruler staggered, then ran to the queen.

Bramble reached Moon's side, panting, wild-eyed.

The queen caught the ruler around the waist and leapt into the air. Moon shoved Bramble behind him and spun to watch the queen, certain it was a trick. But she spread her wings, caught the wind, and vanished into the night.

CHAPTER SEVENTEEN

Bramble choked on her first attempt to speak, then managed to gasp, "So what was that?"

"I don't know. Are you all right?" Gripping her shoulder, Moon could feel her trembling.

"Sure." Bramble wiped an arm across her face. "I need to get back to Delin and Merit."

"Why'd you come over here?" Moon picked her up and she clung to his collar flanges. "For the symbols?"

"Yes." She tightened her grip as Moon leapt into the air. "Delin didn't have a chance to bring his notes and he couldn't remember the different ways they were all pointing and I wasn't sure which ones he was trying to remember."

Moon landed on the top of the pillar and gauged the distance to the cliff wall. From this angle he saw Merit and Delin, huddled on the ledge, examining something. Merit had made several clumps of vegetation and sea wrack glow, and there was just enough light to make out their shapes. Chime had climbed up about thirty paces and clung to the wall.

Moon crouched low, and Bramble tucked her head down. He pushed off as hard as he could, flapped once for stability and distance, and hit the side of the cliff. He slid down a little, getting a close look at the coral substance covering the rock as it cracked and fragmented under his weight. His claws caught hold and he started to climb toward Chime.

As Moon reached him, Chime scraped at the rock, exposing more carved symbols in the light of a clump of moss he had jammed into a crevice. "Any luck?" Moon asked.

"Not so far." Chime peered at him. "You've got Bramble?"

"I almost got eaten by Fell," Bramble informed him. "I'm climbing down, I need to tell Delin which symbols."

"What?" Distracted, Chime stared at her as she transferred her grip from Moon to the rock face and started down.

"The half-Fell queen is out here," Moon said. From the yelling below at Bramble's reappearance, it was obvious that her decision to jump in the water and swim to the dock hadn't been approved by Merit or Delin.

Chime groaned with dismay, and went back to scraping at the coral growth.

Moon half-twisted around so he could watch their backs, holding on with one hand. From the sunsailer, he heard metal creak and groan under the strain. He asked, "What are you looking for?"

It was a vague question under the circumstances, but Chime answered, "Merit said there was a good chance the door doesn't open from the outside, because when the city was alive, someone would always be there to open it for visitors. They wouldn't want just anybody to be able to get in."

Moon saw movement in the air near the sunsailer, a dark shape, more than one dark shape, just on the edge of the light. Then a blue figure flashed past and hit the dark shape in midair. He gritted his teeth, fighting the urge to fling himself off the rock and join the fight. "That's not encouraging."

"No, but Bramble said nobody leaves a place like this and thinks they aren't coming back. Like the colony tree. So if there wasn't already a way to open it from the outside, they would have made one."

"Maybe they just used magic," Moon said. Looking past the bow of the sunsailer, he saw the distance-lights fall on a row of giant sealings, the massive bodies curving in toward them. A Kishan weapon fired, light blossomed in the air, and a kethel screamed. *It was a chance*, he thought, *we had to take it*. But they weren't going to figure this out in time, if there was a way to figure it out at all. Some of the warriors and the Arbora might escape if they could get to the island and dig in . . .

Exasperated, Chime was saying, "Well, Moon, that's a possibility of course but there's absolutely no point in assuming that—"

Then Merit yelled, "It's here!"

Chime hissed and half-climbed and half-slid down the wall. Moon dropped after him.

Delin and the two Arbora crouched on the ledge. Merit held up a clump of wet sea wrack spelled for light, illuminating some still barely visible chipped and cracked carvings. Moon swung down beside Chime on the ledge. He had no idea what they were all staring at. He said, "How do you know that's it?"

Merit said breathlessly, "It's the same symbols on those pillars, the ones we think meant 'opening.' They're around this hole, and we think it's like the hole in the center of the flower-thing at the forerunner city."

Bramble turned to him, her expression elated. "There's old damage, like turns ago someone dug at it, trying to get in."

Delin urgently motioned Chime closer. "Chime, you try it. You know about it from the other city."

Moon thought they had all lost their minds. It didn't look anything like the flower-thing that had guarded the entrance to the underwater forerunner city. It looked like a hole in the rock face, possibly dug by one of the worm-like coral creatures who had infested the cliff wall.

Chime slipped past Merit and Bramble, splashing in the water lapping over the ledge. He tried to peer into the hole. "Can't see anything, and there's no way to get a light down there without blocking it. Anybody have a stick, or do we have to send someone to the boat?"

Delin dug through the satchel slung over his shoulder. "Try this." He handed Chime a long thin metal rod with a hook on the end. "I confess I brought it with this possibility in mind."

Moon hissed under his breath. The sealings were closer to the sunsailer and he couldn't see any Raksura in the air. He couldn't see any Fell in the air either, which could be fear of the Kishan weapons or the knowledge that the sealings were about to do their work for them.

260

Chime took the rod and inserted it into the hole. Moon held his breath. After a long moment, Chime hissed and pulled the rod out. "There's no catch in there."

Delin took the rod back. Chime planted both hands on either side of the hole and leaned on the rock, muttering, "This has to be it."

It didn't have to be it. This was a very old city, and they had always known it might have nothing to do with the forerunners. That Callumkal might be wrong and Vendoin right, that it was a foundation builder city. Even if it had been forerunner, that didn't mean it would open the same way as the other city. And there were two Arbora and a groundling here and Moon and Chime could only save two of them when the sunsailer sank, and he had no idea where Jade and Stone and the others were.

Then Chime leaned into the wall, pressing his cheek against it. He said, "Oh, wait. I hear something."

"Hear or 'hear,'" Bramble asked, her claws flexing nervously.

"It's like . . ." Chime's voice was barely audible over the wind and the growing rush of sealings moving through the water. " . . . breaking rock, someone, something breaking . . . I don't think it's forerunner, I think it's something else . . ."

The Arbora froze. Moon stared, then realized Chime's left hand was half atop one of the symbols. There was a duplicate of that symbol on the other side. Moon nudged Merit and pointed.

Merit twitched in realization and carefully reached to move Chime's left hand all the way onto the symbol. His claws clicked against the rock. "The Fell are wrong," Chime said clearly.

Merit waved urgently at Bramble. Her teeth bared, she gently moved Chime's right hand all the way onto the symbol on that side. Then Chime said, "Oh, Moon was right, it is magic."

The cliff cracked and shuddered underfoot. Moon clung to the rock with his claws and caught Merit before he fell backward off the ledge. Bramble grabbed Delin. Broken rock and coral fragments rained down on their heads and the water below the ledge dropped with a gurgling whoosh. Then the cliff slowly, ponderously, started to swing inward.

Moon clung to the rock and to Merit, equal parts astonished and appalled. It wasn't the whole cliff, it was a large section of it, at least a hundred paces wide and almost as tall. Bramble had said the door was big enough to get the sunsailer through, but Moon hadn't thought it would be this big.

The door swung in toward a great dark tunnel in the escarpment, a channel in the bottom rapidly filling with water from the sea. Inside it was as dark as an underground cavern, the air flowing out of it stale and tinged with salt and a faint scent of plant rot.

"The sunsailer," Delin said, his voice faint. He stared into the darkness, wide-eyed. "They must come in, before the Fell . . ."

Moon had never seen Delin this overcome before and he was fairly sure he didn't like it. Bramble said, "Chime, can you close it? Once we get the groundlings inside—"

Chime gasped, "I can barely hold it open, so yes, I think I can close it."

"Stay here," Moon told them all. He made sure Merit had a good grip on the rock, then moved down the ledge and leapt upward.

The wind caught him and almost sent him right through the open doorway. Moon flapped frantically, rolled, and managed to get himself under control. He flew toward the sunsailer, careful to circle around it and stay out of the distance-lights, in case any of the Kishan were a little too quick to fire. He spotted Callumkal out on the upper deck directing the weapons. And there was Jade, circling above the sunsailer, with Briar and Balm flanking her. Further out, Stone swept past.

He drew near Jade and shouted, "The door's open! Chime's holding it open!"

She circled around and her spines flared as she saw it. She called to the warriors, "Briar, go get Root and River! Balm, you and Song go to the Arbora!"

As the warriors shot away, Jade dropped toward the sunsailer. Moon waited to make sure Stone was headed back this way, and then followed Jade down.

They landed on the steering cabin roof. Jade said, "Tell them. I'll keep watch."

Moon dropped to his knees and leaned down to see through the window. Rorra held the steering lever, grimacing with the effort of keeping it steady. He knocked on the glass. She flinched, then glared at him. He pointed emphatically toward the escarpment. She leaned sideways to see around him, and her eyes widened. She mouthed something that wasn't in Altanic and then turned back to the steering lever.

Moon pushed to his feet. "Are the Fell fighting each other out there or am I hallucinating?"

Jade said grimly, "If you're hallucinating, then we're all doing it with you."

Stone passed overhead then abruptly doubled back. Moon and Jade ducked as he came in low. He shifted and dropped down onto the cabin roof. He staggered and Jade caught his arm to steady him. Stone said, "That gets a little harder every time."

Moon swayed as the sunsailer jerked sideways. Metal groaned as it started to turn toward the escarpment. Hopefully the Fell hadn't realized that the door in the escarpment was open. The distance-lights were pointed toward the sky and the island, and it would be hard to see the door in the dark from where most of the Fell were still flying. Hopefully all the dakti who had managed to get close were dead. He asked Stone, "Could you tell what the Fell were doing?"

Stone didn't take his gaze off the dark sky. "It has to be two different flights— Look out!"

Moon spun around and spotted the shapes streaking past overhead. Rulers, at least five of them, aiming for the city's doorway.

Moon jumped straight up into the air, almost into the chest of the first ruler. It grabbed at him and Moon ripped upward with his disemboweling claws. Jade shot past him and tore into the rulers above. Then a wash of displaced air told Moon that Stone was aloft. The rulers scattered.

Moon twisted in the air, ripping his claws free of the ruler's stomach and shoving it away from him. It flapped unsteadily and turned back toward the island, but he didn't have time to finish it off. He caught the wind and looked for the remaining rulers. They were about a hundred paces off the stern of the sunsailer, near the stone platform with the pillars, trying to regroup.

Jade swept down toward them and Moon tilted his wings to get above her, then they both dove in tandem.

Jade hit one and drove it straight into the ruler flying below it. Moon swerved at the last instant to land on top of another and rip its wing webbing. Stone slammed through again, knocking the three remaining rulers out of the sky. Then Moon felt the air change and knew something was about to slam into him from behind. He flared his spines.

A weight struck him, jolted him hard enough for his wings to lose the wind. He snapped them in and rolled, and heard a distinctive dakti shriek right in his ear. He felt the tug on his spines and realized the stupid miserable thing had impaled itself so deeply it couldn't pull free.

Moon snarled and spun again, and its claws scrabbled at his back, trying to get past his spines and scales. He was going to have to take it down to the stone platform and scrape it off.

As he dove for the platform, the dakti apparently gave up on survival and yanked itself further down on his spines, reaching for his head. Moon slapped claws away from his eyes and cupped his wings, hoping the platform was where he thought it was. Then suddenly the weight was jerked away and the dakti's angry shriek abruptly cut off.

Moon tumbled, snapped his wings in at the last instant, slammed into the stone dock, and rolled. He landed in an awkward crouch and looked up.

The half-Fell queen stood on the edge of the dock, holding the bleeding dakti by the neck. She tossed it into the water.

Moon sprang backward and almost rammed into a pillar. Then Jade landed between them.

For a long heartbeat, they were all frozen, crouching, ready to attack or flee. Then the Fell queen said, "You saw what I did." She was speaking to Jade.

Jade said, "I saw. That's why you still have your head."

The Fell queen flicked her tail, an oddly Raksuran gesture. Teeth gritted, trying not to breathe too loudly and upset the fragile balance of the situation, Moon wondered if she had much control over her spines, if she used them to express emotion and communicate. Or if she didn't know how.

The Fell queen eased to a standing position and Jade copied her, the two moving in time with each other. The Fell queen said, "I want to talk." She spoke Raksuran, but her pronunciation was oddly accented.

Jade said, "How did you control the sealings?"

Yes, Moon thought, *keep her distracted.* Out of the corner of his eye he could see the stern of the sunsailer moving toward the doorway.

The Fell queen answered, "That was the other flight. The sealings aren't under control, the progenitor asked them to attack you. She found their spawning ground. Now they have to do what she says."

So they were right, it wasn't one flight nesting in two different places, but two flights. *That . . . doesn't necessarily help*, Moon thought.

The Fell queen stepped to the side, tilting her head as if trying to see Moon better. "I don't want to fight."

Jade's spines flicked. "You know, that's what all Fell say. So unless you have something more interesting to add—"

"We chased away the other flight. You've seen it."

Jade said, "So you don't want to share your prey. How does that not surprise me?"

"I don't want prey. I want your help."

"We've heard all this before. You're hardly the first to try this."

Moon, his senses hyper-alert, felt something change in the water lapping over his claws. It might just be a wake from the sunsailer's passage, but the angle and the force of it was wrong. Jade hadn't given any indication she had noticed.

The Fell queen tilted her head, another Raksuran mannerism. "The other flight wanted something in the city. Let us come in with you."

Jade laughed. "We're going into the city to get away from you. Surely you noticed that."

"But you don't know what's inside. We know what the other flight told us."

"Then tell me. Prove I should listen to you."

The Fell queen hesitated, and the moment stretched. For a heartbeat, Moon actually thought she was going to tell them something important, something real. Then she bared her fangs in a gesture more Raksuran than Fell, and said, "You don't want to listen. I told you—"

Water fountained up beside the platform as Stone lunged across it at the half-Fell queen. Jade leapt to the top of the pillar, and Moon scrambled up beside her, just in time to see the Fell queen fling herself into the air. She tumbled across the water, flapping frantically, then managed to get enough height to catch the wind.

Stone stood up, spreading his wings, but the Fell queen turned away, arrowing off toward the island. Jade growled, quivering with the urge to give chase. Moon glanced back toward the door to see the stern of the sunsailer was all the way inside. "Jade, we need to go."

She hissed in reluctant agreement, and shouted, "Stone, the door!"

Stone launched into the air. Jade leapt upward and Moon followed, letting the wind catch him and push him toward the sunsailer.

He saw Bramble and Delin waiting on the deck with half a dozen armed Kishan. River, Root, and Briar were up on the cabin roof. He couldn't see Balm and Song, but Chime must still be down on the door ledge. And where was Merit?

Jade dropped onto the stern deck first and furled her wings in to give Moon room to land. Moon skidded across the deck and stopped himself on the rail. He saw with relief that Chime and Merit were both down on the ledge, with Balm and Song beside them. Above him, Stone snapped his wings in and shifted to his groundling form, and landed beside him in a crouch.

Kalam ran toward them. "You made it! We were afraid—"

"So were we," Moon admitted. Bramble flung herself at him so hard he staggered back a step.

Stone straightened up and let his breath out in a hiss. Bramble let go of Moon and flung herself at Stone.

The sunsailer's stern cleared the door and Jade shouted, "Chime, let it close!"

Merit tugged on Chime's arm and pulled him away from the wall. Chime staggered and almost went into the water. Balm caught him, lifted him off his feet, and leapt to the railing. Moon reached up and she dropped Chime into his arms, then stepped off the rail.

Annoyed, Chime said, "You can put me down, I'm fine."

Moon's heart thumped in relief as he set Chime on his feet. Chime seemed ruffled and tired, but not hurt. Song arrived with Merit and jumped down from the railing. Nerve-rackingly slow, the great door started to swing backward, moving to shut off the opening. The Kishan distance-lights focused on it. This side was a smooth stone of mottled browns and grays, gleaming damply in the light.

Watching the door, Jade said, "Careful. If one gets in—"

The door was almost shut when a dakti slipped through the narrow opening. It froze in the light, clinging to the door, staring at them as if it hadn't expected them to be watching. A Janderi fired her weapon and fire blossomed in its chest. It collapsed and fell into the dark water.

The door shut with a rumbling thump that seemed to go on for a long time.

Moon leaned on the railing. His wings were a heavy weight and he wanted to shift to groundling, but he was afraid if he did, he would just collapse on the deck and not be able to get up. Jade didn't need a collapsed consort right now.

"That was close." Chime gripped the railing so tightly, the scales over his knuckles were swelling.

It was still close; they hadn't escaped, just changed the level of danger. Moon hoped it was a little less, at least at the moment.

The distance-lights moved across a high curved ceiling, down to huge arched doorways that led off into empty, echoing halls. The scents were all dank stone and saltwater and rotting vegetation. The thrum of the sunsailer's motivator sounded oddly loud. It was punctuated by the Kishan's hurried footsteps and their shouts as they checked for wounded and made sure no one had fallen off or been snatched away by Fell at the last moment.

Moon squinted into the darkness. It still didn't look anything like the forerunner city, which was a relief. The stone was a light gray, the sides of the archways carved to form pillars made to look like giant twisted skeins of rope or vine. The curved ceiling was emblazoned with interlocking squares. Staring upward at it was making Moon dizzy. He swayed and leaned on the railing again.

"What do we do now?" Root said, his voice small and hushed.

Jade looked around at the warriors. They had gathered around on the deck, and everyone had scrapes and claw slashes and probably some impressive bruises under their scales. She focused on River, who had claw rips across his chest and was dripping blood on the deck. "Merit, take River inside and do something about that. Balm, I saw you run into that ruler, you go with them."

Balm, who had one hand pressed to her head and was grimacing in pain, protested, "I'm fine."

"Sure you are." Merit took her wrist and towed her toward the hatch. "Come on, River."

River limped painfully after him. Jade said, "Stone, why don't you go with them?"

Stone glanced around at the empty darkness of the hall. "Nah, I'll just stay here." He sat down on the deck with a wince and a partially suppressed groan.

Jade hissed in exasperation. "I know I made that a question, but what I actually meant was—"

Callumkal strode out of the hatchway, Vendoin and Kellimdar hurrying after him. Callumkal gripped Kalam's shoulder in relief and looked around at the Raksura, asking, "You are all well? Everyone made it inside?"

Giving up on Stone, Jade turned to him. "We're well, is your crew all right?"

"We've accounted for everyone, and there were no serious injuries." Sounding overwhelmed, Callumkal said, "We need to talk about what to do next." He looked around, taking in the size of the entrance passage. "For so long, we wanted to get inside this place, and now . . . We have to get out."

Delin, leaning on Bramble, said, "Cities seldom have one entrance. There must be another way out, even if it is concealed."

Moon thought that was probably true, but they would still have to get past the Fell. From the grim atmosphere, that aspect of the situation had occurred to everyone.

Then Callumkal said, "How did you open the door?"

Jade glanced at Chime. "That's a good question."

Chime hesitated and Bramble gave him a poke. "You said it was magic."

"No. I mean, yes, it was magic. No, nothing told me what to do." Chime's spines shrugged tiredly. "There was no scarily persuasive voice."

"That's good," Moon pointed out. "That's really good."

The Kishan were listening with various expressions of confusion and dismay. "Scarily persuasive voice?" Vendoin glanced at Delin. Her armor patches glistened damply and her dress was dripping onto the deck. She must have been near a window when the sealing had started pouring saltwater into the sunsailer. "Like the one that drew the Fell to the forerunner city?"

"Right, there wasn't one." Chime was distracted, obviously trying to find the right words. "It just felt right to touch those symbols. And I didn't feel anything until I was right in front of them, so if Delin and Bramble and Merit hadn't figured out they were the ones we should be looking for, we'd still be outside with the Fell. Before that, it was all just a big dead sea-mount." Chime looked around at everyone. "I don't know why."

Delin interposed, "We are all tired, and some of us are very old. We should rest while we talk."

Stone punctuated this by stretching out on the deck and apparently falling instantly asleep. Reminded of his other responsibilities, Kellimdar said, "Yes, the crew need rest and food as well." He started off down the deck toward the distance-light operators on the nearest balcony.

As Callumkal and Delin turned to go back inside, Moon told Jade, "I'll stay out here with Stone." He understood Stone's reasoning for remaining on deck. If something attacked the boat, he could shift instantly to deal with it. There were four Kishan crew posted along the stern railing, holding fire weapons and worriedly watching the darkness past the range of the lights, but Moon figured they could use the help.

"I'll stay, too," Chime added. Possibly he wanted to avoid further unanswerable questions from Vendoin. In Chime's place, Moon knew he would have.

Jade's spines indicated reluctant agreement. She said, "Everyone else, inside for now." The warriors and Bramble started to make their way toward the hatch, Root stumbling a little with weariness.

Moon went over to Stone and sat down heavily. Chime followed, sitting on his heels to eye Moon worriedly. "Are you all right?"

"Just sore." Moon shifted to groundling, and managed not to hiss from relief as the weight of his wings melted away. The next moment, the pain of every strained muscle and bruise and claw scratch doubled in intensity, and he managed not to hiss again. He rubbed his eyes, tried to focus. "When you touched the symbols, you said you didn't think it was forerunner."

Chime shifted to groundling, muttered, "Oof, ow." He half fell over, supporting himself with one arm. "Yes, but now I can't think why I thought that. Maybe just a different . . . feel? I know at the time it seemed clear, but it's just slipped away."

That's probably a good sign, Moon thought. It seemed more likely all the time that this was a foundation builder city.

The motivator thrummed into life again, and the boat started to move slowly forward. Esankel came out of the hatch, a fire weapon slung over her shoulder, and stood by the railing. She made a soft exclamation of awe as one of the distance-lights swept upward over the great blocks on the ceiling. Moon asked her, "Do we know where we're going?"

"No, they thought it was better to move forward, away from the door, in case the Fell get it open." She turned away from the rail, and lifted her hands in a gesture of uncertainty.

They sat in the quiet darkness for some time, watching the Kishan go back and forth from the hatchway and the steps that led to the upper decks, checking over the sunsailer for damage, shining their lights on the city's walls and remarking softly on the carving.

Moon didn't mean to sleep, but he nodded off at some point. He woke lying on the deck next to Stone, with Bramble leaning over him.

Moon could feel through the deck that the ship wasn't moving. Raksura could sense the position of the sun, even when they couldn't see it, and he knew that outside it was near dawn. Everything was quiet except for dripping water, and the faint movements of the crew. The distance-lights still played over the cavernous space and the water. He cleared his dry throat and said, "We stopped."

Bramble nodded. "They decided that we've come as far as we can without scouting. There's been no sign of the Fell; we're not that far from the door and we'd hear it open. Everybody's been taking turns sleeping, except Vendoin and Kellimdar. They're out there on the docks, copying a bunch of the inscriptions and symbols."

Moon sat up on his elbow. "Docks?" Chime lay curled on his side a couple of paces away, still asleep. Three Kishan were on guard at the stern railing, but Esankel had gone. He heaved himself to his feet and went to the rail for a better look at their surroundings.

They were now in an even larger cavern, in what might be a harbor basin. The rope-like pillars supported archways and sheltered broad stone platforms that did look like docks. There were three to the left of the sunsailer, and two to the right, on either side of a wide canal that led farther into the city. Ramps stretched up from the docks into the shadow past the distance-lights, to openings he could barely see as dark outlines. Vendoin, Kellimdar, and several Kishan stood on one of the docks on this side with a smaller distance-light. Kellimdar was adjusting it to shine on another section of the side of the archway, while Vendoin wrote hastily on a slate. The other Kishan, Moon was glad to see, were all armed with fire weapons and were warily keeping their gaze on the ramps and the water.

Bramble said, "Vendoin thinks she might be able to translate the writing."

Moon frowned at the archway, brightly lit now by the distance-light Kellimdar directed at it. "Uh, what writing?"

"We can't see it," Bramble explained. "It's in colors we can't see. But Vendoin can see it, and so can some of the Kishan, just not all of them. She said it's rare, but they've found it on some of the old foundation builder ruins in Kish."

"Huh." They had encountered a species they hadn't been able to see once, but never colors. Or at least Moon hadn't thought so. If you couldn't see something and no one who could mentioned it, you weren't likely to know about it. "Can Delin see it?"

Bramble snorted. "No, and he's madder than a headless Fell about it, too."

Stone, who was apparently awake, said, "Ha."

Moon turned away from the railing. "Where's Jade?"

"Up in the front, talking with Callumkal."

"Did she ever sleep?" They had all slept a little in the small boat on the way back to the escarpment, but the fighting and difficult flying through most of the night had been draining.

"She said she was going to." Bramble got to her feet. "Are you hungry?"

Moon looked down at himself. There was blood spotted on his clothes, his own and Fell blood. The scratches on his arms had closed up, but the bruises were still all there. He felt like someone had punched him all over his body. "Not really. How are Balm and River?"

"Merit put them both in a healing sleep. Everyone else just needed simples. You should have some tea." She nudged Stone with her foot. "Come on, line-grandfather."

"Ugh," Stone said, or something similar, but let Bramble prod him to his feet.

"What did Jade and Callumkal decide to do?" Moon asked.

Bramble pushed him and Stone toward the hatch. "We know we have to look for a way out, but that's it so far. That's why you need to eat. Go past that room they gave us to the middle part of the ship, then up a level. There's a big common room. Some of the others are there. I'll bring Chime."

Moon found the way down the corridor and up a set of stairs, Stone trailing behind him. There were food odors in the air: cooked fish and waterweed and roots. The stairs opened up to a big room with windows on both sides, with seats built around the walls and more benches fastened to the floor. There was a square Kishan stove in the center of the room, with a pot on the metal frame top emitting fragrant steam. Merit and Delin were there, along with Kalam and Rorra, sitting around on the benches and looking weary and worried.

Balm and River were stretched out on two padded benches at the far end of the room. From their breathing, they were still deep in healing sleep. Moon tasted the air and caught a little blood scent but no sickness or infection. "How are they?"

"River's wounds are healing well," Merit told him. He got up and started to fill a couple of metal cups from the pot. "I'm going to wake Balm in a little and check on her."

Moon sat down on a bench. His back muscles twinged. Stone plopped down next to him and yawned.

Merit handed them both cups. "It's Kishan tea," he explained. Stone sniffed it and winced.

"It's not as good as yours," Kalam offered, "but we have a lot more of it."

Moon downed half the cup. It had a dark smoky flavor that wasn't unpleasant. "How's the boat?" he asked Rorra.

She sighed. She had a darkening bruise on her forehead and the skin under her eyes looked swollen. "The steering is pulling to the right. But we're still floating." She added dryly, "We'll be comfortable until the food and water run out."

Kalam said, "The sunsailer had just filled its water tanks from the spring on the island, so . . ." He looked around at everyone and shrugged a little. "That won't be a problem for a while."

Delin stirred. It was hard to tell past the weathered gold of his skin, but Moon thought his face looked a little sunken. He gestured toward the windows. "When we search the city, we will surely find a way out."

Rorra said, "But we have to find it before the Fell get in. And this place is very large. It must fill the entire escarpment."

Delin nodded. "That is a succinct description of our problem."

Bramble came in with a yawning, bleary-eyed Chime. They were followed by Song and Root carrying wooden trays and accompanied by a strong scent of food. Moon tried to get up to help but was still moving so slowly that they had set their burdens down on the benches by the time he was on his feet. Song began to pass out bowls, saying apologetically, "It's all cooked. You're supposed to eat it with these little scoop things."

It was a thick broth with fish, crunchy white and red roots, something green and leafy that tasted like salty sea wrack, and a thick piece of bread in the bottom. The sight of it woke Moon's stomach and he finished off three bowls before he took another breath. Food had been a good idea; he already felt much less bleary and slow.

All three groundlings were still on their first bowl. Delin was unsurprised, but Kalam and Rorra had initially looked puzzled at the number of bowls. After watching the Raksura eat, they evidently understood. With Stone on his fifth bowl, Kalam asked, "Do you want me to get some more?"

Stone, still eating, shook his head. Moon said, "No, this should be enough." It was enough for now, mostly because everyone had been catching fish off and on during the day. But if they were trapped here for longer than a few days, flying around searching this place and expending energy, it was going to become a problem.

Jade walked in, trailed by Briar. She stopped to check Balm and River, then sat down next to Moon. He said, "Did you eat?"

She began, "I don't need—" and Moon handed her a bowl. She looked down at it for a moment, then reached for the scoop.

Briar took a bowl from the tray. "We've been talking about searching for the way out," she said, while Jade's mouth was full.

Jade nodded, swallowed, and added, "We need to start as soon as you're ready." She watched Moon for a moment. "Are you ready?"

He was a lot more ready now than he had been before the food. "Sure."

Bramble was refilling everyone's cups with tea. "About that. You need to let me help you."

Merit seconded that, collecting empty bowls to pile back on the tray. "Bramble figured out which symbols to look for to get in here, and you might need her help figuring out other things."

Delin said, "I will help, as well."

"You don't look so good," Chime told him, before Moon could. "I think you need to stay here and rest."

"I will look worse if I am eaten by Fell," Delin countered.

Jade eyed them, and finished chewing. "Well, you're right. We'll take Bramble and Delin."

With Callumkal watching worriedly, the Raksura leapt from the deck down onto the nearest dock. The party was Moon, Jade, Stone, Song, and Briar, with Root and Chime carrying Bramble and Delin. Rorra was a last-moment addition and was travelling under her own power, with one of the flying packs salvaged from the wreck of the flying boat.

As Moon landed, his spines wanted to shiver and he refused to let them; it was too easy to imagine something waiting in that dark, watching them. The warriors set Bramble and Delin down so they could get their lights out and so everyone could stare warily around at the immense shadowy space. Rorra had a small version of a distance-light mounted on the shoulder of her pack, and it cut sharply through the darkness. Merit had spelled a collection of the metal cups and the Kishan had contributed some net bags of glowing moss. Bramble whispered, "It's scarier without the groundling boat," and Briar hushed her.

"I think I agree," Rorra murmured, tugging the strap of her pack.

Rorra was here because Kellimdar and Vendoin had seemed to want a member of the Kishan party to go along, and Callumkal had given in to placate them. Moon thought they were more suspicious of Delin than the Raksura, not wanting a rival scholar to have a chance at any discoveries. Kalam had volunteered to go, but in the face of Callumkal's obvious fear for his safety, Rorra had offered to go instead. This was actually helpful, since if they found anything underwater that needed exploring, it would be easier for her to do it.

Merit had stayed behind with Balm and River, to give them time to recover fully in their healing sleep. He also intended to scry. Moon had heard him tell Bramble, "You go find some more doors you shouldn't and I'll stay here and fail to scry anything worth knowing."

On the far side of the boat, Vendoin, Kellimdar, and their guards were lifting into the air with their flying packs, going to copy the writings on the walls above the other docks. Though Vendoin had told Jade, "From what I see so far, these inscriptions may be standard greeting texts we've seen before, in the builder ruins in Kish. But it's that inscription—" She had nodded up toward the broad arch above the central hall, her armor plates cracking with her excitement. "—that may truly prove the most valuable. It's in a prominent spot, and I am sure I have never seen it before."

Stone was in his winged form, and had paced a short distance down the dock to the ramp. Jade said, "Forward first." It was obvious that the likeliest spot for another opening was at the opposite side of the escarpment from this one. If they were lucky, the canal leading away from the basin would cut straight through the city to another hidden doorway. Of course, the Fell were bound to think of that, too. "Bramble, you go with Stone."

Bramble shouldered one of the moss-light bags and went to Stone. He held out his hand and she scrambled up his scales to a secure position next to his collar flange. Stone leapt up to the first pillar along the edge of the canal, and then to the next, just out of range of the sunsailer's lights. Bramble's lighted net swung wildly, then stilled as she steadied it. Moon squinted to see, but couldn't spot anything but the carved surface of the pillar, and the water stretching beyond.

"Ready," Jade said. Moon glanced back at Delin and Chime. Rorra tugged at the strap on her pack, and it pulled her upward, her boots hovering a few inches above the pavement.

"Here we go again," Chime muttered as he picked up Delin.

Jade sprang into flight and Moon leapt after her with the others.

CHAPTER EIGHTEEN

Moon took the last position in the group, wanting Chime and Delin to be closer to Jade and Stone, and wanting to keep an eye on Rorra in case her pack failed. And to make sure nothing came out of the dark to snatch anyone away.

After several jumps from pillar to pillar, the light from the sunsailer faded, making the hall ahead look like a dark and slowly shrinking tunnel. The rest of Moon's senses could tell they were still moving through a cavernous space. The lap of water against rock, the click of claws finding purchase on the stone, an occasional half-heard sound from the ship behind them all struck faint echoes from distant walls.

Then Bramble's light jerked and Stone hissed. Moon froze, his claws gripping the edge of a pillar. Everyone stopped. Carrying Delin, Chime had landed just above Moon. Rorra maneuvered her pack close to his shoulder.

After a moment, Moon heard what must have alerted Stone. Claws scrabbled on rock below them, near the edge of the canal. Jade, on the pillar just ahead, turned back and tapped the spell-light hooked around her pack, and then pointed toward Rorra. Interpreting this, Moon whispered, "She wants you to use your light and try to see what it is."

Rorra hovered closer, gripping the light mounted on the shoulder of her flying pack. Her voice low, she said, "Where is it?"

Holding on with one hand, Moon pointed to where he thought the scrabble had come from. Rorra angled the light and squeezed it, and the illumination suddenly doubled. It formed a thin shaft, throwing light down onto the edge of the canal. It showed only empty pavement and lapping water, but movement just on the edge of the darkness made Rorra twitch the light over.

Something huddled on the pavement, something at least the size of a small warrior. It had multiple spiky limbs, and a protective shell in bright colored stripes, red, yellow, blue. So many antennae stood out from the head that Moon couldn't see any features, if it had eyes or a mouth. Two curved claws so sharp the light glinted off their edges shot out from the tangle of limbs, then the creature slid off the pavement into the water.

Rorra moved her light around, searching for more, but as far as they could see there was no movement. That still left a lot of dark space down there that they couldn't see. "Well, we're not alone in here," Chime muttered.

"No swimming," Moon agreed. They hadn't seen any waterlings like that around the island, so the creatures might live in the city. All this water was coming in from the open sea some way, probably through channels buried deep in the rock. "Seen anything like that before?" he asked Rorra.

Eyeing the dark water, she said, "No, not that large. There's a tiny version something like it in the shallows near Vesselae that can snip your fingers off if it gets the chance. I would think a large creature with claws like that would be extremely deadly."

Moon thought so too. Ahead, Jade hissed a command and they continued on.

They passed a long section where there were no archways leading off into the depths of the city, just the supporting pillars and the ledge running along the side of the canal. Moon could tell the hall wasn't quite straight, but curved gently toward the left and the eastern end of the escarpment. Then Bramble's light jerked up suddenly and stopped. As Moon drew closer, he saw Stone had landed on a bridge or gallery, stretching across the hall. The canal extended below it, but seemed to open up into a large space. *I really hope this doesn't dead-end into another basin*, Moon thought. But this city was huge; surely it couldn't function with just one entrance.

The others caught up one by one and Moon reached them and landed beside Chime and Delin. It wasn't just a bridge, it was a junction. Standing on Stone's shoulder, Bramble held her net-light up as high as she could, revealing a giant seven-sided space, with tall doorways in each wall.

Chime set Delin on his feet and stepped over to a large oblong of crystal set into the floor. He crouched to peer down through it. "So does the main canal split into seven branches, and one of these hallways follows each branch?"

Jade flicked a spine in Root and Song's direction and they both jumped over the edge of the bridge. After a few moments they climbed back up and Song reported, "Seven canals, each right below one of these doors. They aren't nearly as tall and wide as the hall we just came up, and it would be tricky to fly along them. They all look big enough for the groundling boat, though."

Jade said grimly, "Yes, but which one do we follow?" She turned to look at the doors. "There isn't a middle one. That would have been helpful."

There were a few dismayed hisses as the realization penetrated. All the doors were set at angles, none obviously a continuation of the main hall.

Rorra stepped to the edge of the bridge to look down at the canal, angling her light to let her see the sides. "If the halls parallel each canal all the way along, that's easier than having to trace them by water. Particularly if the canals are inhabited by those waterlings. It's just a matter of picking the right one."

"'Just a matter?'" Delin echoed.

"I didn't say it was an easy matter," Rorra admitted, stepping back.

Jade showed her fangs in a brief grimace. "So we may have to follow each one to see if there's an outer door at the end."

Moon didn't think the task was that enormous. "The city's tall, but it isn't that wide. It would take, what, maybe a couple of hours to cross the top? The outside walls taper in, but not that much. So searching each canal shouldn't take that long."

"They might connect to each other," Chime added. "That should help, too."

Jade paced away. "It would still be better if we picked the right one first."

With Bramble on his shoulder, Stone moved to the first door, letting the light fall down it a little. It was a hallway, on a smaller scale than the big one that led here, with carvings on the arching walls and maybe pillars farther down. Stone moved to check each door, but the halls seemed all the same. There were bands of carving around the doors, but they were all the same size, and nothing seemed to indicate one door was more important than the others. Bramble reported, "I don't see any of the symbols we found on the entrance." She added wryly, "That would have been handy."

"Maybe we should have brought Vendoin to see the writing," Root said. "I mean, if there's writing."

Delin stood near a pillar, examining the carving. "She would still have to translate it, which takes time. And the Hian interpretation of foundation builder language is greatly disputed." His voice dry, he added, "I heard a great deal about that on the way to the Reaches." He looked around again, squinting in the dim light. "The designs are asymmetrical. And the entrance was toward the eastern end of the escarpment, not in its center. There is less room for the canals on the eastern side."

Jade's tail lashed slowly as she considered it. "So it's more likely some of these canals dead-end, or get smaller."

Briar said, uncertainly, "There's enough of us. We could split up to search each. That would take less time."

Bramble snorted. "There's stories that start that way and they all end 'and then they were eaten.'" Stone grunted in agreement.

Everyone was looking at Jade, waiting for a decision. Trying to give her some breathing room, Moon said, "Do you want to go back and wait for Merit to scry?" He didn't expect her to say yes, considering how badly Merit's attempts to scry had been going.

"There's no telling how long that will take." Jade hesitated, her tail still moving slowly. "Chime, which hall should we start with?"

Moments like these were when Moon felt Chime's former life as a mentor came in handy. A warrior would have balked at taking the responsibility; at this point, Moon would have picked a door at random. Chime moved forward, studying each doorway intently. "Asymmetrical," he murmured. "And the gate into the city was toward the east, and a lot of these carved designs have a focal point toward the left . . ."

Moon, with Jade, Stone, Rorra, and the warriors, turned to stare at the nearest carvings. Bramble and Delin just nodded. Once it was pointed out, Moon could see that many of the carvings seemed to look better if you tilted your head to the left, but he had no idea what that meant. Chime finished, "So I'm guessing we should try that door first." He pointed to the one third from the left. He turned to consult Bramble and Delin.

Bramble said, "It could be that one or the one to its right, but . . . Yes, I think we should start with it."

Delin nodded agreement. "Your theory is sound, Chime."

"What just happened?" Rorra asked Moon.

He said, "I have no idea."

The hall wasn't tall or wide enough to make flying or leaping feasible, and while a bounding gait would cover ground faster, it wasn't a good way to travel through a place as strange and potentially dangerous as this. So they walked.

Moon was worried this might be hard on Delin and Rorra, but Delin seemed more interested in trying to study the wall carvings their lights revealed, and Rorra didn't seem fatigued. Moon still meant to remind Jade to call for a rest sooner than she normally would need to.

Every fifty paces or so there was another oblong crystal inset in the floor. The glass was cloudy with age, but still allowed a dim view down to the canal below, just enough to see Rorra's distance-light glinting off the water. With the others, Moon kept tasting the air, but all he could detect was saltwater, rock, nervous Raksura, nervous sealing, and Delin. Keeping his voice low, Chime said, "This isn't the worst place we've ever explored. If it wasn't for the possibility of a monster locked up in here somewhere, this wouldn't be so bad." He was clearly trying to keep his spirits up, because even as he said it, his spines twitched uneasily.

Walking ahead of them, Briar added, "And that we might starve to death if we can't get past the Fell."

"Right, I forgot about that one," Chime said sourly. "Thanks for reminding me."

"Remember the foundation builder writing," Delin said. "This place is probably not of the forerunners. Unless they took control of it somehow, before or after the foundation builders departed."

"Then why did it let Chime open it?" Bramble asked.

"Good question," Delin said wryly.

Ahead, Stone stopped, and Bramble held up the net-light.

A staircase twisted up a pillar, leading up through an open shaft in the ceiling. Across the hall, an opening showed another set of steps curling down to the canal below. Moon ducked around Stone's big furled wing to see the steps. Each was broad and flat across the middle, with two raised sections to either side, one a little higher than the other. Delin and Rorra moved up beside him, and Rorra said, "More than two legs? Or just decorative?"

"I don't know." Delin leaned into the stairwell, holding his light. "Odd."

Stone set Bramble down, then shifted to his groundling form. Rorra flinched away from the abrupt transformation, but Delin just stepped closer to take advantage of the unobstructed view. Bramble's frills brushed Moon's scales as she pushed between him and Chime to see.

Briar, Song, and Root looked down the other set of stairs, trying to angle their lights to see more. Thinking of the size of the escarpment, Moon said, "I wonder if the city really fills the whole mountain. It's a long walk up to the top, and we saw buildings through the glass up there."

"We can't get the boat up stairs. Come on," Jade said, not patiently.

The others stepped away reluctantly. Moon had to admit, it was intriguing. He wanted to see the top of the city, wanted a better look at the shadow-shapes sealed under the glass. With a long look at the stairs, as if he was reluctant to leave them as well, Stone said, "We're coming."

Root added, "It's not like anyone wants to find the monster."

Stone gave Root a nudge to the head, then shifted back to his winged form.

They moved through the darkness with their lights throwing shadows on the walls and the graceful lines of the off-center carvings. Some distance along, Rorra stopped to drink from her water flask, and made Delin take a drink as well. Moon and Chime stopped with them, just in case something terrible chose that moment to leap out of the shadows. Ahead, Jade noticed and slowed the group's pace so she could keep them in sight. Rorra stoppered the flask and put it back in her pack, saying, "You really think it's too dangerous to split up? It seems so empty."

Moon twitched his spines uneasily. "It's too dangerous."

Chime told her, "The creature in the forerunner city made us and the Fell see things that weren't there."

As they started walking again, she said, "But we don't think one is here now, do we? This is so different from the city you described."

"The creepiness is the same," Chime said.

Some time later, Moon saw Root catch up with Jade. He asked her something in a plaintive tone. She stopped, and pulled affectionately on one of his frills. She turned back and said, "We'll stop for a moment. Root's hungry."

Stone set Bramble down, and shifted to groundling while she dug in her pack for the food she had brought along. They had some bread and some of the dried sea-weed that the Kishan swore was almost as good as eating meat.

Moon turned to ask Rorra and Delin if they wanted any when Rorra swayed and caught Delin's shoulder. "Sorry," she said, and put a hand to her head. "I feel ill."

Moon stepped over to take her arm to steady her, and caught the scent of blood. "Are you bleeding?"

She frowned at him. "No."

He looked down and saw a dark spot just below her left knee, above the top of her boot. "Yes."

"What?" She stared at it, uncomprehending.

"Sit down, here," Delin urged her, and he and Moon helped ease her down.

Sitting on the floor, Rorra let out a breath and admitted, "That feels better." Moon helped her unbuckle the boot and ease it away from the cloth of her pants. Where the fabric and leather had rubbed against her skin, there was a bleeding sore. Rorra swore in Kedaic, and said, "This happens sometimes when I have to walk all day. But I didn't feel it until just now." She touched it carefully and winced. "And we haven't been walking that long."

It must have been there a while. Now that it was in the open, Moon could catch a scent of infection off it. Except that he was sure it hadn't been there when Rorra had removed her clothes and boots to swim in the sea only yesterday.

Chime and Bramble shouldered Moon aside at that point, both proffering medical advice and bandages and simples. Moon left Rorra to accept their help or fend them off, and went over to Jade. "What's wrong?" she asked.

"She has a wound, she must have gotten cut during the battle," Moon said. That was the only explanation he could think of. Except he didn't know how Rorra could have been hurt without it tearing the tough material of her clothes. And it had looked like a chafing sore. "Is Root all right?"

"Just hungry," Jade said, frowning absently.

Still chewing a seaweed cake, Root had gone over to help Bramble hold her pack open. She and Chime were putting together a quick simple for Rorra. Bramble had been carrying extra supplies for Merit and it was coming in handy. It wouldn't have the same effect as a simple made with mentor's magic, but the combinations of herbs and distilled oils still helped healing.

"I'm hungry too," Briar said, keeping watch on the darkness ahead. "And thirsty."

"So am I." Moon rubbed his eyes. He felt grit at the edges of the membranes under his eyelids, but that was probably because of the sand in the air outside. Now that everyone was talking about it, he realized his stomach felt empty and his throat was dry.

Briar said, "We ate before we left. It's only been an hour or so." She flicked her spines, suddenly uneasy. "Hasn't it? My wings feel heavy, like I've been walking forever."

With relief, Song said, "I thought it was just me."

Moon stared at them, then met Jade's gaze. He knew they were sharing a near identical expression of disbelief. Moon tried to sense where the sun was outside the rock of the escarpment, and felt nothing. *Uh oh*, he thought.

Slowly, as if dreading the answer, Jade said, "Stone, how long have we been in this corridor?"

Stone, who had been staring absently down the dark cavern of the hall, turned and ambled back to them. "About an hour." He saw their expressions. "What?"

Moon said, "We're all hungry and tired like we've been walking for more than a day, and Rorra has a chafing sore on her leg that wasn't there earlier, and it's already infected."

Stone took that in. Then he groaned, "Shit."

Delin stepped up beside Moon and said quietly, "I fear you are right." He rubbed his neck below his beard. "I shaved while we were preparing to leave, not knowing when I would have the chance again. I am not a young man, to bristle with hair after barely an hour's time."

"So when did it happen?" Jade said. Her voice was even but she was holding her spines neutral with effort. "After we picked this corridor?"

Briar's spines twitched in agitation, and she turned to Song. "Do you remember how many stairwells we've seen? I was going to count them, just to make sure we could find our way back if there was another branch in the hall. Bone is always going on about the warriors not paying enough attention to tracking, so I was . . . But somehow I didn't count them."

Song shook her head. "I didn't think of that."

Stone said, "Bramble, get over here."

He hadn't raised his voice, but something in his tone made Bramble cross the distance in a single bound. Chime, helping Rorra fasten the bandage, turned to stare, startled. Stone asked Bramble, "How many stairwells?"

"Uh." She blinked. "I thought I was counting them, but I can't remember . . ." She looked around, spines lifting in suspicion. "How long since we've seen one? Or one of those insets in the floor?"

Song said, "I know I was checking those, and so was Root, to make sure we were still above the canal." She tasted the air. "I can smell the saltwater, so it's still below us—"

"Enough." Jade held up her hands, claws spread. "We know what's happened—we know what we think happened—how do we fix it?"

"I just don't think we should move anymore," Chime said, wearily. "We don't know where we are."

Moon nodded grim agreement. They had shifted to groundling to conserve their strength when they had started back down the hall. But after walking for some time, they hadn't even reached the last stairwell again. That was assuming the stairwells were real, and not part of this trap.

The unchanging darkness and no sound except for their own movements and breathing was beginning to weigh on everyone. Moon found himself wondering how long Merit's spells on the moss bundle and the cups would work. If they would be trapped here long enough for their lights to fade.

Chime had been more upset than anyone else, blaming his erratic extra senses for not warning them. Though Root had pointed out, "You thought it was creepy, everyone did. Maybe you just couldn't tell the difference between ordinary creepy and this."

Whatever this was. Chime had said, miserably, "Maybe that's why I picked this hall."

Moon had squelched that quickly. "Whichever one we picked, this would probably still have happened."

Jade added, "Yes, there's no point in a trap like this if there are six ways to avoid it."

Now Stone turned to Jade and said in frustration, "Maybe I should go on alone. Try to . . . get ahead of it."

Moon thought that was a terrible idea. "We don't know what 'it' is."

Jade flicked her spines in a negative. "I don't want us to split up. You might be still stuck like this, but unable to find us again."

It sounded all too possible to Moon. And it must have to everyone else too, because Root edged nearer to Song, Bramble tucked Stone's arm under hers, and Briar gently herded Delin and Rorra closer to the middle of the group. Chime, already standing shoulder to shoulder with Moon, said, "Yes, it's too big a risk."

Stone half snarled but said, "I know, I know."

Jade stood there a moment, her gaze on the shadow at the edge of their lights. "So, trying to go back didn't work."

"We don't know that we are even moving," Delin pointed out. "We may be walking in place."

Rorra added, "At least we know we're actually walking. If we were lying on the floor dreaming this, we might get hungry, but I wouldn't have gotten a sore." With a simple plus a feather-soft stretch of cloth Bramble had brought, Rorra's skin was now protected. Chime had suggested she float along with the flying pack, but she wanted to conserve it, since they weren't certain how long they would be stuck here, and the moss that made its spells work wouldn't last forever.

"So we know we're standing up and walking, even if we aren't making any progress," Jade said. Her gaze fell on Bramble, who was bouncing a little, stifling impatience. Jade said, wryly, "Go ahead."

Bramble said, "It's just I know it sometimes bothers all of you when I get out of hand—"

Moon said, "Bramble, this is just the kind of situation where we need you to get out of hand."

All the Arbora liked stories, and making up stories, and speculating on everything from the motivation of rival courts to every type of intrigue that existed. Bramble was particularly good at it, often to excess. Stone gave her an encouraging nudge forward and she said, "First thing I thought of was that spell you all were trapped in that time in the city in the mountain-thorn." Everyone nodded, and Chime started to object, but Bramble continued, "Of course this isn't the same. Here, time is clearly passing, our bodies feel it passing, we're hungry and tired, it's just that something keeps confusing our heads, making us think we haven't been here that long. But it's not something affecting our memories, because of course otherwise we wouldn't remember that we had realized something was wrong."

Bramble paused for breath, then continued, "So I think this is protective, to keep people from getting any further into this city. And I think it started after we passed that last set of stairwells and the last window down into the canal channel, because since then nothing has changed, the corridor looks the same. I've been trying to see if the carvings are changing, but a lot of them are just repeating patterns, and the light's too bad to tell."

"That's good," Chime said, startled.

Song poked him in the arm. "Don't sound so surprised."

Moon said, "It means Jade's right, splitting up won't help." He wanted to make sure everyone understood that part. A situation where anyone who had separated from the group was still trapped, but alone and unable to find the others, was a nightmare he didn't intend to participate in.

Delin had his fingers tangled in his beard, staring into the distance, deep in thought. "I feel your reasoning is sound, Bramble. If we are some short distance after the last stairwell, what do you think it was that triggered this trap? Was it merely that we stepped over some line imperceptible to us, or was there some object?"

"There wasn't anything on the floor," Chime said, "so if it was an object, it had to be on the walls."

Stone turned away, looking up. "So if we're in a short stretch of hallway, walking it over and over again, we might be between two of Bramble's objects, both mounted on the walls."

"They aren't my objects," Bramble protested.

"No, not your objects, and we don't know that they're actually there." Jade studied the walls. "But if they are, we can't get out from between them by going forward or backward—"

"We need to try going up," Moon finished. "This city isn't designed for people who fly. They may not have thought about that when they made the trap."

They all looked up. The glow from their lights only went up so far, the dark stretching up beyond. Moon felt a prickle down his spines. The darkness seemed to take up more space than it had before, as if the ceiling was higher. "If you're right," Bramble said, "it means this city definitely wasn't built by our forerunners, and it also wasn't built by people who were enemies of our forerunners. If they were trying to trap people who could fly, they'd have put a top on the trap."

The other thing Arbora liked were sweeping conclusions. Moon wasn't sure Bramble was right about what it meant, but it would be interesting to find out.

"A point to think about," Chime said, his spines twitching uneasily. "We might end up in a situation where we're climbing endlessly, instead of just walking endlessly."

The other warriors stared at him, appalled. Stone grimaced. Delin said, "One of you will be carrying me. It will be your decision."

"We'll risk it," Jade said. "Root, take Delin."

"We need to hurry." Stone stepped away and shifted.

Bramble hung the net-light on one of Stone's claws and Stone started up the wall. Jade leapt up next, Bramble starting up behind her. Root followed with Delin, then Song, then Rorra used her flying pack, staying close to the wall. Then Moon started up with Chime and Briar.

They stayed together in a tight group, furled wings just brushing, Stone's tail hanging down to curl up just below them. Moon glanced down and saw darkness seem to fill the space below them like muddy water poured into a bowl. He thought about dropping one of the lighted cups to see if the floor was still there, but if they were stuck here much longer, they might regret the loss of any light source.

"We should be getting close to where the ceiling curves," Chime whispered.

Moon squinted, trying to see it above them, but the net-light bounced around too much as Stone climbed. Under his scales, his skin itched with nerves.

They climbed past a carving of something that might be a stylized sun, the rays streaming off to the upper left, and Moon was sure they must be near the curved ceiling, but he couldn't see anything but wall above.

He was looking up when Stone's form suddenly rippled, as if Moon saw him through a haze of heat. The ripple flowed downward over the others, then Moon's body went numb. The wall spun and there was a roar in his ears, inside his head. His claws slipped on the stone. Above, Jade shouted, "Keep climbing, don't stop!"

Moon scrabbled to keep his grip on the wall. He couldn't feel anything, couldn't tell where his claws were or how hard to grip. Beside him Chime started to slip down the wall and Moon grabbed his shoulder and gave him a shove upward. Briar, near to sliding helplessly herself, grabbed Chime's wrist and tried to pull him up with her. Bramble skittered down the wall almost on top of Moon and he caught her by the frills and shoved her up again.

Then Rorra grabbed Briar and jerked her up, dragging Chime along with her. Chime's tail slapped Moon in the face and Moon grabbed it, and was pulled straight up the wall with them.

His ears popped and the world was suddenly right side up again. There was a ledge just above his head and Jade leaned down from it, grabbed his collar flange, and hauled him up and over.

Moon braced himself on the floor, still shaken. A quick glance around showed him that the others were all here, in various states of disarray, and that this wasn't a ledge, but a large space, a gallery looking down on the hall below. The walls he could see were carved with the same sort of designs, the ceiling also curved. It hadn't been here before, he was certain of it; whenever Stone had held the light up, it had reflected off a solid curved ceiling. He said, "We were right."

Jade squeezed his wrist and stood. "Bramble, remind me to thank Bone for insisting you come along."

Bramble clambered to her feet and lifted the net-light. "You would have gotten here eventually, I just shortened the trip a little," she said, but her spines flicked in pleasure.

Chime crawled to the edge of the gallery and looked down. "I can't see the hall we were in, but it must be down there."

Rorra pushed to her feet, swaying as she got her balance. "There's one of those stairwells, going down. The last we passed, perhaps?" She took a step nearer, peering into the dark, and pointed toward the far end of the room. "And there's one going up."

"Careful," Delin said, as Bramble gave him a hand up. "Do not get too close to the downward stairs. We know the trap extended up some distance."

Moon got to his feet, giving Chime and Root a hand up. Briar and Song were already standing, looking around the room cautiously. Stone hooked the net-light around a claw and took a quick turn around the big room. Then he shifted down to his groundling form. "There's no way out of here but those stairwells."

Jade considered the stairwell that led downward warily. "I don't think we can risk it. It must go straight down to the hall we just left."

"Back into the trap," Delin agreed.

"I don't want to do that again," Root said fervently. There were murmurs and spine twitches of agreement all around.

As the others talked, Moon took one of the lights and went to the wall, following it all around the room. Briar and Song trailed behind him. There was nothing that indicated any secret ways out, not even a crack. At the opposite side, Stone met him with a dry expression. "I tried that already."

"I know." Moon controlled a spine twitch of frustration. He lowered his voice. Briar and Song were standing close and watching worriedly. "The chances of what's up there being . . ." Another terrible prisoner, another creature so dangerous a whole city had to be abandoned to imprison it. And whoever might have left it here wasn't nearly as good at making impenetrable prisons as the forerunners.

"Yeah. There's a chance." Stone looked away. "I wish they'd just killed the damn things."

There had to be some reason they didn't, Moon thought.

"So the trap must have been there to protect that stairwell," Chime was saying, his scaled brow furrowed.

With a growl in her voice, Jade said, "I suppose there's no way to tell the trap that all we want is to get our boat out of this damn city."

Rorra shook her head in frustration. "No, they clearly thought anyone who came in here after the city was deserted would be searching for whatever is up there."

"We have to go up, don't we?" Root said, with a bleak droop of his spines. "What if there's another trap?"

"We can't stay here." Jade turned to the stairwell. "We've already been gone too long."

Bramble's expression was grim. "The others will come after us. They'll follow our scent right up that hall."

Moon exchanged a look with Stone. Then Jade said what they were both thinking, "I just hope they haven't already. I hope Merit was able to scry this."

Merit had felt the sun cross the sky high above the sea-mount. He and everyone else on board had gone from impatience for the Raksura to return to the certainty that something was badly wrong. His scrying was more frustrating than ever, and had yielded nothing but flashes of darkness. *I have to get closer*, he thought. He glared at Balm and River. *Whether some people like it or not.*

The two warriors had both woken up angry, and after nearly a full day of increasingly anxious waiting, they wanted to kill each other. After listening to them argue, Merit wanted to let them.

"I can move faster alone," Balm said to River, her spines lifted dangerously. "I don't need to be slowed down."

Balm wanted to go after Jade and the others by herself, which might have seemed sensible on the surface. If everyone who went into the city disappeared, reducing the number of people going in might be a good idea. But Merit didn't think it was practical. What if she needed to send someone back for help? What if she ended up trapped somewhere because there wasn't anyone to help her at the right moment? It was why Raksura never traveled alone.

River's reasons for objecting were entirely different. "You don't trust me," he growled. "What do you think I'll do, rip your throat out and leave you somewhere?"

Balm eyed him coldly. "Why don't you try it now, so I can kill you and get on with finding them."

Merit hissed, annoyed. "Balm, you don't really think that." He had expected Balm to be half out of her mind with fear for Jade and Moon and the others, but River was almost as bad. And neither wanted to admit it.

They both ignored him. River said, "I don't want to fight you. You're the one who wants that, because you think it'll erase what happened to you, how the Fell used you. I'm not the only one who remembers that, Balm."

Balm's spines went rigid with fury. Merit agreed that it was too close to home and also an unfair strike. Merit said, "River, that's not helping." *Stupid warriors*, he thought. He needed to be more sympathetic to Chime's situation; it must be agony to be like this now after living all your previous life as a sensible Arbora.

Again, they both ignored him. Kalam stood in the doorway, watching anxiously. Callumkal had been in and out as they waited, increasingly worried, trying to make his own plans with the other groundlings. He had said grimly, "At least we know the Fell can't get in, or they would have been on us by now." Unable to wait for the Raksura to return, a group of Kishan were getting ready to take their flying packs and try to follow the canal to find a way out.

Balm stepped deliberately close to River, and he bristled. Balm said, "You made sure everyone remembered it. You took advantage of what it did to me, treated me like nothing to prove to your idiot followers how strong you were—"

River sneered. "You let me."

It wasn't doing Merit any good to think what Jade, Moon, or Stone would do in this situation. If they were here, this wouldn't be happening. He asked himself what Flower would do.

As Balm's claws flexed, Merit shoved in between them. He was in his groundling form, small and vulnerable. Balm was wearing a copper bead necklace and River a bronze armband Pearl had given him. Merit slammed a hand on Balm's chest and grabbed River's arm. He didn't quite hit his targets, but he got close enough.

Both yelped and flinched violently away from him. Balm ripped her necklace away over her head and River clawed his armband off. Both stared at Merit. "What—" Balm began. "You—" River started.

Merit said, "Don't make me do it again."

There was a moment of stunned silence. River touched his armband where it lay on the floor, and jerked his hand away. Balm muttered, "I didn't know you'd do it in the first place."

"You've never been idiot enough to make me," Merit said. Warriors tended to forget that rocks and cups weren't the only thing mentors could spell for heat. "I know you're afraid for Jade and the others, but that's no excuse. This is what we're going to do. The three of us will go look for them. I need to be closer to them, on the route they took, so I can scry about what happened. Now get your packs and get ready to leave."

Balm and River exchanged a look. Merit held his breath, afraid they might comment on his recent lack of success in scrying. But they both turned away, too angry with each other to think of it.

Kalam said, "I want to go with you. My father will let me take one of the levitation harnesses, so I won't slow you down."

River had gone to get his pack, his movements stiff with offended pride. Balm picked up hers, threw a wary glance at Merit, and told Kalam, "If you can't track by scent, there's no way you can help us."

Kalam wasn't deterred. "Some of the sunsailer's crew are suspicious because the other Raksura didn't come back. They think they're searching the city with Rorra and Delin, looking for artifacts instead of the way out. If I go with you, it'll show them my father still trusts you."

Balm grimaced. "Oh."

Filling his waterskin from the cask against the wall, River shook his head. "That's stupid. What artifacts? We don't know anything about this place."

"They think Delin does." Kalam waited for further objections, then said, "I'll go get my harness."

Balm hesitated, and glanced at Merit. "Should we take him?"

Merit wished for an instant he hadn't seized control of the search party in such a dramatic fashion. It was a little daunting. But he didn't suppose Balm and River would remain subdued for long. And Kalam had been friendly to them during the whole trip; Merit didn't see any reason they shouldn't trust him. "He might be able to help."

River made a skeptical noise but didn't argue.

Within a few moments they were out on the deck, Balm and River having quickly assembled their supplies, and Merit making sure he had his simples and anything else he might need. They had taken some more of the little metal cups and Merit spelled them for light. The little glows of illumination seemed ridiculously inadequate next to the dark well just beyond the Kishan lights, but it was all they had. Merit wished he could spell the huge walls for light, but that was far beyond his abilities.

Kalam appeared with Callumkal, trailed by Vendoin, Kellimdar, and some other Kishan. He was pulling on the harness that went with the flying pack, and had a belt with tools and pouches strapped around his waist. Vendoin was fitting a harness over her armor patches. "Vendoin wants to come with us," Kalam explained.

Merit hesitated, and looked at Balm. Balm lifted a brow, the tilt of her spines clearly saying *you decided you were in charge*. River's expression was sour.

Merit controlled the urge to snarl at both of them. Vendoin had a flying pack, so it wasn't any extra burden. Hopefully there wouldn't be any time for her to ask him annoying questions and act surprised at his answers. And if it made the Kishan happy and made it easier for Callumkal, so much the better. He said, "Yes, she can come."

Callumkal seemed gratified and Kellimdar surprised. Callumkal said, "Take care." He squeezed Kalam's shoulder.

As the groundlings got ready, Merit heard Vendoin speak to Kalam in Kedaic, saying, "Once we leave, they will send some crew members in packs up the canal. They don't trust the Raksura."

Tightening a last buckle, Kalam didn't look up. "They didn't betray us. Something's wrong."

"At least we all agree on that," Balm said in Raksuran, in Merit's ear. She lifted him and they took flight into the dark.

CHAPTER NINETEEN

The stairs just kept going up, which at first was terrifying. Moon was certain they had escaped the neverending hallway just to be trapped in the neverending stairwell. Rorra gave Delin a lift on her harness, and the Raksura used their claws to climb. Stone, stuck in his groundling form while the stairwell was this narrow, was the only one who was relatively slow. The uneven steps and the way they made you want to lean to the left didn't help, either. Ahead, Moon could see Jade's spines getting even more rigid as she tried not to betray any emotion.

Then her spines twitched and she said, "There's a landing!"

Moon hissed with relief. It meant they weren't, or probably weren't, in another trap. Moon crowded up onto the open space with Stone. It was a landing, with the stairs continuing to curve up on the far side. To the right was a large crystal-filled window, more than twelve paces wide and nearly taking up the whole wall. "This looks like a door that was filled in," Jade said, tapping her claws on the crystal.

The glass was murky and clouded. Moon stepped up and pressed his light against it, trying to see what was on the other side. Chime leaned past him and chipped at the mortar on the edge with a claw. Rorra, taking advantage of her flying pack, hovered up over everyone else's head to see. Just enough light permeated the glass to let Moon get a murky view of a larger room with a stairwell going down. There was a doorway, too, leading into darkness. He said, "You're right, it was a door."

"The edges aren't smooth," Chime reported. "It's not like those other crystal panels, the windows down to the canal."

Moon thought of the crystal that enclosed the top of the city. Maybe that had been added later as well, an extreme measure to protect against attack. Delin squeezed in around his arm to examine the glass and said, "They wanted to block access to something in this part of the city, so it may only be approached from this stairwell."

It means they thought they might come back, that they might need whatever they left up here, Moon thought. It meant there might not be a dangerous creature trapped in an eternal prison, but something that had been useful, something to be protected. It might also mean the builders or whoever had already returned at some point in the dim past and retrieved it, and just not bothered to disarm the magical trap protecting it. Moon found himself hoping for the latter; it would be easier to deal with.

Jade made a fist and struck the glass. It made a dull thump. "Stone, can you break this?"

Stone glanced around the space and grimaced. "I'll try. Everybody out of the way."

Jade turned toward the stairs leading up. "Come on."

It gave them a chance to rest, sitting around on the steps while Stone shifted and tried to first push the glass out, then to dig at the wall around it. After the first moments of hope, Moon could tell it wasn't going to work. Rorra said tiredly, "I think the Kish might have tools that could get through there. Of course, they're all back on the sunsailer."

Stone shifted back to groundling and hissed in annoyance, tucking his hands under his armpits. "Can't budge it."

Moon hopped back down the stairs. "Are you all right?"

"Just broke a claw," Stone said.

"Let me see," Moon insisted.

Growling, Stone showed him. He had broken three claws, the wound showing on his groundling form as bleeding from under the fingernails. His knuckles were darkening with bruises. He glared over Moon's shoulder as the others crowded around. "Not everyone needs to see."

Bramble dug another cloth out of her pack and said, "Quiet, line-grandfather. Somebody hold a light for me."

Chime got the healing simples out again and Bramble wrapped Stone's hand while Stone hissed impatiently. Moon exchanged a look with Jade. There wasn't going to be another way out. They would have to follow these stairs to wherever they led.

They continued upward, moving faster now that they had some confirmation that this wasn't another trap. Climbing beside Moon, Chime said, "I don't know why I'm not hearing or feeling anything. I should have some idea about this place, this magic that's here. Not that I'm complaining about not being able to hear any frightening voices, for example. But if my stupid ability was ever going to be any help, you'd think now would be a good time."

You would think that. Moon said, "It's got to mean something."

"Perhaps . . ." Delin said, holding to Rorra's harness as she hovered behind them. "You sense magics which are inimical or simply strange, is that it? You don't feel it when Merit scrys or heals, do you?"

Chime told him, "Right, it's always something very different. Sometimes harmful, sometimes just different."

"Perhaps this is not different," Delin said.

"Yes, but . . . Huh." Chime went silent, considering it.

"It would be nice if these people left some carvings of themselves behind," Song grumbled. "Then at least we'd know if they were like us or not."

"I don't think they were like us," Briar told her, hooking her claws around a wall carving to pull herself up. "If they were, they had very odd taste in stairs."

Merit held onto Balm as they leapt from pillar to pillar, River following and Kalam and Vendoin using their flying packs. They found the junction of seven canals quickly enough. As Balm set Merit down on the ledge, he tasted the air deeply. He didn't catch any scent but traces of Raksura, sealing, and groundling. But there was something about this place he didn't like.

"They could just be lost," Kalam said, as he maneuvered his pack down to the floor. He sounded more hopeful than Merit felt the situation warranted. "This place may be a maze past this point."

"If they weren't sure which way to go, they could have followed their own scent trail back here," Balm told him. "And we can't be confused about direction. We always know where south is."

"Are you certain?" Vendoin directed her light up at the carvings. "This place seems very confusing. And these designs . . . They are so intriguing . . ."

Ignoring them all, Merit sat down on the pavement, shifted to groundling, and pulled his pack around. "I need to scry. Can we tell which door they took?"

River was already casting back and forth between the doorways. He stopped in front of one to the left and said, "They took this one. With that sealing with them, they might as well paint arrows on the floor."

"Everybody be quiet so Merit can scry," Balm said, more pointedly than necessary.

Out of the corner of Merit's eye he saw Vendoin start to speak and Kalam shush her. You could scry using a variety of things, shapes and patterns and movement in water, air, blood; it was all up to the individual mentor. Flower had liked to use wind shear, and birds in flight, if possible. You could also focus on individual objects, and Merit felt he was particularly good at that. This time he was scrying on a place, on this junction and the doorway the others had chosen. This place knew what had happened next.

His sense of his own body, of the cool damp air in his lungs, all the scents of salt and familiar Raksura and unfamiliar groundlings, the texture of the layer of cloth between his groundling skin and the chill stone, went away. The visions came between his eyes and the view of the dark doorways, the scraps of carving and the dust motes visible in the spell-lights and Kishan lamps. Balm sat with Kalam. River was a little distance away, his head drooping as he dozed. Vendoin had taken out a small book in a leather wrap and was writing in it. Merit felt the mental drift of scrying, and a sensation like a wall crumbling, as if something had stood between him and the visions and had now dissolved. As he slipped into the space where the images lay, ghosts of color crawled across the walls, the painted designs and writing only Vendoin could see. Not warnings, but a last message: *it lies here, take care, you know our reasons . . .*

Merit twitched, aware he had just spoken. Balm sat up straight. River flinched awake and the groundlings watched him wide-eyed. "What did I say?" Merit demanded, his voice coming out in a dry croak. The words were still floating around in his head, and he didn't think there was time for them to settle so he could recall them himself.

Balm told him, "You said, 'Bramble's wrong, it's not a trap, it wants them to find it.'"

"Right." Merit shook his head, trying to wake himself up. "Something was there, blocking me, but it's gone now." He scrambled to his feet and shifted. The others stood, confused, hopeful. Merit shook his spines out and asked, "How long was I scrying?"

River answered, "Maybe an hour, a little longer. You know where they are?"

Merit nodded. "They had to go up. We just have to figure out where they're coming down." This was going to take more scrying, but at least he knew he was on the right track.

Moon and the others kept climbing, passing more landings, all with blocked-off doors. They tested each one, more carefully this time, just to make sure none of the crystal barriers had been inserted badly and were weak enough to dislodge. Moon was frustrated almost beyond bearing and he knew Jade was as well. This stupid trap had herded them right into the place it was supposed to be protecting.

"Do you think the sunsailer is still where we left it?" Chime said wearily when they paused to rest.

"I hope they haven't done anything stupid with it," Rorra replied. She was sitting on a step, making sure the bandages cushioning the top of her boots were still in place. "They must be searching for us by now, and for the way out."

Delin sighed, stretching his back. "They may think we have betrayed them, and are searching for artifacts."

Moon had already thought of that earlier. The trust between the Raksura and most of the Kishan was still fragile, and this wouldn't help. But apparently Rorra hadn't. She stared, surprised and offended. "Why would I betray them?"

"Because they're so obsessed with getting answers to their questions they can't imagine anyone feels different," Moon said.

Rorra shook her head, still upset. "I have worked with Callumkal since I— Since I came to Kish."

Obviously trying to console her, Root said, "Maybe they think we killed you instead."

"I'd like to kill every wall in this stupid city," Jade muttered. "Come on, we need to keep moving."

They kept going up, and Moon started to wonder if they would reach the top, find an empty room, and have to start back down and try to defeat the neverending hallway again anyway. They were hoping there was a way into a different part of the city through here somewhere, but there was no guarantee of that. He thought mentioning this out loud would be more than Jade's temper could take at the moment, so he didn't. And he just hoped Root didn't think of it and blurt it out.

Then he caught a scent of something different, cooler air, maybe a trace more salt. Ahead Jade's spines flicked as she caught it too. She said, "There's another landing up here. I think— It might—" Then she leapt ahead.

Stone took the last three stairs in one step. Lunging after them, Moon jumped up onto a landing that opened into a passage with a curved ceiling. The others crowded up behind him.

It was such a shock to see something different, they all just stood there. The glow of the spell-lights didn't reach very far, but Rorra directed her distance-light around, revealing more carved walls and a dark space at the end of the passage.

Jade started forward cautiously. Moon tasted the air and caught more salt. There was something different, not quite fresh, but not as heavy with rock and stale water. There was a draft coming from somewhere ahead.

Moon felt the tension he had been holding in his back and shoulders ease a little. Whatever happened, at least they weren't in a box-trap at the top of the stairs.

"How far up are we?" Delin asked softly.

Bramble answered, "Not near the top. We're well above the sea, though."

"And deep inside the rock," Chime added. His spines twitched uncomfortably. "The city's heart?"

Bramble drew breath and Jade said, "Let's not speculate." She started forward. "Chime, if you get any sense of something—"

"I'll say so right away," Chime assured her.

"Feel free to yell," Moon murmured. Chime moved a spine in assent.

As they moved through the passage, the lights revealed stone shelves built out from the walls, though their placement seemed random and they were all empty. *So did they store things here?* Moon wondered. Again, it was hard to know what something might be meant for when you didn't know what the people who had built it looked like.

The lights started to reveal glimpses of the chamber ahead. Moon was expecting carved stone and emptiness; it was all they had seen so far. But the lights glinted off broken ceramic and smashed fragments of stone. Rorra pulled the distance-light off her shoulder strap and held it up. Jade said, "So something else got here before we did."

The chamber had apparently held a number of objects on carved stone plinths of various heights. The plinths had been overturned and most smashed, and all that was left of the objects was a mix of intriguing debris: broken crystal and pottery of all different colors, stained with mud and mold, and small scattered pieces of bright metal.

Delin groaned. "This is disappointing." He sighed heavily. "I will hate to tell Callumkal of this."

Stone stepped forward, picked his way carefully through the room. Moon followed with the others. Rorra's light showed a doorway on the far side, so hopefully they could keep going until they found a stairwell down, or the source of that draft. His foot brushed something soft, and he nudged it cautiously with his claws. It was a pile of some disintegrating substance, with folds as thin as an insect's wing. "This was fabric, maybe?"

Chime crouched over another moldy pile, studying it closely, holding his spell-lighted cup almost on top of it. "I see incised markings. I think these were books."

Delin made a pained noise and clapped a hand over his eyes. Moon sympathized. And they didn't even have anyone like Vendoin here, to tell them if there was writing on the walls that explained what these ruined objects were for.

Stone had almost reached the doorway. Normally Stone liked to poke through remnants like these, the abandoned remains of strange people, but now the path ahead seemed to hold all his attention. "This isn't good. This is salt mud. It came from the sea bottom."

That stopped Moon in his tracks. It couldn't be a flood, not so far up in the escarpment. "So what's it doing all the way up here?"

"Odd." Bramble twitched, shedding nervous energy. "There wasn't any mud in the stairwell."

"Yes." Rorra pivoted, shining her light over the walls. "Something got in here. But the mud is all dry, I think, so it wasn't recent."

Bramble nodded agreement. "And that's a relief— Root, what have you got?"

Moon turned. Root stood near the center of the chamber, holding something of dull silver-colored metal that was shaped like a cage or a frame for a piece of glass or crystal inside. Root said, "This is pretty. We should take it."

There was a moment of startled silence. Moon felt his spines prickle uneasily. They had no reason to suspect anything was wrong but . . . Moon thought something was very wrong. It was like the air in the room had changed. Chime said, "Uh . . . I don't feel anything, but . . ."

"I feel something," Stone said, and his tone made all the warriors twitch. Though Root seemed not to notice. "I feel anger. Root, put it down."

"But the groundlings are going to take things," Root said, not looking up. "Why can't we take this?"

Watching warily, Delin said, "I would not recommend it. If it is a compulsion, like the call that drew groundlings and Fell to the forerunner city . . . Root, put the object down."

Root ignored him, an extremely un-Root-like thing to do. Frustration and fear in her voice, Song said, "Root, you heard Stone, put it down!"

Moon took a step closer, wondering if he could knock the object out of Root's hands without touching it.

"Root," Jade said, and Moon felt the tug on his own heart. It was the queen's power, the connection between her and all the court. He knew he must only be sensing the edge of it; all Jade's concentration, sharpened by fear for his safety, was directed at Root. "Root, put it down."

Root's head jerked up and he stared at her, startled, his spines drooping. Then he looked at the thing in his hands and set it on the nearest broken plinth. He said, "That was weird. Why did I want that?"

Moon hissed in relief. There was a nervous flutter of spines around the room. Stone's body still radiated tension. Jade said, "Root, come here. Everyone out, come on, this way."

Root took a step forward and Moon moved, hooked his arm and pulled him away from the plinth. Chime and Song hurried to reach Jade and Stone, with Bramble taking a wide path around the plinth. Rorra, ever practical, used her pack to lift off the floor, picked up Delin, and navigated them both over the debris and down to the door beside Jade. Briar came last, shepherding Bramble ahead of her.

The passage past the room was wider but longer, and Moon could feel more moving air. He was still holding onto Root's arm, and Root whispered, "Moon, I don't know what happened. Am I in trouble?"

"Yes," Chime snapped. "If that was the thing the trap was protecting, it's dangerous."

"I'm talking to the consort, not you," Root said, sounding more like his normal self.

"No more trouble than usual," Moon said. He hoped so. They might have just averted a disaster.

"Do we tell Callumkal about this?" Rorra asked Delin. Moon noted she hadn't switched to Kedaic, which meant she didn't care if the Raksura understood her. "If it's dangerous, I'm reluctant."

Delin said, "First we must escape this city, and the Fell. Perhaps they have followed the Kish to this city, believing it to be forerunner, and will leave it when we do. If so, Callumkal and the others will wish to return and examine this place in more detail. I also . . ." He hesitated, and then sighed. "This is a long-winded way of saying 'I don't know.'"

Moon didn't know either. The silver and crystal object was the only thing in the shattered room that had stood out, and it had been near the plinth left of the center. Whatever had destroyed the books and other objects hadn't taken it, but then maybe whatever had dragged that sea bottom mud up here wasn't sentient, and had just been looking for food. *If that thing is what the Fell want* . . . The Fell queen had seemed to imply that it was something specific, that the Fell weren't just chasing rumors of power associated with ancient ruined cities. *But then how did they know it was in here?* Unless Callumkal and the other Kishan had known, and had kept the knowledge from Rorra, and the Fell had discovered it from them somehow.

"There's dried mud on this floor," Stone said. Moon could feel it underfoot, but just as a slight gritty texture. Stone was in his groundling form and the skin on the bottoms of Raksuran feet was tough, but still more sensitive than scales.

Bramble stopped to examine the mud on her foot claws. "It's got to be turns old. Doesn't it?"

"Doesn't mean what brought it in isn't still here," Stone said.

"We know waterlings can get in here," Moon said. You would think they would stay in the lower part of the city, in the canals, but maybe some had gotten curious. "If they can get in, we can get out."

The passage slanted toward the left, and they passed several smaller rooms, the floors covered in layers of dried mud but empty of debris. Chime said, "I'm still afraid we're going to turn a corner and there's going to be . . . one of those things."

"I think if we were going to find one, it was going to be in that room," Jade said. She glanced back and Root's spines drooped again.

Then Stone said, "Wait."

Everyone stopped. Moon tasted the air and caught a trace of rotting sea wrack. Stone turned to Jade. "It's close."

She tilted her head to listen. Moon couldn't hear anything from ahead. But the draft felt stronger. Jade said, "Stay here."

Moon stepped past Chime and Bramble, just as Stone drew breath to speak. Jade said, "I was talking to the consorts, too."

Stone subsided with an annoyed hiss. Moon managed not to object as Jade started ahead down the passage, a single spell-light to guide her. As the passage curved to the left, her light disappeared.

Stone tasted the air again, his head tilted to listen. Moon glanced back at the others, their worried expressions and the tired angle of everyone's spines. Delin's face was drawn and Rorra seemed more gray than she had before. He didn't think it was a good sign. Chime leaned against the wall, Bramble rested her head on Song's shoulder, her eyes half-closed. Briar was last behind Root and Song, keeping a wary watch back down the passage. They needed rest and more substantial food than the rations in their packs. They needed to not be trapped in this endless maze.

The movement of air in the passage was the only thing to signal Jade's return; she had shoved her light into her pack. Moon saw her expression and the grim set of her spines and knew things had just gotten even worse. Her voice low, she said to Moon and Stone, "Something is getting in and out of this place, but I'm not sure we're going to be able to."

Lying on his belly, Moon looked over the edge of the air shaft. He swallowed back a hiss. *Yes, it's worse.*

They had left the others and he and Stone had followed Jade as the passage narrowed and they began to see faint natural light ahead. The passage met a large vertical shaft, with a little light falling down it that must originate at the top of the escarpment and the crystal-sealed portion of the city. From the quality and scent of the air, it wasn't open to the outside. But below this level, the shaft was occupied.

The inhabitants clung to the sides of the shaft, and at first Moon could only see thick, rough, scaled bodies of silver and blue, glowing with prickles of blue light, like burning coals buried in their flesh. And claws, like the kind crabs and shellfish had, big bulky razor-sharp things on the ends of their limbs. And there were a lot of limbs, some with hand-like structures with smaller claws, which they used to hook themselves to the wall. As Moon watched, an eyeless head lifted up and yawned, and revealed that the distended jaw was full of a myriad of needle-like teeth. These must be the creatures who had explored these rooms, destroyed the objects left behind. Fortunately, they all seemed to be asleep, or drowsing. The few who were moving were languid and seemed barely aware.

Moon wriggled silently back from the edge to where Jade and Stone waited. They retreated farther down the passage, out of earshot of the air shaft's occupants, and Moon said softly, "At least we know there's no neverending hallway trap at the bottom of that shaft. They have to be eating something."

Stone said, "They're probably from the ocean. Eyeless waterlings don't live in seas this shallow."

Moon nodded. "They must have washed up here in storms, and got in through the passages that are letting the water in. They probably only go out at night."

Jade hissed impatiently. "I really don't care how they got in, or what they do when they aren't blocking our way out. How do we get down past them?"

"We don't," Stone told her. "We go up. If there's one air shaft, there's more. Before they sealed off the top of the city, that's how they kept the air moving through here."

"We have to go while it's still daylight," Moon added. "They probably start moving around at dark. There's a chance they might clear out and go to some other part of the city, or go outside, but we just can't risk it."

"That makes sense." Jade dropped her spines in chagrin. "I should have thought of that."

"That's why you have us," Moon said, and thought, *we really need to get out of here*. They were all getting too exhausted to think straight. Jade had told the others to eat and rest while they were waiting, but that wasn't going to be enough. And it was never good to stay too long in enclosed spaces with no fresh air. If this place had been originally designed to be ventilated from the outside, then having all those openings closed off wasn't helping.

Jade squeezed his wrist. "Right. I'll go up and see if I can find an opening to another level."

"Let me do it," Moon said, keeping his voice casual. The image of Jade slipping and falling because she was too tired to climb made his chest constrict. "This is why you brought me."

Jade said, wryly, "I brought you for sex."

"Ha." It was good she could still joke but he hoped it didn't mean she was getting loopy. "Sex and climbing walls."

Stone said, "Jade, he's right. The warriors are exhausted, and if the connecting passages are this size, I can't fit into them. We can't risk losing the queen."

Jade growled under her breath. "I don't care if he's right, I'm going. You two get ready because if I wake the waterlings it's not going to matter."

Moon drew breath to argue and Stone punched him in the chest. Jade, already turning to creep back to the edge of the shaft, didn't see. Rubbing the injured spot, Moon waited until she was out of earshot to whisper, "You said I was right!"

"She doesn't need an argument right now. Neither do I," Stone said pointedly.

"Fine." One reason to send someone ahead was that they needed to know if moving into the shaft would rouse the waterlings. If it did, it would be very, very bad. "Why don't you go back to the others and get ready to die horribly when the waterlings swarm us?"

"Why don't I," Stone said, and turned back down the passage.

Moving quietly, Moon went to the edge of the shaft. Jade had slipped out to cling to the side and cautiously moved upward. The rock was heavily pitted and made for easy climbing. It was just the sleeping waterlings that were the problem.

Moon gripped the edge and leaned out, trying to see if there was an opening to another passage. The light from above was faint, but it was just enough to throw shadows. And there, about fifty paces up and on the far side of the shaft, was a door-sized square shadow.

Jade had seen it too and climbed toward it slowly, obviously being careful not to make any noise louder than the gusty exhalations of the sleeping waterlings. Like sealings, they probably weren't scent hunters, and hopefully their senses weren't as acute out of the water as in it.

Jade reached the door and swung inside, and Moon retreated back down the passage. He let his breath out in relief and scrubbed his face with the heels of his hands. Time passed excruciatingly slowly, then Jade climbed back inside the passage so suddenly and silently Moon flinched. She drew him further back, and said quietly, "That's it. It leads to an open hall with several stairwells heading down. There were other openings farther up, but the less time we spend in that shaft the better."

It was good news, until Jade stumbled and caught Moon's arm to steady herself. When she pulled away he caught her wrist and said, "On the boat, did you sleep? Don't lie."

She bared her teeth and he bared his back. Then she hissed, frustrated. "The sunsailer's crew was starting to panic and Callumkal needed help. They had to see we weren't afraid, they had to see— I slept for a little while."

Moon hesitated. He was trying to think how long that meant Jade had been awake. They had all napped in the boat on the way back from searching for the Fell nest, but that hadn't exactly been undisturbed rest. She said, "It was a mistake, I should have slept more. There's nothing I can do about it now," and pulled away from him.

They followed the passage back to where the others waited. Moon's mind was racing for a solution, anything to make it easier for Jade. They just couldn't afford to stop here longer, not so close to the waterlings. *I should have made sure she had a chance to rest*, he thought, furious at himself. The terrible thought of returning to the colony and his clutch without Jade stopped his breath for a moment. He couldn't let that happen.

Stone had already told the others about the air shaft and what was in it. While Jade described the climb and the potential way out, Moon crouched down beside Bramble. "Do you still have some food? Jade hasn't eaten."

Bramble, far more expert than Moon at reading spines and expressions, went still for a moment, then pulled her pack around to dig through it. "There's some of that dried seaweed, and Acama on the sunsailer said this bread stuff with the red flakes is supposed to be a stimulant but I don't think it works on us."

Jade was saying, "It's not a long climb, but we'll need to move fast."

Rorra leaned forward. "You all can't fly in that shaft, but I can. I can take you up one by one. It will perhaps be quieter."

Jade tilted her head in acknowledgment. "We can start climbing, and you can come back for each of us in turn. That should cut down on the time, and the faster we get away from those waterlings, the better."

Delin frowned in concern. "Will your pack last? The substance within will need to be renewed at some point."

Rorra shifted around. "Check the levels for me. We weren't long getting to the junction, so it should still be at least half full. It's a good thing I didn't try to use it in the endless corridor, or it would be empty."

As Delin tugged at various things or peered into parts of the pack, Moon told Jade, "Eat something. Everyone else did."

Jade grimaced but didn't argue. She bit into the piece of dried seaweed Moon handed her and said to the others, "Just be quiet, and everything will be fine."

While Jade was chewing, Bramble turned to the others and said, "Rorra, you're going to have to take Stone."

Stone growled in annoyance but didn't protest. With the passages too small to accommodate his shifted form, it was the best solution. Rorra just nodded. Bramble added, "And I think Jade should go first."

Thankfully, Jade let Bramble sort out the order everyone should go in. Moon figured as an Arbora she was the one in the group most likely to still be able to think straight. Arbora were stronger than groundlings or sealings and didn't need nearly as much sleep as the Aeriat. At least, he hoped this was the case. It would be nice to have someone in the group who could still think straight.

Everyone put their lights away in their packs, and they moved quietly up the passage toward the opening. When Jade slipped out into the shaft, Moon felt every nerve in his body tense. Rorra tugged on her pack's strap, lifted off the floor of the passage a little, and turned to Stone. His voice low, he said, "I'd rather you go out first and then I'll jump to you."

Rorra whispered, "Hah, no thank you." They managed a very awkward embrace and Rorra ducked out into the shaft.

Chime pulled Moon back a little, and whispered, "Is something wrong with Jade?"

"Just tired," Moon said, with a grim *I'll tell you later* look.

Chime winced, said, "Oh," and didn't ask anything further.

Bramble, crouched at the opening, motioned for Root to go next, then for Chime to follow him. Moon let out the breath he had been holding when she signaled that Jade had reached the doorway successfully. Rorra came back for Delin, and Song and Briar moved forward for their turn. Below the waterlings murmured in their sleep, and Bramble turned around to Moon and mouthed the words, "This is terrifying."

Moon nodded. His nerves were so tight he thought his spines were going to snap. Song went next. Rorra returned, and Moon pointed for her to take Bramble. Bramble glared, because her plan had included Moon going with Rorra, but Moon wasn't going to leave an Arbora in this passage alone, even for a few moments.

Once Rorra and Bramble were moving upward through the shaft, Briar climbed out. Moon waited for her to get far enough away, then started his climb. The air in the shaft was heavy with the acrid scent of the waterlings, far more so than the passage. Moon realized it was their breath, rising in the cool unmoving air, and his spines twitched involuntarily. He concentrated on not letting his claws slip on the pitted rock.

Rorra and Bramble floated up to the opening and Stone reached out to take Bramble, then to pull Rorra inside. Then Song reached the doorway and climbed in. With some way still to go, Briar climbed silently, her pack slung back over her shoulder so it wouldn't bump the wall. They made it around the curve of the shaft and Briar was almost within reach of the doorway. Moon was about ten paces behind her. Then from below, something groaned.

Moon flinched and froze. It was a low wail that rose in pitch as it rose in volume. It ended in a gasp, and Moon looked up at Briar. There was just enough light to see her wide-eyed expression. *Our luck just ran out*, Moon thought. He flicked his spines and tail, telling her to keep moving, and Briar resumed her climb, moving with less caution and more speed.

Below, bodies slid over each other as the waterlings stirred. Another groan split the air and it was answered by a chorus of breathy exhalations.

Moon climbed, glancing down. Light glinted on the scaled forms as they stretched and uncurled, their claws clicked on the rock. Above, Briar swung into the opening and then Rorra suddenly dove out. She maneuvered down level with Moon, and he flattened his spines so she could put an arm around his waist. Forcing himself to let go of the wall to grab onto her shoulders took an extra moment of effort he knew they couldn't afford. His weight made her sink down for a breathless heartbeat, then her pack lifted them both up.

Something seized Moon's lower leg, a weight dragged them down. Snarling, he looked down to see a waterling clung to the wall just below them. Rorra must be looking down too because the distance-light on her shoulder shone down on the creature. Its upper half was vaguely groundling-shaped, with a blue-scaled torso and an oval eyeless head. The two largest claws, one of which had closed around Moon's leg, were where a groundling's arms would be, but more limbs sprouted below them, and the lower body was much wider, extending out to accommodate six clawed segmented limbs. Moon raked the claws of his other foot across the creature's claw, but they glanced off the hard surface. He growled, "Rorra, let go."

Rorra, struggling to support his weight, gasped, "No."

There was no time to argue. Moon grabbed her shoulders and shoved out of her grip. The waterling yanked him down straight toward its mouth, its distended jaw opening wide, fangs gleaming. Moon flung his weight sideways and grabbed the clawed limb at the joint, then twisted it down. He fell and hung upside down, supported only by the creature's abused joint. The waterling screamed as its joint popped out and Moon slammed into the wall, dangerously close to the creature's lower limbs. He jerked free of the slack claw and scrabbled away along the wall.

More waterlings scrambled up the wall toward him and he climbed rapidly up past the screaming injured one. It flailed at him with its remaining claw then abruptly fell backward and down the shaft. Moon looked up and saw Jade on the wall just above where the creature had been, snarling in fury.

"Go, I'm coming," Moon yelled and climbed faster. Then Rorra dropped down and this time Moon let her grab him. As they lifted up, Jade turned and climbed toward the opening.

Jade reached the edge and pulled herself inside. Rorra lifted up even with it, and Jade caught Moon's arm and dragged him in. As Rorra caught the edge to pull herself after him, a waterling rose up behind her and claws snatched at her waist.

Moon and Jade were off-balance, in the wrong position, and even as Moon tried to lunge for Rorra, he knew neither of them would be able to reach her. Then Stone stepped on him, flattened him to the floor, and leaned out the opening. He reached past Rorra, seized the creature's head, and twisted sharply. The audible snap echoed off the walls and the creature dropped, lifeless. Stone snatched Rorra out of its grip, Jade grabbed Stone around the waist, and they all tumbled forward into the passage on top of Moon.

Smushed on the bottom, Moon couldn't do anything but hold his breath as the weight was lifted. When Jade climbed off him, he gasped to fill his empty lungs and staggered to his feet. Chime grabbed his arm and pulled him down the passage. Jade was hissing, "Go, go, move, hurry!"

Moon followed the others down the dark passage. Beside him, Rorra muttered, "I didn't know Stone could do that. Not as he is, I mean. Not large."

"That's why we try not to argue with him," Chime told her, breathless with nerves.

Behind them, Stone snorted derisively.

Moon said to Rorra, "He's got really good hearing, too."

Light bloomed ahead as Song and Briar dug their lights out of their packs again. They were in a passage larger than the one below, and the others made way for Jade as she moved forward to lead them. Root glanced back, whispering, "That wasn't fair! We did everything right, nobody made any noise, and they know we're here anyway."

"This place is awful," Bramble agreed.

"Keep moving," Moon urged them. Behind them, he could hear a sliding, scraping movement growing louder, closer. *They're following us.*

Something had woken the waterlings, but Moon would swear they hadn't made enough noise to wake a sleeping fledgling. Maybe the waterlings had felt faint vibrations through the rock. Or maybe they were sensitive to Rorra's distinctive scent and interpreted it as an attack.

Jade led them past several dark doorways, then the corridor suddenly opened up into a large chamber and the welcome sight of an open stairwell leading down. Jade said, "We need to keep going, I don't want to risk this one."

"You don't think we came far enough from the trap in the hall below," Delin clarified, breathing hard as he jogged after Bramble. "That we might enter it again if we go down now."

Rorra directed her distance-light across the space and they saw it was only the first of several large chambers. "She's right, we should keep going, there are more stairwells ahead."

"Faster," Stone said. "They're not far behind us." Then he shifted.

Rorra used her pack to lift up and shoot forward to scoop up Delin. The warriors and Bramble started to bound, covering ten to twelve paces in a single jump, and Stone was careful not to outpace them. The combination of stronger flying muscles and fear could have let Moon outpace all of them but he stayed in the rear, making sure the rest didn't fall behind. He was sure Jade would have objected to this but fortunately she was a little too busy at the moment.

They crossed two large halls, their lights revealing half-seen carvings and shapes. In the second, Bramble yelped a warning and they slid to a halt. Rorra's light swung around to catch a giant face looming from the end of the hall, but it was made of stone. "Statue," Jade said. "Keep moving!"

They surged forward again and Moon was left with an impression of a smooth triangular head, no visible nose, with small eyes to either side. It might have been a sculpture of a builder, or maybe just something from a story. And now he could hear the rasp of claws on the stone floor, the swift slide of heavy bodies. "They're in the first hall," he said aloud. They could hide the lights, look for a doorway to another route, but the chances of being trapped in one of these dead-end passages or rooms was far too great.

Ahead, Jade reached the next stairwell. She called out, "Down, down this way! It's got to be far enough."

Moon threw a glance back and saw roiling movement in the shadows. It had to be far enough, because the waterlings moved too fast. With Delin still holding onto her, Rorra dropped down. Bramble, Chime, and Root dove after her. Jade motioned for Song and Briar to follow. From below, Bramble called, "Stone, the stairs turn down here and it's too narrow for you!"

Stone snarled, and shifted to his groundling form, saying, "This shitting place!"

Jade caught Moon's arm and half-shoved him down the stairs. She grabbed Stone and jumped after him.

Moon hit the first landing in a crouch, waited for Jade, then dove down the next set of stairs with her. The lights flashed sporadically as the Raksura jumped and dove and scrambled and jumped again. Rorra's distance-light was mostly steady, Delin directing it toward the stairs so they at least had some idea where they were going. This would be a bad time for someone to run into a wall and stun themselves.

Moon heard the rush of movement above them, the scaled bodies slapping into the walls, claws scraping as the waterlings flowed down the stairwell like water. An acrid stench of rot and fish filled the air.

Below, Bramble took a tumble down the stairs but rolled to her feet at the bottom and kept going. The waterlings were gaining on them. *We're going to have to stop and fight to give the warriors a chance*, Moon thought, then Rorra shouted, "Light ahead! Someone's down there!"

I hope it's someone we know. Moon hit two more landings, as ahead Song missed and catapulted herself shoulder-first into the stairs. Root stopped and half-started back. Briar yelled, "Keep going!" and scooped Song up and jumped down to the next landing.

Two more landings and there was just enough light for Moon to glimpse a familiar scaled face looking up at them from the bottom of the stairwell. *That was Balm*, he thought. He wondered if he was hallucinating. *How did they find us?* And it really didn't matter, because even if River and Merit were with her, three more Raksura weren't going to be much help against what was after them. Beside him, Jade gasped, "No, no, not them too—"

Rorra and Bramble yelled warnings, and Balm's voice echoed up, "Come on, it's all right, just hurry!"

Maybe they had a plan. Moon hit the next landing with Jade and said, "Just trust her!"

Stone gritted out, "Listen to him."

Jade growled in despair and they jumped for the last landing. The others reached the bottom and bolted through a tall archway out into a hall. Moon spotted Balm, Merit, and— Kalam, braced just outside the door holding a Kishan fire weapon that was almost bigger than he was. River was braced behind him, ready to steady him when he fired the weapon.

Moon and Jade dove down the stairs together, Moon breaking left and Jade to the right. She let go of Stone as they rolled across the pavement of a broad hall, and Stone came to his feet, already shifting into his scaled form. Moon landed hard and rolled into a half-crouch. Still by the doorway, Balm looked up the stairwell. Merit stood a short

it meant the waterlings were still coming. Though hopefully far more slowly.

Ahead, lights swung around and started to disappear down another stairwell. Moon, Jade, and Balm reached it to find Kalam and River waiting. Kalam asked, "Should I shoot again from here?"

"No, the boat's not far," Balm said, with a glance at Jade. "We'd have to wait for those things to catch up."

Jade's spines signaled agreement. "Keep going, maybe they won't follow us to the boat."

Maybe, though Moon doubted it. But Balm was right that this wasn't a good place to make another stand. The stairwell was much wider, and the waterlings could spread out across it and avoid Kalam's weapon.

They started down the uneven stairs, Balm telling Jade, "You were right about this hall being the way through the city, but you have to go along the canal to avoid the trap. There's a lock, though, and the Kishan are trying to get through it. The other canals are connected, but they all dead-end—"

"Merit scryed all this?" Jade asked as they hit the next landing.

"Not all of it. We thought it would be Fell chasing you," Balm said.

Moon hissed as he cleared the next set of stairs. He hoped Merit hadn't actually scryed Fell inside the city. They had about all they could handle now.

They reached the archway at the base of the stairs and found Vendoin already there, waiting with four Janderi, all armed with smaller versions of the fire weapons. "Are those creatures still coming?" Vendoin called as the Raksura spilled out onto the pavement. They were on a walkway paralleling a canal, and Moon's sense of direction said it was the one they had tried to follow from the hall above. That had certainly seemed like a good idea at the time.

"They're still coming, but not as quickly," Jade answered. The Raksura gathered around, breathing hard from exertion, spines twitching. Rorra and Delin hovered nearby. To the watching Kishan crew, they probably seemed unmoved. To Moon, everyone looked exhausted and half-shattered by nerves. Jade shook her spines out. "Where's the boat?"

"It's up this canal, not far." Balm glanced at her, obviously worried.

"We need to hurry," Kalam said. "They said if they get the lock open before we get there, they'll go on without us."

"Your father is going to leave you behind here?" Jade asked, startled and skeptical. Moon found the idea unlikely too.

"Well, no," Kalam admitted. "But I don't want him to have to go against everyone."

"Fair enough," Jade said. "Let's go."

CHAPTER TWENTY

It was a long walk before they saw the sunsailer's lights. If the water-lings had made a serious effort to catch them, they would probably have all been eaten because Moon wasn't sure they could have moved fast enough, even with the Kishan weapons as cover. Stone shifted to ground-ling about halfway along, and said quietly to Moon, "They're following us, but they're up there, in that hall above us." He jerked his chin up.

"Why?" Moon wondered. "Are they just that territorial? Or hungry?"

Stone hissed under his breath. "That's a good question."

The lights grew brighter until Moon could see the battered sunsailer floating in the canal. It faced a huge mold-covered metal door stretched across the hall, blocking the way. From the curving pillars on each end, and the huge gears built into the sides, it looked as if it was meant to raise up to let boats pass below. But it was so old, the dark patina glinting under the lights, and it looked like the mold might be eating it.

"Oh, that's perfect," Chime said, weary and sour.

"And the other canals are blocked?" Moon asked, glancing back at the others.

Sounding irritated, River answered, "Yes, they all stop further back. This is a stupid city."

For once, Moon agreed with him.

The Janderan on guard on the deck saw them and called out. A group was on the walkway, examining or working on one of the pillars. Lights flashed as they turned and Moon spotted Callumkal.

He came toward them, relief plain on his face. "We thought you were lost in this place—"

"We knew where we were, we just couldn't get back," Jade told him. Moon could hear an edge of irritated defensiveness in the husky quality of her voice, though he was fairly sure the Kishan couldn't.

A ramp had been stretched from a break in the boat's railing to the walkway. Moon was glad to see it, since he wasn't sure most of them could have made the jump right now. His calf and knee, where the waterling had grabbed him, was one solid ache. As Rorra and Kalam told Callumkal about the waterlings, Moon trudged up the ramp with the others to the deck.

Kellimdar was there, sorting through a pile of tools with two Janderan. He seemed unflatteringly startled to see them. "You returned? We thought . . ."

He let that trail off. Bramble plopped down on the deck and said, "What, you thought we'd decided to live here?"

This part of the deck was brightly lit and littered with metal tools of obscure purpose and coils of various sizes of line, and several jars of the moss. The Kishan had obviously been working on the lock for a while. *At least we won't starve now*, Moon thought wearily. He just hoped the waterlings tasted good.

The others followed them up the ramp and a Janderi woman started to help Rorra take off her harness. Delin staggered toward the hatchway, and Merit hurried to help him. Callumkal stood with his arm around Kalam's shoulders, obviously nearly overcome with relief that he was alive. He said, "What did you find? Was Merit right about the trap?"

Jade turned to answer, though her spines were drooping and she had clearly used up every ounce of energy she had left. Moon decided he was going to take drastic action. He stumbled a little, then shifted to his groundling form and collapsed. Jade caught him with a startled hiss, and Moon went limp. It wasn't difficult. Losing the weight of his wings after all this time made him dizzy, and every muscle ache acquired in all the previous hours increased tenfold.

He heard Callumkal, Kalam, and Vendoin make exclamations of concern and dismay, and Jade said, "I need to—"

"Of course, go on," Callumkal urged her.

Jade lifted Moon and he heard the hatch swing open. The light visible through his eyelids faded and he felt the change in the air as she carried him inside. He heard the others trailing after her, then Chime asked worriedly, "Is he all right?"

"Yes," Jade said, her voice tired but dry. "I was particularly impressed by how he rolled his eyes back in his head before he fell over."

"It worked, didn't it?" Moon said under his breath.

They turned into a cabin and a moment later Jade deposited him on one of the padded benches. He opened his eyes and caught her arm. She shifted to her Arbora form and he drew her down next to him. She curled around him, said, "Balm, wake me if something happens," and fell instantly asleep.

Balm smiled in relief. "I will." She squeezed Moon's shoulder and left the cabin.

Stone and Chime had followed them in. Now Chime said, "I think I'll be right here," and pulled a cushion down to curl up on the floor. He shifted to his groundling form and groaned.

Bramble ducked in, glanced around as if counting them, and then ducked out again. Moon wasn't sure where the others had ended up and had to resist the knee-jerk urge to get up and check on them.

Stone leaned over for a close look at Jade. Satisfied, he said, "I'm going to go collapse dramatically on Rorra," and walked out.

"I think Stone likes her," Moon said through a yawn.

Already half-asleep, Chime sighed. "It wouldn't be the oddest thing that happened on this trip."

The next thing Moon knew, Merit was leaning over him, saying, "Are you awake?"

"No." Moon rubbed his face. To his relief, Jade was still curled around him, breathing heavily. He knew it was night outside the city again, that they had only been asleep for a few hours. The bright liquid lights hurt his eyes and his throat felt raw. He managed to rasp, "What?"

Merit was in his groundling form, frowning with worry. "The Kishan think they might be able to get the lock open. I have to talk to you and Jade before we leave the city."

From the floor, Chime said, "Why do they call it a lock? Why would you build a river for a boat and then put a lock on it?" He sounded woozy and half-conscious.

Merit ignored him. "It's about my vision. I need Chime to hear this too. And Stone, but he's still asleep and I'm afraid to wake him."

Chime wondered, "He's sleeping with Rorra?"

Merit's jaw set. "Hold on." He turned around, leaned over Chime, and shook him hard.

"All right, all right," Chime protested. "Stop, I'm awake!" Chime sat up, his hair sticking out in all directions. He blinked and groaned. "What were you saying?"

Moon carefully moved the arm Jade had around his chest and sat up a little. "What about your vision?"

Merit crouched beside the bench. "You all thought that trap you ran into was meant to keep anyone from going up into that part of the city, right?"

Moon nodded. Jade stirred and muttered in her sleep. Scratching his head vigorously, Chime said, "Mmmhmm."

"But instead you realized you could climb or fly out of it, that only someone who could climb or fly like a Raksura could get out of it," Merit said. "From what I saw in the vision, it wasn't a trap, it was a— a trail sign. It was telling you where to go."

"But—" Moon hesitated. *It took us to a place where there was only one way to go, and once we were through it, there were open stairwells and halls.* "Go on."

"That's what I saw in my vision," Merit said, his expression anxious. "Any groundlings who walked into it would be stuck. I think there might be a way out for them, I'm not sure what it is. But if you knew to take one of the paths through the city, and you were told that at the right point, something would show you the way . . ."

Chime was wide awake and staring. "I didn't have any warning. I mean, my . . . power, my sense, whatever it is, I didn't have any warning."

Merit turned to him. "Because it wasn't a trap. And I think maybe it was hiding from me, from my scrying. The closer we came to this city, the less I could see. It was like I'd forgotten how to scry. Once you all walked into that hall, suddenly my vision was back."

"So you think it was meant for Raksura?" Moon said. His skin was prickling with unease.

"Or forerunners." Merit shook his head and shrugged. "Maybe the foundation builders were their allies, and something happened, and the builders had to leave. But they left something here for the forerunners, and left a way to show them where it was. Maybe what the tiles with forerunners on them at the outside dock area were saying was 'if you're a forerunner, go down one of the halls above the canal and you'll find it.'"

Chime frowned, frustrated. "But what was supposed to be up there? The waterlings destroyed everything in that room we found, except that thing Root picked up."

Moon said, "Uh . . ." They all stared at each other.

Jade said, "This shitting city," and sat up. "Are the waterlings still out there?"

Merit told her, "Stone said they were in the hall above the boat. He's up on the roof of the top cabin, so he could listen to them while he slept."

Jade prodded Moon to move. "I have a bad feeling."

Moon had a bad feeling too. He sat up and moved over for her. This would explain why the waterlings had woken so suddenly, when they had done nothing to disturb them. "You think it made the waterlings come after us? That whatever attracted Root to it also attracted them?"

Jade climbed over him. "I think for an ancient object that had a magical trap guiding Raksura-like beings straight to it, it gave up way too easily when a Raksura picked it up."

They went to the upper deck common area, the one with the cooking stove, where the others had gone to rest. Balm and River had been keeping watch out on the deck, but the other warriors and Bramble were here. They were all mostly awake now, in their groundling forms and still bleary-eyed. Delin was here too, awake and making notes in one of his books, half-lying on a bench with his bare feet propped up on a cushion. A pot of water was heating on the stove and there was a bowl of something that smelled like pickled melon that Bramble was trying to get the warriors to eat.

First Moon had gone up to the top deck of the ship to get Stone, who reluctantly rolled off the cabin roof, yawned, and stretched. "Now what?" he asked.

"Are the waterlings still up there?" Moon asked. "Because we think we know why."

As Moon and Stone followed Jade and Merit into the cabin, everyone looked up, and Bramble held out the bowl of melon. She said, "I'm making tea."

Jade said, "Wait, we need to talk."

Chime hurried down the corridor with Balm and River behind him. Once they were all together, Jade slid the door shut, lowered her voice and said, "In that room we found, where the waterlings had destroyed almost everything except the silver cage thing Root picked up."

Everyone nodded except Balm and River, who must have only heard parts of what had happened. Root ducked his head and tried to look unobtrusive. Jade finished, "Did anyone else pick it up?"

Moon looked around the room. In the dark, in the confusion, with everyone waving their lights around at random, it would have been easy for someone to slip the object into a pack. Especially if compelled to by an influence that had made them immediately forget what they had done. Moon had already checked his own, Jade's, Chime's, and Stone's packs, which had been dumped in the cabin downstairs, even though he didn't think it was likely to be there. Moon had walked out with one hand around Root's arm, and the others had all been in the front part of the room, too far ahead to get back to where the object had lain without anyone else noticing. And Rorra had been carrying Delin, though he suspected the spell was like the trap, and had been aimed at Raksura, or a species related to Raksura.

The warriors and Bramble stared at Jade, confused. "No," Song said, a little hurt. "You said not to."

"Why would we—" Bramble began, then went still as the implications hit her. "You think—"

Delin sat up all the way, dislodging his cushion, alarmed. "You think the compulsion caused someone to take it?"

Jade said, "Check your packs."

The packs had been dumped by the wall and Briar got up to pass them over to the others. The packs didn't hold much, most of the warriors having only brought what they thought they might need on the search for the way out of the city, leaving the rest of their belongings on the sunsailer. Song turned hers out, revealing a still-glowing cup, a nearly empty waterskin, a crumpled spare shirt, a little pouch for flints, and some fragments of cloth waterproofed with mountain-tree sap that had been wrapped around food. Bramble's and Root's packs all held variations on the same, though Root squeezed his eyes shut with trepidation before he dumped his out. Briar sat down, opened hers, and stared down at it. "Jade . . ."

Moon stepped between Bramble and Root, and crouched beside Briar. Inside her pack was the dull silver cage, the crystal gleaming faintly in its center.

Briar's eyes were wide with horror. "I— I didn't— I don't even remember—"

Moon felt a surge of sympathy for her. He knew it hadn't been her fault and he hated to see anyone singled out like this. He told Briar, "You couldn't help it. And you were right behind me and I didn't see you." He looked up at Jade. "This thing really wanted out of there."

"It's not your fault, Briar," Jade said. Her jaw was set, as if it was taking a lot of effort not to hiss. Or maybe scream. Moon wanted to scream a little himself. They had been tricked into taking this object with them and there just couldn't be anything good behind it. They had come here to prevent the mentors' vision of a massive Fell attack on the Reaches from coming true, and he had a bad feeling they had just made that vision more possible.

Watching Briar's pack nervously, Song said, "You think it made those waterlings come after us?"

Delin climbed off the bench and limped over to look more closely at the object. "Possibly whatever influence it projects that drew us to it also drew them, as an unwanted side effect. It may explain their attraction to the city, why they came here from the ocean. Possibly it also drew the Fell." He looked up at Jade and added bluntly, "You understand we will be accused by the Kishan of stealing this thing, for our own purposes."

325

Jade grimaced. "We came here to prevent the Fell from getting inside this city, because we were afraid there was something dangerous inside it that they could use against us. That was our purpose. All I want to do is leave this thing here."

"Can we put it back?" Balm asked, obviously thinking furiously. "We could get back up there . . . Except for the waterlings . . ."

Stone leaned against the wall, sighing wearily. "It's too late for that. If the trap was meant to guide forerunners to this thing, it would work for the Fell, too."

"But what is it?" Chime asked helplessly. "What does it do?"

No one had an answer for that. Moon said, "If we were forerunners, I guess we'd know. Or be able to figure it out."

Chime stepped over to peer cautiously into the pack. "I wonder if the Fell know, or if they just think it's a weapon, like what the creature in the forerunner city offered them."

Delin's face, already wreathed with new lines from exhaustion, wrinkled further in consternation. "Perhaps this was what it meant to offer them."

There was a general moment of silent dismay. They couldn't just leave it in poor Briar's pack, so Moon started to reach for it. "No, better not to touch it," Delin said.

Root rubbed his hands on his pants anxiously. "I touched it."

Briar winced. "I must have touched it too."

"Well, nobody touch it anymore," Bramble said. "Here." She pulled a leather bag out of a supply pack. "Tip it into this."

Moon took the pack and managed to work the object out and into the bag Bramble held open without touching it. As Bramble laced the top down, Chime asked, "But what do we do with it? I know the Kishan will want it, or think they want it, but whatever it is or does, we can't let them have something that's going to attract Fell. They'll never get home alive with it."

Jade rubbed her temples. "I don't know. Unless we just drop it in this canal."

Moon didn't think that would work. "If the Fell get into the city when we get out, it might draw them to it, like it did the waterlings. And us."

"We could drop it in the ocean." Root looked up at Jade. "It's not far from here, is it?"

Moon stared, then exchanged a look with Chime. Chime said, "That's not a bad idea."

"The ocean's deep, right?" Root continued. He turned to Stone. "Deeper than the sea-mounts are tall. And there aren't any sealings."

Jade's spines flicked thoughtfully. Stone stared absently into the distance, considering it. He said, "I've never heard of sealings going into the ocean, or any talk of anything out there that had any interest in shallow-sea dwellers or land-dwellers. Except to eat them." He folded his arms, leaning back against the door. "It isn't a bad idea."

"We don't even know what it is." Delin sounded depressed. He made his way back to the bench and sat down heavily. "There were carvings in that room. I should have stopped to record them. Or we should have brought Vendoin, to copy any writing on the walls that we were unable to see."

"There wasn't time," Bramble told him. "The waterlings destroyed the books that were in there. Those were probably important too. And all the other broken things in that room."

Moon added, "It might not even work like it's supposed to anymore." But he was thinking of the freshwater sea and the bridle that had been used to control the leviathan there. It had still worked after all these turns, even though the magisters who had originally constructed it were long dead.

Jade flicked her spines in decision. "If we get out of here, if we get past the Fell, we'll drop it in the ocean." She glanced at Merit. "Merit can scry on it in the meantime. Maybe he can get some idea if that will work or not."

Merit nodded, and he looked less alarmed at the prospect than he would have a turn or so ago. Merit had gained a great deal in confidence since Moon had known him. Jade turned to Delin. "From what you've said, I'm assuming you don't intend to tell Callumkal."

Delin's frown deepened a little. "I feel it is something that should be hidden and left alone. My passion is to know and describe living species; the past draws my curiosity but it does not mean as much to me as it does to Callumkal and Kellimdar and Vendoin. And as much as I would like to understand its purpose, this object was not meant for us.

If Merit is right, it is meant for people who are as dead and gone as those who built this city."

Everyone twitched a little in relief. Bramble said, "We don't tell Rorra? I mean, she's a sealing, she might know things about the ocean, like where we should drop it."

Jade dipped her spines in a negative. "I don't want to ask her to choose between us and Callumkal. Besides, she's known him a lot longer and she might choose him."

Delin nodded once in grim agreement. Moon didn't say anything. He had the uneasy feeling they were making a mistake. But he had no idea what the right course would be. Telling Callumkal seemed to be asking for trouble, and leaving the object here in the city for the Fell to find was too dangerous.

Still miserable, Briar said, "I'm sorry, Jade."

Jade sighed, but stepped over to sit on her heels in front of Briar. "No one is blaming you," Jade told her. "We were stuck with this thing as soon as we walked into that trap. If it hadn't been you, it would have been someone else."

Moon caught the ironic expression in River's eyes, as if he was thinking of the reaction if he had been the one to pick up the object. He was probably right.

Stone said, quietly, "Rorra's coming."

A moment later Moon heard her steps in the corridor. Stone slid the door open and Rorra looked inside. She had changed her clothes and her natural scent was overlaid by oil soap and something astringent, probably a healing salve. Her face was still hollow-cheeked with exhaustion. She frowned at them all, and said, "Is something wrong?"

"We're just discussing the situation," Jade said. "Is there any progress on the lock?"

Rorra's frown turned annoyed. "They're talking of blowing it up. I wanted to warn you."

Moon, Chime, and Stone followed Rorra up to the bow, where they had a good view of the lock. "They know this canal goes all the way to an outer door?" Moon asked Rorra.

She jerked her chin toward the lock. "They explored using the levitation harnesses. Past this point, there's a short passage, then a basin that looked to them like a port, and another door in what must be the outer wall, like the one we came through."

Moon hoped they were right about it being the outer wall. Knowing the waterlings were out there somewhere in the dark made the shadows and empty spaces even more forbidding. It would be a relief to get out of here, even with their unwanted souvenir.

Below them on the pavement, a weary Magrim said, "The problem is that it isn't locked in place, it's just so old the gears have been eaten away and it's too heavy to lift without them." Several of the crew were gathered around the curved pillar that supported this half of the lock, the exposed bits of their dark skin stained green with mold. More Kish-Jandera were stationed nearby with their fire weapons, guarding the workers.

Callumkal stood on the pavement with Jade. He was telling Kellimdar, "I don't want to bring the city down on top of us. Using this mixture in an enclosed space is—"

"But we have no choice," Kellimdar said. He sounded weary and his blue skin had flushed dark in spots. "We can't go back. There isn't enough power left in the moss reserves."

From this vantage point, Moon had a better chance to see the lock. In the glare of the distance-lights, it looked thick and heavy, an insurmountable barrier. Beside him, Chime said around a yawn, "If we're going to be killed by the escarpment collapsing, I'm going back to sleep with the others."

Jade had told the warriors to get more rest while they were waiting. If the waterlings attacked, somebody had to be in good enough shape to fight them. Jade needed more rest too, but Moon thought the few hours of sleep had helped.

"If we don't get crushed, the Fell will be on us as soon as we get out," Stone pointed out.

That rankled a bit. "We weren't much help with that," Moon said. Finding the way out of the city quickly hadn't come to much, thanks to the trap. It would be nearing dawn outside.

"If the door opens at all," Chime said. "If it has that coral growth on it, it might be stuck. And that's if the mechanism is inside the rock like the other one, and not exposed to metal-eating mold like this."

"You all are such a cheery bunch," Rorra said.

Stone's voice was dry. "That means so much, coming from you."

"He only talks like that to people he likes," Moon said. Rorra's frown turned a little alarmed.

Below, some of the Kishan began to collect their tools and lights to carry back aboard. Others moved along the base of the pillar, placing something on it or next to it that Moon couldn't quite see. One lifted up in a flying pack to attach something higher up on the pillar. In the light from the boat's large lamps, it looked like the same stuff that came out of the bolts that the fire weapons used. Rorra pushed away from the railing. "We're going to need to move backward. I should get up to the bridge to help."

"Bridge?" Chime asked, watching her go.

"The steering cabin," Moon translated. He wondered if they were going to shoot at the lock.

The Kishan continued their work, and Kalam came up the ramp carrying one of the moss containers. He asked Moon, "Are you well? When you collapsed, I was— We were all very worried."

"I just needed to rest," Moon said, conquering a surge of guilt. "Thanks for helping Balm and Merit save us."

Kalam looked away, either uncomfortable with the praise or the situation or something. Possibly the smell; Moon knew he needed a bath and clean clothes very badly, but there hadn't been time. He eased back a step. Kalam said, "It was . . . I just did . . . What anyone would do." He seemed to realize he was still holding the moss container. "I need to put this up." He hurried away down the deck.

Chime sighed heavily. "What?" Moon asked him.

Chime pointedly turned back toward the railing. Amused, Stone muttered, "Kids."

"What?" Moon asked again. He had no idea what was going on. *I'm starting to remember why I don't like Raksura.*

Jade, Callumkal, and Kellimdar walked up the ramp back onto the deck, and the other Kishan followed with the last of the equipment. "We're nearly ready," Callumkal said.

Stone stood up straight, his head tilted, listening. Moon froze with the other Raksura, but he couldn't hear anything over the low noises of the boat. Stone said, "You need to hurry. The waterlings are moving."

Kellimdar said, "Are you sure?" but Callumkal strode immediately for the hatchway.

"We need to move the ship back from the lock." Callumkal called up to the Kishan on watch on the deck above, "Alcon, warn the fireguards!"

"Can you tell where they are?" Jade asked Stone. "Are they making for the canal?"

Stone, his expression distant as he listened, said, "Can't tell exactly. They're moving down out of the hall above us."

If the waterlings got underneath the boat and attacked from there, it could be disaster. Moon told Chime, "Go warn the others."

Chime bolted toward the hatch. Moon moved along the railing, staring into the shadows past the sunsailer's lights, trying to spot movement.

The crew pulled up the ramp and slid a panel across the opening. The deck thrummed as the motivator started up again. Stone hissed, "I can't hear them through that."

It was possible to filter out some sounds, but the nearness of the stone walls concentrated the motivator's sound, until the thrumming was vibrating in Moon's bones, and in all the delicate structures of the ear that made distance hearing possible. Stone shifted, his dark scaled form blooming into being as some of the Kishan near the railing flinched away. Moon swayed as the boat jolted. A high-pitched noise joined the thrumming and the sunsailer started to move backwards up the canal, away from the lock.

The rest of the warriors spilled out onto the deck. Bramble and Merit peered out of the hatch behind them, then retreated back into the corridor when Jade twitched her spines pointedly. "Spread out along each side of the boat," she told the warriors.

Kellimdar shouted from the upper deck, "Crew, get back from the railing! The creatures are in the water." The Kishan still on the bow deck ran to the hatch, and others on the first and second decks scrambled to get up to the lights and weapon balconies.

Then Stone growled a warning and the first waterlings came over the side.

Stone tossed the first three off the boat and snapped a more persistent two in half. Fire-weapons struck the ones climbing the sides, then Moon's focus narrowed to the two trying to get past him into the hatch.

He ducked snapping claws, wrenched waterling joints, and ripped open the upper part of a jaw that got far too close to his face. Another balanced on the railing and Moon slammed it off the boat. He landed back on the temporarily clear deck to hear, "They're dropping from above!" It was Briar, yelling the warning from down the port side.

Stone leapt straight up. The deck rocked under Moon's feet and one of the distance-lights swung up to follow Stone. He landed on the arch directly above the boat and swept off the clump of waterlings climbing along it.

A loud pop sounded from the lock pillars, echoing off the stone walls. Fire blossomed at the base of the pillar and shot upward. It struck the other patch of the explosive mixture and someone on the deck above yelled something in another language. Moon suspected it meant "Get down!" and he flung himself flat.

The blast blotted out his hearing and the wood and metal beneath him rocked with the disturbed water. Moon had been expecting a hail of hot metal shards, but there was nothing. Ears ringing, Moon shoved himself upright. He let his breath out in a hiss. *Oh, no.* The lights shone on the lock, still intact.

Then the pillar creaked and groaned, and the gears started to move. Slowly, the panel blocking the canal began to move upward. The Kishan hadn't blown it up, they had just jolted it loose. Moon thought it was probably a better solution. Then a waterling threw itself over the bow and swarmed up the front of the cabin, heading for the Janderan operating the fire-weapon and light on the deck above.

It was Magrim, and he couldn't swing the fire weapon down far enough to shoot the waterling. He stepped back, trying to draw a smaller handweapon from his belt. Moon leapt and hit the waterling's torso from behind, dug his claws into the join where its head met its short neck. He caught a glimpse of Magrim's startled expression as

Moon threw his weight backward and yanked the creature off the railing.

The problem with that tactic was that Moon landed flat on his back, the waterling on top of him. To buy himself time to recover, he bit the waterling in the neck and felt its scales crack under his teeth. It shrieked, decided to run, and tore itself off him and dove for the railing.

Moon rolled to his feet and let it go as it appeared to be the only waterling with any sense; the others were flinging themselves at the sunsailer and being shot by Kishan or mauled by Raksura. The panel was still in motion, high enough now for the boat to pass under it. The deck thrummed again as the boat surged forward.

Three more waterlings came over the bow and Magrim's fire-weapon killed one, wounded the second, and Moon dealt with the third. He danced around the deck, dodging claw snaps, until he could close with it. As he slung its body back into the water, he realized they were out of the canal and entering some larger space.

The sunsailer's lights flashed around a cavern, as big as the entry harbor on the far side of the city. Moon caught glimpses of pillars stretching up, huge dark hallways leading away from platforms extending out over the dark water. But he couldn't see the door. No, there it was, the outline of it incised into the far wall. But there was no platform alongside it, and no sign of the carvings or the mechanism to open it. Moon thought, *we're in trouble*. He hoped the builders hadn't removed it, that taking away the mechanism hadn't been an attempt to defend the city from whatever had caused them to abandon it.

The sunsailer surged forward and the deck swayed underfoot from suddenly choppy water. Moon dealt with another waterling and looked for the outer door again, still wondering how they were supposed to open it. Above, near the steering cabin, someone shouted in horror. The big distance-light swung around and shone on the water in front of the door.

The dark water swirled violently, waves rocked the boat and crashed over the bow, spraying Moon with saltwater. He shook it out of his frills and backed toward the hatchway. The deck jerked underfoot and suddenly became a slope, as the pressure of the water dragged it sharply down and pulled the vessel forward toward the whirlpool. Moon dug his foot claws in to stay upright. The water was full of waterlings, the lights reflecting flashes of their bright blue scales, but they were all caught in the suddenly rushing current. The deepening whirlpool pulled them down toward the center. Just like the sunsailer.

We're going to sink, Moon thought. They might have time to get at least some of the crew away. No, he had forgotten the flying packs. With those they might have a chance to get everyone to safety. Moon started to turn, to head up onto the deck above to find Jade and Callumkal. But then the big light on the port side of the sunsailer made a slow sweep across the walls. They were covered in waterlings.

The creatures fought their way out of the less violent current around the edge of the basin and streamed up the walls, clustered on the platforms, on the floor of the hall. More appeared on terraces and balconies in the upper part of the chamber, climbing up, still trying to get above the boat. Moon stared in sick dismay. The chamber was alive with the creatures. If the Raksura and groundlings left the boat, there was nowhere to go.

"Moon—" The shout was from overhead and Moon snapped out of his horrified contemplation of the large hole forming in the churning water ahead. Magrim was yelling and pointing. "Close the hatch!"

Right, or we'll die faster. Moon turned, climbed back up the steepening slope toward the hatchway. He snapped his claws through the strap holding the metal door open and slammed it shut. There was a lever on the outside and he gave it a turn, and felt a locking mechanism jolt inside. Water washed up from the bow and he leapt up, caught the wall over the hatch, and slung himself over the railing.

Magrim braced there, staring wide-eyed at the water. He said, "I meant go inside and close the hatch!"

"I know," Moon told him. But there were still at least three Kishan out here at the fire-weapons and lights and he didn't want any desperate waterlings to jump onto the boat at the last minute and eat them. Even if they were all about to drown. "Do you know what caused that?"

Magrim grimaced, still staring at the whirlpool. "It must have been the lock. When the gears blew, they must have been connected to some opening in the bottom of the basin."

Probably, and it had obviously been an ill-considered decision, but as part of the group who had attracted the waterlings' attention, Moon wasn't going to point fingers. He said, "Just hold on. Maybe it'll stop." He didn't think it was going to stop but there was no point right now in saying so.

He looked up toward the steering cabin, visible from this angle, and through the window saw Rorra, Kellimdar, and three other Kishan shouting, gesturing, and wrestling with something that was probably the steering mechanism. He realized the background roar was the sunsailer's motivator, desperately fighting the current.

Moon went to the edge of the railing and looked back along the boat, but couldn't see anyone out on the decks on this side, except the Janderi at the big fire-weapon post on the third deck. There was another Janderan on the far side, grimly keeping a big distance-light pointed toward the whirlpool. Moon hoped all the Raksura had gotten inside already. And that everyone was still alive.

A thump on the deck above made him flinch but it was only Stone, now in his groundling form. He jumped down next to Moon, and frowned at the whirlpool. "So that looks pretty bad."

"Where's Jade and the others?" Moon asked. He wrapped his claws around the railing. Despite the furious efforts in the steering cabin, the sunsailer drew closer to the circle of rushing water, the deck sloped more steeply.

"They're inside, on the lower deck. Waterlings were climbing up the stern, but they left when this started. Kalam told everyone to get inside and lock the doors." Stone asked Magrim, "You want to go inside?"

Magrim shook his head. "The crystal in the ports isn't made for this. It's going to break. If I'm going to drown, I'd rather do it out here than inside."

Moon would rather do it with the other Raksura, but he wasn't sure there was time. Then Stone said, "Delin doesn't think we're going to die."

The sunsailer jerked sideways and Moon gripped the railing as he nearly slammed into Stone. The motivator jittered and sputtered. He raised his voice over the roar of water. "Does he?"

"He thinks this is happening for a reason," Stone explained. He ducked as a huge gout of water splashed up over the decks. "He admitted it might not be a good reason."

Then the bow dipped and the boat surged forward straight into the darkness at the center of the whirlpool.

CHAPTER TWENTY-ONE

Moon wrapped one arm around the railing and the other around Stone's waist. He saw Stone grip the railing and grab Magrim's arm. And then water rushed up at them.

After five heartbeats of nothing but saltwater and blind terror, the wave passed. Moon was dripping wet, salt stinging in the cuts and abrasions in his scales from the waterlings' claws. It was dark and he was huddled against Stone's side, tucked under his arm. He blinked water out of his eyes and looked for Magrim. He was still here too, tucked under Stone's other arm.

The sunsailer's distance-light swung wildly, allowing glimpses of dark curving walls, streaked with white mineral deposits and patches of mold. The light steadied, proving the operator had managed to survive, and swung to illuminate the way ahead. The sunsailer raced down a dark straight channel filled with water, which rose as the basin behind them emptied into it. Moon retrieved his scattered wits, flattened his spines to keep from cutting Stone's arm, and said, "Delin thinks this is the way out?"

It made a strange kind of sense, at least for this place. Only one boat could take it at a time, and the lock was there to prevent others from being pulled out of the canal while the water was draining into the opening. Forcing the lock to move must have made the passage open as well.

"Right." Stone's voice was tight and strained. He hadn't been as calm about this as he had pretended. "We couldn't get all the groundlings off the boat, and there were enough waterlings to eat us all if we tried, so we decided to risk it."

"'We,'" Moon asked. Not that he was arguing.

"Me and Delin," Stone admitted. "We didn't have much of a chance to discuss it with anybody else."

Magrim, who had been cursing steadily in Kedaic, now said in Altanic, "We must be past the wall of the escarpment by now. Perhaps the Fell won't know where to look for us."

He was right. Moon said, "I wonder how it goes back up?"

"That's a good question," Stone said.

Magrim said, "I hope it's not jammed shut, like the lock."

Moon glanced up at what he could see of the curved ceiling overhead and hoped so too. But the outer door on the far side of the escarpment had still worked, so he thought the chances were good. He hoped the chances were good.

Stone twisted around to look up at the steering cabin. "There's Jade."

Moon looked, squinting past the spray of saltwater. In the lighted cabin he could see Jade looking out the window, beside Rorra and the others working at steering the boat. He thought he could see Callumkal and Kalam in the rear of the cabin. The one thing that was clear was that Jade didn't seem pleased to see him and Stone out here.

Moon turned back toward the dark onrushing tunnel. "We're going to hear about this later."

Stone leaned forward, eyes narrowed, staring toward the end of the tunnel. "Maybe."

Some distance ahead the darkness of the tunnel gave way to something deeper and blacker, that the light couldn't penetrate. *Not a wall*, Moon thought. *Not a wall would be good.* The image of the boat jammed up against an unmovable barrier while the tunnel filled up . . . But the tunnel wasn't filling up. This water was going somewhere.

Then Stone said, "It's another chamber."

Magrim groaned.

As the end of the tunnel approached, the distance-light began to show detail. They headed toward a big cavern filled with oddly still water, and it didn't seem to be much lower than the tunnel.

Moon braced himself against Stone as the sunsailer shot out of the tunnel and dropped a few paces. The deck jolted with bone-rattling impact and water fountained up on all sides. The thrumming ceased as the motivator cut off and the boat slewed around in a circle as Rorra and the others managed to stop its headlong progress. The distance-light swung around, frantically at first, then more methodically as nothing immediately terrible happened.

The chamber seemed circular, but water ran down the walls and Moon couldn't see if they were stone or metal. But the light kept catching white and blue reflections off the water, the colors of whatever material was under it. And where was the water coming from?

Then the boat jolted again, and the water trembled, suddenly choppy with ripples and little disturbed waves. A window opened somewhere above and one of the Kishan yelled something in another language. "She says, 'Look up, look up,'" Magrim translated.

The light swung upward in response and lit a ceiling of light-colored material, all in delicate folds, like the outer petals of an elaborate flower. Staring upward, Moon hissed in astonishment. "That's forerunner."

Stone stared. "You're sure?"

"Yes!" This was just like the flower-shaped doorways and carvings they had seen in the underwater forerunner city. There had been nothing like this in the builders' city.

The sunsailer jolted again, and it, the water, and whatever the water was resting on began to move upward. Moon drew a sharp breath. "Oh. Oh, I hope—" The outer door in the forerunner city had needed a forerunner, or a half-Fell half-Raksura close enough to forerunner, to open it, unless you could find and manipulate a hidden lock. If this was set up the same way . . .

Then the flower carving trembled and the petals folded back in a complex spiral. Past it was darkness, but it was the living darkness of a cloud-strewn night sky. Moon sagged against the railing, the release of tension making him weak. "No, it's letting us out." And it wasn't going to dump half a sea's worth of water on them, either. The chamber stretched all the way up to the surface.

Faintly, apparently reeling from the shock that they were going to live, Magrim asked, "You hope, what? Did you think it would crush us?"

"Nothing, just, nothing," Moon said, feeling his spines twitching with relief.

Stone nudged him. "Climb up to the steering cabin and tell them we need to turn our lights off. We should be downwind, and if we're far enough away from the escarpment, the Fell may miss us."

"Right." Moon detached himself from the railing and Stone, and made the jump up onto the next cabin roof. He crossed it, and climbed up the next level to the steering cabin.

Jade was already pushing open one of the windows. "Get in here," she demanded.

"Tell Callumkal to tell the crew to turn off the lights, so the Fell won't see us," Moon said first. "Stone thinks we might be far enough away."

Jade hissed in irritation and turned to relay this to Callumkal. Kellimdar poked his head out the window and said, "We should have thought of that." He seemed a bit loopy from shock. "Is everyone all right out there?"

"I think so. I was with Stone and Magrim in the bow," Moon told him. A Janderi hurried out the door at the back of the steering cabin and from the opposite window, Callumkal called down to the Janderan on the other side of the boat to cover their lights.

"Ah. Thank you, all of you." Kellimdar awkwardly patted Moon's claws, and withdrew into the cabin.

As an apology for doubting Raksura in general, Moon would take it. It was more graceful and heartfelt than some apologies he had received in the past.

The forward distance-light went out, then the two closer to the stern, then the lights in the windows along this side. The whole chamber was still moving upward, the rush of water down the sides slowing as it neared the surface. The petal door was nearly all the way open.

Jade stepped back to the window. Moon said, "So it looks like these people knew the forerunners."

"Moon—" Jade hissed in annoyance. "Move over."

He moved sideways along the steering cabin wall and Jade climbed out the window. She asked, "Why did you stay outside?"

"I don't know." Moon didn't want to argue about it. Like Magrim, he hadn't wanted to drown inside the boat, and he was just enough of an optimist to think there might have been some last moment way to save them all that he could have accomplished or helped with. It didn't make a lot of sense, a good consort would have gone to huddle inside, but there it was.

Jade leaned over to look closely at him, then apparently decided to drop it. She sat back against the side of the cabin. "Well, we're alive. And we're downwind."

"And the forerunners were here," Moon said.

"That too," Jade agreed, looking upward grimly.

They were only twenty paces below the surface now. Moon heard a couple of doors open, and two Janderan stepped out on the lower deck to get ready to operate the big fire-weapon there. Toward the stern, Balm, River, and Briar hopped up on top of the rear cabin, their spines twitching nervously.

The boat lifted up level with the surface and the water churned under them. There was Fell stench in the wind, and Moon twisted to look back toward the escarpment. It was a vast looming shape, dark against the stars of the night sky. The sunsailer was about three times the distance from it that the island had been. Watching for movement, Moon spotted a kethel wing framed against the lighter clouds, just for an instant, as it passed around the side of the escarpment. "They're circling it," he said. "Wonder which flight won." He thought of the Fell queen, trading Bramble for her ruler. It was hard to remember sometimes that Fell rulers, and perhaps the progenitors, did care for each other, unlike the way they treated their dakti and kethel.

"I'm not sure it matters." Jade leaned into the window. "Don't start the motivator; the Fell might hear it."

"Yes, we'll let the current take us into the ocean." Rorra appeared in the window. "Did the walls drop down, can you see?"

The words "into the ocean" made Moon's spines want to twitch. He felt like they should have a much larger boat for that, maybe one as big as the island, but there wasn't much choice. He craned his neck, trying to see if the door had closed and the chamber was sinking down again. It had filled with water to push them to the surface, and then once it closed, the water must drain away somewhere. They were lucky it still worked after all this time, but then the forerunner city's defenses had still worked as well.

The swirling water was calming. "I think so," Jade told Rorra.

"Then we should start to move." Rorra pulled away from the window and went back to the steering lever.

In Raksuran, Moon said, "It's too bad we can't use the motivator yet, because if that crystal thing does attract Fell, the faster we get away the better." They needed to be farther away from the escarpment than the Fell could fly in one stretch. If there were no islands out here to rest on, then the Fell wouldn't be able to follow them.

Jade's spines signaled grim agreement.

The boat turned gradually away from the shape of the sea-mount and toward the limitless dark where the sea met the ocean. The sails on the two central masts started to unfold, opening out like huge fans.

The scale of the escarpment was so large it was hard to tell if they were moving away from it or not, with no other landmark to measure their progress by. But after a while, Moon realized he could feel the forward movement of the boat. There was no sound but the wind, and the occasional footstep or quiet Kishan voice.

Moon wasn't aware he had drifted off until Jade nudged him. He jerked awake and she said, "Go inside and sleep, before you fall off the boat."

"Hah." He managed to uncurl his cramped legs. The escarpment didn't look any smaller, but he could tell maybe an hour or more had passed. The sky was still empty and the clouds clearing away, only a few wispy ones to obscure the stars. The boat moved faster, the current still pushing it along. "You're the one who needs more sleep."

"When we're a little farther away." Jade leaned away from the cabin wall and rolled her shoulders to ease the tension in her furled wings. "I'll send Stone and some of the others after you. Balm and River are in better shape than the others; they can take the first watch."

Moon climbed awkwardly inside the steering cabin. Callumkal was holding the steering lever, and Esankel, Kalam, Vendoin, and Rorra sat on the benches against the wall, drooping with exhaustion. Kalam had fallen asleep, his head on Vendoin's armored shoulder. Keeping his voice low, Callumkal asked Moon, "Nothing in the air?"

"No. Not so far." He hesitated, not sure he wanted to know. "Are we in the ocean now?"

Rorra stirred a little and said, "We're in the Blue Drop, where the sea meets the ocean. At dawn, you'll be able to see it."

Moon didn't ask how she knew, whether it was because she was a sealing or a navigator. He stepped out of the steering cabin into the dark passage beyond, and found his way down the stairs.

On the lowest deck, where the cabins didn't have windows, some of the lights were still lit. All the Kish-Jandera he glimpsed through the doorways were asleep, lying on bench-beds. In their cabin, Merit and Bramble were curled up together on a bench, and Delin sat on a floor cushion, a sheaf of papers in a leather folder on his lap. He was frowning intently at the wall. As Moon came in, he blinked up at him, as if he had been so absorbed in something, he had forgotten anyone else was alive. Delin shook his head a little, and said, "All is well?"

"So far," Moon said around a yawn. He crossed the cabin and sank down onto an empty bench, and shifted. He winced; his shoulders ached, his back ached, everything ached. The wind had dried his scales, so at least there was no water to transfer to his clothes. But the salt made his skin itch. "Did you see the flower door? The forerunners must have made that whole passage for the builders."

Delin still seemed distracted. "Yes, they were obviously allies. It is perhaps not as unexpected as we supposed."

Moon nodded toward the papers. "What are you reading?"

Delin patted the papers. "Vendoin had some translations I wish to look at." He pushed to his feet. "She is still in the steering cabin?"

Moon nodded, and lay down on his side. Delin said, "I will take it back to her room, then."

Moon yawned again. "Did she figure out what the inscription on the wall said, the one up on the arch where we first came into the city?"

Delin paused in the doorway. "It said, 'If eyes fall on this, and no one is here to greet you, then we have failed. Yet you exist, so our failure is not complete.'"

Delin slipped out while Moon was still trying to understand that. He fell asleep, wondering why Delin had chosen a time when everyone else was bracing for a Fell attack to read Vendoin's translation.

Sleeping heavily, Moon was only vaguely aware of it when the sunsailer's motivator thrummed into life. Not long after that, Jade climbed onto the bench and curled up with him.

He woke knowing that it was well past dawn. He sat up carefully and disentangled himself from Jade. Merit and Bramble were gone, but Chime, Root, and Briar occupied the other benches.

Moon managed not to wake anyone as he slipped out of the cabin, though he was still off-balance and bleary. He went down the passage toward the bow, found his way through a crew area filled with sleeping bodies, and then out the door onto the deck. Stone was out there, leaning on the railing, but it was the view that caught Moon's attention first.

The water was a deep dark blue, and the sky above it a limitless horizon. The boat crested gentle swells and was moving southeast, its motivator fighting the current to keep them from being pushed farther out into the ocean. He moved to the railing and leaned beside Stone. The wind had changed and it was absolutely devoid of anything but water and salt. It made Moon realize just how much the scattered islands had added an undercurrent of sand and greenery and other scents to the sea winds. They had never been far from land or a reef or one of the shallow zones. Here, there was nothing.

Then motion caught Moon's eye several hundred paces off the starboard stern. Water fountained briefly, then a great shape rose up. Sunlight glanced off bright silver scales and a delicate multi-colored array of feelers concealing the top of the creature's head. There were three of the crab-like waterlings from the city clamped in its long jaw. It sank back below the surface before the ripples from its appearance reached the boat to gently rock it. Moon wanted to make a noise but his throat had temporarily closed up.

Stone said, "Some of the waterlings followed us from the city, but that keeps happening." He added, "Rorra says we're still on the fringe."

Moon reminded himself they had traveled over water this deep before, water also filled with menace, in the freshwater sea, but somehow it wasn't the same. Even if it was vast, the freshwater sea was surrounded by land, and fed by rivers, and somehow that made a difference. He fought his flight instinct down and managed to say, "Did you sleep?"

Stone rolled his shoulders and stood up straight, still propping himself up on the railing. "Out here. The Fell missed us completely. Getting out of there unnoticed was what that underwater tunnel was meant for."

Moon tried to remember that last harbor basin and what had been in it, if there had been any more clues they hadn't had time to notice. "The Kishan were right; there was a door in the outer wall of the city, like the one we came in through. So the tunnel was added after the city was built." Maybe at the same time the top of the escarpment had been sealed off. "And the foundation builders knew the forerunners, and they were friendly enough for the forerunners to build that for them."

Stone turned and leaned his back against the railing, to look up at the steering cabin. Moon was still a little too edgy to turn his back on the deeps yet. "Delin and Callumkal and the others have been discussing that. They don't know what it means, but they've been discussing it."

Speaking of the city and what they had found there . . . "We need to drop the . . . thing soon." Moon glanced around the deck. There were still Kishan at the weapons' posts and on watch for the Fell. "Is it deep enough?" If they were lucky, maybe one of the giant oceanlings would eat it.

"I don't know." Stone jerked his chin toward the cabin. "Rorra's up now."

Moon turned. Rorra was on the deck above, gazing out toward the ocean. She had a map case tucked under her arm. "I'll go talk to her."

Moon shifted and leapt to the railing. Swinging over it, he shifted back to groundling. Rorra rubbed her eyes and said, "I'm glad I'm used to that now." She still looked tired, though her face was less gray and her eyes not so sunken. She had clearly slept in her clothes, and her hair was unraveling from her braids.

"Are we in the ocean or still on the fringe?" Moon asked.

"We're still in the fringe." Rorra opened the map case and propped it against the railing to unfold light wooden pieces. "We're here." She pointed to a spot some distance from the escarpment and traced it along the big wavy path that marked the transition between the sea and the ocean. "We'll be moving in this zone until we get to this point." She tapped the map. "It would be safer to stay in the fringe, but to do that we'd have to turn back landward. If we keep our heading and cut across this section of the deeps, we can reach the sea again much more quickly, and we'll be moving away from the escarpment and hopefully the Fell the entire time."

Moon nodded. "When will we get to the deeps?"

"Probably around sunset, and we'll make the crossing during the night, hopefully reaching the sea again by morning." She began to fold up the map, a grim set to her expression. "I hope the deeps aren't as dangerous as the rumors say. Ocean-going ships should be much bigger than this one."

It sounded perfect. By the middle of the night they would be well into the deeps, and too far out for the Fell to reach. Someone could easily stroll out on deck and drop the object over the side. As long as nothing appeared to eat the boat, this would be easy. "You should get some more sleep."

"I don't—" Rorra yawned, wide enough that Moon could see the characteristic sealing fangs in her side teeth. "Probably." She frowned down at the lower deck. "Why is Stone staring at us?"

Moon leaned on the railing, and decided since they were lying-by-avoidance to Rorra about the object, he might as well tell the truth about this. "I don't know. We think he likes you, though."

Rorra stared at him, astonished but oddly not appalled. Then she got her frown back into place. "What does that mean?"

"Nothing." Moon shrugged, a little. "He's always liked groundlings. But he's just so old, he doesn't usually get that interested in people we meet."

Rorra's frown was now confused. "How old is he?"

"Older than all of us put together. But not as old as the escarpment." He pushed away from the railing. "I'll let Jade know what we're doing."

Moon met with Jade in the cabin they had been sleeping in. Stone had come in from the deck, and Chime, Balm, and Delin sat around on the benches, with Merit and Bramble on the floor. It was a little crowded, but the cabin on the upper deck with the stove was also used by Callumkal and the others, and taking it for a private conference would be a lot more noticeable.

Once Moon told everyone what Rorra had said about their route, Jade moved her spines in agreement. "Good. We'll drop the thing overboard tonight, once we're well into the deeps and out of the Fell's range."

Stone said, "Are you sure you don't want me to fly it out now and do it?"

Jade exchanged a look with Balm, and lifted her brows. She asked Stone, "Do you think it's safe? From what we've heard, it isn't."

Delin agreed. "You may call attention to us from whatever dwells further out, and the large waterlings who float on the surface, waiting for prey."

Sounding horrified, Chime said, "Are there really waterlings like that?"

Delin nodded. "The stories of the Kish and sealings and others who mapped this coast in the past turns are not pleasant reading."

Merit, holding the satchel with the object in it, clutched it nervously. "I don't think you should do that, Stone. I could scry, but—"

"It's too obvious for scrying. What are you going to tell Callumkal?" Moon asked Stone. "That you're going to sightsee?"

Stone sighed. "Fine, we'll wait till tonight."

Jade told Merit, "If you're rested, try scrying anyway. Maybe we're close enough by now that you can see whether this is a good idea or absolutely the worst thing we can do."

Bramble sat forward. "Is that settled? Because there's another problem."

Jade said, "It's as settled as it's going to be right now. Go ahead."

Bramble's expression wasn't encouraging. "There isn't much food left. Igalam, the Janderi who's in charge of the supplies, and I went down into the hold to sort out how much to bring up. He wanted me to show him how much we'd need. But when he opened the door, the smell was rank. Some of the ceramic containers of the pickled fish and the grain flour for bread had broken on the bottom, probably when the boat fell getting in and out of the tunnel. The Kishan can't eat them now. I don't think our stomachs are as delicate, but they don't smell like they'd be fit for us, either."

There was a moment of worried silence. Chime said, "Did everyone get hungry when she said that, or is it just me?"

It wasn't just Chime. Moon said, "We'll be back in the sea by tomorrow, and it'll be safe to go fishing." Safe but maybe not too profitable. From what he had seen on the way out here, the big fish that made good meals tended to be in the currents between the islands. It might be two or three more days before they found a good spot to fish. It had been more than two days since their last big meal, and while the smaller meals of fruit, bread, and fish helped, they couldn't live on them and still fly and fight.

Bramble said, "That's what I told Igalam, that when we could hunt, we could bring in enough food for the whole boat."

"Does he think if we get hungry we're going to eat the crew?" Stone asked, and not sarcastically. This question had occurred to Moon, too. They had been getting along well enough with the ship's crew, helped by the fact that the more familiar flying boat crew were aboard. The number of Kishan who shied away from him when he passed them in a corridor had dropped drastically since they had fought off the Fell and taken refuge in the city. But this was the kind of fear that could destroy that limited trust.

Bramble winced, but gave the question serious thought. "I don't think so. He seemed more annoyed that this had happened, and wondering what to do about it. He's still trying to figure out how long what we have will last."

Then someone rattled the door and slid it open. "Jade." Root peered inside. "There's another flying boat coming."

Delin sat up, hopeful. "Perhaps it is Diar and Niran."

Root flashed his spines in a negative. "It's not a wind-ship."

Delin grimaced and swore. "That would have solved several problems."

Moon thought Delin meant something more than the shortage of food. Though it probably wasn't obvious to anyone who didn't know him, Delin seemed more rattled now than he had when they were being attacked by Fell. Moon started to ask what was wrong, but Esankel came down the corridor to tell them about the flying boat, and there was no time for it.

The flying boat hung in the air about fifty paces above the sunsailer's stern. The Kishan were all happy to see it. "It's from Hia Iserae," Callumkal told them, leaning on the railing as if the relief had made his legs weak. "The Hians, Vendoin's people."

This flying boat was shaped differently than the expedition's ruined one, and was longer and sleeker, without the ridge up the middle, but was made of the same mossy material. Vendoin and Kellimdar had already gone up to it in the flying packs to explain their situation.

"How did they find us?" Jade asked. Moon thought it was a good question. They stood out on the deck with Stone and Delin, with the others told to stay inside until they could be assured that the new groundling arrivals wouldn't shoot at them by accident.

"We had shared the location of the city with them, though I didn't think they meant to join the expedition this season." Callumkal turned to gesture at the steering cabin. "Their ship is powered by the same varietals of moss as the sunsailer. The varietals have an affinity for each other, and clever horticulturals can use this to locate ships."

"I see," Jade said. It was unexpected, but at the moment it was hard to see it as a bad thing. The more fire-weapons there were to fight off the Fell, the better.

Beside him, Moon heard Delin make a hmph noise under his breath. Delin would clearly have preferred a wind-ship with his family aboard, and Moon had to admit that would have made the situation much less fraught.

Rorra came out of the hatch, squinting up at the flying boat. "I hope they have supplies they can give us."

"That's what Kellimdar and Vendoin are asking about now," Callumkal told her.

Jade asked, "So are we keeping to the same course, and crossing back into the sea tomorrow morning?"

Looking up at the flying boat again, Callumkal gestured an absent assent. "As long as they have no new information to make us decide against it."

"They shouldn't," Rorra said. "They came up from the south. It will be interesting to hear if they spotted any Fell from that direction."

"Interesting?" Callumkal commented dryly. "This voyage has been interesting enough."

Stone glanced at Moon, his expression opaque, and headed back toward the hatch. They would still be sailing across the deeps tonight and still have the opportunity to get rid of the object. Merit had already retreated to a corner of their cabin to scry on it, with Bramble and Song guarding the door to make sure no Kishan walked in on him.

"They're coming back," Jade said, watching the flying boat.

Vendoin and Kellimdar were returning in their flying packs, another Hian following. Callumkal said, "Don't worry, Vendoin and Kellimdar will have explained about you. The Hians are not very excitable people; they won't be afraid."

Jade gave that a serious nod. "Good."

The flying packs didn't manage the wind very well, but the ground-lings landed on the deck without ending up in the water. Vendoin shed her pack and said, "This is Bemadin, captain-navigator." Bemadin nodded as Vendoin named everyone for her. She bore a close resemblance to Vendoin, at least as far as non-Hians were concerned, though she was taller and her body heavier. She stared as Vendoin named Jade and Moon, though like Vendoin, it was hard to read her expression.

When the introductions were complete, Bemadin said, "I am glad we could find you. As I told Vendoin and your colleague Kellimdar, we are anxious to hear what you discovered before the Fell forced you to leave."

Callumkal said, "It's a long way back. We'll have plenty of time to show you all the inscriptions we copied."

"And we will be bringing down supplies to see you through to the next port." Bemadin added, "Perhaps you would all join us for evening meal." She turned to Jade. "I invite the Raksura, as well. I have never met any of your people before, so I am anxious to get to know you."

"Ah." Jade managed to look pleased by the prospect, which was something of an achievement for Raksuran diplomacy. It wasn't an appalling idea, it was just that Moon didn't think Jade or any of the others were ready to take on a new group of groundlings, not while everyone was tired and tense. "I feel our time would be better spent here, helping the Kishan guard their boat. We don't know what we'll encounter on this stretch of ocean."

"That's true," Callumkal said immediately. He didn't look as if he was in the mood for diplomatic visiting, either. "Perhaps in a day or so, once we are safely back into the sea, and farther away from the Fell."

"That would be best," Kellimdar agreed readily.

"That's right, best just to send some supplies down for tonight," Vendoin said, giving Bemadin a friendly pat on the arm. "Some fresh food would be welcome."

She was right about that. Bemadin said, "Very well, I will have the supplies moved immediately, and we can be underway again."

As they began to discuss the arrangements, Moon managed to wander away down the deck with Delin, and after a moment Jade followed. "This worries me," Delin said, keeping his voice low, even though he was speaking Raksuran. He twisted his fingers into his beard, a sure sign of agitation. "This sudden appearance."

"You think Vendoin was planning to betray Callumkal, take his work, or something." Moon looked off toward the horizon, as if they were worriedly discussing the prospect of being eaten by oceanlings.

"Perhaps, perhaps that." Delin frowned at the deck, and Moon had the impression that of all the things he was worried about, that ranked fairly low down on the scale. Delin looked up at Jade. "We must take care tonight, when disposing of the object. Perhaps Merit will have some insights for us, as to how best to proceed."

"We'll take care." Jade put a hand on his shoulder, and turned to steer him toward the hatchway. "You get some rest."

Hians in flying packs carried down the round containers of supplies, and by mid-morning the sunsailer got underway again, the flying boat trailing along after it. Moon spent the time napping off and on and taking turns on watch with the warriors. Three times they spotted movement in the distance, as oceanlings far larger than the boat broke the surface and submerged again. It was nerve-racking, but being able to catch up on sleep, and not worrying about the lack of food, made the tense situation easier on everyone. The Kishan were starting to look better too, taking time to rest and clean up and change their clothes.

"I'll be glad when this is over," Chime said. He was sitting back to back with Moon on the top cabin as they took their turn at watch. Stone was on the lower stern deck, and Balm was up in the bow. At least the day had stayed clear and bright, the sky blue and cloudless, the sun glinting off the limitless ocean. The wind was fairly gentle, and still carried nothing but the scent of saltwater.

"Is it ever going to be over?" Moon didn't like to bring this up, but it was worrying him more and more as the day progressed. "The Fell aren't going to stop looking for that thing. If that's what they were looking for."

"There's still too much we don't know," Chime admitted. "We don't know if it really drew them to the city or not. I'm hoping the Fell sit around outside the escarpment until they all die of old age."

Moon didn't think that was likely. Especially with a Fellborn queen involved.

Late in the afternoon, Merit finished scrying and came up to join them in the upper cabin. Bemadin had sent down some containers with cooked food, including a stew with big pieces of fish in a spicy brown sauce and fruit in sweet syrup, apparently two Jandera favorites. Igalan, the crew member in charge of supplies, had made sure Bramble had been given enough for all the Raksura. Both dishes were surprisingly tasty, probably because both the fish and the fruit were much fresher than what they had been eating on the boat for the past few days. Briar, having already eaten, had gone outside to carry a portion up to River, and to take a turn at watch so Song could come inside to eat.

"Did you get anything?" Jade asked, as Merit slumped down on the floor. His expression wasn't encouraging.

Merit sighed. "No, it was all confusing. I saw the ocean, I saw the Fell, the city, but it was all fragments. I don't think it's the same as before, where the trap in the city was clouding everything." Bramble put a bowl of food in his lap and he took a bite. "I think there's just too much happening right now."

"Fragments are what you get when there are too many possibilities," Chime explained to Delin. He took Moon's empty bowl and his own and put them in the stack near the stove. "They're usually just images of things that have already happened."

His mouth full, Merit nodded confirmation.

Jade grimaced and set her empty bowl aside. "At least there's nothing to change our plans."

"No, I think we should do as we have already decided," Delin said, so firmly that everyone stared at him.

"I'm glad someone is sure," Chime prompted, but Delin ate some more fruit and didn't respond.

Song stepped into the cabin then, reporting, "Stone is coming this way with Rorra."

Moon leaned back against the cabin window in frustration. They wouldn't be able to discuss this in front of Rorra. Not that discussing it was helpful.

Bramble readied two more bowls and handed them to Stone and Rorra as they came in. Stone sniffed skeptically at his, but tasted it anyway. Rorra took a seat on a bench and started to eat. Between mouthfuls, she said, "So what do you all think about Bemadin's sudden appearance?"

Jade said, dryly, "I'm glad we're not the only ones who noticed how sudden it was."

Rorra's nod was grim. "If they were going to show up, it would have been nice if they had done it while the Fell were trying to kill us."

"What does Callumkal think?" Moon asked. Chime hadn't finished his fruit, and Moon stole a piece. Chime glared at him.

Rorra grimaced in frustration. "He is very 'diplomatic.'"

Stone leaned against the wall, giving in reluctantly and eating the fish and sauce. "Tell them what you told me about the Hians."

"You know they were driven out of their old territory into the Kishlands because of the Fell?" Rorra asked.

"Vendoin spoke of it a little. And Delin mentioned it," Jade said.

Delin, who had leaned back against the bench and started to drift off to sleep, snorted at the sound of his name but didn't wake up. *That's probably for the best*, Moon thought. Delin clearly needed the rest.

Rorra said, "The territory they live in now is heavily forested, and has deep gorges, and is very difficult to view from the air, if you see what I mean."

Balm nodded understanding. "Lots of cover."

"Yes. For a long time, the Kishan scholars who study the builders have believed there are more builder ruins there. Turns and turns ago, they discovered fragments of a road leading that way, and some of the other writings they found referred to something—people, trade perhaps—coming from that direction." She waved a hand, setting her bowl aside. "I don't recall all the details, but Callumkal and others believe it likely that there is at least one ruined foundation builder city in that region. But the Hians say they have searched, and it isn't there."

Chime was frowning absently. Jade said, "Maybe it really isn't there."

"Maybe. There seems no reason to hide it if it is. But it has made for some disagreement between the scholars of Hia Iserae and the Kish-Jandera." Rorra blinked and rubbed her eyes. "I should go back to the bridge."

As she got to her feet, she stumbled a little. Moon caught her hand to steady her. He said, "I'll go with you. I'll take another turn on watch so River can come in and rest."

Jade gestured assent. Chime was already curling up to sleep, and Bramble and Merit were both yawning. Stone was still eating, frowning at his bowl.

Moon walked with Rorra to the stairwell. The corridors seemed quiet, but then everyone was probably eating while the food was still warm. As Rorra started up the steps, he told her, "You probably need more sleep, too."

"Probably, probably." She waved a hand absently.

Moon went on down the corridor toward the bow. He passed an open doorway to a cabin, but the several Janderan and Janderi inside were all asleep on the benches. Everyone breathed deeply, the sleep of the exhausted.

Moon was almost to the bow and the second stairwell when he caught a scent in the air. He couldn't identify it immediately, which seemed odd in itself. But it was coming from the draft down the stairs. It was just strange enough to make him want to investigate. He started up the steps.

The scent in the air was blood, mingled with something else.

As Moon reached the top of the stairs, his shoulder bumped the wall as he swayed sideways. *A wave hit us*, he thought. But then his head swam and he realized it was him.

He grabbed a rope handle at the top of the steps, put there for unsteady groundlings, and pulled himself up. He blinked, not understanding why it was suddenly so hard to keep his eyes open. Someone lay in the passage, slumped against the wall. It was a Janderan, and Moon thought he recognized the red-trimmed jacket the figure wore. He stumbled forward and slid down the wall, and carefully lifted the man's head. It was Magrim, and his dark eyes were open and staring; the warm fluid on Moon's hands was blood, from the deep gash in Magrim's throat.

A soft step on the deck made him look up. Vendoin stood there. She said, "Unfortunately, he didn't like the food."

CHAPTER TWENTY-TWO

The world spun and Moon couldn't sit up, couldn't see, couldn't shift; the feeling was terrifyingly familiar. *It's Fell poison*, he thought. *Somehow they have Fell poison.*

He tried to shove the looming figures away but hands seized his wrists and dragged him down the corridor. The edge of a hatchway scraped his hip, then he was dumped onto the deck again. Footsteps moved away, then he heard the door slide shut. From the corridor there was quiet talk but he couldn't make out the words. One of the voices was Vendoin's. Then a set of footsteps moved away, but he could sense more than one groundling just outside the door.

Someone patted his face, whispering, "Moon, can you hear me?"

It was Rorra, her scent laced with anger and fear. He dragged his eyes open. She half lay beside him, supporting herself on trembling arms. Her gray skin had light and dark patches, and there were deep bruises beneath her eyes. She looked like she was dying. She said, "It was the Hians. Vendoin betrayed us. They poisoned the food."

"I know," Moon croaked. He managed to lift his arm and hold it close enough to his eyes to see his skin. His snarl came out as a weak groan. Yes, there was a faint ghost-pattern of scales, his scales, imprinted on the dark bronze of his groundling skin. He tried to shift again but nothing happened. It was like reaching for something that wasn't there. This was Fell poison. It must have been in the food. It had no scent, and the weedy taste had been disguised by the spices.

He gripped Rorra's forearm, and managed to lever himself up a little. Squinting, he made his eyes focus enough to see they were in a cabin he didn't recognize, with cases built against one wall packed with Kishan books. He knew they hadn't left the boat, so this must be one of the cabins on the top deck, just below the steering cabin. Then he realized that what looked like a blurry heap of clothing lying at the base of the wall was actually three unconscious Kishan. One was Kalam, and the other two facing away were Callumkal and Kellimdar, all sprawled on cushions pulled off the benches. Sickness tainted the air and their breathing was far too quick and shallow.

"It's made everyone sick, or unconscious," Rorra was saying, her voice thick and choked, as if she was controlling nausea by force of will. She twisted awkwardly to look toward Kalam and the others. "I tried to prop them up so they wouldn't choke. The Hians just threw us in here."

From another cabin somewhere nearby, Moon could hear someone being violently ill, and someone else groaning. Rorra seemed coherent enough even if she looked terrible, but she was sprawled awkwardly on the floor. He said, "Are you hurt?"

Her expression went from dismay to thwarted fury. "It wasn't working on me fast enough so they took my boots."

With the boots missing, there was no support for her fins and the missing part of her leg. He said, "They killed Magrim. I found him in the corridor."

Rorra made a sound that was half-growl of rage, half-sob. "Why are they doing this?"

Moon was still trying to figure out how they were doing it. "Most simples meant for groundlings don't work on Raksura. Fell poison shouldn't work on groundlings." This didn't make sense. *Jade, Chime, Stone, all the others* . . . Some of them had already been falling asleep when he had left the cabin. Delin had been unconscious already but everyone had still been so tired, Moon hadn't thought anything was wrong.

Rorra shook him and he blinked, realizing he had almost drifted off. She asked, "What's Fell poison?"

"It comes from the Abascene peninsula, from old Kiaspur. The groundlings there drank it and when the Fell ate them, it poisoned the Fell." He couldn't believe it had worked on Stone so easily. *Maybe it didn't. Maybe he's hiding, planning something. And why am I still awake?* His body felt like a useless pile of disconnected limbs, and the urge to just slump to the deck and sleep was powerful, but he could fight it. He should be unconscious, like the others. Maybe because he had been given the poison before, back in the east, he had some resistance to it.

Rorra made a noise of disgust. "Letting the Fell eat them? That's mad."

"I don't think they knew that that was what was going to happen ..." Moon shook his head, trying to hold back the creeping darkness at the edges of his vision. *But where did the Hians get Fell poison?* Unless they had had it all along. The Hians had supposedly gone to Kish to get away from the Fell attacks in their old home. "But it still doesn't make sense. If Fell poison did this to groundlings, the Fell would know something was wrong, they wouldn't eat them."

Rorra winced, tried to drag one leg into a more comfortable position, and forced herself upright again. "Maybe the Hians used two different poisons, combined them. But why, I don't, unless—" She froze. "They're going to use us to kill the Fell."

They stared at each other. Moon thought, *If she's right* ... A voice in the corridor spoke and they both flinched, then Vendoin slid the door open.

She stepped inside, and another Hian moved past her, carrying a limp Janderi body. As the Hian deposited it beside Kellimdar, Moon saw it was Esankel. Her chest moved, though her breathing was rough and uneven. Rorra crawled to her immediately and rolled the woman onto her side. She glared up at Vendoin and demanded, "What did you give us?"

Vendoin's face was as opaque as ever, the bone plating her skin like partial armor, her expressions too different to be interpreted. She said, "I didn't mean for any of you to be harmed. We always carry the shapeshifter poison in our ships. We thought it would work against the Raksura, but combined it with a sleep drug for the Jandera and others. For some, it did not work as intended." Vendoin lifted a hand in a gesture like a shrug. "Most Jandera plant preparations and distillations are ineffective on Hians, so we are inexperienced at administering them." She cocked her head, looking at Moon. "You are not as affected as the others. Perhaps you have had the shapeshifter poison before?"

Moon didn't answer. He didn't want Vendoin to get the idea to give him another dose. And there was no telling what the effect would be of putting the Fell poison together with another simple.

Rorra grimaced in disgust. "You killed Magrim. And others? Why? Why would you do this?"

"I didn't kill him. One of Bemadin's crew panicked, when she found him still awake."

Moon hissed in disbelief. If all Hians reasoned that way, there was no talking to them. "You're not stupid. You knew this could kill all of us, but you didn't care."

Vendoin seemed unmoved, at least as far as Moon could tell. There was nothing different in her voice as she said, "That is unfair. We have tried to be as careful as possible."

"He's right, you're lying," Rorra said. "You didn't care if you killed us all. What about Avagram? He was in good health before we left. Did you poison him? You wouldn't want a Kish arcanist suspecting you. What do you want? Why did you do this?"

As if it was obvious, as if it was what anyone would do, Vendoin said, "We thought the city held an artifact that we wanted. A powerful artifact, that Hians or Jandera could not obtain for themselves."

Moon felt his heart sink right down to his stomach. An artifact. That couldn't be obtained by groundlings.

"What artifact?" Rorra was baffled. "No one found an artifact. There were only writings and carvings and . . ."

Footsteps approached from down the corridor, and then another Hian stopped in the doorway. She held the object, the silver cage with a lump of dark quartz-like mineral suspended inside. The sunlight falling through the window touched it, but the crystal didn't glint; it just absorbed the light. "Ahh, you have found it," Vendoin told her.

Rorra stared at Moon. "But no one took it. It was in the ruined room when we left and found the waterlings."

He said, "There was a spell on it. Briar picked it up and hid it in her pack, and didn't remember doing it. We didn't figure out she had it until we were back on the boat."

Vendoin regarded them both with what Moon thought might be amused disbelief. "You truly didn't know this was in the city? Or what it is?"

Rorra watched her warily. "No. You obviously do. Tell us."

Vendoin touched the silver cage, her fingertips barely brushing it. "We believe Hia Iserae was one of the places where the last of the foundation builders fled. The inscriptions there are far more complete than those at any of the sites found in Jandera. They spoke of this artifact and how to find it. I and the other scholars in Hia Iserae helped Callumkal organize this expedition because of it, though he knew nothing of our reasons. But I suspected that the protections the builders had left on it would not let me take it from the city." She told Rorra, "I tell you all this so you can explain to the others. We will leave you and the crew here on this ship, and you will be able to return to shore once the plant distillations wear off. I wish our reasons known and spread as widely as possible."

Moon managed to say, "So why do you want it? What is it?"

"I fear it would be cruel to tell you," Vendoin said, with no irony whatsoever.

Rorra stared at Vendoin, disbelieving. "Cruel? After what you did to Magrim?"

Moon's throat was so dry he wasn't sure he could talk. He knew nothing of Vendoin; everything she had shown them so far was just a mask, a performance to keep Callumkal and Kellimdar and the others happy and listening to her and cooperating with her so she could manipulate them. He said, "It's a weapon, isn't it? The weapon the Fell wanted. So use it. Use it now."

Vendoin looked at the artifact and seemed regretful. "I thought I would be able to." Moon thought, for an instant, she had reconsidered. But she continued, "The inscriptions on it tell me that there are other things I must do first." Vendoin gestured and the Hian with the artifact turned away and moved hurriedly down the corridor. Two others stepped in and moved to gather up Callumkal. Vendoin told Rorra,

"We will take Callumkal and Delin with us, as well as some of the Raksura." She nodded to Moon. "Your mentor, Merit, of course, and it has become obvious you will make the best hostage." She added to Rorra, "Be sure and tell everyone you encounter what we have done. Now it is time to go."

The Hians moved forward and Moon couldn't do anything but try to make them regret it.

Clinging to the hull of the ship only a few paces above the waterline, River thought, *I should have a plan. Stupid Moon would have had a plan.*

Briar had reached him just in time to collapse unconscious, her bronze skin already showing the distinctive markings of scales, the sign of Fell poison. He had thought at first that all the groundlings were betraying them, and hidden her in the shelter behind the distance-light on that side. But when he had climbed down the hull to make his way back to the cabin where the others were, he had seen the Kishan unconscious or sick. Then dozens of Hians had come down from the flying boat, and it was obvious they had poisoned everyone.

The Hians had the smaller fire weapons, and he couldn't kill them all. There had to be a clever way out of this; he just couldn't think of it.

He was stuck, climbing along under the windows on this side of the sunsailer, trying to hear what was happening, and waiting for an oceanling to pop up and scrape him off the hull. Then he heard Moon and the sealing, talking to Vendoin.

River took his chance and quietly climbed up to cling just below the window. If one of the Hians in their flying packs flew past this side, he was dead. He knew they would kill him. He had caught the scent of groundling blood in the air flowing out of the ship's upper corridor; if the Hians would kill other groundlings, there was no reason for them to hesitate at killing Raksura.

He heard Moon's weak growls and the Hians struggling to drag him out of the cabin. Then nothing.

He cautiously edged up and peered inside. Rorra was gone as well.

The Hians had left the door partly open and all River could scent right now was sick groundlings, sealing, and Moon. He shoved the window open and slung himself into the room.

He stepped quickly across it and took a careful look out into the passage. It was empty, except for Rorra, who had apparently crawled to the stairway leading up to the steering cabin and was trying to drag herself up it. She had only made it to the third stair. The Hians had taken her boots, revealing the mangled and missing fins at the end of one leg and the scarred stump on the other. River didn't care about sealings one way or another, but that was pure cruelty. And she was the closest thing he had to an ally.

He stepped silently down the passage and touched her shoulder.

She twisted around with a strangled yell before she saw who he was. "Some warning would have been nice," she gasped, pressing a hand to her chest.

River crouched on the floor. His arms and legs still shook from a combination of nerves and the strain of hanging off the metal hull by his claws for so long. "The Hians are leaving?" He wasn't sure what to do. He could follow the flying boat, maybe even hang onto its hull, until he could find a way to free Merit and Moon. But he hated to leave the others here and helpless until the poison wore off.

"Yes, with hostages." Rorra pushed her hair out of her eyes, and he saw the pale skin of her hands had been abraded by the metal steps. "They said they were going to take Moon. You didn't see him?"

River hissed. "I can't get over to that side without being seen. They have fire weapons!"

"I know, I know." Rorra held up a placating hand. "I'm not complaining."

River remembered about her communication scent, the need to filter it out. *Good, something else to feel inadequate about*, he thought. "You can use the fire weapons, right? If I follow the flying boat, can you take care of the others, and get the ship back to the sea?"

"Yes. But I'll need my boots, so I can walk. The Hians left them in the steering cabin." She added desperately, "We have to hurry. I think the poison is killing the Jandera."

River grimaced as he pushed to his feet. Merit was the only one who could help with that, and the Hians were taking him away. "Stay here." He slipped past her up the steps.

Moon growled, clawed, and managed to bite one of the Hians, despite getting slammed and scraped against the walls of the passage and stairwell. They dragged him out into the bright sunlight of the deck and dropped him, skipping out of arm's reach. He lay there, panting, what was left of his strength nearly gone, and he hadn't even been able to delay them much.

He managed to roll over. The flying boat hung low in the air, about a hundred paces above the surface of the water, and a dozen Hians in flying packs moved upward toward it. One attached straps to the still unconscious Callumkal's harness and dragged him up off the deck. Two more came out of a hatch lower down, carrying smaller bodies. Moon squinted and realized they were Delin and Merit. Another Hian came out carrying Bramble. He hissed helplessly. "You're leaving the others to die."

Vendoin said, "No, we will leave them, but they are free to recover and return to land. I want word of what we have done spread as widely as possible."

"Why are you taking Bramble?"

Vendoin made an irritated gesture. "Bemadin thinks you are too dangerous, that we should only take the wingless ones."

Moon wanted to rip her throat out. The sunsailer was drifting farther into the ocean, and Rorra was the only one who had shown any sign of recovery. He said, "Then give Rorra her boots so she can get up to the steering cabin and get the boat back to the sea."

Vendoin ignored him, watching as Delin, then Merit and Bramble were lifted up toward the flying boat. Then she gestured and two Hians moved toward Moon. One carried a small flask. They were going to give him more Fell poison. Moon shoved himself back on the deck, desperate to stand. Another dose might make him unconscious or kill him.

Then he caught the Fell stench on the wind.

His reflexive attempt to shift was useless. He was still trapped in his groundling form and there were Fell close by. Too close for the Hians to fight them off. *So this is how it ends*, he thought. The Fell would either eat them all and die of the poison, or realize the danger and wait until it wore off before feasting. He said to Vendoin, "You might want to drink that yourself."

She stared down at him. Then her head jerked up and she spun around to scan the sky. To the southwest, dark shapes cut across the wind. Moon spotted a ruler and a small swarm of dakti, with three kethel following further back. They must have circled around to approach from upwind.

Vendoin fell back a step, then shouted a warning to the other Hians. She said, "How are they here? We should be too far out for them to reach us!"

Maybe the Fell wanted to reach their prey more than they feared falling out of the sky from exhaustion. "Too bad you don't have any Raksura to fight them off," Moon told her.

She looked down at him, lips drawn back in a grimace. "We're not leaving without you." She made a sharp gesture.

The two Hians lunged in and grabbed Moon's arms to haul him upright. He twisted to pull away. One grabbed him from behind and lifted up off the deck, dragging Moon with her. The few other Hians still on the deck lifted into the air.

As they moved upward, Moon eyed the flying boat above and the water below, trying to make a decision. The only reason to take him along was to keep him drugged and helpless and keep Jade and the others at bay by threatening to kill him. The Hians could do the same with Merit and Bramble, but they might not realize that. He twisted his head around and tried to sink his teeth into the arm holding him.

Then the Hian jolted sideways as a heavy impact knocked both her and Moon back over the sunsailer's deck. He got a bare glimpse of a dakti's wing, then with a cry the Hian let go of Moon. Instinct made him go limp to minimize the damage, but he landed with a stunning impact.

Rolling over, he bit back a groan. His whole body felt numb. Lying on his back he saw the dakti tear the Hian's pack off, then fling her overboard. It darted away toward the upper deck. Three other Hians dropped toward the water as dakti tore and harried them.

Vendoin shot upward to reach the railing of the flying boat. A kethel swept past as she scrambled aboard. Other Hians ran to get to the fire weapons on its bow and stern. The weapon on its top deck swung around. Moon didn't see it shoot the wooden disk, but the kethel slipped sideways and the fire stream passed it, missing completely. The Kish-Jandera were obviously better marksmen.

Moon tried again to shift, but again nothing happened. He shoved himself up to his hands and knees and crawled to the wall. It was instinct to seek shelter, but he thought that would only delay the inevitable. There was no fire weapon on this deck that he could reach, nothing he could do. He tried to force himself to his feet, using the metal wall as a ladder. His head swam again and his knees gave out, and he sank back to the deck.

Two more fire streams shot out from the flying boat, but these kethel were just too quick. They darted in and away again. *They're fighting smart*, Moon thought. More like Raksura than Fell. As the last two Hians reached the boat's railing, it turned from the sunsailer and started to lift up and away.

Several dakti landed on the sunsailer's deck barely five paces away and Moon thought, *this is it*. But they approached slowly, cautiously, staring at him.

Moon waited for them to figure out that he was helpless. Then the ruler landed on the railing.

She wasn't a ruler. She was the half-Fell queen.

She called to him, "Should we chase the flying boat?"

It took Moon several heartbeats to realize she was actually asking him, expecting an answer. It was tempting to send them after it, but Merit, Bramble, Delin, and Callumkal were on that boat, helpless. He said, "No. Let it go."

She didn't make any gesture, but the three kethel broke off, curving away from the Hians' flying boat. Moving fast with the wind, it headed out over the ocean.

The queen hopped down from the railing, and shifted. Her form flowed and blended into a figure who could have been mistaken for a

Raksuran warrior. Except her skin was bone white, like the groundling form of a Fell ruler, and her dark hair was long and straight. She stepped closer, and he saw there were patches of dark scales on her cheeks, down her neck and shoulders. What looked like heavy braids in her hair might actually be frills. It was like a queen's Arbora form blended with a ruler's groundling form. She wore a loose dark tunic, patched and stained around the hem.

She stopped a few paces away, then dropped to a crouch to get eye level with him. Four dakti hunkered on the deck nearby, apparently to listen. She said, "What happened to you?"

Under the circumstances, it was a reasonable question. Moon said, "It's a poison. If you eat anyone on board this boat, it will kill you." The poison dulled all his physical reactions, so his frantically pounding heart and the tightness in his breathing was like something that was happening to someone else.

"We weren't going to eat anyone anyway. We're not like that." She tilted her head a little. "Why . . . Why?"

Moon pushed back against the wall, slowly, using it to keep him from slumping over on the deck. "Why are we poisoned?"

"Yes, why?"

Moon couldn't think of a reason to lie. The more she understood about the poison, the better. "The groundlings who came in the flying boat gave it to everyone."

She took that in. "They are fighting you over the city?"

"Yes." He wasn't going to give more detail than that.

She said, "We were fighting over the city. We made the other flight leave. They attacked the groundlings near the city, and you killed most of their kethel. You saw that." She waited for a response, and when Moon said nothing, continued, "They hate us, because we're not like them. We were supposed to help them. But we changed our minds."

Moon wanted to keep her talking. "Why?"

"We saw you." She tilted her head. "Are you a consort?"

He thought about saying no. But she had seen him in his scaled form on the city's dock, and this might be a test to see if he would lie to her. "Yes."

"Our father was a consort. He told us some things but not enough." She lifted her shoulders, looking toward the water. "We followed the waterlings from the city to find you. That was smart, wasn't it?"

He needed to change the subject, get her away from thinking about consorts. "Why were you at the city?"

"The other flight. We were with the other flight. They said there was a weapon inside. They heard it from some groundlings, in a groundling place." She twitched, lifting her shoulders again as if settling the wings she didn't have in this form. "They take a groundling, take their mind, and put a ruler inside, and then the groundling tells them whatever it knows—"

"I know about that."

She twitched again. "That flight had heard from other flights that there are good things in old cities, but you need groundlings to get inside. But the other flight might have been lying. They didn't say Raksura would be there."

Moon debated the wisdom of arguing with her, but if he was only delaying the inevitable with this conversation, he would rather she killed him outright. "You're lying."

Her white brows drew together and she dropped her gaze.

"You split from the other flight before you saw us. You captured some gleaners and forced them to build you a floating hive, then you ate them. You're not different from the other Fell."

Instead of getting angry, she looked away, her gaze moving along the boat's deck. "They weren't groundlings. We don't eat groundlings."

"They were people. And you're still lying."

She recoiled, still refusing to meet his gaze. "No one told me they were like groundlings! It's hard! I don't know what to do!" The dakti hissed at her. She hissed back, but grudgingly calmed herself. She added, as if determined to make sure everyone understood her rebuttal, "No one told me."

It struck Moon, suddenly and horribly, how much this was like a conversation with stubborn fledglings. "How old are you?"

She looked at the dakti again. Then turned back to Moon as if one of them had answered some unspoken question. "Twenty turns."

Twenty turns was barely old enough for an Aeriat to leave the nurseries. But she was still lying. "You know how to tell the difference between animals and people."

She shook her head, but said, "We did break from the other flight, but it was earlier, back on land. We followed them here but we didn't fight them until we saw you." She tossed her head, clearly upset. "So it was partly not lying. They said we were a mistake. It was a mistake to make us. They said it didn't work, they didn't need us anymore." The dakti all hissed in sad chorus.

Moon couldn't believe this. The equivalent of an Aeriat fledgling was in apparently complete command of a Fell flight. "You're all part Raksura."

"No." She looked up at the kethel. "Several."

So there were some Fell still with them. "The ones who aren't part Raksura obey you."

"I killed the progenitor." She ducked her head, shy and proud. "They like me better. I know to do things. We stole the other flying boat, the little one on the island, while the other flight's kethel was tearing apart the big one and getting killed. The dakti made it work, and we used it to follow the waterlings who were following you." She waited, as if hoping Moon would compliment this strategy.

"Tell him," a soft, deep voice said. "If you wait longer, it's worse."

Moon flinched, staring. It was one of the dakti who had spoken. It said again, "Tell him." It wasn't a ruler speaking through it. Its lips were moving; it was speaking with its own voice.

She told it, "Maybe not. Maybe later." She jerked her head toward Moon. "He's sick now."

The dakti had to be part Raksura too, even though it didn't look like it. Moon had seen rulers show intense emotion when another ruler was killed, but he had never seen one treat a dakti as anything other than something to use and discard, never seen dakti seem to care about each other. Moon said, "Tell me what?"

The Fell queen stirred uneasily. The dakti said again, "It will be worse later." The other two hissed in agreement.

She looked down at her curled toes, and said reluctantly, "One of the others is dead."

The others. Moon went cold. But maybe she meant . . . "One of the other groundlings."

"No. Other Raksura."

No. Not that. Terror made Moon's voice come out as a rasp, "You killed them."

"No!" She held up her hands, flexed as if her claws were still there. "No. Tilen saw Raksura through the glass, all sleeping. He wanted to see closer and climbed inside. He saw one was dead and went out again and told me."

"It's true," the dakti said.

Moon couldn't think. *It's a mistake. It's not true.* But Vendoin had said *I never meant for any of you to be harmed.* He had thought she meant Magrim and maybe some of the other Kishan. He said, "Show me."

River slipped back down the stairs, took Rorra's arm, and hauled her into the cabin, hissing at her to be quiet when she tried to speak. He put her down and dropped the boots beside her, staying in a crouch to keep out of view of anything flying past the window. His heart pounded with terror, the pulse beat in his ears so loud it interfered with his hearing. It took effort to keep his voice even. "The Fell are here."

Her eyes widened. "I thought— I heard the shouts and hoped the Raksura had woken and were fighting the Hians."

River moved his spines in a negative, keeping part of his attention on the window. A kethel circled in the distance but no dakti climbed past the opening. He didn't know why he was telling this to a sealing, as if she could help, but without her he was completely alone. "The Fell killed some of the Hians, but others got away. I saw them from the windows in the steering cabin." He had watched as best he could while scrunching his body into the back corner of the cabin, trying to blend with the wall so the Fell didn't see him through one of the big windows. He was still alive so he assumed they hadn't spotted him. The Fell's arrival had ruined his partially formed plan of following the flying boat until he could free the prisoners or report back to Jade where they had been taken. "The Hians took Bramble and Merit and Delin away with them."

Rorra hauled her boots on, hurriedly buckling the straps. "But not Moon?"

"They tried; he's still on deck." Moon might have survived the fall, but River didn't know how he could survive the dakti. "Are you still willing to use the fire weapon?"

She got her feet under her, and he reached down and caught her arm to help her stand. She wavered and he held on long enough to make sure she wasn't going to collapse. "Yes, it's our only chance."

It was a terrible chance. River had himself and one sealing who had been poisoned half-unconscious. But the alternative was to sit here and wait for the Fell to eat them. "Come on."

Fear gave Moon the strength to shove to his feet. He leaned on the wall to steady himself as the dakti surrounded him and the Fell queen moved down the deck toward the rear hatchway. He managed to get inside without falling but the stairway to the upper level loomed ahead. He grabbed the railing and tried to pull himself up but he was still so weak his muscles just refused to lift him. Hesitantly, the Fell queen reached for his arm. When he didn't move to stop her, she took his arm and helped him up.

Moon swallowed with a dry throat and let her, gripping the railing to steady himself. Her skin felt dry and too warm. Not like Shade, who felt exactly like another Raksura.

They reached the upper passage and Moon pulled away from her, and staggered down to the open cabin door.

He heard breathing. It was labored, but they were breathing. Jade lay slumped on the floor in front of the bench, in her Arbora form, as if she had been trying to stand and collapsed. Her chest moved with her panting breath. Relief let Moon manage a step forward.

The others were all in their groundling forms, their scale patterns visible on their skin. Stone had fallen over onto the bench and Chime was curled on the floor. Balm lay sprawled near Jade. He couldn't see if they were breathing and lunged forward to land on his knees near Chime. Frantically he felt for the pulse at their throats, finding faint movement. They were all alive. He twisted around, looking for the others.

Root and Song lay behind the stove, stretched out on the floor.

At first his eyes refused to see it. Root lay on his back, his breath a faint flutter like the others, and Moon wanted to see Song the same way. But there was a stillness to her body, an awkward stiffness to the way her limbs lay.

He crawled to her and touched her face. Her eyes were open, blank and staring and beginning to cloud. Her skin was waxy, the scale pattern partially faded from the bronze. Her blood was already cooling. She had been dead before the Fell arrived. There was blood mixed with vomit on her chin and chest.

Not really aware of what he was doing, Moon took the tail of his shirt and started to clean her face. Part of his brain was still working and he thought, *Briar isn't here. River isn't here.* Had they escaped? He knew Briar had eaten the poisoned food. They might be lying in a corner somewhere, left there by the Hians . . . He hoped they hadn't fallen off the sunsailer.

Another dakti slung into the room and Moon flinched away from Song. The other dakti gathered around flinched too. The newcomer chittered at the Fell queen and the others hissed in response. The queen pushed to her feet and looked down at Moon. "Another flying boat is coming. This one has Raksura."

Moon stared at her, uncomprehending. A flying boat with Raksura? *Niran and Diar. It might be them.* But had someone from the court come with them?

"They were following us, like we followed the waterlings." She hissed, but apparently at herself. "I was stupid." She looked down at Moon. "You come with us."

Panic penetrated the numb shock. "No, I need to stay here."

She hesitated. The dakti who had brought the news chittered in alarm. She said, "Better if you come with us. You can tell us what to do."

If he could reason with her . . . "The Hians who left on the other flying boat have the weapon that was hidden in the city. I have to tell the other Raksura so they can stop them."

She stared at him, her brow furrowing, and blinked in distress. She looked at the dakti. The one that seemed to be her advisor said, "Possible."

The queen stood there, frozen for a heartbeat. Then she flowed into her scaled form, and said, "Bring him."

Moon tried to stand but the dakti surged forward and grabbed his arms. Panic took over and he fought, tried to bite, but they half-dragged, half-carried him out and down the stairs, out onto the deck.

Outside he couldn't see anything in the air but the kethel circling overhead. He couldn't believe the flying boat, whoever was aboard it, was coming toward them and not fleeing as fast as it could.

The dakti were too small to fly with him. They put him down on the deck and the queen started toward him. Moon yelled, "No, stay away from me!"

To his surprise she did stop. She shook her head, confused and determined all at once. "We won't hurt you! We won't eat groundlings! We're not like Fell!"

"You're stealing a consort, just like the Fell who made you!"

"No, it's not— That's not— We need— We need something!" She flung her arms wide, confused, hopeless, determined. "We need help!"

Moon said, desperately, "Not from me!"

She hesitated, breathing hard. Moon had a moment to think that she would listen to him, that she would leave. Then she lunged for him.

A flash of green scales exploded out of the hatch and struck the Fell queen in the back. *It's River*, Moon realized in astonishment. She staggered forward, then tossed River off.

River rolled and came up in a crouch, just as the distinctive thunk-whoosh of a fire weapon sounded almost from above.

It was the big weapon just below and behind the steering cabin. The fire shot out in a long stream. The dakti shrieked and scattered off the rail as it moved toward them. The weapon swung up and pointed toward the kethel arrowing down from above.

The queen snarled and pounced at River. River ducked the first blow, tried to lunge in at her belly. Blindingly fast, she clawed him across the chest and flung him away. River slammed into the wall, then fell forward and hit the deck boards so hard he bounced. The queen tensed to strike again. Moon shoved forward and flung himself over River. "No!"

Caught in mid-lunge, the queen stopped, her claws scraping against the deck. Moon stared up at her, expecting her to tear them both apart.

River might already be dead. He wasn't moving and the coppery odor of fresh blood hung in the air.

But Moon saw the instant when the blank rage went out of the Fell queen's eyes and her expression turned to turned to confusion again. She stumbled back a step and looked up at the kethel. The one stooping over the ship immediately broke off, and the others circled back upward.

A dakti perched on the rail chittered to her. Her head jerked up and her gaze went to something in the sky to the west.

She snarled, threw one last look at Moon, then surged for the railing. She leapt into the air, the dakti leaping with her.

Watching them catch the wind and shoot upward toward the waiting kethel, Moon stared in bewilderment. He didn't understand what could have made her give up and leave.

Then a large queen and half a dozen warriors thumped down on the deck from above. For an instant, Moon didn't recognize any of them. Then the queen turned to him and he saw it was Malachite.

CHAPTER TWENTY-THREE

Moon tried to stand, but he was lying on River and there was no place to put his weight without hurting him. Then a male warrior caught him around the chest, lifted him up, and helped him to his feet.

Moon stumbled toward Malachite. "We need mentors. The Hians gave us all Fell poison, and a sleeping simple for the groundlings, it killed Song, they took Merit and Bramble away on a flying boat— They have a weapon from the city—"

Malachite lifted a hand and two warriors bounced into the air, flapping up to catch the wind. Moon thought they were going after the Fell, which was suicidal. Then Malachite said, "I've sent them for Lithe. The wind-ship isn't far away. Which way did the flying boat go?"

Moon pointed. Malachite selected two warriors with a flick of her tail and said, "Locate it."

They took to the air, but Moon knew it wouldn't help. The flying boat was already out of sight, it would have changed direction as soon as it was away from the Fell. Warriors couldn't possibly fly fast enough to find it. "They won't catch it, you have to go after it!"

"If I leave, the Fell will return within moments," Malachite said. Her tail flicked again. He had never been able to read her expression, even after spending time at Opal Night. It would have been easy to say she was unconcerned, unaffected, except for the fact that here she was, having travelled from across the Reaches and the coast and the sea and halfway into the ocean to be here when he needed her.

The warrior who had helped Moon had been leaning over River, trying to find breath or pulse. Now he reported, "He's alive."

Malachite reached to touch Moon's face, and he stepped back. A female warrior caught his arm and steadied him, and he dimly realized it was Rise, Malachite's chief warrior.

Malachite said, "Are there still Fell aboard, or Hians?" Six more warriors dropped down to land on the flying boat's upper decks.

Moon started to say no, then realized he had no idea. "I don't know. I don't think there's any Fell, but I don't know if all the Hians were able to leave. The Hians— They're silver gray, with patches like rock on their heads and skin." He remembered something else she needed to know. "The Fell were part Raksura. They had a queen."

Malachite took this information in with opaque calm, and stared off into the distance, the direction the Fell had fled. She said, "Search this craft."

Warriors on the upper decks scattered to climb down and enter the hatchways and open windows.

Rorra stepped out of the nearest hatchway, slowly, wary at all the strange Raksura. She saw Moon and the relief on her face was obvious as she limped toward him. She still looked sick and exhausted, but had one of the smaller fire weapons slung across her back. "Is River—" She saw him lying on the deck, the warrior crouched beside him.

"He's alive," Moon told her. He pointed to Malachite. "This is my mother."

Rorra stared at Malachite. "Oh." She turned back to Moon. "Are the Fell coming back? I can get to the larger weapon stand now—"

Malachite said, "The Fell won't come back while I'm here."

Rorra hesitated, eyed Malachite, then said, "That's good, then."

A dark shape that might have been the model for the forerunner depicted on the foundation builder city's tiles dropped to the deck suddenly, and Rorra flinched. It carried a small Arbora still in her groundling form.

It was Shade and Lithe. Moon thought he was clearly hallucinating all this, but if he was, he didn't think everything would hurt quite so much. Shade set Lithe on her feet, shifted to his groundling form, and flung himself at Moon. He caught Moon in a hard embrace, buried his face in Moon's neck, and said, "Are you hurt? You look terrible."

Moving toward River, Lithe demanded, "Is that your blood or his?"

"His, he needs help. The others are inside, unconscious from Fell poison," Moon told her, gripping Shade's shoulders to steady himself. Shade smelled of clean Raksura and salt wind and something indefinable that was somehow clearly the court of Opal Night, or maybe their shared bloodline. If Moon had been able to feel relief, he would have felt it then. Lithe knelt beside River, motioning a warrior to help her roll him over so she could get at his wounds.

A shadow fell on the deck and Moon twitched and looked up. But it was a wind-ship, coming around above the sunsailer's bow.

This one was easily twice the size of the sunsailer, the hull long and slim, made of what looked like lacquered wood but was a plant fiber, much stronger. The fanfolded sails on the two central masts were closing as it came about above them.

Then things started to happen very fast and in a dream-like fashion that Moon found vague and unpleasant.

Golden Islanders in climbing harnesses dropped from the railing of the wind-ship and Moon had a confused memory of trying to explain to Niran about the object Vendoin had said was a weapon and what had happened to Delin and about Rorra's distinctive scent while simultaneously introducing her to all his relatives. Lithe had River carried inside and went to help the other Raksura.

In the common room, Moon insisted on showing Malachite what had happened to Song. Malachite had hissed in regret, and made Moon let Rise gather Song up and carry her away. Moon had followed her, aware the Golden Islanders moved through the ship with the warriors, trying to help the Kishan crew. At some point Shade cupped Moon's face and said clearly, "Moon, you need to lie down."

Moon ended up back in the common room with Jade and the others. They were all still unconscious, and even with Lithe tending them, Moon didn't feel easy until he had checked to make sure each was still breathing. With the help of a couple of warriors and Shade, Lithe had moved everyone except Stone to pallets on the floor. Stone had been left stretched out on the bench, with a couple of cushions tucked around him. "I don't have any experience with line-grandfathers," Lithe said, "but I feel like it's not a good idea to move him."

Briar had been found and brought in to recover with the others, and River had had his wounds cleaned and been put into a healing sleep in a nest of cushions and blankets. Shade made Moon sit down on a cushion near Stone, while Lithe tried to get him to drink a cup of something. He said, "Is that a simple?"

"No, it's just tea. More simples are the last thing you need," Lithe assured him.

Moon took the cup. When he drank it he realized how abraded his throat was. No wonder he sounded so hoarse. It was suddenly a little easier to think, and he asked, "How are the Kishan?"

Lithe's expression told him it wasn't good news. She got to her feet and said, "Ivar-edel, the Golden Isles healer, said that so far she's found four dead, and some of the others seem very badly off. I'm going to go help her now."

As she went out the door, Moon tried to get up and follow her. He had no idea why, or where he thought he was going. Shade caught his arm and urged him to sit again. Moon said, "Where's Song?"

Shade winced. "They took her to an empty cabin, where they're putting the others who died."

Moon sank back down on the cushion. "Right." He closed his eyes and his head swam. "How did you find us?"

"We went to Indigo Cloud, and then we caught up with Diar and Niran. We followed the map out here, then we caught Fell stench. It was from the ocean, so we knew the Fell had to be looking for groundlings or Raksura."

Moon managed to get his eyes open again. He didn't want to sleep yet. "You wanted to come? Malachite didn't make you?" He was too groggy to put it into the right words, but if any consort should want to stay far away from the Fell, buried in the safety of a powerful court, it was Shade.

"She didn't want me to come, I insisted." It would have been an unbelievable statement from anyone else, but Shade was one of the few people who could actually talk Malachite into things. Shade lifted his shoulders a little, half-shudder, half-shrug. "Our mentors had the same vision as yours, right before Jade's message arrived. I thought, if we need to get into the city, and it's like the other one and I'm the only one who can open it, I have to go." He added, a little reluctantly, "And . . . I just had to do it to make sure I could."

"That was brave." It was one of the bravest things that Moon had ever heard of anyone doing.

Shade seemed reassured. Maybe he had expected Moon to disapprove of his decision to come. Moon was too loopy to judge anybody's decisions about anything at the moment. Shade said, "I didn't feel brave at Indigo Cloud. But Ember invited me to have tea, so it was all right."

It didn't surprise Moon. "Ember always knows what to do." He rubbed his face, trying to stay conscious. "The Fell were part Raksura. There was a Fellborn queen only twenty turns old."

"You told us, about her and the dakti." Shade's brow furrowed. "You said she killed the progenitor. You don't think . . . Maybe we could talk to them, to her?"

Moon hesitated. He only vaguely remembered telling them about the Fellborn queen, so he wasn't sure his opinion was worth anything right now. "I don't know." He remembered how desperate the queen had been. Like he had been desperate, not that many turns ago, a lost fledgling with no idea who or what he was. But he also remembered the paralyzing fear at the possibility of being taken away by Fell, so intense despite the drugs and sickness. "Maybe I should have tried harder, but—"

"No, no. I meant all of us with Malachite. The Fell queen tried to take you away." Shade twitched uneasily at the thought. "We have to be careful."

Through the deck, Moon felt a gentle thrum. "They got the motivator started."

Shade said, "Niran was going to try to help Rorra get the boat moving again so we can get out of the ocean."

Right, that was important, Moon remembered. Being carried further into the deeps wasn't going to help anything. "We're going after the flying boat?"

Shade watched him with concern, as if worried what his reaction might be. "The warriors couldn't find it. But Rorra thinks it must be going back to Kish."

Moon slumped a little. He had known the warriors were too late to catch the Hians, but hearing it confirmed was painful. If Rorra wasn't right . . . And even if Rorra was right, Kish was a big place.

On the bench above him, Stone made a faint noise, as if trying to wake. Moon shoved himself up and leaned over him.

The scale pattern on Stone's skin had perhaps started to fade a little, though it was hard to tell, and it hadn't been nearly long enough. He tried to explain this to Shade, who said, "Why don't you lie down with him? It will help keep him calm."

That sounded like a good idea, but Moon hesitated. "You'll keep watch?"

Shade said seriously, "I will."

Moon lay down beside Stone, and sank into sleep.

Moon slept off and on, listening to Stone's steady heartbeat and the motivator's thrum. He was aware when Stone stirred, rolled over, and curled up around him, but didn't really wake.

Moon woke finally, far more alert, to realize it was night and the liquid lights had been adjusted to a soft glow. *Song's dead*, he remembered again, and squeezed his eyes shut until his self-control returned.

He pushed up on one elbow. Shade sat on a cushion near the stove, and Rorra, bleary but conscious, sat on a stool nearby holding a cup of tea.

Stone was deeply asleep. Chime, Briar, Root, and Balm still lay unconscious but they had rolled over, changed positions. Moon could see River's chest move with his breathing. Jade was missing.

His voice a rusty creak, Moon said, "Where's Jade?"

"She woke a little while ago and went to talk to Malachite," Shade said, watching him worriedly. "She's very upset."

Moon moved Stone's arm off his waist and began the slow process of sitting all the way up, and possibly standing in the near future. Every bruise had settled into a sustained ache, but at least his head was clear. A memory tugged at him, an echo of something someone had said. In another moment he had it; it had been Callumkal, when the Hians had first arrived. "Can we find the Hian flying boat the way it found us? With the moss in the motivator?"

"We thought of that," Rorra said, her voice hoarse. "But Magrim was the only one who knew enough about the moss varietals to do that."

Moon wanted to growl. He hadn't believed Magrim's death was some sort of avoidable accident before; now it seemed sure that he had been killed deliberately, on Vendoin's orders.

Then Stone snarled and sat bolt upright. Shade and Rorra flinched. Moon grabbed Stone's shoulder and said, "It was the Hians. They gave us Fell poison."

He watched the blank, blind rage in Stone's face turn slowly into awareness and recognition. Stone's gray brows drew together as he focused on Moon, then on the wide-eyed Shade, and then Rorra. His voice a gravelly rasp, he said, "Malachite's here."

"The Fell found us," Moon told him. "She drove them off. She's outside now, with Jade."

Stone looked at the others' unconscious forms, tasted the air. "Where's Song and Merit? And Bramble?"

The words stuck in Moon's throat for a moment, and he had to force them out. "Song died. The poison killed her. The Hians took Merit and Bramble away, with Delin and Callumkal, maybe back to Kish. We're trying to find them now."

Stone stared at him. Then abruptly shoved to his feet. Moon grabbed his wrist, and said, "Don't leave!"

Stone blinked, his expression clearing. He said, "I just want to see Song."

Moon let go of him. He didn't know where that outburst had come from. It wasn't as if Stone could fly anywhere at the moment; the faint scale pattern was still on his skin.

Rorra pushed herself upright, wavering a little. She looked exhausted and sad. "I'll show you. And tell you the rest."

Stone squeezed Moon's shoulder almost hard enough to hurt, then followed Rorra out.

Shade let out his breath and reached for the kettle.

Moon told him, "I'm going to find Jade." He shoved to his feet and went out into the passage. Under one of the brighter lights, he examined the skin of his forearm. He could still see the faintest impression of scales in the bronze of his groundling skin. He resisted the urge to try to shift. He wouldn't be able to yet and he didn't want to waste his slowly returning strength.

He had to grip the railing to get down the steps. The ship sounded more like it normally did, with voices and movement audible from down the corridors. Though some of the muted noise he could hear were groans and Kishan being very ill.

Moon heard familiar voices ahead, then Kalam stepped out of a doorway. Moon leaned against the wall to let the dizziness pass. Kalam had to know about the artifact or weapon or whatever it was by now, know that the Raksura had brought it onto the sunsailer.

Kalam came toward Moon. He looked terrible, his cheeks sunken and his eyes clouded. He said, "They took my father."

"I saw it."

Kalam stepped forward and almost fell into Moon's arms. Moon said, "We'll find him."

Kalam looked up, and suddenly he had pulled Moon's head down and was pressing their lips together.

Kissing wasn't something Raksura did, though Moon had seen it in some of the different groundling communities he had lived in. He had been careful to avoid it; even in groundling form, his teeth were too sharp. Moon gently disengaged Kalam and said, "That can't happen. You're too young." He used the tone that worked best for firm commands to fledglings.

Kalam buried his face in Moon's shoulder for a moment. Moon said, "I know they killed Magrim. Was anyone else . . . ?"

Kalam stepped back, and pressed his hands to his face briefly, a gesture of apology. He looked up and said, "Kellimdar died, and three others of the crew, Viandel, Hith, and Semdar." He sounded wounded, and bewildered, and angry all at once. "Do you think the Hians will kill my father?"

Moon took a sharp breath. "I think they wanted hostages." He hoped that was what they wanted.

Niran stepped out of another doorway, with Lithe and Esankel, the Janderi navigator. Frustrated, Niran said, "We searched this Hian person's quarters but she left nothing behind."

Kalam said, "We've known Vendoin for five turns, since I was a child. How could she do this to us?"

Moon didn't have the answer to that. It had sounded as if all the Hians, not just Vendoin, had been planning this ever since Callumkal and the other Kish-Jandera scholars had found the map to the city. He pushed off the wall and started forward again. "The Fellborn queen said the other Fell flight heard groundlings talk about a weapon in the builder city. Did Callumkal know about it?"

"No, no one did. No one . . . It must have been the Hians." Kalam lifted his hands helplessly, trailing after him. "And the Raksura. Why did you hide it from us?"

Moon stopped and faced him. "We didn't know it was there until we found it. We didn't know what it would do, and we were afraid of it." It was the bare truth, and he hoped it was enough for Kalam. "There was a spell; it tricked us into taking the weapon back to the sunsailer. We just wanted to get rid of it in the ocean, where the Fell wouldn't find it."

Lithe watched Kalam carefully. "It wasn't why your people wanted to get into the city?"

"No, I swear it." Kalam lifted a hand in helpless frustration. "I've seen my father's work, I've traveled with him, I'd know if there was any idea about a weapon. If it is a weapon."

"Vendoin believed it was," Esankel said, wearily. "I'm sure she believed it. Would she have done all this if she hadn't?"

Moon looked away. He was standing by the doorway to the other room the Raksura had been using and found himself looking at Delin's bag, tucked under the bench next to Stone's pack. Delin. Delin who had gone through Vendoin's things and then became even more insistent that the object from the city should be dropped into the ocean as quickly as possible. He pointed at the pack. "Delin looked through Vendoin's notes when she was up in the steering cabin. Maybe he copied something. He was suspicious, I think. I didn't realize it at the time . . ."

Niran snarled, "Of course he was," and went to snatch up the pack. "I'll send this up to Diar so we can examine it all. Perhaps grandfather left us some clue or message."

Moon knew Niran's fury was mostly terror at what might happen to Delin. He turned away and went down the corridor to the hatch.

Guarding it was a young Golden Islander. She said, "They're on the stern deck."

He nodded to her and stepped outside into the night. The cool salt-scented wind was like being dashed with cold water. The outside lights had been dimmed and shaded to help conceal the boat's position from the Hians and the Fell and whatever else might be after them. The reassuring shadow floating above them was the wind-ship.

Jade and Malachite stood near the stern railing, their spines outlined by the faint moonlight. Jade was still in her Arbora form, and Malachite had her wings.

He heard Jade say, "I shouldn't have done this. I've done everything wrong."

Moon stopped in mid-step. He hadn't thought Jade would take it that way. He didn't know why he hadn't thought it. *Of course she would.* Queens thought they were responsible for everything.

With just an edge of sarcasm to her cool voice, Malachite said, "So you should have ignored the dreams and the augury and waited like an animal in a trap."

"Waited for help." Jade looked toward the water and the silver glimmer of the ship's wake. She added, almost not grudgingly, "Waited for you."

Malachite's spines took on a skeptical angle. It had to be for Jade's benefit. Malachite seldom betrayed any recognizable emotion unless it was deliberate. "Was I in the augury?"

"No, but—"

"All this is hardly over. We've seen nothing of most elements of the vision." Malachite flicked a spine. "Moon."

Moon moved forward and Jade turned toward him. He couldn't think of anything to say, and just folded himself into her arms.

When he looked up, Malachite was gone. Jade muttered, "She's up on the roof of the second deck, looming over us."

"I thought you two were getting along better." Moon buried his face in her frills. "When Root wakes up, we have to tell him about Song."

"I'll do it," Jade said. Her grip on his waist tightened, almost enough for him to feel her claws. "I don't know why she died, and not the rest of us."

Moon knew. The Hians had dumped her and Root on the floor like garbage, with no concern for what might happen. The poison had made Song sick and she had choked on her vomit. Even Rorra, a sealing, had been aware of this danger and had crawled around half-conscious making sure the others with her had been propped up.

Chime staggered out of the hatch and headed for Moon. Jade let Moon go and he caught Chime, who stumbled and wrapped his arms around him. He muttered into Moon's neck, "Stone told us about Song, and the Hians."

"Are you all right?" Moon asked him.

"I feel sick, and you smell terrible," Chime said miserably.

Jade patted Chime's back. "Let's go inside."

When they got back up to the common room, Lithe, Rorra, Kalam, and Shade were in the corridor. Shade was telling the other three, "I thought you all should talk."

Inside the room, Stone sat on the bench. His face was drawn and exhausted. Raksura didn't show age the way most soft-skinned groundlings did, but there was something in Stone's face right now that revealed the weight of many, many turns.

The others were awake, sitting around on the floor, still bleary and sick, the scale patterns visible on their skin. Root was curled up in a ball, his head in Briar's lap, and she was stroking his hair.

"They killed Song, and stole the Arbora and Delin." Root sat up suddenly, his face etched with pain. "They took the weapon I found and we don't know where they are."

"Root—" Moon began. "You didn't find the weapon—"

"It found you," Jade said firmly. "It wasn't your fault. It wasn't Briar's fault."

"I told you that," Balm said. She sounded as if she was barely holding on to her own composure. Briar looked wretched. "Listen to your queen."

"But we can't find them," Root persisted. "They stole Merit so we couldn't find them."

Then Stone said, "But they didn't know about Lithe." He watched the group just outside the door.

Lithe was saying, "But it's the moss, correct? The moss is from the same plant, and the two have an affinity."

Moon's heart thumped, and he stepped closer to listen. The others fell silent.

"Yes, that's it," Kalam said. He gestured in frustration. "But Magrim was the only one who would have been able to use our moss varietal to find theirs."

Rorra explained, "Magrim was a horticultural, which is someone who can manipulate the stored sunlight in the moss for different tasks, like making it release light, produce the lift for a levitation harness or an air-going sailer, or to draw water into a motivator. The rest of us can tend those things and keep them working the way they should, but he knew how to make them."

Everyone was listening now. Chime took a step toward them, his brows drawing together.

Hope making her voice tight, Jade said, "Manipulate the moss for light. Like a mentor could."

Moon realized he was holding his breath. If there was still a chance . . .

Lithe turned to them. "Yes, that's what I was thinking." She asked Kalam and Rorra, "Can you explain to me exactly what you would do to find the flying boat if Magrim was here?"

Kalam glanced at Rorra. "I've seen it done but . . ."

Rorra thought it over, frowning absently. "There are several varietals of moss for the motivator. Magrim would have been able to choose the varietal that we share with the Hians' ship. Then it would be put into a growth liquid, and the moss would start to grow in the direction of the other ship."

"Maybe," Chime said, his voice thick. "Maybe—"

"Maybe," Lithe agreed. She asked Rorra, "Can you do the second part without him? The growth liquid?"

"Yes, that's part of the necessary tending—" Rorra stopped, suddenly hopeful. "You think you can find the varietal?"

"I was going to scry to try to pick up their direction. But I thought we might try this first."

Moon followed Lithe and Rorra and the others to the stern and the steps down to the motivator chamber. Jade had let Chime and Stone come along, but none of the others, telling them to stay and rest. She had said quietly to Moon, "If nothing comes of it, it'll just be . . ." She didn't finish the thought.

Just be another blow on top of all the others, Moon thought. Shade had stayed behind with the recovering warriors, still keeping watch the way he had promised.

The chamber took up the whole stern of the sunsailer, its air filled with heavy green scents and a salty acrid odor, and the sound of the steady thrum and rush of water from the motivator just on the other side of the hull. All across the back wall were large webbed containers for the moss itself, and gray-veined vines that looked unpleasantly like tentacles wound all through it. They led out through an opening in the back wall. Rasal and another Janderi woman had some of the small containers open. Rasal seemed well enough, though the other woman swayed on her feet.

Looking around at it all, Niran said, "I'm not sure I understand the mechanism. The motivator is a creature, which is eating the moss?"

Chime said, "No, it's a plant that's eating the moss."

"Eating the heat the moss produces," Rorra corrected. "Rasal, we need samples from all the core moss varietals. I'm going to get the growth liquid out."

"There's three tens of varietals," Rasal protested. "We'll never be able to tell which is the right one."

"We might," Rorra countered, going to a set of pottery jars against the far wall. They were all tied up to wooden racks, their lids carefully strapped down. "Lithe here is a Raksura arcanist and may be able to tell."

Rasal and her helper exchanged startled looks, then started to pull various tools out of a storage box. Lithe sat down on the floor nearby. After a moment, Chime went to join her. He said, softly, "I know I can't help. If you want me to go—"

"No, I want you to stay," Lithe told him. "You know more about groundling magic than I do."

After watching them carefully snip pieces of moss out of various containers while Rorra laid out even more containers and more tools, Moon found a seat on the steps. It was becoming rapidly obvious that this process wasn't going to be instantaneous. Stone settled beside him, while Jade and Niran started to pace.

Rorra carefully put the first sample into a pottery cup of unpleasantly acrid fluid and presented it to Lithe. Lithe cupped it in her hands, and they waited. The fifth time Niran almost tripped on Jade's tail, Moon decided he couldn't take it anymore. This was going to take forever, might lead to nothing, and the intense scents were beginning to make his stomach protest. He told Jade, "I'll be up on deck."

As he went up the stairs, he realized Stone was following him. He went out the first hatchway, onto the stern deck. There were two of Malachite's warriors on top of the cabin overlooking it, and he could sense the presence of more nearby. The wind was still cool, sweeping away the Fell stench that still lingered over the sunsailer. Moon went to the railing and sat down where he could see the wake. Now it was outlined against the dark water by the little blue glowing bugs or plants that lived in the sea. It was a sign the water was now shallow enough that they were safe from giant oceanlings, though it could give their location away to anything in the air. But between Malachite and her warriors, the wind-ship, and the Kishan who were recovered enough to work the fire weapons, Moon wasn't too worried about that.

Stone sat next to him, hissing under his breath at either stiff muscles or the leftover effects of the poison. Moon said, "I'm sorry I . . ." He wasn't sure how to finish that sentence. "I'm just sorry."

"Me too," Stone said. Then he admitted, "I don't know what we could have done differently."

"Me neither." They had been suspicious, just not of the right people. And now Song was lying cold because of it. "Jade doesn't know why
she died. She thinks it was just the poison. But you saw her."

Stone looked out at the water. "Whatever happens, none of the
Hians on that flying boat are going to live through this."

"Whatever happens," Moon agreed.

Moon wasn't sure how long they had been sitting there, when
Chime bolted out through the hatchway. He crouched beside them,
saying breathlessly, "Lithe found it. She found it. It was the eighth sample, it triggered a vision of the Hians' flying boat. They're going to grow
it now so it'll show the direction in the liquid. It'll grow toward the
moss aboard the flying boat."

Stone let out a breath of relief. Moon swallowed down the urge to
growl. He hoped Vendoin was afraid. He hoped she knew they were
coming. He said, "Let's go back inside."

About the Author

Martha Wells is the author of over a dozen science fiction and fantasy novels, including the *Books of the Raksura* series, *Star Wars: Razor's Edge*, and the Nebula-nominated *The Death of the Necromancer*, as well as short stories, nonfiction, and YA fantasy. Her books have been published in seven languages. Wells lives in College Station, Texas, with her husband.

Visit her website at www.marthawells.com.